# THE RELICS OF ILLAYAN

KATHRYN KNOWLES

MAD
ENDEAVOUR

This is a work of fiction. Names, characters, places, and incidents are the product of the author's imagination or are used fictitiously. Any resemblance to actual events, locales, or persons, living or dead, is coincidental.

Copyright © 2021 by Kathryn Knowles

Illustrations copyright © 2021 by Kathryn Knowles

Cover Design by Maria Spada

Edited by Marion Lougheed

First Mad Endeavour Edition: November 2021

All rights reserved.

The scanning, uploading, and distribution of this book without permission is a theft of the author's intellectual property. If you would like permission to use material from the book (other than for review purposes), please contact info@madendeavour.com. Thank you for your support of the author's rights.

Identifiers:

ISBN 978-1-7778470-2-9 (hardcover)

ISBN 978-1-7778470-0-5 (trade paperback)

ISBN 978-1-7778470-1-2 (ebook)

Mad Endeavour

www.madendeavour.com

*For Nanny, as with everything I do*

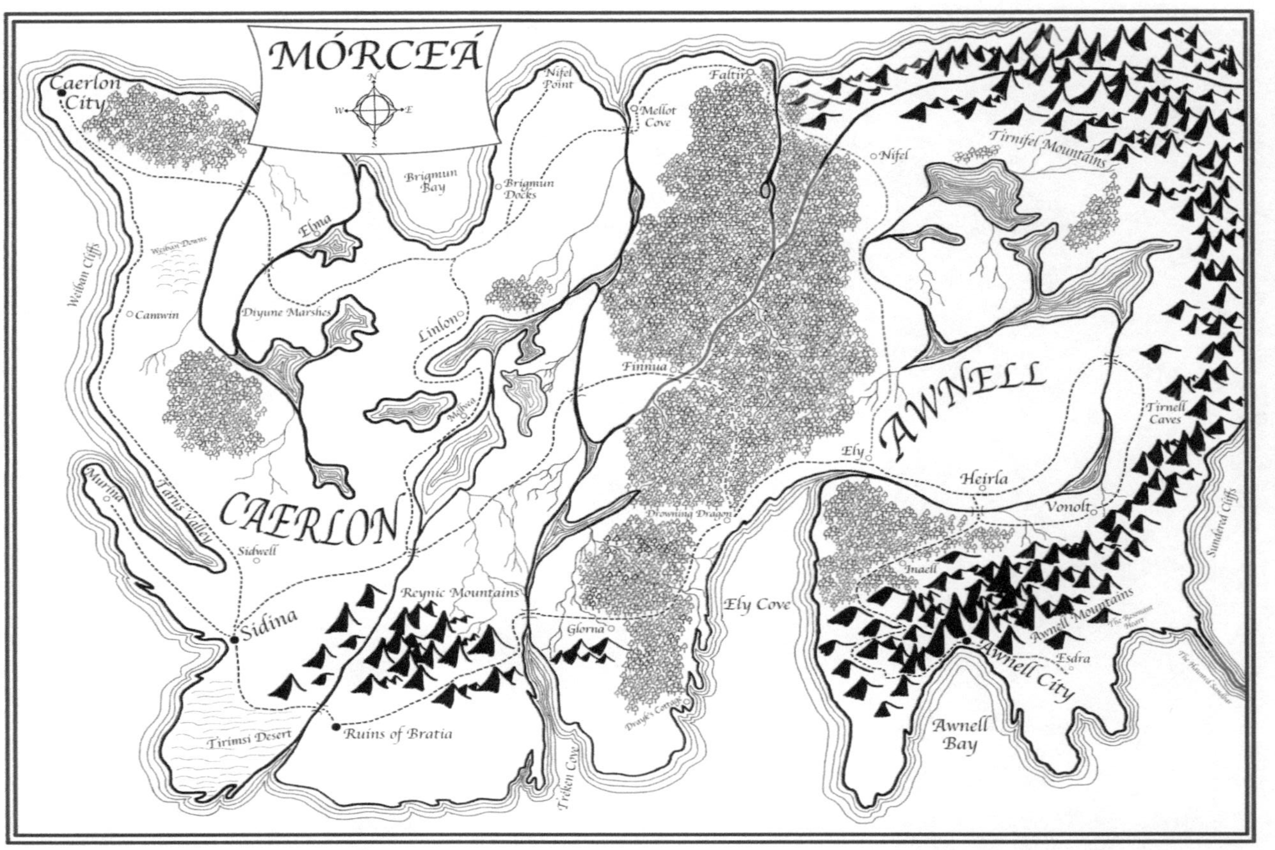

MÓRCEÁ
N
W E
S
Caerlon City
Nifel Point
Faltir
Mellot Cove
Brigmun Bay
Brigmun Docks
Nifel
Tirnifel Mountains
Elma
Weiban Downs
Diyune Marshes
Canwin
Linlon
Melfosia
Finnua
Awnell
Caerlon
Murina
Tarus Valley
Sidwell
Drowning Dragon
Ely
Heirla
Vonolt
Tirnell Caves
Sundered Cliffs
Weiban Cliffs
Reynic Mountains
Glorna
Ely Cove
Inaell
Awnell Mountains
Esdra
Awnell City
The Roseman Heart
The Haunted Sandbar
Sidina
Tirimsi Desert
Ruins of Bratia
Treken Cove
Drake's Corridor
Awnell Bay

# PROLOGUE

## FEHLA

# RAIN FALLS

Fehla had seen enough executions, some public rituals staged for entertainment and intimidation, and others private slaughters born of anger and hate.

She had no intention of letting this turn out that way.

The rain lashed against the walls as the wind howled, ripping at the shutters and threatening to tear them from their hinges. Lightning cracked through the sky, momentarily illuminating the room.

There hadn't been a storm this wild in months and Fehla was having trouble shaking the feeling it was a bad omen.

"Your Majesty, you should lie still." The physician watched her with mingled pity and fear in his eyes. "The damage is extensive. It's a wonder you survived."

"We don't have time, Grante," she said, shivering as she swung her legs off the bed and grabbed hold of the bedpost beside her head. Her entire body was crying out against the effort of trying to move, but she had to ignore it. There would be time to rest later.

She hauled herself to her feet and stood there, waiting for her legs to stabilize. A wave of dizziness crashed over her and she teetered, clutching the post so she wouldn't fall. She closed her eyes, waiting for the sensation to pass, and when she opened them again, she found Grante hovering beside her nervously.

"I'm fine," she muttered, taking a shaky step towards the dressing table in the corner of the room.

Grante had left his supplies on the table and the stench of the inducing tonic was so strong it curled her nostrils from a distance. She wretched and covered her mouth. Her stomach was empty, but the heaving motion was excruciating.

She passed the cheval mirror by her wardrobe and caught a glimpse of her reflection for the first time in days. Her hair was matted and sweaty and her eyes bulged out from the dark orbits that betrayed her lack of sleep. Her nightdress was half-drenched in sweat and stained with blood along the hemline.

She grimaced at the mirror and turned her attention back towards the dressing table where a small wooden box lay waiting.

Somewhere nearby, she heard a door slam and an instinctive fear shot through her, causing her to hasten her pace. As she took a larger stride, she cried out in pain and clutched at the edge of the table for support.

"My lady." Grante hurried forward, looking terrified. "Let me help you."

Fehla brushed away his comment with a dismissive wave. "Here," she said through clenched teeth. She opened the box to reveal a necklace.

It was a simple yet elegant golden chain bearing a gemstone that, as far as Fehla knew, was the only one of its kind. The heavy pendant was walnut-sized and shaped in a tapered oval, but it was the stone's colour that made it truly unique. It was pale and almost translucent, but also iridescent, with infinite colours that danced and sparkled in the light of the candles. Sometimes Fehla thought it looked like a glittering ocean, and at other times it was closer to a cloudy sky at sunset. It was the most beautiful necklace she'd ever owned, and its colours seemed to deepen and intensify over time, so that now it shone brighter than ever.

Fehla had lived surrounded by magic for many years and she knew how to recognize it. But this necklace was something stronger than mere magic. Like life and love frozen in glass.

"It's"—the physician looked at the queen with reverence—"it's exquisite."

"It was my mother's—my birth mother's." Fehla tried to smile, but it twisted into a pained grimace. "And her mother's before that. It has been passed down through my family from mother to daughter for generations. It is the only family heirloom I have, and whenever I wear it, I feel as if my mother is here, my sister... as if my entire family is here with me. And now I-I want my daughter to have it. When she's old enough." Her voice shook and she took a deep breath.

"Of course, Your Majesty." Grante took the box from her and stared at it.

A faint whimpering sound was coming from the cradle beside the bed. Fehla had to close her eyes to resist the urge to rush over to it.

"We need to hurry," she said.

The darkness outside was thinning. Grante was supposed to be gone already, but the entire ordeal had taken longer than expected, even with all the inducing herbs.

The castle would be waking up soon, and King Casréyan was due to return home later that morning. Fehla had orchestrated the delivery to coincide with his trip to the Ruins of Bratia, but she hadn't counted on it taking this long. Fehla couldn't let anyone discover the truth. She couldn't let Casréyan see his daughter.

The physician's eyebrows pinched in commiseration. "My

queen, have you considered—" He broke off, fidgeting anxiously.

"Considered what?" She didn't look at him as she spoke. Instead, she began making her way back towards the bed, wincing as she stepped.

"Have you considered perhaps... running? You could just take them both and leave." He sounded desperate and spoke in a rapid whisper, as if afraid of his own words. "I could help you," he urged.

Fehla laughed. It was a mirthless laugh, full of resignation and bitterness. "No, we can't run. No matter where we'd go, he'd find us and he would kill us all. I know he would." She pressed her lips together in determination. She'd made her decision months ago and there was nothing Grante could say to change her mind.

Casréyan had never wanted children. Deluded into believing he'd live and reign forever, he didn't believe he needed them.

But the chaplain had convinced the king to marry and sire an heir.

*Just one heir*, he'd told Casréyan. *Just in case.*

Fehla suppressed a snort and shook her head. *If only she'd known...*

But it was too late for that now.

"You remember Schlana," she said, giving Grante a hard stare as she continued moving slowly towards the bed. "She was a good woman, quiet and discreet, and she kept Casréyan's attention away from me for a time." Fehla shut her eyes, blocking out the image of Schlana's mangled corpse, and the countless others before her. "They all do... for a time."

Casréyan was determined to have only one heir, and he'd already demonstrated how far he'd go to ensure it. How far he'd go to protect his throne.

"I'm the queen. That gives *me* some protection at least. But my children—" She broke off, trying not to imagine the consequences if her plan failed.

"My lady—"

"You promised me you would do this," Fehla said pointedly, as she arrived at the bed and glanced down at the faces of her two sleeping children cuddled together in the cradle. They were so small, so peaceful. "This is my only option." She cleared her throat, turning her gaze towards the opposite wall, trying to ignore the pain she felt inside and out.

The physician sighed in resignation. "Very well." He bowed his head as he crossed the room to the cradle and lifted one of the sleeping babies out of it. "Are you sure you don't want to hold her, Your Majesty? Just once?"

Fehla shook her head rapidly, keeping her eyes trained on the wall across from her. They stood together in silence. Both overcome with the weight of what was happening, they listened to the rain pound against the walls and the thunder growl in the distance.

When Grante spoke again, his voice was firmer. "I give you my word, my queen. I will protect your child and deliver her to safety far away from here. She will live a normal life somewhere Casréyan will never know about her."

Fehla nodded, still not looking at him, fighting back tears. "Go now."

"Very well."

The door to her chambers opened and closed quietly and she took a deep, rattling breath, trying to calm herself.

After a while, she peered down at the cradle where her son slept peacefully and reached in, lifting him out. As she pressed the little bundle to her chest, tears began to stream down her face.

# PART I

**1**

———

## A FRIEND, A SISTER

Catanya closed her eyes, waiting for the sense of calm that her surroundings usually gave her. She loved this secluded beach. She loved the smell of salt water and the sound of waves breaking against the rocks. It was her favourite escape—somewhere she could retreat to be alone with her thoughts, somewhere she felt safe.

But today it wasn't working.

She opened her eyes and stared down at the sketchboard on her lap. How many times had she drawn this beach, trying to capture its raw beauty?

It was a narrow coastal inlet, hidden at the north edge of the forest where the earth tilted away from the tree line. The beach was a blend of rocks and sand, strewn with an assortment of driftwood and seashells that gave it a wild, untameable quality. It was this quality especially that appealed to Catanya. She'd spent years trying to capture that sense of freedom on the page, never really succeeding.

But this latest effort was the closest she'd ever come. Perhaps because she finally understood how trapped she was, she could appreciate its defiant wilderness.

*Just stay here, Catanya. Keep your head down and everything will be alright.*

Catanya rubbed her forehead, wishing she could forget everything.

She had been sitting on this beach for hours, trying to sort out her emotions. Her mind was reeling. She was having trouble processing everything that had happened these last few days. It was too surreal. No matter how many times she replayed her conversation with Genna and Grante, a part of her still didn't believe it. Or *couldn't* believe it.

She needed to keep herself distracted.

Catanya shuffled the sheaves of parchment on her lap, searching for one with a square of clear space, then she laid it on the sketchboard and snatched up a fresh pencil.

She traced the pencil across the sheet, outlining the shape of a man's face with round, weary features and worry lines on his forehead. She'd met Grante for the first time a few days ago, but she never forgot a face, and that meeting had been particularly memorable.

Catanya's hand trembled, causing her next pencil line to jut out at an odd angle, slicing through the image.

Grumbling under her breath, she rubbed the page with her thumb, trying to blot out the line, but it just smudged into a grey and black blotch on the page.

Frustrated, Catanya tore the corner off the page and crumpled it into a ball, tossing it away so it landed in the sand nearby. Then she started rifling through the sheaves again. She lingered on a page with a series of images she'd drawn the day before. Images of things she'd rather not remember.

The shining chalice and the old man in the shadows.

And *him*.

Catanya snapped the sketchboard closed and laid it down in the sand. She ran her hands through her hair, hugged her knees to her chest, and felt her pulse quicken yet again.

She longed to forget, to go back and pretend none of it had happened, but she couldn't.

Catanya shuddered involuntarily as the memories of that fateful night came rushing back. The dizziness and pain had been excruciating, and then that strange, blinding light...

She tried to push the memory away, not wanting to remember what had happened next. She didn't want any of this.

Catanya groaned and rested her chin on her knees, gazing out at the ocean. The water shimmered like a sheet of textured glass, giving the impression it stretched on forever. She wondered, not for the first time, what lay beyond the horizon.

Hesitantly, Catanya reached down and opened her sketch-board again, flipping through the pages to one at the back.

It was a busy page, filled with drawings that flowed together, pouring out from the centre: faces, horses, birds, trees, and more, all surrounding a long cedar lodge with several carved columns supporting its roof, and a series of dormer windows overhanging a lush garden.

Camlee Lodge, a home for orphaned girls in the small village of Faltir.

*Orphaned girls. Right.*

Catanya gazed at the image of the home that had never truly been hers. Her resolve began to strengthen. She climbed to her feet, ignoring the slight tremor of her muscles, and stepped across the damp sand towards the ocean. The waves rushed at her feet, drenching her bare toes and the hemline of her dress, and tugging at the sand beneath her.

One by one, she lifted her sketches off the board and laid them in the water, watching as the pencil lines bled together, and the thick parchment wilted and drowned, bearing her past into the depths of the ocean.

When the last page had succumbed to the undercurrent,

she returned to her spot on the beach, pulled on her shoes, and sat down to watch the sun set.

After a while, she heard a rustling noise coming from behind her. She turned to see a familiar young woman emerging from the forest, her long brown kirtle catching on the brambles and branches as she moved.

"Here you are," said Diyah, relief in her voice as she yanked her dress free from the thorns. "I've been searching for you for ages." She reached the edge of the trees and began to descend the steep, rocky slope towards the beach. "What are you doing?" She stumbled to a halt at the base of the incline.

"I'm just... thinking." Catanya squinted towards the setting sun. Diyah sat down in the sand beside her. She was observing Catanya closely, and Catanya knew what was coming next. "I'm fine," she said before her friend could ask the question. "Really, I am."

Diyah snorted. "Well, that's not true," she said, turning her gaze out towards the water. "But we can pretend it is, if that's what you want." She flashed a warm smile.

Catanya laughed and felt a burst of affection for her. "Thank you."

Diyah nodded, and they settled into a comfortable silence.

Catanya and Diyah had known each other their entire lives. They'd grown up together at Camlee Lodge, and from the moment they'd met as children, they had been inseparable.

Catanya could hardly remember the years before Diyah arrived at the lodge. It was as if those years belonged to someone else's life. She and Diyah had been together forever. Catanya couldn't imagine her life without her.

She glanced over at her friend. Diyah's wavy blond hair was shining in the sunlight and her silhouette was unusually vibrant, set against the beach like a perfect sculpture.

Any other time, Catanya would have started a new sketch. She'd spent hours of her life drawing her friend's face.

Diyah was widely regarded as the most beautiful woman within miles of Faltir. Her hair fell in perfect curls that framed her face, and her wide brown eyes had a permanent shine in them that seemed to convey an enticing charm. But what most people saw as flirtation, Catanya recognized as a sign of her friend's fiery temperament and impatience. Capturing that on the page was always a satisfying challenge.

Catanya smiled to herself and turned her attention back out towards the water.

"What is it?" Diyah eyed her curiously.

Catanya shook her head, still smiling. "Nothing, I was just remembering a few years ago... the celebration when you officially came of age." Catanya wrestled back a laugh. "What did the villagers say about you again? What did they call it, the Murina Passion?"

"Yes, that's it." Diyah rolled her eyes. "People born in Murina are strange, volatile creatures. Didn't you know that?" She sniffed and tugged at the leather strap wrapped around her shoulders, holding her work satchel in place. "Apparently, refusing to be paraded around the village in a ridiculous dress is unthinkable."

Catanya laughed at the scowl on her friend's face. "Oh, of course it is. Ladies of Faltir should be proper and polite." She sniggered.

"Oh, right. Because that's how you behaved when you had to do it?"

Catanya pulled an expression of mock offense. "What? Doesn't every lady show up to her celebration two hours late, unkempt and covered in pencil smudges?"

They grinned at each other and laughed.

"Oh, sometimes I wonder about this place, you know?" grumbled Diyah, running her hand through her hair. "I've never understood how they can be so small-minded."

Catanya sighed and looked around at her surroundings.

Faltir was located at the furthest reach of the kingdom, nestled in the foothills of the Tirnifel Mountains. A thick forest blanketed the rolling highlands, and the many peaks and valleys gave way abruptly to the border of the northern sea.

"It is beautiful here though," she breathed. "It's a peaceful place, full of simple people who aspire to lead quiet lives." Catanya shrugged. "It's not what I would want either, but it seems to make them happy... I suppose you and I have just never truly belonged."

"Definitely not."

Catanya couldn't help but smile at the defiance in her friend's voice. Diyah had always been driven, determined to effect change in the world. But Catanya was more artistic and imaginative, spending hours drawing, painting, and crafting, and trading her works at market.

Catanya often dreamed of setting out on her own, selling her works to pay her way. The romance of it spoke to her—living as a wanderer, travelling the world and seeing the countless wonders from her childhood stories.

She wanted to watch the tides of Brigmun Bay vanish, and to visit the Ruins of Bratia where the famous battles were fought. The great cities of Caerlon, Sidina, and Awnell called to her to walk their winding streets. She yearned to trek across the Tirnifel Mountains and discover what lay beyond them and she wanted to swim in the warm waters off the coast of the Tirimsi Desert. She longed to explore the far reaches of the kingdom, to learn its secrets.

Catanya had been thinking about this a lot lately. She'd spent her entire life dreaming of distant places and imagining grand adventures. Now that she knew the truth, she finally understood why Faltir never felt like home to her.

But it was one thing to fantasize about leaving, it was an entirely different matter to actually do it.

This wouldn't be easy.

"So"—she cleared her throat—"did Lady Genna send you to find me?" She grabbed a handful of sand and felt the coarse grains slip through her fingers.

Diyah exhaled heavily. "She's worried about you. We both are."

Lady Genna managed the lodge where Catanya and Diyah grew up. She was a strict, demanding guardian who opened her heart to every girl in her care. She loved them all like she was their mother.

Until recently, Catanya had never realized how much she owed Genna for taking her in and giving her shelter all this time. She had never known how dangerous her presence was for everyone around her.

Catanya turned to study her friend, a twinge of guilt nagging at the edges of her affection. She couldn't bear to imagine what would happen to the people she loved if anyone discovered the truth about her.

She grabbed another handful of sand, letting the grains slip away to reveal a small pink seashell in her palm. With a sudden wave of sadness, she flipped the shell over in her fingers, running her thumb across its ridges.

"You're going to leave, aren't you?" asked Diyah, without taking her eyes off the setting sun.

For a moment, Catanya was taken aback, but then she shook her head and snorted. Diyah could always tell what she was thinking without her having to say it.

"I have to," Catanya said as she tossed the shell back onto the sand. "I know Genna and Grante think I should stay, but I can't. Now that I know... I'm sorry." Catanya fought to keep her voice level. As much as she loved Genna and the other girls at the lodge, there was only one person she'd really miss in Faltir.

Diyah didn't respond.

They sat in silence, watching the sun inch closer to the horizon. It reflected off the rippling surface of the ocean in a sparkling, watercolour imitation of the sky. The pinkish hues of the clouds brushed the vivid blue canvas as it melted into a blur of orange and red. The sunset was exquisite, and the brilliance of the colours reminded Catanya of the necklace she used to wear.

She frowned and rubbed her neck, wishing she still had it, as if, somehow, it might have given her the answers she needed.

"Well." Diyah climbed to her feet and shook the sand off her dress. "If we're going to leave, we'd better do it sooner rather than later." She held out her hand to Catanya, who stared at it in disbelief.

"*We?*"

"I'm coming with you." Diyah's tone was matter-of-fact, a steely glint in her eye.

Catanya opened her mouth to protest, but Diyah cut her off. "There's no point in arguing with me. I'm coming with you."

"But Diyah—"

"I don't want to hear it. I don't care where you came from or who your parents are. It's you and me together, *we're* family. And I'm not going to lose my family again. I can't—I *won't*."

Catanya wanted to protest, but once Diyah had her mind set, there was no winning an argument with her. And Catanya couldn't help feeling a surge of relief. She reached out and took Diyah's hand, pulling herself up to her feet. "Are you sure?"

Diyah shrugged. "We're in this together, Catanya. We always have been. I don't know what's going to happen next, but whatever it is, we'll face it together. Besides," she continued with a thoughtful frown, "it could be rather exciting. Think about it. We can go anywhere. Faltir was never big enough for us, anyway."

"True." Catanya grinned and bent down to collect her sketchboard and pencils. Something akin to excitement bubbled beneath her fear and anxiety. "And together, you and I are capable of anything."

"Oh, I'm counting on it." Diyah's face was alight with enthusiasm. She had the familiar air of confident determination she wore whenever she was facing a new challenge. "So, where do you want to go? Somewhere we can find work? I was thinking Sidina, although maybe that's not far enough. Hmm... Awnell City? We can ask Genna. She might have connections..."

Diyah chattered on happily about leaving, without requiring much response. Catanya suspected her friend was trying to keep her distracted, and she loved her all the more for it.

They climbed back up the slope and into the forest towards Camlee Lodge, where Lady Genna would be waiting for them. It wouldn't be easy to convince Genna to let them go, but they owed her an explanation after everything she had done for them.

The sun had set behind them and shadows engulfed the forest, making it much colder than the open air of the beach had been. Catanya was looking forward to regaining the comfort and warmth of the lodge. By now, the younger girls should be finishing their chores and winding down for the evening, and if they hurried, she and Diyah could join them for one last cup of tea before bed. After that, they would be free to talk with Genna undisturbed.

Over the years as Lady Genna aged, she'd started relying on Catanya and Diyah more. The eldest girls at the lodge had always been expected to help educate and guide the younger ones, but recently Catanya and Diyah had taken on this role almost completely.

Including themselves, there were currently twelve girls living at the lodge. When Catanya was young, there was half that number. It seemed like a sign of the difficult times how many girls needed shelter nowadays.

Catanya was the oldest—her twentieth birthday had come and gone earlier that year—followed closely by Diyah, but the other ten girls had not yet reached adolescence. They would be a handful for Genna to manage on her own.

But it was better this way. It was time for Catanya to leave. She didn't belong in Faltir anymore. She wasn't sure she belonged anywhere.

"Do you hear that?" Diyah broke through Catanya's reverie.

Catanya stopped to listen. Somewhere nearby, she could hear the low thunderous pounding of hooves against the earth.

"Horses?" She raised her eyebrows.

Then another sound sent a chill down her spine. Somewhere ahead of them, people were screaming.

"That's coming from the lodge!"

They broke into a run, careening through the forest towards their home.

As the lodge came into view, they saw people running in every direction as a deep, angry voice shouted, "Round everyone up! Kill anyone who resists! She's here somewhere, so find her!"

Catanya saw one horseman chasing a tiny figure that was running as fast as its little feet would allow.

"No, Alli!" she cried, dropping her sketchboard and launching forward to protect the girl. But before she had taken two steps, it was too late. The rider's sword sliced through Alli's fragile frame, and she crumpled to the ground, motionless. The rider barely slowed his pace.

"Catanya!" Diyah grabbed her friend and pulled her back into the trees. "They're here for you. You have to leave, now!" Diyah's face had drained of colour. She was shaking with anger and grief as she tried to restrain her friend.

"No, let go of me. We have to help!" Catanya struggled against Diyah's grip.

"If they catch you, then we're all dead! Look at them, Catanya. Look at their uniforms."

Reluctantly, Catanya turned to look at them.

The men were dressed in brilliant purple surcoats that stretched down to their knees above their glistening hauberks. Their sleeves and hemlines were bordered with gold embroidery, and their billowing capes were fastened at the side with a circular brooch. Across their fronts, they bore the clear image of the royal crest and royal insignia, which depicted a large bell-shaped chalice encircled by a wide, ornate crown.

Catanya recognized the violet and gold colours of Caerlon and understood what her friend was trying to tell her.

"Fírkon," she breathed in a low, terrified voice.

The fírkon were the elite soldiers of Caerlon. They were the kingdom's most highly trained and ruthless warriors, and if they were here in Faltir, it could only mean one thing.

"He knows... Cadyan knows." Catanya thought she might be sick. She retreated a short distance into the trees, feeling helpless.

"You have to go," whispered Diyah. "Go now before they find you. I'll help Genna and the others. Maybe I can distract the fírkon long enough for you—"

"What?" Catanya snapped back into focus. "No!" She grabbed her friend's arm to stop her.

"Yes!" Diyah wrenched her arm out of Catanya's grip. "I'm sorry, but this is bigger than us, Catanya. Don't you understand? You could actually change things in Caerlon—tear everything down and rebuild. Think about it. *You can fight.* You're the only one who has a chance against him. But you have to go now."

"I... I... no..." Catanya's heart raced and she stammered, unable to speak.

"We can't let them find you. Not here, not now. I'm sorry."

Before Catanya could say anything, one of the fírkon spotted them. "Over there!" he shouted, pointing at them.

"Go now!" said Diyah, sounding panicked as she pushed Catanya forward. Then she turned to run out of the trees towards the rider. "GO!" she called, as she disappeared into the chaos.

Catanya's head was reeling, unable to accept what had just happened. She needed to run after her friend, to bring her back. But when she stared at the scene, she spotted a pair of riders heading towards her. Diyah was right.

Catanya turned and took off into the trees.

Panic set in while she ran as fast as she could. Behind her, the sound of horses grew louder. A painful stitch pierced her side, but Catanya willed herself to keep running, to keep going. She owed it to everyone at Camlee Lodge. She owed it to Diyah.

The sound of horses resounded everywhere, and suddenly she realized it wasn't only coming from behind her. Someone was racing towards her from the side. She glanced back and lost her footing, tumbling to the ground just as the huge horse burst through the trees. She rolled over to see the rider towering over her in the patchy moonlight, triumph written on his face as he pulled on the reins to stop his horse. But the beast reared, and with its feet about to descend on top of her, Catanya raised her hands reflexively to shield herself. As she did so, she felt a strange prickling in her arms.

A fleeting but eerie moment of silence blanketed them in stillness before a powerful gust wailed through the trees and a sudden and loud creak rent the air. Then came the ominous groan of roots being wrenched from the ground as an enormous fir tree teetered and crashed down between Catanya and the rider, sending a wave of debris billowing in every direction. The rider jerked his reins to avoid the impact, but the effort unseated him. He fell to the ground, while his horse bolted away in the opposite direction.

Catanya scrambled to her feet, coughing as she inhaled the dusty air. Torn between fear and astonishment, she surveyed the damage. The fallen tree completely blocked the path and the rider was nowhere to be seen. She could hear the angry voices of other soldiers nearby, but she didn't wait to find out what they were saying.

She started running again.

Catanya ran without stopping for what seemed like hours. Her lungs burned and she had sharp pains in her sides, but she urged herself to continue onward. The trees thrashed at her as she flew past, tearing her clothes and cutting her skin. But she didn't care. Her eyes watered and her legs shook, but she kept running until she was deep in the forest, leaving Faltir far behind.

2

# THE CITY OF CAERLON

Diyah stumbled forward, the rope twisting and tearing at the skin on her wrists as someone dragged her through the door to Camlee Lodge. She turned to see Lady Genna, covered in blood and bruises, huddling on the sitting room floor with the remaining girls sheltered behind her. At least four fírkon were standing guard throughout the room. The man dragging Diyah tossed her unceremoniously onto the floor in front of them.

"It's not her," he said before the others could ask. "She's not the girl I saw talking with Grante." He looked down at Diyah. "I don't know who she is, but I caught her trying to help the other girl escape."

"Then I take it she did escape?" asked another man who was leaning against the wall, looking rather bored.

"Obviously."

Diyah exchanged glances with Genna, who exhaled in slight relief. But Diyah had never seen so much fear on her guardian's face. Genna was doing her best to look stoic, but her lower lip was trembling and her eyes darted back and forth, searching for an escape.

Just then an older, grizzled soldier strode through the door, wearing a murderous expression. He had long hair that appeared oily and matted and a dark bristly goatee. Although he was shorter than the other men, he carried himself with a self-important air that declared him as the leader, the maífirkon. He let out a frustrated cry and kicked a nearby chair, sending it careening across the floor until it cracked against the cabinet.

"Well, Slaedir, what do you want us to do with the rest of them?" asked the bored-looking man, indicating the prisoners. He seemed remarkably unfazed by his leader's outburst. "They're hardly going to be much use in the work camps," he added, nodding at the terrified young girls cowering behind Lady Genna who, with her hands and feet bound, was struggling to shield them from view.

"Kill them, I don't care," declared the maífirkon.

"As you wish." The bored man drew his sword.

"No!" Genna screamed and Slaedir backhanded her, sending blood spattering onto the floor.

Diyah lurched towards Genna, but someone yanked her hair and hurled her back so that she skidded across the floor and landed on the other side of the room.

"Diyah!" Genna's voice was strident and angry.

Winded, Diyah rolled over and stared up at the gleaming sword above her, and the impassive face of the man holding it.

"What are you waiting for, Julyán?" snapped Slaedir. "I gave you an order."

But Julyán stood fixed, staring at Diyah with a slight crease in his forehead. "You said she was trying to help the other one escape?" He addressed the man who had dragged Diyah into the lodge.

"Yes, what of it?"

"Well." He deliberated before turning to face his leader. "It occurs to me that she might be useful."

Slaedir's eyes flashed in displeasure. "How so?"

"Information," replied Julyán.

Slaedir scoffed. "You think you can make her talk?"

"Well, I don't intend to give her a choice."

Slaedir's face broke into a cruel smile, revealing his yellow teeth. "Very well, we'll keep her." He crouched beside Diyah, his pupils dilated as he stroked his beard. "Yes... she's lovely, isn't she?" He looked up at Julyán, whose face remained impassive. "We'll take her to the city and if the king doesn't want her, I'm sure someone else will." He raised his hand to touch her chin, but she smacked it away. "Oho. Yes, she'll do nicely. Keep her and a couple of children just in case, but kill the rest."

There was a brief pause, but then Julyán nodded and crossed towards Lady Genna.

"No!" screamed Diyah. She attempted to block him, but Slaedir kicked her hard in the stomach. She coughed and spluttered, rolling on the floor in agony. Blinking tears out of her eyes, she looked up to see the fírkon surrounding her family.

"No, don't hurt them!" Genna struggled to shield the girls. "Just hurt me! You can kill me, but please—" Genna tried to fight, but Julyán was too strong.

"Genna!"

Diyah let out an inarticulate cry and moved towards them, but Slaedir kicked out again, this time hitting Diyah's face and splitting her lip. And as Diyah struggled to reach her guardian, she watched in terror as Julyán pulled Genna's head back and in one quick fluid motion drew his sword across her throat. She was dead before she hit the ground.

The girls were all screaming and trying to escape as the fírkon surrounded them. Diyah didn't know which way to turn, but when Julyán lifted Hahney off the ground, Diyah lost her head and charged at him, hitting, kicking, and elbowing every inch of him she could reach.

"Don't touch them! Don't you dare touch them!"

But even as she screamed and punched, she knew it was useless. She felt arms tighten around her, and something hard struck her head. The last sounds she heard before she fell into darkness were the high-pitched screams of nine little girls who were left completely unprotected.

---

Diyah slid in and out of consciousness for what felt like days. Her brain was hazy, and she was barely aware of anything around her. She thought she felt herself being lifted and dragged, then jostled by horses. At one point, she caught a vague glimpse of a coastline and a campfire, but then she slipped into darkness again.

When she finally awoke, she could hear voices all around her, but she couldn't understand any of their words. Her body felt heavy, and her head was throbbing so painfully it made her feel sick. When she tried to touch it, she realized her hands were still bound by rope. And then she remembered what had happened.

She sat up straight and opened her eyes to find herself sitting on a horse, crossing through a gate in an enormous stone wall. Steady rows of torches illuminated the path ahead. Her jaw dropped as she saw the great city of Caerlon stretched out before her, cast against the black sky like a never-ending maze of flickering lights. The streets snaked and climbed through the hordes of buildings, stacked together like cordwood.

She twisted her head around, trying to take in her surroundings.

"Stay still," said the man sitting behind her, controlling the horse. He had one arm wrapped around her waist, holding her upright.

"Get your hands off me!" She tried to smack his hand away, but the ropes restrained her.

"If I let go, you'll fall."

"Then let me fall. I'd rather be trampled to death by horses, anyway."

The man tightened his grip and ignored her. Diyah twisted and struggled, but it was no use with her hands tied.

"Let me go!" she insisted.

"No."

Diyah cast around and noticed the other riders, three of whom each held a young girl on their horse. She recognized Meya, Gréys, and Hahney. Hahney and Gréys were awake, their eyes wide with fear. But Meya was lying draped over the horse, unconscious, and her face was covered in bruises.

*Three.* Only three were left.

A white-hot rage shot through Diyah and she struggled harder than ever. "You bastards! How could you? They're just children! Let us go!" Diyah cried out in rage and attempted to elbow the man holding her, but he tightened his grip, making it harder for her to breathe.

"Do us a favour and shut her up, Julyán," came another, oilier voice.

*Julyán?* She craned her neck to see his face. Her anger only intensified.

"You!" she shouted. "You killed her! Lady Genna! You killed them all, you loathsome, evil, barbaric—" Something struck her on the side of the head and she was almost thrown from the horse, but Julyán swerved to hold her steady.

"Are you mad? You nearly unseated us both!" he yelled at someone Diyah couldn't see.

"I told you to shut her up!"

Something trickled down Diyah's cheek and she knew she was bleeding. She moaned and leaned forward, struggling to stay awake. She needed to fight.

"We need her conscious!" shouted Julyán.

Fear was creeping in. They were bringing her to the castle and they needed her conscious for questioning. They thought she had information about Catanya and they were planning to torture her to get it.

Her stomach lurched as she looked over at the girls bound and tied on their horses. She couldn't let this happen to them. She had to be smart, she needed to find a way to save them.

The horses carried them up the winding streets and through the entrance of a second, smaller wall, where the city adopted a more spacious and developed appearance. Diyah suspected they had reached the wealthier district of the city, and she turned slowly to watch as an immense grey-stone castle emerged from the darkness.

The castle was mounted atop a large hill, overlooking the ocean to the northwest, the city to the south, and dense forest to the east. The ramparts were massive with curtain walls that measured at least ninety feet tall, connecting the eight enormous towers and countless turrets that reached high into the dark sky as though trying to touch the stars. Dozens of castle guards were stationed along the wall-walk, while the fírkon patrolled the battlements.

The horses' hooves clattered against the wooden bridge as they crossed the ravine into the courtyard and slowed to a halt.

If she hadn't been so frightened and full of blind loathing, Diyah might have been impressed. They had stopped outside the stone stairs leading into a huge keep with dozens of mullioned windows and niches built into its façade. The moon cast an unearthly glow around the stonework and the air was dense with an otherworldly energy. It was as though every spirit who'd ever lived and died in Caerlon was now wandering its streets, restless and alone. It sent a shiver down Diyah's spine.

All around her, the riders were dismounting and then,

without warning, Julyán swung her around and lowered her to the ground beside the horse. He jumped down beside her and put his hand tightly on her arm to keep her from running. She twisted and turned, attempting to lock eyes with one of the girls and assure them everything would be okay. But she couldn't find them amidst the sea of towering men.

"Let's bring this sorry lot to the king," said Slaedir, gesturing to the prisoners. "He won't be pleased to learn that the girl escaped."

Diyah thought she detected a note of fear in his voice.

"Hopefully one of them will prove useful." Then Slaedir crossed in front of Julyán and wrenched Diyah out of his grasp. "I'll take this one." He gave her a nasty smile and pushed her towards the stairs leading into the front door.

The faint whimpers behind her told Diyah that the girls were being forced to follow. As she stumbled up the steps and through the door into the entrance chamber, she could feel Slaedir's breath on the back of her neck. It made her skin crawl.

Diyah's heart pounded in her chest. Any second now she'd be standing opposite a man she hadn't seen in over ten years. They were children when they'd met the first time, but even then she'd known he would grow up to be exactly like his father.

Diyah could remember the encounter as if it were yesterday. It was over a decade ago during Cadyan's first royal tour of the kingdom in honour of his tenth birthday.

She had been walking in the woods outside Faltir, collecting herbs for Elyán, the village physician, when she'd noticed a boy sitting all alone on a fallen log by the side of the river.

She knew who he was almost instantly, with his high cheekbones and neat black hair, not to mention his superior clothes in the violet and golden colours of Caerlon. Her first instinct was to turn around and leave, but then she noticed the scuff marks on his clothes and the faint bruise on his face. He looked so lost and frightened that she took pity on him.

"Are you alright?" she ventured.

He jumped up, startled, spinning around to see who had spoken. Then he jutted out his chin in a haughty look. "Of course I'm alright, and it's none of your business, anyway."

Diyah was taken aback. "Sorry, I didn't mean to pry. I just thought you might be lost."

"I'm not lost!" he snapped, his face flushed.

She tried to ignore his hostile tone. "I-I can help you find your way back to the village."

"Help me? *You* help *me*? Don't you know who I am? I don't need help. Especially not some little girl—some *commoner* like you." He glared at her defiantly.

"That's not a very nice thing to say." She scowled at him. "I was only trying to help." She turned to walk away, but he stepped in front of her, blocking her path.

"I've just told you, haven't I? I don't need anyone's help."

"Get out of my way!"

"You can't tell me what to do! I tell *you* what to do!" he shouted. "You should bow to your prince, you filthy little brat." He knocked the basket out of her hand and littered the ground with all of her herbs, smirking.

"Hey!" She stooped to pick them up, but he shoved her away and then proceeded to stomp all over the herbs, crushing them under his boots.

"Why are you doing this?" Angry tears filled her eyes.

"Because," he declared petulantly, "because I don't have to give you a second thought. You're meagre and... and weak!" He appeared to be casting around for words that were strong enough. "You're just a commoner and I live far above you. I am the Crown Prince of Caerlon." He lunged forward and pushed her. She hit the ground hard and smacked her head on a tree root protruding out of the soil. "Stay down there in the mud where you belong!" he cackled with a self-satisfied gleam in his eye.

More tears burned in the corners of Diyah's eyes. She moved to stand up, but the prince pushed her down with his foot.

"I told you to stay—"

"Let her go!" called a voice from behind them. Cadyan whipped around to see a tall boy with dark, wavy brown hair standing beside the river. The boy was much bigger than Cadyan, and obviously several years older.

"Stay out of it, farm boy." Cadyan sneered and turned back to face Diyah.

"Leave her alone, or I'll make you," the other boy said.

"Make me?" Cadyan snickered and looked at him again.

The boy simply stared back, his expression impassive. Cadyan snorted disbelievingly and raised his leg to stomp on Diyah's fingers. But before he could bring his foot down, the teenage boy hit him hard and sent him flying into the mud. Then the boy took a step forward and held out his hand to Diyah.

"Thank you," she breathed.

The boy gave her a courteous smile and watched Cadyan scramble to his feet. "I warned you," he said.

"Do you have any idea what you've just done?" sneered Cadyan, failing to sound menacing as he spit mud out of his mouth.

"Yes." The boy's voice was perfectly matter-of-fact.

"*Yes?* Don't say *yes*, you rude... you impudent..." His face was red, and he stuttered angrily. "Do you know who I am?" he shouted. "Who my father is? You're going to pay for what you've done."

"What, never been knocked into the mud before?" The boy grinned.

"How dare you!"

The boy's face hardened and he advanced on Cadyan. "How dare I? How dare you hide behind your name and use your power to torment other people? You know, a truly powerful man wouldn't need to make others feel weak so he can feel strong." His eyes glinted in the light and he stood tall and dignified. "So you must not be as powerful as you'd have us believe." He shrugged and turned to walk back to Diyah.

"Watch out!" she called. Cadyan's face had contorted into a mask of rage. He jumped up and charged towards the boy. The boy ducked aside just in time and Cadyan fell face first on the ground. He rolled over, choking and groaning. He had cut his forehead on a rock. Blood trickled down his face as his eyes filled with tears.

"Come on." The boy laughed as he grabbed Diyah's hand and pulled her away into the forest, leaving the injured prince behind.

And in this moment, as Diyah was being forcibly marched towards the now-*King* Cadyan, she couldn't help wishing she were back in the woods with the teenage boy who'd rescued her—the only person she'd ever known brave enough to confront a member of the royal family.

But this time no one was coming to save her. She was on her own.

Slaedir pushed her towards a door at the other side of the chamber. It was an ornate door of ebony with gold inlay, large enough for a carriage to pass through. He pushed it open to reveal a massive throne room.

The ceiling was over thirty feet high, held up with two parallel rows of elaborately gilded stone pillars. Enormous violet banners bearing the Caerlon coat of arms hung every few feet along the aisle, and the dark stone floor echoed with every step. The intricate leadlight windows set high in the walls tinged the room with flickering moonlight, but despite that, and despite the several dozen torches burning in brackets lining the walls, the room still seemed dark and unwelcoming.

Several dozen firkon and courtiers had gathered at the far end of the room, chatting nervously.

And there, reclining arrogantly in his throne, was Cadyan.

Cadyan leaned forward as the door slammed, and the chatter behind him died. When the light hit his face, Diyah had to stifle a cry as she noticed his hair. Nearly all of it had transformed into an otherworldly mixture of colours, reminiscent of the greying one might expect in a man twice Cadyan's age. But these streaks were not grey; they were somehow both silver and opaque with hints of rose, turquoise, and violet. In the firelight of the candles and torches, the colours danced, their shimmering silver-white quality mesmerizing. It looked as though someone had poured a blend of melted pearls and opals over his head. The effect might have been beautiful had it not been combined with his angular face and cruel grey stare. He appeared distorted, nothing like the boy she remembered meeting in the woods all those years ago.

His cold eyes scanned the party as they walked towards him, and then they narrowed as he realized Catanya wasn't there.

"Where is she?" he demanded in a quiet but carrying voice.

"Your Highness—I mean, Your Majesty." Slaedir's face flushed at his mistake. He stepped forward and bowed. "Apologies, my lord. I regret to inform you that the girl escaped."

A dense pause lingered in the air.

"How can that be?"

"M-my lord?" Slaedir faltered and he shrank beneath the gaze that Cadyan gave him.

"How can that be? Are you incompetent?" Cadyan's words were full of malice.

"N-no, my lord! She-she had help!" Slaedir sounded desperate. He pushed Diyah to the floor at Cadyan's feet. "This one, Your Majesty. She warned the girl. She helped her escape."

Cadyan looked down at Diyah with indifference. He showed no sign of recognizing her. "I see. So you want me to believe that ten of the kingdom's most highly trained fighters were thwarted by two unarmed peasant girls with no training and no skills?" He glared at Slaedir, venomous accusation flaring in his eyes.

"No! Your Majesty, It's just—"

"What?" Cadyan spat with rancour.

"Well, we almost stopped her when something... happened."

"What happened?"

Slaedir cleared his throat roughly. "I was about to grab her when a massive tree fell and blocked my path. I was unseated and my horse fled, my lord."

Cadyan stared at him, his face impassive. "A tree fell and blocked your path?" he said with irony. The courtiers behind him laughed.

Slaedir clenched his teeth. "Yes, sir, except"—he closed his eyes as though bracing himself to say what came next—"I don't believe the tree fell of its own accord."

"What are you talking about, Slaedir?" Cadyan's posture stiffened.

"Well, I examined it, my lord. It was a perfectly healthy tree, no sign of rot or decay, and it didn't just fall. Something tore it free from the earth. Some... force."

He looked at Cadyan apologetically.

Diyah's heart raced, as she understood what Slaedir was trying to say.

"A force?" Cadyan gripped the arms of the throne so tight his knuckles turned white.

Slaedir sighed. "My lord, I believe it was the girl. I believe she has magic."

A loaded silence followed this statement. Then, to everyone's surprise, Cadyan started to laugh. It was a bitter, crazed laugh. He sprang to his feet and jumped down off the dais.

"Of course!" He was still laughing. "Of course she has powers! Is this what you've been hoping for all along?"

Diyah didn't know who he was talking to. He was staring past them to someone near the door.

"Well, Mother, tell me, you must be so *pleased!*" he spat. Then he started pacing agitatedly back and forth in front of the dais.

*Mother.*

Diyah twisted to see the woman striding down the aisle towards them.

She was younger than Diyah expected, with a proud face and long dark hair flecked with grey. She wore a heavy burgundy dress made of fine velvet, the portrait neckline adorned with golden vines that climbed down the sleeves, winding tighter until they reached the wrists. A matching circlet of delicate filigree encircled her head.

She presented an impressive figure as she strode towards her son and stopped. "How could you believe I take pleasure in any of the events that are coming to pass?"

Cadyan scoffed. "Well, we all know who set these events in motion, don't we?"

Fehla's face flushed and she glanced at the watching crowd. "I did what I needed to do," she said, holding her head high.

Some of the firkon shuffled and exchanged nervous looks. Cadyan didn't seem fazed to have an audience. If anything, he seemed emboldened by it.

"Oh, and I suppose you *needed* to choose," he said. "To choose which one of us stayed and which one of us left? How *did* you choose, mother?" He paused, his demeanour suddenly calm. "Tell me, how did you choose which child would live the normal life and which one would suffer, cowering under father's rage? How did you decide who would grow up with *him*?" Cadyan was staring at his mother, a mixture of pain and fury in his eyes. "*Tell me!*"

Fehla flinched involuntarily as he shouted it. "It was the hardest decision I have ever made," she said. "Not a day goes by that I don't regret it."

Cadyan's lips curled back into a sneer. "Regret what, Mother, losing her or keeping me?" He scowled and strode over to the fireplace. "Well, at least Father got what he deserved. I made sure of it, and I'll make sure she gets what she deserves too."

"Stop it, Cadyan!" Fehla's face was red with anger. "You're searching for enemies where there are none. You are acting like a spoiled child pitching a fit because he didn't get his way."

"Except I'm not a child, Mother!" spat Cadyan. For the first time, he looked self-conscious, his eyes darting towards the surrounding onlookers. "I'm the king now. And the king always gets his way." He straightened his posture and glared at his mother, daring her to respond, but she didn't take the bait. "Well, let's see. If you won't take credit for this, we'll have to find someone else."

Cadyan strode away from the fire and stood facing Slaedir. "I'm sure you did your best, Maífírkon," he said in an artificial voice. "It's not your fault that your best simply isn't good enough for your new king."

And without warning, Cadyan struck Slaedir hard in the face. Slaedir's nose cracked audibly and blood poured down his chin. The surrounding courtiers gasped and a flurry of whispers broke out, but then Cadyan's eyes burned gold and a horrified silence settled throughout the room.

Slaedir sank to the floor beside Diyah, writhing and struggling to breathe against the invisible force tormenting him, his blood pouring into his open mouth. Then Cadyan started kicking him in the chest, punctuating each of his next words with a blow from his feet.

"You. Miserable. Excuse. For. A. Fírkon."

Muffled mutters and exclamations of shock ran through the room. Diyah heard nervous squeaks from the girls behind her. She turned to see them watching the scene, their faces streaked with tears.

Cadyan stopped kicking and panted as he brushed his ethereal hair out of his face. Slaedir gasped and wheezed on the floor.

"Julyán." Cadyan addressed the other fírkon. "Take the prisoners to the dungeons. Find out what they know. I assume that's why they're still alive?" He glowered at Slaedir who nodded stiffly, still trembling. "Very well. Now stand up and go with them. I expect you won't fail me again. Do whatever it takes to make them talk."

Cadyan spun around and strode back to his throne, where he sat down, looking haughty and displeased. "Get out!" he called to the room at large. All the fírkon and courtiers scrambled for the exit.

Diyah felt someone yank her to her feet and steer her towards the door. Meya, Gréys and Hahney were gathered beside her, their small bodies shaking with silent sobs.

When they passed Fehla, Diyah attempted to get a closer glimpse of the woman she knew to be her friend's mother. The two made eye contact, and Diyah thought she could read defiance in Fehla's eyes. For one wild moment, she thought the queen might stop the fírkon from taking them to the dungeons, but then Fehla averted her eyes, allowing the girls' captors to march them away.

Diyah's head throbbed and she fought the urge to be sick. They were walking down a vast stone corridor, which ended abruptly at a black iron gate. Julyán pushed open the gate to reveal a set of treacherous steps descending into a dark, dank passage. Diyah stumbled when they pushed her down the steep stairs. Only the hand gripping her upper arm prevented her from falling.

When they reached the bottom, two imposing guards blocked their path. The guards wore full hauberks and coifs, with purplish grey surcoats that bore the Caerlon coat of arms. Each of them held a long wooden spear with a sharp, asymmetrical blade that glistened threateningly in the torchlight.

"The king wants these prisoners escorted to a cell," said Julyán.

"Aye, this way."

One of the guards lifted a torch off the wall and unlocked a second iron gate. Behind it, stretching away into darkness, was a narrow passage lined with bars on each side.

A damp, sour smell reached Diyah's nostrils. As they walked down the passage in search of an empty cell, she looked around in horror. She didn't know what she had expected, but it shocked her to see the prisoners chained to the floor. She couldn't bear to think how long the poor wretches had been wasting away in their dark, filthy cages. Some of them had been starved to practically nothing, cowering in the corners of their prisons, shielding their eyes from the passing torchlight, and jumping at every faint sound.

Julyán halted. "This man." He pointed at the nearest cell. "How long has he been lying like that?"

"Why does it matter?" It was Slaedir talking. He sounded bitter as he rubbed dried blood off his face before casting a cursory glance at the man in the cell. "He's vermin, and he's doing what vermin does."

"How long?" Julyán glared at the guards.

"Not sure. Few days. S'been a while since the ships have docked. Can't get rid of 'em, can we?"

Diyah closed her eyes, still fighting the urge to be sick.

"Check if he's still alive," Julyán said.

The guard unlocked the door and approached the motion-less body.

"Oy!" he called. "Oy! You get up, vermin." He kicked the man, but nothing happened. Then he bent down to check for a heartbeat. "Yeah, dead. Ice cold too. Been dead for a while."

"Well, hurry up and remove that corpse," snapped Julyán.

"What does it matter?" asked Slaedir. "Leave it to rot, for all I care."

Julyán's face hardened. "We're going to be stuck down here interrogating these prisoners. Do you want that foul, rotting stench to saturate the entire place?"

Diyah glowered at him with disgust and contempt. He returned her gaze, his face impassive. Then he pushed her farther down the line of cells.

As Diyah stumbled forward, she was surprised to hear someone call her name.

"Diyah? No!"

There was genuine anguish in that cry.

A man rushed forward in his cell, stopping short as the chain on his leg reached its limit. He stared at her through the bars, looking distraught. His round face was badly bruised and bloodied. His left eye was swollen shut, but Diyah recognized him instantly.

"Grante!" she exclaimed. "No! What have you done to him?" She struggled against Julyán's grip, but he pushed her forward so she tripped over the uneven floor.

"Diyah!" Grante called after her, grabbing hold of the bars and straining to keep her in view. "Diyah, I'm sorry. I'm so sorry, they followed me. I—"

"Be quiet, you," shouted a guard as he banged his spear on the bars, rapping Grante's knuckles and causing him to cry out in pain.

"Stop it!" shouted Diyah. She struggled even harder, but it was no use. Julyán pushed her along the corridor, deeper and deeper into the dark, until Grante's cries faded to mere echoes in the distance.

Diyah closed her eyes momentarily, trying to calm herself. Then her heart sank.

*So that was how they'd found Catanya.*

Anger and sadness swirled through Diyah's mind until a painful lump formed in her throat. She didn't know Grante well—they'd only met a few days ago—but that didn't matter. He was a good man. One who'd risked everything trying to protect Catanya.

He didn't deserve this fate.

When they finally arrived at an empty cell, Julyán tossed Diyah away, so that she tripped and fell to the ground. Meya, Gréys, and Hahney were thrown in after her. They hit the stone floor hard, yelping in pain and fear.

"Watch it!" Diyah yelled at the men. She stood up in front of the girls.

"Shut your mouth!" shouted Slaedir. He stepped through the open cell door and continued in his oily voice, "You're about to learn, girly, that around here nothing you say or do matters. You'll tell us everything we want to hear, and then we'll leave you to rot, just like that body back there."

"I won't tell you anything," she spat.

He leaned in closer so only Diyah could hear, "Honestly, pretty, I don't care. I'm going to enjoy our time together either way." He ran his bloody fingers across her cheek and down her neck, smiling as she recoiled. Then he called to the guards, "Shackle them! We'll be back to interrogate them soon." He gave Diyah one last lecherous look, then turned and limped back down the passage, rattling the cell bars as he passed.

The cries and shouts of the other prisoners echoed down the hall as the guards chained Diyah's ankle to the floor. When they'd finished with the girls' chains too, the guards stepped out of the cell, waiting for Julyán.

Julyán stared at Diyah with a blank expression. Then he pulled out a gleaming dagger and walked deliberately into the cell. Diyah tried to back away from him, but she tripped on her new shackles and hit the floor with a resounding thud. She scrambled to shield the girls behind her, but Julyán grabbed her by the arm and spun her around. He bent over her, and in one swift movement, cut the binds around her hands. She stared as he stepped behind her, slicing through each of the girls' binds and collecting the ropes before striding out of the cell. He pulled the door shut with a crash, locked it, and left the dungeon without a second glance.

The guards followed him, taking the light of the torch with them and leaving the prisoners alone in almost total darkness. A small window in a nearby cell provided a meagre ray of moonlight, but it scarcely penetrated the suffocating blackness of the dungeon.

Diyah crawled over to the girls. "Are you okay? Is anyone hurt? Meya?"

"No, Diyah, we're okay." Meya was the oldest of the three girls and Diyah suspected she was putting on a brave face. Diyah reached out to touch her. She needed to examine Meya's bruises, but it was too dark to see any detail.

"What are they going to do to us?" asked Gréys. She wasn't crying anymore, but her fear was palpable. She crawled into the patch of moonlight, her eyes wide as she peered around the cell.

"I-I don't know, girls."

"I'm scared, Diyah," whispered Meya.

Diyah pulled Meya into an embrace, then reached her hands out for Gréys and Hahney. "I know. I'm scared too. But I won't let anyone hurt you, okay?" She looked into their shadowy faces, struggling to make eye contact.

"Lady Genna..." moaned Hahney in a quiet, little voice.

"Why? Why are they doing this? And what do they want with Catanya?"

"Listen to me," said Diyah seriously. "Listen, you mustn't tell them anything about Catanya, okay?"

"But why?"

Diyah cast around for a way to explain without telling the truth. The less the girls knew, the better. "They're searching for Catanya because they think she knows something that might threaten the king. They want to kill her."

"What does Catanya know?" asked Meya.

"I-I'm not sure." Diyah averted her eyes. "I just know they'll do whatever it takes to find her and kill her. If we care about Catanya, and if we want her to survive, we can't tell them anything. Do you understand?"

"Yes."

"Is Catanya going to be alright?" Gréys tightened her grip on Diyah's hand.

"I hope so." It was all she could say.

"Are *we* going to be alright?" asked Hahney.

Diyah sensed their scared eyes on her. Lost for words, she reached out and pulled them all into her arms and held them tightly until they drifted off to sleep.

# 3

# TRAVELLERS IN THE WOODS

Catanya was perfectly content. She was back at Camlee Lodge sitting with Lady Genna and Diyah. The fire blazed in the grate, and the sun was setting outside the window, lending the room a cozy warmth.

As the sun sank lower and the room grew dark, Catanya reached over to light the candles on the table between her and Diyah.

When she moved to turn away, one of the candles slipped off its stick. She automatically reached out to grab it.

"Ow!" She dropped it and shook her hand in frustration. A large welt was forming on the inside of her thumb where the flame had burned her. "Stupid," she muttered, picking up the fallen candle and putting it back on the table to light it again.

"What happened?" asked Diyah.

"Oh, nothing." Catanya hid her hand behind her back, concealing the burn. She didn't want Diyah to make a fuss. Then, avoiding Diyah's gaze, she stood up and crossed to the cabinet where they kept the wine.

"Always getting hurt, honestly I don't know how you do it," grumbled Diyah under her breath.

Catanya suppressed a laugh as she pulled open the cabinet doors to survey the contents inside.

Genna usually kept a couple bottles of spiced wine and haymead, but she only had one of each in the cabinet now. Catanya opened the bottle of wine and poured a generous portion into each of their glasses. She was carrying two of them back to Genna and Diyah, when a wave of nausea and light-headedness washed over her. She sniffed the wine to see if it had soured. It smelled fine, so she handed the glasses to the other women and returned to grab her own.

As she passed behind Diyah's chair, her legs went suddenly weak. She clutched the back of the chair for support.

"Catanya, what is it?" came Lady Genna's voice.

She tried to answer, but the room was spinning. She strug-gled to stay upright. The edges of her vision were turning dark and she knew she was falling. A sharp pain shot through her head as she crashed to the floor. Everything went dark.

*She was standing in a room, surrounded by hundreds of people. But nobody seemed to see her. They were transfixed by the scene in front of them.*

*A young man was kneeling before an ornate altar that emanated a blinding golden light. He seemed familiar, with his thick crop of neat black hair and his cool grey eyes. Even kneeling, she could tell that he was tall, his long legs stretched out behind him under the flowing violet and gold robes.*

*"Cadyan, King of Caerlon, do you pledge fealty to your kingdom's sacred power?" a voice resounded in the dark. A wizened figure in long grey robes appeared behind the altar.*

*"I do." The kneeling man spoke with a clear, firm resolve.*

*"Do you vow to use that sacred power only for the welfare of Caerlon?"*

*"I do."*

*"Do you swear to protect that sacred power from all those who seek it for themselves?"*

"*I do.*"

"*Then rise and claim the powers bestowed by the Elixir of Caerlon.*" The chaplain bowed and retreated off to the side as Cadyan rose and lifted the chalice off the altar, swirling its contents. He smiled, and his face looked distorted in the dazzling golden light that emanated from the liquid. He turned to stare at the congregation.

"*My people.*" He lifted the glowing chalice as if in toast. "*Today you witness the end of one era and the start of something new. I pledge loyalty to the kingdom and its people and I vow to honour my role as your king.*"

He glanced behind him, where an older woman stood watching him, her expression strained.

"*Let us not pretend that my father was the king you deserved!*" called Cadyan. An awestruck silence followed this bold declaration. He turned back to the crowd. "*Let us not pretend he was anything more than a selfish coward, too threatened by his power to use it as he ought to have done. For too long you have been kept at arm's length. For too long you've been kept in the dark. But no more!*" A murmuring of curiosity and interest buzzed through the faceless crowd. "*I will not be so ungenerous,*" he said more quietly, scrutinising the chalice in his grasp. "*No, I will not hoard this power for myself. Rather I will use it to improve the lives of my people!*" he cried. "*I will be a merciful leader and in my reign you will experience my generosity and my gratitude for your fealty. At sundown of every full moon, I will make my power available to you and your requests. Bring what you have to offer and you shall receive what I have to offer in return.*" He paused and stared at the crowd.

"*For Caerlon, for Might and for Glory,*" he called in a ringing voice.

"*For Caerlon, for Might and for Glory!*" chanted the congregation.

"*Long live the King!*" came a genuine cry from the audience.

"*Long live the King!*" The echo came with enthusiasm.

*Cadyan smiled to himself, raised the chalice to his lips, and drank deeply.*

And somehow Catanya tasted its smooth, sweet contents.

*Cadyan closed his eyes and drank until the chalice was empty. Then, as he lowered his arm and opened his eyes, he swayed and teetered. When he reached over to place the chalice on the altar, it nearly slipped from his grasp.*

Catanya could hear panicked voices above her. The blurry faces of Diyah and Genna stared down at her, blanched and alarmed.

And then suddenly she was burning, her entire body scorched by a white-hot flame coursing through her veins. She screamed and thrashed.

"What do we do?"

"I don't know, I've never seen anything like this before!"

The burning reached a peak. It felt like a small, round object was boring a hole into her heart. Catanya clutched at the necklace on her chest and tried to tear it away. But she couldn't move it. When her fingers touched the stone, it sent a shock surging through her that rattled her bones and seared her veins. She squeezed her eyes shut and willed the pain to stop, but the darkness blazed to life with a blinding, iridescent glow.

*The light exploded from him in every direction and he was screaming now too.*

She wanted to reach out to him, to help him, but she was trapped inside her own body, incapacitated and powerless. She was sure they were both dying.

And she almost welcomed it.

<hr>

Catanya smelled the sweetness of the earth against her cheek. Something hard jabbed into her ribs. She was drenched with sweat and shaking as she opened her eyes and sat up, scanning the trees. She groaned as she realized where she was and remembered what she'd been dreaming about.

Since that night, she'd replayed its events over and over again in her mind, trying to understand what had happened. But each time she went through it, she understood less and less.

Taking slow steady breaths to calm down, she brushed her hair off her face. As she lowered her hands, she noticed something odd.

In the uproar of the previous days, she hadn't realized, but now she saw that her burn from the candle was gone. In fact, she couldn't see any sign that her skin had ever been burned.

She racked her brain, trying to remember if the wound had been there the morning after the coronation. She'd spent that entire day working in the gardens, so surely the skin would have irritated her. But she couldn't remember having any trouble that day.

She stared at her hand in disbelief, running her thumb across the spot where the burn should be.

*Always getting hurt, honestly I don't know how you do it.*

Catanya's eyes—already puffy and sore from crying herself to sleep—started to sting. She pressed the heels of her hands against her orbits, wishing she could physically hold the tears back. Losing control wouldn't help her right now.

She cleared her throat gruffly and told herself to focus on the present. She'd been trudging through the forest for days without proper food or shelter, and she needed to keep moving.

It was shortly after daybreak. The forest buzzed with the sound of birds and other wildlife. Thick trees stood on every side and when she craned her neck upwards, she caught a faint glimpse of blue sky through the dense canopy. The forest floor was strewn with twigs and branches, and thick moss grew on the rocks and tree trunks. Though the forest was less frightening in the daytime, it was still an overwhelming expanse of never-ending trees with untold numbers of creatures and predators lurking within it.

Every minuscule sound was magnified by the forest. Every rustle of the underbrush, every snap of a twig drew Catanya's attention. Her muscles were tight with tension as she twitched at each new sound. The forest was confining, and her fear was suffocating.

As she stood up, her legs stiff and protesting the exertion, she made herself take several deep breaths and stay calm. She needed to get out of this forest. The best way to do that was to follow the river south. Eventually, it would lead her to the southern sea, and she knew she could follow the coastline east towards the Kingdom of Awnell and out of Caerlon. She had no plan other than the vague hope that in Awnell she might be safe.

So she started walking again, and though her legs were sore, the pain eased as she moved. She looked up, trying to orient herself. Then, putting the sun at her side, she continued southeast in search of the river.

She walked for hours, until finally, around midday, she heard running water. She pushed through a dense patch of bracken to emerge atop a small hill sloping down to the river below. The river rushed wildly and the smell of rich, moist earth greeted her nostrils as she stumbled down to the riverside. She plunged her hands gratefully into the water and allowed the strong current to pull at her. She cupped her hands and brought them up to her mouth to drink. The water was cold and refreshing, sweet like grass and sun-drenched honey. She hadn't realized how thirsty she was.

After emptying her hands several times, she leaned back and stretched her legs out in front of her. A small pool of water had collected between a cluster of stones. She sat staring at her reflection in its glassy surface.

It was strange. Although she knew it was her face staring back at her, all she saw was *him*.

Catanya had never met Cadyan in person, but his face was forever burned in her memory. The longer she looked at her reflection, the more she saw the family resemblance. They had the same high cheekbones and silky grey eyes. And her long black hair, which had started falling free of its braid, shone in the sun, despite the forest grime matted into it.

Catanya untied her braid, letting the long strands fall into her face. As she began rewinding it, she noticed a silver strand mixed in with her dark black locks.

*Strange*, thought Catanya. She wouldn't have expected her hair could turn grey so quickly. But as she pulled the strand out to get a closer look, she realized it wasn't exactly grey. The hair had a curious shimmering quality, and it reflected the light when she moved.

She had never seen hair quite like it before. She couldn't explain why, but the sight of it put her on edge. Unwilling to look at it anymore, she pinned the strand back and finished tying her hair to conceal the strange iridescent streak.

Then she glanced back down at her reflection and frowned. It was difficult for her to look at herself now.

Unlike her friend Diyah, Catanya had never been considered beautiful, but she had always liked her appearance. Until now. Between her height and the striking effect of her hair with her eyes, she had always supposed she was just a bit too unusual for the people of Faltir.

But now she wondered if subconsciously they'd sensed that something was off about her. Maybe they were afraid of her.

Catanya splashed some water on her face and stood up, glancing around. The river was too wide and wild to cross, which should give her protection on one side, but if anyone approached her from behind, she'd be trapped.

She sighed heavily, weighing her options. Finally, she

decided to follow the river downstream, all the while trying to stay alert to any sounds or sudden movements.

The riverside was rock-strewn and slimy. She stumbled and tripped as she made her way across it, cutting her hands and knees when she slipped on the rocks.

"Ow!" she gasped, examining the bloody gash that had opened in her palm. The cut was full of tiny specks of dirt and it smarted as she brushed the dirt away. She turned and headed to the water. Placing her hand in the river, she let the current wash her wound clean. The cool temperature soothed the pain.

*Snap.*

Catanya froze. Something was moving on the opposite bank of the river.

She glanced across the water and watched the treeline rustling. Overcome with panic, she crouched low and darted behind a large, moss-covered boulder on the edge of the water, where she sat very still, listening. She could hear the faint thuds of feet on the rocks followed by the sound of water splashing. Someone or something was over there. She shut her eyes and pulled her legs in tightly so as not to be seen.

She sat uncomfortably still, waiting for the sounds to stop.

It sounded like only one person.

*But what kind of person would be skulking alone in the middle of the woods? Other than me.* She resisted the sudden urge to laugh. Her exhaustion was making it difficult to think clearly.

After some time, she thought she heard footsteps retreating, so she peered out from her boulder to check. Whoever it was, they were gone now. For the present, she was safe. Still, she had nearly been discovered, and it made her realize just how exposed she was, walking along the riverbank. So she retreated into the trees.

She walked for hours, occasionally stopping to drink from the river, but always returning to the cover of the trees. Her fear mounted again as the sun sank lower, casting the forest into shadow. Owls hooted in the trees, animals scurried through the underbrush.

A sudden chorus of howls and yips burst through the air. Somewhere nearby, a pack of coyotes was hunting its prey. Snarls and the sounds of ripping flesh and snapping bones. Then came the frantic squeals of smaller animals clinging desperately to life.

The sound was disconcertingly close.

Shaking from head to toe, Catanya forced herself to keep walking as quietly as possible, putting distance between herself and the pack of hunters. Eventually the sound subsided, but the echos still tormented her.

It was late when she stumbled upon a small, sloped clearing surrounded by tall oaks. Darkness had fully swallowed the forest. Unable to continue moving, she slumped onto the hard ground with her back against the largest tree so she had a clear view of her surroundings. The cool night air seeped into her bones and she shivered as she wrapped her arms around her legs and tried to sleep.

Catanya had barely shut her eyes when she snapped awake again. She didn't immediately realize what had woken her, but then she heard them. Voices.

She could hear men laughing and a fire crackling through the trees. She sat frozen, listening.

"Good haul this time."

"Aye, on'y I wish they'd put up a better figh' you know."

"Yeah, I do like it when they figh'."

The men laughed.

A sizzling sound came up over the incline, and the smell of roasted venison reached her, making her stomach ache with hunger. For a wild second, she considered running down the hill to join them, but she thought better of it.

"Oy, get a load o' this."

"What is it?"

"That's genuine Sidina silk that is. That'll fetch us a pretty penny."

"An' we can buy all the best spiced wines!"

"An' the company of ladies what are act'ly decen' to look at! Not like las' time! Do you remember tha'? Oh, she was a dog."

"Me, I don' mind how they look, on'y how they feel."

Their whistling and raucous laughter made Catanya's stomach clench. Clearly these men weren't the kind she wanted to encounter alone in the dark forest. From the sound of it, they were thieves.

They continued guffawing and hooting until another man's voice cut through the noise. "Give me that! You imbeciles. If it were up to you, we'd all be dead by now. You know perfectly well that we aren't selling any of this."

"Oh, come on. Nobody'll know if we jus' take a bit off the top."

Murmurs of agreement, followed by more laughter.

"I said no." The man's tone was cool and commanding.

On her hands and knees, Catanya crept across the damp, leaf-strewn earth and peered out from behind a fallen log. She could see the silhouettes of at least five men. Four of them were sitting around a fire, while the fifth stood towering over them. His posture was straight and imposing, and she saw the outline of a sword fastened to his side. He held himself with a firkon's stature, but he bore no sign of Caerlon's colours.

"Oh, al' righ'."

"Yea, 'ave it your way then."

A murmur of reluctant assent drifted through the group, and they handed the silks to the man standing above them.

"Good. Now shut your mouths and put this fire out before someone sees us," commanded the leader. He strode away from them.

"I hate havin' to take orders from him," groused one of the other men, as he stood up and began kicking dirt onto the fire.

"One o' these days, jus' you wait."

Catanya ducked down behind the log, trembling. She needed to leave before any of these men noticed her. They definitely weren't firkon, but she didn't want to cross paths with outlaws in the woods either. It took her several deep breaths before she mustered the courage to move. When she had steadied herself, she crept away from the log and back through the clearing.

She hurried as quickly and quietly as she could towards the river. When she reached the riverbank, she turned and followed it farther south. The moon hung low in the sky, filtering through the canopy and reflecting off the water. She attempted to stay hidden inside the trees as she moved, but it was difficult to find a route in the dark. The branches scratched her, and her dress caught on thorns and brambles, as she stumbled clumsily through the dense thicket. More than once, she had to stop and disentangle herself from clumps of twisted shrubbery.

She continued until the sun began to rise. When she thought she had put enough space between her and the bandits, she slowed her pace.

Catanya was starting to despair about her situation. Her nerves were strained beyond their limits and she was starving and weak. There were all manner of dangerous people and hungry creatures hiding in these woods. She had no food, no weapons, and no way to protect herself.

*Maybe you* do *have a way to protect yourself*, said a timid voice inside her head.

She held up her hands, remembering the tree that had fallen between her and the rider pursuing her back in Faltir. At the time, she hadn't stopped to question it. But now she wondered...

She stumbled along the river until midday, when it branched off into a quiet pond. The sun beat down on her, burning her skin, and she was exhausted from running all night. Her mind was groggy and strained from fighting back her emotions. Caked in sweat and filth, as well as her own blood, she wanted to swim, to feel the water on her skin washing away the pain of the days before.

Forests overwhelmed her, but water... That was where she felt at home.

She staggered to a halt. Then, fumbling to unlace her shoes, she kicked them off and pulled her dress over her head, pausing to examine it. This dress had been her favourite—Genna had bought it for her several years ago when Catanya came of age. It used to be a dark green colour with a simple laced bodice and long sleeves, but now it was ripped and stained, and covered in filth and grime. She shook her head and laid it on the ground trying not to think of Genna, and then she stepped into the water, wearing only her underdress.

The water was cold, but it felt nice on her toes. As she waded farther into the pond, she let the water soothe her aching muscles. She took a deep breath and plunged under the surface. It was bracing and refreshing, as she paddled farther into the pool and came up for air, shaking her sopping hair out of her face. She rested there, treading water and looking at her surroundings, as some clarity returned to her weary mind.

It was beautiful here in this small crop of wilderness. The bright green trees encircled the clear water, and the sun shone down from above, making all the colours brighter and more vibrant. The water sparkled in the sunlight and the whole place seemed magical.

*Magical.* Catanya looked down at her hands again, wondering what powers they held. She lifted them up and imagined using them to influence the motion of the waves. She ran her hands through the water and pictured the movement of the ocean she'd left behind in Faltir. With her hand above the pond, she made a curve in the air. To her surprise, the water formed a perfect arc as it followed her gesture.

In her astonishment, she forgot to kick her feet and got a mouthful of water. She marvelled at her hands, hardly believing what she'd seen. Then she raised them both into the air as a small tunnel of water rose between them. She rotated her hands in a circle and watched the tunnel spin like a whirlpool.

Catanya stared at the whirlpool, mesmerized, until a thought crept unbidden into her mind.

*I wonder if* he's *ever done something like this.*

She felt a strange prickling sensation in her fingers. Her heart pounded. Crippling dread dampened the impulse to push her magic further, and the whirlpool evaporated.

Catanya was staring at the spot, hands outstretched, listening to her heart resume its normal pace, when something crunched behind her. She dropped her hands under the water and twisted to see what caused the sound.

There was a man watching her. He was holding an apple and leaning against a tree near the edge of the pond, looking nonchalant, the corners of his mouth curved up in amusement.

Catanya's body tensed and her heart raced. How long had he been there?

"What did you see?" she demanded, surprised at the authority in her voice. Then she cast around, trying to spot any others. But he appeared to be alone.

The man chuckled, lifting his hands up in an apologetic gesture. "Honestly, I didn't see anything," he said. "You were already in the water when I arrived."

"What?" Catanya was confused for a moment until she realized what he meant. "Oh!"

She laughed involuntarily at the misunderstanding. He obviously hadn't seen the whirlpool.

The man smiled widely and peered around the clearing. "What are you doing here?" he asked.

Catanya followed his gaze, frowning. "What do you mean, *what am I doing?* I should have thought that was obvious." She splashed her hands in the water, too exhausted to care about her tone.

"Right, yes. Well, I mean, what are you doing all alone, in the middle of nowhere with"—he spotted her discarded dress —"with tattered and—" He stooped to look closer. "Is that blood?" He gazed up at her, eyes wide with surprise and alarm. "Are you alright?"

"Yes. I'm perfectly alright," said Catanya stiffly. She watched him through narrowed eyes, trying to decide what to make of him. He didn't seem like a threat, but she couldn't be sure.

"Where is the rest of your party? Wait, you're not travelling alone?" He sounded shocked, as he glanced around.

Catanya didn't respond.

"Where are you from?" he asked, a line forming between his brows.

"You ask a lot of questions..." She trailed off, eyeing him guardedly. He seemed genuinely concerned, but Catanya wasn't sure she could trust her weary brain to judge.

"Look." The man raised his hands in a peacekeeping gesture. "I don't mean to be rude, but it seems to me like you could use some help."

"I don't need any help," she blurted.

He scoffed and started eating his apple again. "You mean to tell me you are out here all alone, with blood-stained clothes, cuts all over your face, and you don't want my help?" He arched his eyebrows.

"Well." Catanya cast around for an excuse. "Well, I... I'm not—"

"Look, you don't have to tell me what you're doing if you don't want to," he said in a gentle voice. "But at least let me leave you some new clothes." He gestured to a large bag he'd left by the tree. "And I imagine you haven't eaten for some time, since you don't seem to have any provisions with you. I'd be happy to leave some food, or we can share a meal, and then after that, if you don't want my help, we'll go our separate ways."

Catanya thought for a moment. How long had it been since she'd eaten something? Her stomach ached as it growled. "Alright," she mumbled. "One meal."

He smiled at her, and there was an awkward pause until Catanya said, "Okay I'm coming out now."

"Right. Right!" A flush crept up his face. "I'll just—I'll wait over there then, shall I?" He pointed behind the trees. "Here." He rummaged through his pack and pulled out a brown tunic and a pair of men's breeches. "I imagine these will make it easier for you to navigate the woods. Easier than a dress anyway." He laid them down at the edge of the pond before stepping behind the tree to wait while Catanya emerged and dressed herself.

The clothes were much too big for her, but they were clean and they smelled fresh. She pulled the laces out of her dress bodice and used them to tie around her waist to keep the breeches from falling down. Then she rolled up the tunic sleeves to free her hands and sat down to pull on her shoes.

Lastly, she tied her hair back up, hiding the coloured strand as best she could. "Okay," she called to him.

He poked his head out from behind the tree. When he saw her, his face cracked into a wide, infectious grin. "Not exactly Sidina fashion, but I think they'll do the trick."

"Thank you." She shifted from one foot to the other awkwardly and smoothed the front of the shirt.

"My pleasure. By the way, my name is Jémys." He extended his hand towards her. "Jémys Aí-Finnua."

She stared at his hand for a moment, then hesitantly

reached forward. "Catanya Aí—" She stopped herself before mentioning Faltir. "Just Catanya," she said, realizing too late it probably wasn't even wise to give her first name. But at least she could leave Aí-Faltir behind. It had never been her real name anyway.

*Aí-Caerlon.*

Catanya shuddered. She dropped his hand and backed away.

"Well, Catanya." He seemed untroubled by her wariness. "I have a few bread loaves, some cheese, and plenty of nuts and apples. I think I have a bit of haymead left too." He rummaged through his pack, pulling everything out.

Catanya was so hungry that she took everything he handed her without hesitation. She sank into the grass and started ripping off chunks of bread and cheese, stuffing them into her mouth. Jémys sat down to finish his apple and eat some bread as well.

They ate in silence for several minutes. Once her stomach was full and she felt stronger, Catanya was able to take in the full appearance of the man sitting opposite her. He was wearing a dark green tunic, a brown surcoat and cloak, and plain leather vambraces on his arms. He had warm, kind features and dark, wavy brown hair that kept falling in his face, prompting him to brush it away. Although he was sitting, she could tell he was tall. He had long muscular arms and legs and she suspected he might be several inches taller than her when standing—which was saying something, given that Catanya was unusually tall herself. It was difficult to tell, but she thought he must be close to her age, though his bright green eyes seemed to carry significant weight.

She watched as he tore a chunk off the bread loaf. His skin was dark and he had strong hands that bore clear signs of heavy labour. He certainly wasn't a wealthy man.

Catanya was still examining his hands when she sensed his

gaze on her. She looked up. He smiled and handed her the bottle of haymead. She tried to return his smile, but it felt unnatural on her face.

"That looks painful." He pointed at the large gash on her palm, as she took the bottle from him.

"It's fine," she mumbled. "I just tripped." She stared at the cut, feeling strangely unsettled. Why wasn't it healing as fast as her burn had done? In fact, dozens of cuts and bruises covered her body, and there was no sign they were healing any faster than they would have done previously.

Had she imagined the burn entirely?

*Always getting hurt, honestly I don't know how you do it.*

Her eyes prickled and she turned her head so Jémys wouldn't see.

"So..." Jémys's tone was light and soft, like he knew she was upset but didn't want to pry. "I'm getting the sense that you didn't plan this journey into the woods, am I right?"

They made eye contact and Catanya measured him up. Then she shrugged. "No, I didn't plan it." She took another slow swig from the bottle before changing the subject. "What about you? Where are you heading?"

"Me? I'm heading back to Finnua. It's about a four-day walk from here." He gestured through the trees. "Southwest," he finished, swallowing a mouthful of bread.

"And that's your home? Finnua?"

"Yes. That's where my aunt lives and that's where I was born." He started repacking his bag with the remaining food. "I've been gone for a long time so it'll be nice to return home." He fastened the clasp on his bag and peered at Catanya with concern in his eyes. "Where are you headed, then?"

She eyed him shrewdly. "Nowhere."

"Nowhere," he repeated, nodding knowingly. "Yeah, I think I've been there." He flashed a grin.

Catanya held his gaze, debating whether to tell him the

truth. Then she sighed. "I... well, I have no home anymore." She struggled to keep her voice calm, pretending she wasn't terrified.

"Look." His tone was soft. "Why don't you join me? Come with me to Finnua. You can regroup before continuing your journey. It's just—honestly, I don't think anyone should travel alone in these woods. Especially not these days." Seeing the inquiring look on Catanya's face, he continued, "Every day I hear stories of outlaws and bandits in these woods. The higher Caerlon raises its taxes, the more people are driven to thievery and cruelty."

"Hmm." Catanya glanced back through the trees. "I did overhear some men in the woods last night. I suspected they were thieves..." She trailed off, shuddering at the memory. Not to mention the sounds of coyotes howling.

"So, you'll come with me?" His face brightened.

"I—" She bit her lip. The early evening sun hung low in the sky and she didn't relish the idea of setting off alone again.

"You can trust me." Jémys gave her a reassuring nod.

Catanya surveyed him. Her eyes met his, the grey and the green, and she suddenly knew it was true. "Okay, yes, I'll come with you."

He smiled widely. "Great, it'll be nice to have the company."

As they stood up, Jémys lifted a sword off the ground behind him and began fastening it to his belt.

Catanya watched him curiously. She hadn't noticed the sword before.

Jémys finished securing it in place and rested his hand on it. Then, seeing the question on her face, he shrugged. "It belonged to my father. I just carry it for protection. Like I said, these woods can be dangerous." He swung his bag over his shoulder. "Shall we?"

Together, Jémys and Catanya circled the pond and continued through the forest.

4

___

# RAIN AND RECOLLECTIONS

A gentle breeze blew against Catanya's face. As she awoke, curled up on the forest floor, she could smell the delicious scent of something roasting on a fire. The light was dim, still close to dawn. She rolled onto her back and stared at the canopy above for a brief moment before sitting up.

Jémys was crouched a short distance away, tending a fire and roasting a rabbit. When he saw her watching him, he smiled.

"Morning," he said cheerily.

"Good morning." Catanya rubbed her sore eyes and squinted at the spit in the fire. "Where did you get that?"

"I caught it. Not an hour ago... I couldn't sleep." He shrugged. "It's done, if you'd like to eat before we get moving."

Catanya's stomach growled, as though in answer to his question. Jémys chuckled and lifted the spit off the fire and laid it down on a flat stone. He pulled a large hunting blade out of a strap on his leg and sliced the spit and rabbit cleanly in two pieces. Then he handed one half to Catanya.

"Thank you," she mumbled.

She ripped a chunk off the bones with her teeth. It was delicious. She devoured the rest of it, and when she had finished, she felt much stronger and more awake.

"Here." Jémys handed her his canteen. "I filled it up by the stream."

Catanya drank deeply. Despite the constant weight of her grief and fear, she couldn't deny her gratitude for her new travel companion.

They packed up the rest of their things and extinguished the fire, kicking dirt over it to cover their tracks. Then they climbed down the hill towards the river, where they refilled the canteen before setting off.

The sky was overcast, and the wind was cool as they continued their journey through the woods. As long as they kept moving, they didn't notice the cold, but whenever they stopped, the air would seep into their bones, causing them to shiver.

After several hours of walking, the cloud cover had grown thick, and the forest was nearly as dark as night.

Catanya eyed the gloomy sky. "I think it's going to rain."

As she said it, somewhere far above them came a deep rumbling noise. The sky ignited and a loud crack like a whip exploded in the distance. At first it was only a gentle drizzle, then steadily more drops fell until a torrential downpour was drenching them.

Desperate, they ducked under a broad oak whose canopy covered them. The storm raged harder, so they had to shout over the noise.

"I think we should wait it out," called Catanya.

"I agree. There's no sense trying to walk in this. We'll be drenched through and freezing."

Jémys slid down to sit against the tree. He leaned his head back and closed his eyes, running his hand through his damp hair, looking frustrated. Catanya hesitated before settling next to him. She leaned forward and hugged her knees into her chest to keep her legs out of the storm. There wasn't much room under the canopy, so they were sitting quite close together, closer than Catanya would have done otherwise. She was having trouble keeping her arm from brushing up against his.

The storm raged around them. The wind howled and tore through the trees, whose roots quaked in the strain of trying to stay upright. There were constant flashes of light and ear-splitting cracks, as the lightning broke through the sky. The violence of the storm reached a fever pitch, and the rain slammed into the ground like falling rocks, as the thunder roared and raged through the forest, unleashing a wild, pent-up fury.

Another flash of light illuminated the sky and Jémys opened his eyes and exhaled heavily.

"What's the matter?" asked Catanya.

"Nothing, I'm just anxious to reach Finnua and this isn't exactly what I had in mind." He gestured to the storm.

"Why are you so anxious to return?"

He looked at her, his face close to hers. She could see the rain dripping from his hair and down his face.

"My aunt is in Finnua and she struggles. Especially now..." His voice trailed off, sounding bitter. He brushed his hair out of his face. "But it's not only her," he continued. "Now that Caerlon has increased the taxes again, the entire village is struggling. I worry about them all. I worry they won't be able to get by... Especially my aunt."

He leaned forward so he was shoulder to shoulder with Catanya and he started pulling grass out of the dirt, twisting it through his fingers.

"I've always taken care of her," he said. "I take these odd jobs to earn more money so I can help her."

"What sorts of jobs?" Most young men Catanya knew in

Faltir were farmers and apprentices. She was curious to hear what other options existed. And conversation helped to distract her.

He shrugged. "Anything. Everything. I just finished building ships in Brigmun Bay. That wasn't so bad."

Genuine interest broke through the din of her melancholy. "Brigmun Bay?" she asked in awe. She'd heard stories, but nobody she knew had ever seen it before. "Is it true what they say about the vanishing tides? Does the bay really disappear?"

Jémys chuckled. "Well, it doesn't actually disappear, but the water drains out of it almost completely, so it seems like it does. The shipwrights have to do everything during those hours, racing against the rising tide. It's intense work, but it pays well, and I always return to Finnua for the harvest so I can help my aunt in the busiest time."

"Where are your—" She jumped. Something had moved in the trees nearby. She waited tensely until she realized it was just a red squirrel scrambling up a tree to escape the storm. Sighing, she relaxed a little. When she shifted her attention back to Jémys she realized he hadn't moved at all. He was watching her, his eyes tight in an odd, almost pitying expression.

"What?" she asked, more defensively than she'd intended.

"You're very jumpy," he commented. "I've been noticing it since we started travelling together. You seem nervous."

"Oh, I—well, I don't feel at home in the woods, to be perfectly honest," she mumbled, averting her eyes. "Any cramped dark place... I prefer to be in the open air, closer to the ocean."

"It seems like more than that though." Jémys was frowning at her. "What are you so scared of?"

She turned her eyes to meet his and saw them filled with concerned interest. The damp forest underlined their colour so that the already bright green was more vibrant against his dark complexion.

She sighed and looked down. She couldn't tell him the truth, it wasn't safe, but she needed to get some of it off her chest. "My home," she said, deciding to tell part of her story, "it was attacked. Raided by... by mercenaries on horseback."

She glanced up at him and saw shock written on his face. "Mercenaries? Do you know who they were? What they wanted?"

"N-no. I have no idea..." She averted her eyes. "But they killed... they killed..." Her voice sounded thin and shaky. She took a deep breath, wrestling back her tears. "It's all gone now. Possibly even the entire village. I don't know for sure... but I think everything... everyone. I think I'm the only one who escaped. Just barely."

Jémys waited for her to steady herself before responding. "That's awful, I'm sorry. I can't even imagine..." He put his hand on hers and frowned thoughtfully. "But I can say, I know what it's like to suffer a devastating loss. To feel so shattered and broken you think you'll never recover. But you will, I promise. You will recover."

She stared at his hand. It was warm and strong and she was surprised at how comforting she found it.

He squeezed her hand reassuringly before pulling away.

"I was so helpless," blurted Catanya, taking herself by surprise. She couldn't explain it, but something about Jémys encouraged her to be open. "I just stood there and watched, I couldn't do anything to help them. Everyone I cared about... and I did nothing. I didn't even fight. I wouldn't have even known how."

"Well..." Jémys lifted a small twig off the forest floor and snapped it between his fingers absentmindedly. "I can show you, if you like." He scattered the bits of twig onto the rain-drenched ground and nodded earnestly. "I can teach you how to fight if you want... I learned a long time ago how important it is. We live in dangerous times, and I think everyone should be able to protect themselves."

"You do?" She hadn't expected him to say that.

"Yes, I do. Between mercenaries, criminals, bandits—even the firkon..." He shook his head and slumped his shoulders. "We have to protect ourselves because nobody is going to do it for us."

They sat in silence, watching the rain pound against the forest floor. Small pools of water were collecting in the mud around them like shards of broken glass, and the falling raindrops sent ripples swirling in every direction.

"If you don't have a home anymore," said Jémys after a while, "maybe you'll decide to stay in Finnua when we arrive. I can help you find a new home and work."

Catanya was surprised at the kindness of his offer. "I—I'm not sure that's the best idea." She lowered her head, wishing she could give him a different response.

Jémys frowned. "Why not?"

Catanya fiddled with the sleeve of her baggy tunic. She had never liked lying, and she wasn't very good at it. "I just—I don't think I should stay in Finnua," she mumbled. "I think I should keep moving."

"Keep moving?" He looked at her inquiringly.

Catanya didn't know how to explain without telling him the whole truth, so she stayed silent.

"Well," Jémys shrugged, "that's fine, if it's what you want. But I imagine you might feel differently when you get to Finnua." He grinned at her.

"I'm sure I will," she said quietly.

The rain had eased, and the sky was clearing, so they started walking again. The ground was damp beneath their feet and the mud clung to their shoes forcing them to move at a slower pace.

They walked in silence for some time. Catanya's mind wandered over the last several days' events. She wanted to believe that Genna, Diyah, and the girls were safe, and that the firkon had left everyone in Faltir behind once they'd realized she'd escaped. But she knew that wasn't true. She knew they were most likely dead—or worse.

With every step she took, reality sank in. By hiding her all these years, Genna and her brother Grante had been committing treason in the king's eyes. The penalty for treason was death. But how could she be dead? How could Genna—the woman who'd raised her, who'd loved and protected her—how could she be dead? Genna was one of the strongest people Catanya had ever known. She had single-handedly raised an entire home full of orphaned girls. There was no way she'd surrendered without a fight. Maybe she and the girls had escaped.

Catanya sighed and rubbed her forehead.

Even if anyone did manage to escape, they were likely lost in the woods, just like her. And what chance did the young girls have of surviving? None of them knew how to find food or shelter. Even Genna would have trouble finding her way, and she wasn't exactly young anymore. No, they wouldn't survive. Not without Diyah.

*Diyah.* Catanya's eyes filled with tears. She hated herself for abandoning her friend, even though it had been Diyah's idea. But what would the firkon do with someone who had helped their fugitive escape? Would Diyah be executed for treason too?

That thought left a gaping hole in Catanya's heart that nothing could fill. She needed to think about something else, to keep her mind from focusing on everything she had lost. But she couldn't. No matter what she tried, her mind kept spiralling and circling one haunting thought: none of this would have happened if not for her.

If Catanya hadn't gone to live there, the firkon never would have attacked Camlee Lodge. It was all her fault.

*And my mother's fault,* she thought bitterly. She wanted to blame someone else, and it was satisfying to blame it on the woman who had abandoned her. Though she knew her mother had supposedly done it to protect her, she was still angry. And she didn't feel very protected.

Catanya and Jémys walked for another hour, the wet ground beneath them squelching and clinging to their feet. The mud weighed them down while the damp branches whipped at them, scattering droplets that soaked through their clothes.

Catanya was thinking how tired she was, when her foot slipped in the mud and she fell backwards. She slammed into Jémys so the two of them crashed sidelong into a bristly pine tree.

"Sorry," she groaned as they disentangled.

"It's okay." He laughed, brushing needles out of his hair. "I don't think we should try to go any farther tonight." He looked around warily and scraped his boot on a rock to get the mud off. "It's getting dark, anyway."

Catanya agreed. Her muscles ached, and she was cold and exhausted from the constant battle with her emotions.

So the two of them began searching for a spot to make camp. It was difficult to find anywhere that wasn't drenched, but eventually they found an elevated area with great slabs of moss-covered slate woven through the sodden ground.

"It won't be the *most* comfortable night, but it'll be better than trying to sleep sopping wet and shivering," said Jémys, sitting down on the nearest slab.

They set about struggling to get a fire started. It took them a while to find dry wood for kindling, but by the time darkness set in properly they had a sizeable blaze to keep them warm.

They sat on damp logs by the fire, eating some more bread

and cheese, when Catanya finally asked the question she'd been wondering all day. "So if you were going to teach me to fight, where would you start?" She was curious to hear what he had to say, and admittedly she liked the idea of traditional weapons much more than using whatever powers she might have.

She contemplated how vulnerable she felt, and how vulnerable everyone at Camlee Lodge had been. Maybe if they'd known how to defend themselves, they could have prevented this from happening.

"Well." Jémys swallowed the mouthful of bread and cheese and surveyed her appraisingly. "We start by giving you a weapon." He twisted around and started rifling through his pack for something. When he turned back, he was holding a hunting blade. "I always carry a spare, just in case. Here."

He flipped the knife around and handed it to her. It was a six-inch dagger with a simple wooden handle. She ran her finger over the blade to feel how sharp it was.

"Thank you," she said a little uncertainly.

"Here's the sheath for it, it's too small for my leg so it'll probably be a good fit for you." He handed her the leather case.

She strapped it to her thigh and secured the knots so it wouldn't fall off. Then she stood up and kicked her leg out a few times to check. It seemed secure.

"Now, that blade isn't the best, but it'll do for now," continued Jémys. "You should get something more effective if you're planning on taking any more dangerous jaunts through the woods alone." He chuckled as he reclined on the stone behind him.

"Like a sword?" she asked dryly, staring at the impressive blade he had laid on the ground beside him.

"Maybe," he said with a smile.

"Um, I still don't know how to use this thing." Catanya

pulled the dagger out of its sheath and fumbled, nearly dropping it.

Jémys chuckled. "I'll show you when the sun is up." Then he craned his head and looked at her across the fire. "Unless you desperately want to fight me in the dark?"

"No." Catanya grinned. "No, I can't say that I do." She twisted the blade around, feeling its weight in her hand.

"Good, neither do I." Jémys lay back down and crossed his arms behind his head.

They lapsed into silence, listening to the gentle buzz of the forest. The insects and animals were emerging after the storm. Water droplets trickled between the leaves. The storm had cleared the clouds from the sky, so the stars shone brightly, reflecting off the beads of water and giving the world a shimmering quality.

"You know," Jémys raised his hand up to the sky and traced a pattern of stars above his head, "when I was a child, my father used to tell me the stars were connected to the Spirits. They watched over us, protecting us from harm. I really believed him," he murmured, letting his hand fall to his side.

"But you don't anymore?" Catanya glanced up at the stars and wondered if they were indeed watching over her. She liked that idea.

Jémys shrugged. "I don't know." He sounded sad. "But I used to love stories like that. Stories of magic and Resonance, the Natures... the times before the Quiescence Wars."

"Really?" Catanya fidgeted with her sleeve as she thought about her own powers.

"Yeah." Jémys was still gazing up at the sky. "I always liked the idea of people using Resonance for good, you know?" He glanced at her and smiled sadly. "Not like what we have now."

"What if—" She bit her lip, trying to find the right words. "Do you think anyone like that still exists? People who can use Resonance for good?"

Jémys exhaled audibly. "I doubt it," he muttered. "As much as I love the stories, that's all they are. Stories. The king's the only one with magic now. We can't go back, so we have to protect ourselves."

Catanya tried to swallow but her throat had gone suddenly dry.

"I have this sense that we're on the verge of something," continued Jémys quietly. "Something dark."

Catanya's stomach clenched. "Like what?"

Jémys lifted himself up on his elbows to look at her. "Honestly? I think Caerlon is on the verge of collapse—on the verge of chaos. I had hoped the king's son might be different, but now I'm not sure."

"Well, I'm sure," said Catanya. "I'm sure he's worse." She was surprised to hear the anger and bitterness in her voice and she was inexplicably ashamed. She tried to convince herself it was the shame of knowing she was related to such a horrible family, but something about that didn't ring true.

Jémys nodded, unfazed by Catanya's tone. "I know I was being naïve," he said, staring transfixed at the fire. "The rumours were all over Brigmun Bay. The way Casréyan died... They're saying it was Cadyan who did it."

This took Catanya by surprise. She had heard that Casréyan had died mysteriously, but she had assumed it was some unknown illness. It hadn't occurred to her he might have been murdered.

Had Cadyan killed his own father?

*Our father*, she thought, and she shivered before trying to push the thought out of her mind.

"I guess it was silly to hope that Cadyan would be any better," grumbled Jémys. "They're all the same, aren't they? These people, they call themselves our kings and queens yet they do nothing to actually help us. No, they just hoard power and use it to inspire fear and force us down in the mud. And then they call themselves strong and mighty." He grimaced like he'd tasted something sour. "No, a proper leader—someone who is truly strong and powerful—doesn't need to prove it by pushing others down or making them feel weak." The flames danced in his eyes and he glanced at Catanya, who nodded in agreement.

She was impressed with how firm his principles seemed, and something about his words was familiar to her. She recalled an evening ten years ago when Diyah had described her encounter with Prince Cadyan in the woods, and the young man who helped her that day. Catanya racked her brain, trying to remember how Diyah had described him.

*Well, he was tall, really tall. And he had dark brown hair and such beautiful eyes.*

And what was it he'd said to the prince?

*He said, 'A truly powerful man wouldn't need to make others feel weak so he can feel strong.' Or something like that.*

Catanya could almost hear her friend's voice, and it made her ache. Diyah had been so awestruck and impressed that day. They were only children when it happened, but Catanya had always remembered the story.

She surveyed Jémys, wondering. Could it be possible?

"What is it?" he asked, looking a little self-conscious.

Catanya hadn't realized that she'd been staring at him for so long. She could feel the mixture of nostalgia and sorrow on her own face. "Sorry, I was just lost in thought." She looked away embarrassedly. "We should get some sleep."

She stretched her arms as she stood up. She stepped over to one of the larger slabs of rock and lay down. It wasn't comfortable, but it was dry. Within a few minutes, the fatigue won out and she drifted off to sleep.

5

———

# A CAULDRON AND A WHIP

"Tell us what we want to know and the pain will stop."

"No."

Diyah was hanging from her arms in the cell. The back of her dress had been torn open, and the ragged, tattered fabric hung off her in shreds. The skin on her back was raw and flayed. There were deep, bloody gashes along her shoulder blades, where the whip had been used. She could feel the blood trickling down her spine and dripping onto the stone floor, where her feet slipped and slid as she struggled to stay upright.

Her wrists were bruised and burned from the pressure of the shackles. Her arms had gone numb. The pain was worse than anything she'd ever experienced, but she was determined not to show weakness. She wouldn't let them break her.

"Well, at least I'm enjoying myself," announced Slaedir, as he wound his arm back for another strike.

A swish and a crack, and Diyah screamed. The other girls huddled in the corner, crying silently with their heads buried in their hands. Diyah had told them not to watch.

"Oh, I love it when they scream for me, don't you, Julyán?"

Slaedir groaned and wrapped his arms around Diyah's waist, pressing his body against her from behind. Then he lowered his voice and whispered in her ear, "Almost as much as I love the whimpers and moans." He inhaled deeply and squeezed her tighter.

Diyah's skin crawled and she felt sick to her stomach. She clenched her jaw and urged herself to stay quiet as the pain in her back reached a new level.

"You know, Casréyan always wanted the first taste, but our new king doesn't seem interested. I bet he wouldn't mind if I were to sneak in there first." He moved his hands towards Diyah's legs. "What do you want to bet Cadyan doesn't even notice?"

"Let go of me," snapped Diyah, trying to shake him off, but he only tightened his grip.

Slaedir laughed. "What do you say, Julyán? Want a taste when I'm done? Or do you prefer them younger?" He gestured to the girls in the corner.

Diyah let out an infuriated cry, rage and revulsion coursing through her veins. She wrestled even harder against Slaedir's grip, feeling the open wounds on her back expand and contract with every movement. Then she threw her head back and it collided with Slaedir's face.

He backed off, swearing and gripping his already tender nose. "You bitch," he spat at her. "You're going to pay for that."

Another swish and another crack, and Diyah felt a new patch of skin erupt in agony, but she was determined not to scream.

"I've seen something like this before," said Julyán, speaking for the first time. He seemed not to have registered the exchange happening around him. He was sitting in a chair near the cell door, holding Diyah's shoulder satchel in his hand, turning it over and examining it curiously. "Are you a Heiltúir?" he asked, a faint trace of wonder in his voice.

The question surprised Diyah. As the chain suspending her twisted, she glared at him from under the matted hair that had fallen in her face. She said nothing.

Slaedir scoffed. "A Heiltúir? You mean those ancient healers? *Her*?"

He laughed and thrashed her again, paying no attention to his aim. The whip glanced off her shoulder and one of the knotted tails slashed across her face, splitting open her eyelid and lip.

"Oh, whoops, there goes that pretty face," he sneered, grabbing her chin and pulling her face up to within an inch of his. "Such a shame."

Diyah struggled to pull herself free, but his grip tightened, causing even more blood to ooze out of her wounded lip.

"I'm telling you, that's what this satchel means," Julyán continued, as though there had been no interruption. "See this mark here." He held it up to show Slaedir the embossed symbol on the front. A small cauldron with an elaborate letter H engraved on it, set inside a circle of ancient Awnle writing and designs. "That's the mark of the Heiltúir. They were said to carry these satchels full of ancient remedies. Look." He pulled out the herbs to show Slaedir. "I thought all the Heiltúir were gone."

Slaedir stepped back impatiently from Diyah. "So what?" He gave Julyán a hard stare. "Who cares if she's a healer?"

Julyán frowned. "Not just any healer. The Heiltúir were the elite, with healing abilities unrivalled by anyone. They were long believed to be sorcerers. In fact, most of them were killed during the Quiescence Wars in an attempt to extract their powers. But it didn't work. No healing magic was ever discovered, and no one has ever learned their secret. But whatever it was... it was in their blood and it died with them. All that hereditary expertise was lost, but..." He looked at Diyah with newfound interest.

Diyah was surprised by his knowledge of her ancestors. Few people she'd met were even aware the Heiltúir existed. She'd certainly never met anyone who knew the legends about their history well enough to recount them.

Julyán studied her with a shrewdness that scared her almost more than Slaedir's cruelty. She felt vulnerable and exposed. She didn't like how much Julyán already knew about her, and she could see the wheels turning in his head as he contemplated ways to use this new information.

"It doesn't matter," snapped Slaedir. "We have a job to do. So unless you're thinking something in that pouch will make her talk, I suggest we get back to work." He waved the bloody whip in front of Julyán's face.

Julyán turned to stare at him, as though he'd only just registered Slaedir's presence. But then he nodded in agreement and lowered the satchel.

Several minutes and countless lashes later, Diyah was having trouble staying conscious. Her knees had buckled completely, and she thought her wrists were going to break from the strain of holding her weight.

Slaedir was sweating when he paused to stretch his arm out in front of him. "Oh, she's a tough one," he said with glee. He rolled up his sleeves and brushed the grimy hair off his forehead. Then he spun her around to face him again. His face bore an eager expression. It seemed like the longer Diyah held out, the more delight he took in hurting her.

Diyah's vision blurred, so his face swam in front of her. She didn't think she could handle any more pain.

"M-master Slaedir?" came a hesitant voice from the shadows.

A guard was standing near the door, watching the interaction and trembling with what could have been either fear or excitement. Diyah couldn't tell. She could barely see straight.

"The ship will be docking shortly, sir. How many should we

take?" His eyes seemed glued to Diyah's bloodied frame as he addressed the maífírkon.

Slaedir looked around the dungeons. "Take them all. If they can stand, they can work."

"Except the physician," interjected Julyán. "His execution has been set."

These words broke through Diyah's agony. They were going to execute Grante. "No," she gasped, choking on her own raspy throat, as she tried to muster the strength to resist, despite how futile she knew it was. "No, you can't!" Her broken lip smarted and bled, but she didn't care.

She couldn't feel her arms anymore, as she struggled feebly against her chains. Only the sound of the metal clanging told her she had moved.

The young guard gawked at her, his face contorted with mingled intrigue and revulsion. "And what about them, sir?" He gestured towards her and the girls.

Slaedir turned back to look at them, a callous smile on his face. "Oh, no," he purred. "I'm just getting started with these ones."

There was a sudden commotion outside, and another guard said, "Forgive me, Your Majesty, we did not expect you."

"Get out of the way!" There was a bang as the guard went crashing into the bars beside him. "Honestly, how long does it take to get information from one simple peasant girl? It has been days!" Cadyan appeared in the door to the cell, flushed and shaking with anger.

"My lord, we are making excellent progress." Slaedir straightened up, striding out to meet his king.

"Progress?" Cadyan stared at him with outrage. "Look at her, you imbecile! She's half-dead and you haven't gotten anything from her."

"Well..." Slaedir squeezed the whip in his hands, and ran his fingers through the bloody knots. "As I told you before, there are more effective ways to break a woman's spirit. If you will allow me to—"

"Ugh!" Cadyan seemed to suppress a shudder as he brushed past Slaedir into the cell. "I knew I shouldn't have left this to you." He gave Slaedir a hard glare. "I need a military leader with intelligence and insight. Not a desperate mongrel, yipping at my heels and making excuses for his failures."

Slaedir's jaw dropped, and his eyes bulged at the insult. He seemed to be struggling not to retort.

Exhausted and delirious, Diyah couldn't resist the urge to laugh. She spat at Cadyan's feet and snarled, "I'll never tell you anything." She struggled to breathe as she tried again to stand upright, wincing at the excruciating pain overwhelming her. Then she looked him straight in the eye and hissed, "You'll have to kill me." And in that moment, she welcomed the idea of dying. They were going to kill Grante and surely she'd be next, so why delay the inevitable? She wanted it to be over.

Cadyan's face screwed up in disgust as he surveyed her. "Very well," he said through gritted teeth. "This is a waste of time. Kill her. Kill them all. Or send them to the work camps with the rest, I don't care." He threw his hands up in the air.

Diyah was suddenly alert again as a wave of panic flooded through her. Horrified, she strained to look at the girls huddled in the corner. In her exhaustion and agony, she had almost forgotten about them. But she couldn't die now—she needed to stay alive for them. She had to help them. She struggled to put her weight on her feet, but her knees shook and she fell, straining her already weakened arms.

"Wait." Julyán's voice was slow and measured. He was looking at Diyah with a quizzical frown. "I know how to make her talk." He held her gaze without flinching.

The cold, calculated expression on his face sent a shiver down her spine.

Slaedir snorted and gave Julyán a sceptical sneer. "Is that so? How?"

Julyán tilted his head, but kept his eyes on Diyah. "Them." He pointed towards the girls in the corner. "Hurt them."

There was silence and then Slaedir spoke, "The children?" He studied Diyah longingly, as though he'd rather go another round with her.

"Yes," said Julyán matter-of-factly. He seemed to be watching Diyah for a reaction.

Her heart was pounding so loudly it rang in her ears. She hoped against all hope that they wouldn't listen to him.

Slaedir glanced at his king, who was wearing a sour grimace. Cadyan shrugged and jerked his head.

"Alright, then." Slaedir strode over to the corner and pulled Gréys up by the hair. Gréys screamed and tried to resist, while the older girls struggled to grab her. But Slaedir was too strong. He dragged her across the floor and threw her down at Diyah's feet.

"No, stop! What are you doing?" Diyah fought to stay on her feet and pulled at the chains that bound her, but she was too weak.

Gréys attempted to scramble away, but Slaedir kicked her. She cried out.

"Don't touch her!" shouted Diyah.

Gréys tried again to escape, and Cadyan made a sound of impatience. He clapped his hands together and she slammed to the ground, gasping and crying and unable to move.

"Thank you, Your Majesty." Slaedir inclined his head.

"Get on with it." Cadyan waved his hand and an unnatural silence pressed upon them, dulling the whimpers and cries.

Slaedir flashed Diyah a nasty grin.

"No..." She watched in horror as he raised his arm and brought the whip crashing down on Gréys's shoulders and neck.

Gréys screamed.

"Stop it!" cried Diyah, struggling even harder against her binds. "Stop it! She's just a little girl. She doesn't know anything." Diyah's eyes filled with angry, exhausted tears.

"Tell us what we want to know!" shouted Slaedir, with a second, harder crack of his whip. Gréys was sobbing uncontrollably now. Although the sound was muffled by Cadyan's magic, it still made Diyah's stomach churn.

Slaedir raised his hand to strike again, but Diyah yelled, "Alright! Stop!"

Everyone looked at her.

"I'll tell you whatever you want to know, but please... please don't hurt them." She could have endured anything herself, but she couldn't let them hurt the girls. She felt sick at the idea of betraying her friend, but she knew if Catanya were in her position, she'd make the same choice.

Catanya would do whatever was necessary to protect the people she loved. So Diyah knew that, wherever she was, Catanya would forgive her for what happened next.

Slaedir kicked Gréys aside and stood facing Diyah. Cadyan strolled into the cell to examine her, his eyes glinting madly in the torchlight.

"Start from the beginning," said Cadyan. "Tell me everything."

So Diyah talked, hating herself for every word she spoke. Her pain and exhaustion made it difficult to focus, but she needed to say something. And she was determined not to offer them any more information than necessary—determined not to reveal anything that might help Cadyan track her friend.

She told them what she knew about Catanya's arrival at Camlee Lodge. How Catanya grew up believing her parents were dead and how, until recently, she had never known her true lineage.

"How did she learn the truth?" Cadyan's voice was quiet but cutting.

Diyah hesitated. She wasn't sure what Cadyan knew already. She needed to be careful.

"L-Lady Genna told her." She closed her eyes, trying not to think about her dead guardian.

It was half true. It had been Genna and Grante together who told Catanya the truth. Grante had arrived in Faltir shortly after the coronation, to check on Catanya. He'd explained how the elixir seemed to malfunction when Cadyan drank it, and nobody could explain why.

"Genna?" Cadyan frowned at Slaedir.

"Grante's sister," he explained. "She's dead now."

Cadyan nodded indifferently and Diyah felt a sudden and profound hatred for him. She would never understand how someone could be so broken—so cruel.

"What I don't understand is why," said Julyán slowly. "Why they risked it after all these years?" He glanced over at Slaedir, forehead creased. "She was hidden, wasn't she? Nobody except Grante knew where to find her, so why risk everything by returning? And why tell her the truth now? Unless—" He broke off, frowning thoughtfully as he looked back towards his king.

Cadyan seemed to understand what Julyán was thinking. His face contorted into a mask of rage, and he glared at Diyah. "Well?" he snapped.

Diyah faltered, frowning. "W-what?" she asked, not sure how to respond.

Cadyan's nostrils flared. He advanced farther into the cell, his eyes locked on Diyah. "Why, after all these years of lying, did they decide to tell her the truth?"

"I-I don't know," stammered Diyah, recoiling from him.

Cadyan's eyes narrowed. "You're lying."

"N-no, I'm not," said Diyah, trying to feign ignorance. She was afraid to tell him the truth about what had happened. She couldn't give him added reason to hunt Catanya, and this might be her last important secret—the only thing that could possibly save them all.

There was a pause as Cadyan stared at her and then, without turning his gaze, he spoke, "Slaedir, kill the child."

Slaedir grinned savagely. "With pleasure." He lifted Gréys up by the neck, choking her as he pulled a dagger from his belt.

"Wait! No—stop! I'll tell you!" cried Diyah frantically. She tugged at her chains, ignoring the agonizing pain in her back. She waited with bated breath as Cadyan nodded and Slaedir lowered his blade, loosening his grip on Gréys. Diyah took a deep breath before continuing, choosing her words carefully, "Genna told her because she had to... she couldn't hide it anymore. Something happened to Catanya. Something *strange*." She knew that Cadyan already suspected Catanya of having powers like his, but she had hoped to avoid giving him any information that might confirm it.

"*Strange*?" Cadyan's nostrils flared even wider.

Diyah closed her eyes in resignation as she thought back to that evening. "There was this light," she said, her parched throat rasping painfully. "This bright golden light and it surrounded her—lifted her off the ground. I couldn't see anything. It was blinding, and she was screaming in pain... and when it ended, she was lying unconscious on the floor."

Cadyan stared at her, his eyes bulging with rage and alarm. "When was this?" A muscle twitched as he clenched his jaw. When she didn't answer right away, he shouted, "WHEN?"

Diyah flinched, and her body exploded with pain. "The night of your coronation."

There was a long silence, as everyone in the room turned their gaze towards Cadyan. Diyah thought she could tell from their expressions that they were all thinking along the same lines. She remembered Grante's description of the coronation.

"Where is she now?" Cadyan seemed eerily calm.

"I-I don't know. Honestly I don't," she added, seeing the suspicious look on Cadyan's face. "I have no idea where she might have gone." Neither she nor Catanya had ever spent much time outside Faltir, and Diyah couldn't imagine anywhere was safe for her friend, now that Cadyan was searching for her.

Cadyan and Julyán exchanged almost imperceptible glances before Cadyan nodded. Turning to Slaedir, he said, "Get her down from there."

"Yes, my lord." Slaedir tossed Gréys aside and hurried to unshackle Diyah's hands, letting her fall to the ground where she bruised her knees on the hard stone floor.

"Come." Cadyan beckoned to Julyán and Slaedir to follow him. "And you," he barked at the guard who was standing there, gawking at them. "Don't you have prisoners to transport? Get these rats out of my city and shipped to Bratia. We're running out of time."

The guard jumped as if he'd been hit with the whip, and hurried to round up the prisoners from the other cells.

Diyah struggled to crawl across the floor to where Gréys lay, huddled in a ball and trembling.

"Shh," she whispered, brushing the hair out of the little girl's face. "You're alright. You're going to be alright. I've got you."

Meya and Hahney crept forward to join them, their faces blotchy and streaked with tears.

Diyah's body shook uncontrollably. Every so often, a spasm made her twitch, aggravating the throbbing wounds on her back. But she needed to stay strong for the girls.

She could hear Cadyan barking orders as he stormed out of the dungeon, followed by Slaedir.

There was a loud clang as Julyán swung the cell door closed behind them, causing Diyah to flinch painfully. She glared up at him, filled with loathing and contempt.

He turned the key, locking them in, and then hesitated briefly before tossing her Heiltúir satchel back through the bars. It fell to the ground an inch from Diyah's face. She stared at it, startled. She looked up to see him turn his back and stride out after his king and his maífirkon.

**6**

---

# ELIXIR, RELICS, AND GOLD

Cadyan was pacing back and forth in a private parlour near the Great Hall. It was late and the low-hanging sun cast a reddish-orange glow through the room. Dust was visible in the air, lingering above the comfortable furnishings. But Cadyan was too preoccupied to care.

He'd spent his entire afternoon pacing this room, running over what that girl in the dungeons had said. He couldn't understand why any of this was happening.

Cadyan had lived his entire life waiting to take the throne and finally claim the powers that came with it. But they were supposed to be his—*only* his. How had the elixir affected her too?

His *sister*. He snorted and shook his head.

He'd been king for little over a week, and already his position was in jeopardy. Why was any of this happening? What had he done to deserve this?

An abrupt knock broke the silence, and he flinched at the sound.

*Habit.*

"Enter," he called. It was about time. He'd sent for them all ages ago.

The door opened to reveal Julyán and Slaedir, accompanied by a much older man wearing a heavy, grey robe.

"Your Majesty," croaked the chaplain as he stepped forward, closing the door behind him. His thinning white hair hung in wisps off the sides of his head, and he had a fragile air about him that Cadyan detested. But in this instance, the man's age was actually an advantage. He had served as the royal chaplain for years—beginning in Cadyan's grandfather's reign—and he knew more about the kingdom's traditions than anyone.

If anybody could give him answers, it was the chaplain.

"You've explained the situation to him?" asked Cadyan, turning his back on them to gaze out the window. In the court-yard below, he could see one of his grooms leading two horses back towards the stables and a small group of fírkon clearing away the day's weapons and targets. It seemed wrong to see everyone behaving so normally.

"We have," replied Julyán.

"But, my lord, what does it mean?" asked Slaedir.

Cadyan rolled his eyes. "It means that my *sister* does indeed have powers like mine." He spat the words as though trying to expel them like a poison. He hated admitting it, but there was no way to deny it anymore.

"How is that possible?" asked Julyán.

"Well..." The chaplain's voice rasped and grated. "From the description the prisoner gave, it sounds as though your sister underwent the same process as you, my king."

"Indeed." Cadyan pursed his lips. "But how can that be?"

It made no sense. She was nowhere near him or the elixir when he'd taken it, and there was no chance she could have taken it too. It wouldn't have worked even if she had.

"Well..." Julyán addressed the chaplain. "To your knowl-edge, has Caerlon ever had two living heirs before?"

The chaplain frowned. "Once. A few generations ago... but there are no accounts indicating they both received powers. The way the elixir functions..." He shook his head. "It's impossible. There are steps—precautions to ensure only the chosen heir, the drinker, is affected. I am mystified..."

"Hmm... perhaps..." Julyán trailed off, lost in thought.

"Perhaps what?" Cadyan turned around to look at him. He found the chaplain's lack of answers irritating, so whatever theory Julyán had was better than nothing.

"Well, my king, perhaps something connects you and your sister—something beyond the physical."

"Like what?" asked Slaedir a little sceptically. His mind had always been annoyingly slow and unimaginative.

"I don't know." Julyán frowned, shaking his head. "But whatever it is, it might be out of your control, my king."

"Out of my control... no." Cadyan's eyes narrowed and his voice was scarcely a whisper. "I don't think so. I'm going to find her and I'm going to kill her. Slaedir." He whirled around to face the man. "You will organize search parties. Send them out along all the major roads. Search every village for her. She can't stay hidden for long, and when she resurfaces, I want her brought here, alive."

"Yes, my lord."

"And post a reward for her capture. I want her found, and I don't care who does it. The more people searching, the better."

"Yes, my lord," said Slaedir with a resentful undertone. "Let's go, Julyán."

"No. Julyán will remain here with me," said Cadyan. "I have something else I want him to do."

"Something else?" Slaedir looked from his king to Julyán with raised eyebrows.

"Yes," said Cadyan with a warning edge. He had never liked Slaedir. It offended him that this imbecile had raised himself to maífírkon and retained the post all this time. And as the reigning maífirkon throughout most of Cadyan's life, Slaedir had been a faithful lackey for his father, King Casréyan.

But Casréyan was finally gone. Now that it was Cadyan's turn to rule, he was eager to remove everyone who'd been loyal to his father—everyone who'd made his own life miserable.

It would be a long time before Cadyan forgot the gleeful sneers on Slaedir's face whenever his father had berated and abused him.

Cadyan clutched absentmindedly at his left forearm. The permanent damage from repeated breaks and injuries had all been healed when he'd taken the elixir. He was stronger than ever. Soon everyone would understand what that meant.

"As you wish, my lord," replied Slaedir. He bowed stiffly and exited the room, all while glowering in Julyán's direction.

Cadyan smiled smugly to himself before turning his attention towards the chaplain. "Now, as for you, I trust you will keep a close watch over the strongroom and the elixir. Double the guard and notify me of any unusual activity."

For centuries, the Elixir of Caerlon had been the world's greatest treasure—the king's rare and precious birthright. But somehow Cadyan's legacy had been compromised. His glory had been usurped, and he was determined to take it back, whatever the cost. He hadn't spent his entire life living in fear, weak and vulnerable, dreaming of the day when he'd finally have power, only for it to be taken from him once he had finally attained it.

The chaplain left, and Cadyan sighed. "Now, on to another pressing matter. Come." He beckoned for Julyán to follow him out of the room.

Admittedly, Cadyan's first motive in keeping Julyán behind was to aggravate Slaedir, but he had a second motive too. Julyán was a good soldier, intelligent and methodical, and Cadyan was eager to involve him in more strategic matters. He was confident that Julyán would be a great asset to him. The next

Maífírkon Tournament would happen in the spring, and there was a strong chance Julyán might win and claim the title for himself.

Julyán would make a fine maífírkon—and an excellent ally for a new king.

It was a wonder Cadyan hadn't noticed him before, but then again, he never paid close attention to the fírkon when his father was around. He'd hated them then.

But now they were *his* fírkon. Only the best would suffice.

"You impressed me today," said Cadyan, as they walked side-by-side down the corridor towards the throne room. "You know, Slaedir has been maífírkon for quite some time now. He served under my father for many years, before me. I can remember as a child, watching the tournament when he first won his title. It was impressive—in fact, I used to be afraid of him." He paused, thinking back on how Slaedir had treated him as a child. "But Slaedir's performance of late has left much to be desired," he continued, somehow simultaneously pleased and irritated. "How long did he interrogate that girl without success? And yet, with one suggestion from you, we got all the answers we needed. Yes, well done, well done, Julyán."

"Do you think she has any more useful information for us, Your Majesty?" asked Julyán, showing no sign of having just received praise from his king. Cadyan had to admit he admired that about him. With Julyán, there was no obsequiousness. He was forthright and honest.

"Oh, I believe she might prove useful still," replied Cadyan. "We'll let her stew for a while, shall we? And if she dies, it'll be no great loss, I'm sure. Now follow me, I have someone I want you to meet."

He pushed open the door and marched towards his throne, where two men stood waiting for him. The first was a middle-aged man in a heavily faded fírkon uniform. The second was a severe, grizzled man sporting tall boots and a long black coat.

"Ah, excellent! Bordlun, Osrin, you're here." Cadyan clapped his hands together expectantly.

Both men gaped in shock as they took in the vastly altered appearance of their king.

It had taken Cadyan some time to adjust to his changing hair, and although he had hated it at first (and it unnerved him that he still didn't understand why it had changed), he had actually come to like its new appearance. It set him even further apart from the rest of Mórceá. Its shimmering, magical quality served as a constant reminder to everyone of his power.

"Your Majesty." The men quickly modified their expressions and bowed. Then the grizzled man, Osrin, turned his sharp eyes towards Julyán.

"It's Julyán, isn't it?" asked Bordlun, following Osrin's gaze. He extended his hand in greeting, a bland smile on his face that made him look rather stupid.

Julyán inclined his head in response, but made no effort to take his hand.

"Bordlun is the fîrkon responsible for the excavation of the Ruins of Bratia," explained Cadyan. "He supervises the work camps and the slaves."

"I remember," said Julyán quietly.

"Oh, that's right." Bordlun snapped his fingers. "You used to be one of our young guards, didn't you? Must've been almost four years ago that you left. Been working your way up through the tournament ranks, I see." He grinned in approval.

Julyán's expression soured. He didn't respond.

"And Osrin handles transport between Caerlon and the camps," continued Cadyan, ignoring the interruption. "He captains one of the fastest ships in the seas. No other ship can match it."

Osrin finally moved his gaze away from Julyán to address Cadyan. "Aye, she's fast," he said. "But it takes a seasoned captain to helm her." He smirked at the compliment he had given himself.

"Well, tell me then." Exhausted, Cadyan flung himself down onto his throne. "Has there been any progress?" He ran his hands along the throne's wooden arms, feeling how coarse and ordinary the material was. But a king's throne should be a symbol of his power, a symbol of his status. Cadyan deserved something more spectacular than this.

"I'm afraid not, Your Majesty." Bordlun shifted uncomfortably and cleared his throat, drawing Cadyan's attention back. "The area is vast and we need more workers."

"Nothing?" Cadyan felt the sting of disappointment and irritation.

"Well, not nothing." Osrin gestured to the massive crates behind him. "Tha' one's gold. You've got jewels in this one. And here." He lifted the lid off the third crate, its hinges creaking fiercely, and let it swing back with a thud.

Cadyan leaned forward, expecting to see other rare jewels or metals, but what he saw instead surprised him. The crate was full to bursting with papers and odd trinkets.

"What is it?" He asked, approaching the crate.

"S'not our job to know that," said Osrin, picking at a spot on his chin. "Figured you'd want a look though."

Bordlun stared at him like he was mad, before turning to address his king. "Your Majesty, we did finally penetrate one of the inner cave-ins and we found an ancient chamber with a skeleton inside—looked like he might've starved to death, trapped there—and all this debris. I don't know what any of it is. The papers are in a language I don't recognize..."

"It's ancient Awnle," said Cadyan, lifting out the nearest parchment to read it. The paper was worn and delicate, and he thought the writing style resembled a journal entry. His knowledge of Awnle was poor, since he'd never paid very close attention to his lessons with the chaplain, but he could pick out certain words. *Reicog,* war, *Éalure,* escape… but then something halfway down the page jumped out at him. *Maílehr Illayan.*

Cadyan felt a jolt of excitement.

"Julyán, fetch the chaplain immediately." His voice tremored as he scanned the paper, trying to take in more of its meaning. His heart pounded, and he received another jolt each time he recognized a word.

*Córune.*

Crown.

*Siou.*

Stone.

*Rinne.*

But Cadyan couldn't place that word.

"Rinne." He ran his hand over the text, as if hoping the touch would tell him its meaning. "Rinne, siou, córune… *córune.* The crown… this is it."

"My lord?"

Cadyan looked up, moderately bewildered to find Bordlun and Osrin still standing there, staring at him. Julyán hadn't yet returned with the chaplain.

"What else did you find?" Cadyan clutched the parchment in his hand, as he leaned over the crate and began lifting out other items with a cautious reverence. There were stacks of papers similar to the one he was holding, and from the rotted strings dangling off their sides, Cadyan suspected they'd once been bound together in a book. There was an old lantern that amazingly still held oil; several rusted daggers; shards of broken clay that used to form assorted pots; a copper chalice that had turned green; a plain iron ring; and several jars of sickly substances that had most likely gone rotten centuries ago.

But no crown and nothing he would call a stone.

There was a loud bang as the door opened and closed, announcing Julyán's return with the chaplain.

"Chaplain," called Cadyan eagerly.

The old man looked surprised to see him suddenly excited.

"Come look at this." Cadyan strode to meet him, holding out the paper. Then he waited impatiently as the chaplain scanned it. "Well?"

The chaplain's eyes widened. "I don't believe it," he breathed, apparently torn between awe and fear.

"What does it say?"

"*I'm trapped,*" read Julyán. He was standing behind the chaplain, but he could easily read the parchment over the old man's head.

"You read Awnle?" said Cadyan, astonished but impressed nonetheless.

"Some," Julyán replied without taking his eyes off the page. "*I'm trapped, I've been cut off from the others and I will surely die.*" He halted, squinting at the writing. "I can't make out the next part."

The chaplain cleared his throat and began to read, translating as he went.

"*I'm trapped, I've been cut off from the others and I will surely die. The enemy descended upon us with great vengeance and determination, as our master foretold. The soldiers defended the city bravely, but they bore no weight against our enemy's power or the tides of his supernatural war. He has grown strong. Too strong. Maílehr Illayan fears that Caer has lost what little humanity he had left, and if he succeeds in his quest to unite our master's relics with the siphoned Resonance of his elixir, he will destroy us all. We cannot allow that to happen.*

"*If everything has gone according to plan, Maílehr Illayan should have departed by now, bearing to safety the crown and the stone. I must hope my master's flight was more successful than my own. I was tasked to protect the ring and bring it to Illayan before the migration of the mountain. But I have failed. I have failed in this most important task, and my punishment will be my solitary demise and the damnation of my spirit to this festering cavity of our long-doomed age. I can only hope my body, and this cursed ring on my finger, will lie desiccated and forgotten in this vault—the tomb of our fallen city—and never be found again."*

There was an extended pause when the chaplain finished reading.

"Ring," spluttered Cadyan, rushing back to the crate. "Rinne means ring!" And there *had* been a ring—a plain, nondescript, metal ring.

Cadyan rummaged through the debris until he finally found the item he was searching for, buried under a pile of clay shards. It was a crude, unpolished metal band with a flat surface, almost resembling a signet ring. But it was made of iron or some other common metal. The flat top bore the faded echoes of an ancient design that Cadyan couldn't make out. It was utterly unremarkable, but as he held it in his hand, he thought he could feel its power tingling as it recognized his own.

Without hesitating, he placed the ring on his finger and held his breath, waiting for something to happen. But nothing did.

Cadyan tried to ignore his disappointment.

"What is this ring supposed to do? What is its power?" He looked at the chaplain for answers.

The chaplain's forehead creased. "I'm afraid I don't know, my king. I am only aware of the crown. There are countless records and reports of its magic, its immortal properties. The other relics were mere conjecture until now... the ring and the stone... I can't fathom what powers they might hold." The chaplain eyed the ring on his king's hand with awestruck eagerness. "If the crown truly brings immortality, then imagine what these might do."

Cadyan studied his hand with excitement. "We need to find out."

"Perhaps there's more information in these papers." Julyán knelt down to inspect the pile.

Cadyan nodded. "Chaplain, take all this to your study and sort it. Bring me every piece of information you can find about these relics. I want to know everything about Maílater Caer, his teacher, Illayan, and whoever wrote these journal entries. I want to know what power this ring holds, how it works, and most importantly, I want that crown."

"Yes, my lord." The chaplain bowed. After instructing two guards to reload the crate and follow him, he scurried out the door.

Cadyan could barely contain his excitement. He was closer than any king before him. If he could find that crown, then it wouldn't matter what happened with his sister. Nothing would matter ever again.

"Bordlun, we need to double the work force in Bratia. I want that entire place searched. I need that crown now more than ever."

Bordlun and Osrin exchanged mildly curious glances.

"What is it?" snapped Cadyan. Their sedate attitudes irritated him.

"Well, pardon my asking, Your Majesty," said Bordlun. "But are you sure these relics really do what the rumours claim? Your father searched for them his entire life and his father before that. But what if it's just a story? What if they're just useless objects? I mean, that ring looks like a piece of scrap metal, and this supposed crown of immortality... well, it sounds a little far-fetched, don't you think?" He gave Cadyan an apologetic look.

Cadyan frowned at him. "Far-fetched?" There was a tense silence as he stared at Bordlun, sizing him up. Then he flicked his wrist and one of the other crates behind Bordlun sprang open. The heaps of gold inside it floated into the air like leaves on the wind.

Everyone stared, transfixed, as the gold slowly melted before their eyes, until a stream of shimmering liquid fluttered around the room like an ethereal ribbon.

"If *I* exist, why not the crown?" hissed Cadyan. "And if the crown exists, then I promise you, I will find it."

"Of course, Your Majesty." Bordlun eyed the gold with a mixture of terror and envy on his face, as it drifted towards him and lingered threateningly above his head.

Cadyan observed Bordlun with narrowed eyes, enjoying the fear he was creating. "Go find Slaedir," he commanded. "Tell him you need more slave workers and he should bring as many as he can gather from outlying villages, then return to the ruins and scour them top to bottom. That crown is there somewhere, and if you report here again empty-handed, well..." He shrugged and waved his hand so the gold ribbon writhed like a serpent. "Better to wield the whip than be under it, don't you agree?"

The colour drained from Bordlun's face. "Y-yes, my lord," he stammered. Then he hurried towards the door, keeping his eyes trained on the molten gold above him as it continued to curl and swerve through the air.

When the door had shut behind him, Cadyan turned his attention towards Osrin. "Now, there should be several dozen prisoners awaiting your transport outside. Make sure you don't wear them out before they get to the camps." Cadyan sneered and clapped his hand on Osrin's shoulder, letting the ring press between his fingers and the man's leather coat. "I want you to sail faster than ever before. There's no time to waste."

Osrin's face contorted as if he were trying not to speak, but he couldn't help himself. "Aye, sir. Faster than ever before. No time to waste." He repeated the words almost involuntarily and then shook his head like a dog trying to cast off water.

Cadyan grimaced and dropped his hand. "Very well, you can go," he declared in exasperation.

Cadyan waited for Osrin to leave before turning to face Julyán. "I cannot tell you how frustrating it is to rely on such people. That's why I'm so pleased to see the way you handle yourself. You're sharp. You use your brain." Cadyan walked back over to his throne and stood there, surveying it. "Surely a man of your intelligence will understand..."

"Understand what, Your Majesty?"

Cadyan didn't reply right away. He lifted both hands above his head, and made a sweeping gesture. The molten gold that hung in the air like a sparkling fog draped itself over the carved wooden throne, encasing it in shimmering metal until no sign of the wood remained. He assessed it from every angle. When he was satisfied, he turned back to face Julyán. "What do you think of the Relics of Illayan? Do you believe the legends are true?"

Julyán paused thoughtfully before answering. "I do, Your Majesty."

Cadyan was pleased to hear it. He ran his thumb over the ring on his hand. "They belong to me," he declared, envisioning himself with all three objects in his grasp—how strong they would make him. "I'm sure you can appreciate that it's not enough to be powerful. No. I need more than that. I need to be unstoppable... *invincible*." He held up his hand to examine the ring again. "And when I finally have all the relics—especially the crown—that's exactly what I'll be. I will be the eternal King of Caerlon."

# 7

# AN ENCOUNTER WITH OUTLAWS

The forest looked brighter the morning after the storm, its colours so vibrant that everything seemed more alive. Sunshine filtered through the trees, and the fresh breeze was invigorating. The ground had dried overnight. Catanya and Jémys could start walking again.

The fine weather seemed to brighten Jémys's mood. They were making good time, and it seemed the closer they got to Finnua, the more cheerful he became. He walked a few feet ahead of Catanya, and every so often he would glance back at her and smile. Whenever he did, his eyes crinkled and large dimples appeared on both of his cheeks. Catanya couldn't help but smile back. She liked Jémys. He was kind, and she enjoyed his company.

"I'm glad I met you," she called as they walked.

He turned around and walked backwards as he said, "I'm glad I met you too." Grinning, he faced forward just in time to avoid walking into a tree. He ducked sideways awkwardly to avoid colliding with the low-hanging branches.

Catanya laughed. Her heart seemed a little lighter as she walked with Jémys through the forest. She felt safer with him around. His presence was reassuring, and his easy cheerfulness distracted her from her grief.

Around midday they stopped to eat again. Jémys caught another rabbit using his snare.

"So you tie the loop like this?" she asked, holding the snare for him to check.

"Exactly like that. And then you hang it somewhere you know the animal will have to pass through it. The more it tries to free itself, the tighter the snare will get."

"That's so simple."

The rabbit they'd snared was roasting on the fire, and while it cooked, Jémys used the time to show Catanya how to hunt.

"It doesn't always work—and rarely as fast as it did today," he said. "We were lucky. It's best when you have a few days to track an animal. Or if you know an animal will pass through an area, but you can't always be certain."

"No, I know. But it's a good skill to have, anyway." Catanya had never needed to hunt before. In Faltir, the local butchers and fisherman had always provided enough for the villagers.

"True." Jémys looked at her appraisingly. "Okay, take out your knife."

He tossed the snare aside and stood up, beckoning for her to follow him. Catanya pulled the blade out of its sheath and held it gingerly.

"Now, as for fighting..." He grabbed her hand and wrapped it around the blade more forcefully. "Grip it tight like this. And if you're going to strike, strike fast and aim well. Avoid the areas like the chest—it takes a lot of strength to plunge a knife through someone's chest. It's best to aim for the stomach or the throat. Or to use your opponent's weight against them like this —come at me like you're going to hurt me."

"Um, okay." She stepped forward with her knife out. Jémys blocked her arm with one hand, ducked down, and jabbed upwards with the other—stopping right before the knife reached her chest.

"See? If someone comes at you like that, you can let their weight be the force that plunges the blade through their chest."

"What if I don't want to kill anyone?" she asked, alarmed.

"Oh, in that case you should probably do your best to avoid people who want to kill *you*. Either that or become a very fast runner." Jémys laughed.

"Oh, very amusing."

Catanya bent down and lifted a large stick off the ground, holding it out like a sword. "What about swords?" she asked, waving the stick to indicate the blade he had strapped to his waist.

"Swords?" he repeated, grinning widely. He pulled out his weapon and held it up in front of his face.

Catanya had never examined a sword up close before. Its blade gleamed in the sunlight and she could tell from a glance it was sharper than any blade she'd ever seen. It had a shallow, curved cross-guard with engravings that matched the ones on the handle, and it shone in a way that suggested its owner maintained it well.

Jémys lowered the blade, grinning, and tapped it against her stick as if daring her to fight.

Catanya backed away.

"Oh, come on," laughed Jémys, softening his posture. "Just give it a try." He raised his eyebrows encouragingly.

Catanya suppressed a laugh and shook her head. "Okay…" She raised the stick in front of her face, trying to mirror his stance. Then she stepped forward to strike. But in one swift movement he spun his sword around the stick and forced her to lunge in a different direction. She stumbled, panting, and tried again. This time, he blocked her strike with his sword. He was smiling as he blocked every attempt she made to hit him.

They both laughed, as Jémys spun his weapon once again to send the stick flying out of her hands.

"I concede!" she gasped.

He let out a bark of laughter as he re-sheathed his sword and watched her struggling to catch her breath.

They sat down to eat, and after a few minutes, Catanya asked, "So where did you learn to fight?"

Jémys chewed his food for a moment. Then he swallowed. Looking down at his hands, he replied, "My father taught me."

"Oh, and where is your father now?"

"He's dead," said Jémys calmly. He was gnawing flesh off a rabbit bone, his eyes trained pointedly away from Catanya.

"Oh, I'm sorry. I didn't realize... I didn't mean to pry." Catanya toyed with her food.

"No, you're not prying. It's no great secret. We—my aunt and I—don't talk about it very much, but mainly because I think it was always too painful for her. He was her older brother and when he died, Nelle, my aunt, was heartbroken. She loved him so much—admired him. And he took care of her, you know? And then suddenly she was alone, taking care of me, a lost and confused young boy." He threw the bone he had been chewing into the fire.

"How did your father die?" Catanya asked.

Jémys looked at her and smiled mildly. "He was a fírkon—I know." He nodded when he saw the shock on Catanya's face. "But he didn't have a choice. He came from a family of soldiers, a noble family, and it was expected of him." He sounded bitter now, and he threw the remaining bones into the fire, watching as they blackened and cracked.

"He never truly wanted to be one of them. He was always away from home, away from his family and fighting to uphold laws he didn't believe in. But he was a proper soldier, and an experienced fighter. He kept his head down, never rising through the tournament ranks—he never sought more power.

And for most of my childhood, everything was fine. He would come home for weeks at a time and teach me to fight, or tell me tales of honourable heroes fighting for justice. I think he always believed the world would become a better place for his children—he believed the next generation would inherit something better... well, I guess he was wrong."

"What happened?" Catanya's voice was quiet.

Jémys inhaled slowly. "I don't know exactly, but I think the maífirkon ordered him to do something... something truly awful." He paused and brushed the hair out of his face. "But my father refused," he said, eyes gleaming with pride. "He tried to leave, but someone betrayed him. He was executed for treason."

"Oh, Jémys, I'm so sorry."

Catanya reached forward and put her hand on his. He stared down at it and smiled. "Don't be sorry," he said. "It's not your fault. You're not responsible for the evil inside Caerlon."

Catanya shifted uneasily.

"Besides, it was a long time ago and I've made my peace with it," he added.

"What happened to your family after your father was killed?"

"My aunt was all I had left. We had no income and our family was stripped of its noble title, of course." He let out another sharp laugh.

"So that explains why you weren't enlisted as a fírkon then?"

Jémys looked down and shrugged. "I suppose," he muttered. "But more importantly, it's why my village struggles so much. They have no lord to support and protect them. Most of the fírkon are corrupt, borderline mercenaries, but they're still responsible to their lands. Few villages the size of Finnua have no lord. It makes things... difficult. I try my best, but there's not much I can do."

Catanya remembered all the meetings Lady Genna had with her late husband's steward. She couldn't imagine how much harder everything would have been if Faltir hadn't had Lady Genna's support.

"I've never spoken about this with anyone," said Jémys, sounding mildly surprised. "Like I said, my aunt would never talk about it, or *couldn't* talk about it. So I learned early on not to mention it and not to ask questions. I couldn't stand to see the pain on her face when I did. But I never realized..."

"Realized what?"

He raised his eyes to meet hers. "I never realized how nice it would be to talk about it with someone. I loved my father. He was a good man, honourable and true... and I think it's an insult to his memory that I've avoided talking about him all these years. It may be painful, but the memories are how we keep them alive with us, aren't they?"

Catanya held his gaze. She wasn't sure what to say. Of course they had to keep the memories of the ones they'd loved and lost alive within them. It *was* painful, and it *was* difficult, but it was also so important. Catanya thought about her loved ones and how she'd been trying to avoid thinking about them. Jémys was right, that was an insult to their memories.

"Come on," Jémys interrupted her reverie. "We should keep moving. We're not far from Finnua. I expect we'll arrive tomorrow if we make good time this afternoon."

They walked for hours, chatting happily about Finnua and the people who lived there. The more Catanya learned about Jémys, the more she understood what a truly decent person he was. He told her stories of his youth in Finnua—how he helped on his neighbours' farms, and how the old widows who lived on the village outskirts would invite him over for meals and chat nostalgically about their younger years.

Catanya thought the residents of Finnua sounded like a happy, simple lot, not unlike the people of Faltir. Except she had the sense that Finnua was more of a community. Perhaps because Finnua had less outside support, they were more open and willing to lend each other a helping hand. In Faltir, everyone had been guarded. They were never cruel or selfish, but they liked to keep to themselves. Finnua seemed like one massive family, all working together.

Jémys had explained that Finnua was also a farm village. Most of its people owned and operated farms, which they needed to sustain them throughout the year. Unlike Faltir, there were no other towns or villages for miles, which, Catanya suspected, meant everyone in Finnua learned by necessity to rely on each other.

Faltir, however, had always relied heavily on its neighbour, Mellot Cove. Mellot Cove was a seaport town, with a great deal of transient business and industry. Few people passing through the town ever had cause to visit Faltir, but its proximity gave Faltir the opportunity to benefit. As a result, Catanya always considered the villagers a bit too inclined to prioritize their own needs.

But Finnua sounded nice. And Jémys had said he would help her build a home there if she chose to stay. This thought was surprisingly appealing to her—the idea of building a home. She had never dreamed of settling down before, but now that she was displaced and alone, she appreciated the safety a home could offer her. Before all of this, she would have done anything to escape her dull village life. She'd spent years longing for freedom and adventure. But now...

After hours of walking, the sun had set. A faint chill drifted in the air that spoke of autumn approaching. Catanya loved autumn, it had always been her favourite time of year. She preferred the cooler temperatures, and she always enjoyed the harvest. Above all, she loved how the leaves changed colour and the world came alive with crimson and auburn flame. She had spent many autumn days painting and sketching the land-scapes around Faltir.

"I wish I had my paints," she said to Jémys, as he stoked the fire that night. As silly as it might have been, she found herself thinking this a lot lately. If she'd known what was in store for her, she never would have discarded her drawings on that beach or dropped her supplies in the woods. She missed the relaxing sensation of putting images on paper and she didn't know when or if she'd get a chance to do it again.

Jémys looked up at her, the light of the flames dancing on his face. "Paints?"

"Yes, my paints and brushes. This forest is beautiful. I would have enjoyed painting it. I've always been drawn to artistic work. Painting, sketching, pottery..."

"Oh, I see, so you're an artisan." He sat next to her and frowned at the fire. "What about charcoal?" he asked.

Catanya followed his gaze and chuckled. "Yes, I suppose charcoal is easily available to me, isn't it?"

"When we leave in the morning, we should remember to collect some of it for you."

Jémys indicated the burning wood, then smiled at Catanya. She beamed back at him. "Where did you learn how to paint?" he asked, reclining in the grass.

Catanya frowned. "I don't know... I can't remember anyone ever showing me. I found some old, forgotten supplies and just sat down to paint the mountains. And I never really stopped."

"So your parents weren't artisans? Your mother?"

"My mother?" Catanya frowned, unsure how to respond. "I never knew my mother or my father. I was raised in an orphanage."

"Oh, sorry. I shouldn't have assumed. I didn't mean to—" Jémys broke off, casting her an apologetic glance. "What happened to your parents?"

"I'm not sure." Everything she knew about herself was a lie.

Everything she'd believed about her parents... "Well, I guess I know my father died." That *is certainly true*, she thought. King Casréyan had died quite recently. "But my mother... I don't know where she is. I never met her—" Catanya broke off, as a memory flooded into her mind—a memory of a day over ten years ago.

The day she'd met the Queen of Caerlon.

After weeks of pestering Genna, Catanya had finally gotten permission to open a stall where she could sell her handmade crafts and jewellery in the village market. She'd been there all day, brimming with pride and excitement as the villagers praised her work, and she'd already sold half her cart when she heard the news. The royal family would be stopping in Faltir to water their horses on their way to Mellot Cove. They'd been on tour for weeks already, in a custom to mark Cadyan's tenth year and first rite of manhood.

The nervous energy had been palpable. Everyone in Faltir was terrified, whispering words of caution and debating whether to return to their homes. Catanya had been so young that she didn't fully understand, but the adults' uneasiness was catching.

She could still remember the opulent carriage being drawn down the dusty road by four magnificent white horses, flanked on either side by soldiers clad in armour and wearing the royal colours.

And riding ahead of the carriage was the maífirkon, their leader and the most ruthless warrior among them. Everyone knew the maífirkon title could only be earned through a quadrennial tournament, famed for its brutality and carnage. The maífirkon was the second-most feared man in Caerlon. Second only to the king.

Despite their desire to flee to the safety of their homes, most villagers gathered in the square near the stables. They were anxious to greet the carriage and careful to show

Casréyan an excess of admiration and flattery. But Catanya stayed behind at her stall. Genna hadn't given her permission to wander around, and Catanya wasn't interested in the royal family—at the time, she had no reason to be.

It wasn't long before the crowd dispersed. The king and the prince had disappeared along with most of their firkon, leaving the queen to explore Faltir alone. Without the king around, everyone seemed more relaxed. The queen dismissed her guards and strolled through the market, stopping to talk with every vendor. She inquired about their work with genuine interest, offering compliments and making several purchases. Then she reached Catanya's stall.

"What have you got here, my child?" she asked.

"Your Majesty." Catanya remembered curtseying clumsily. "These are some necklaces and bracelets I made using stones and shells I collected by the ocean. And these are various pencil drawings and portraits."

"Well, they certainly are beautiful, aren't they?" Fehla smiled at her. "And what about the piece you are wearing, that necklace? Where did you get that?"

Catanya was wearing her new necklace. Lady Genna had given it to her earlier that week, explaining that it had belonged to her mother, who'd intended it for Catanya on her tenth birthday.

The necklace comprised a single gemstone dangling from a delicate golden chain. It had surprised Catanya to be presented with something so lovely. She'd never seen anything like it before, and when she rotated it in her fingers, the stone had seemed to change colour. It was the oddest stone she'd ever seen. It always seemed alive as its colours danced and sparkled in the light. But despite its multitude of colours, it also had a strangely pearly and translucent sheen.

Surely, the queen had recognized the heirloom she'd intended for her daughter. Had she known who Catanya was?

Had she known she was standing in front of the daughter she'd abandoned?

Catanya racked her brain trying to remember what else the queen had said. She remembered thinking the queen seemed kind—kind but sad. She had asked Catanya her name, and about her home at Camlee Lodge, and then...

"Before I go, Catanya," she had spoken her name with deliberate emphasis, "I should very much like to buy one of your bracelets." Then she'd selected one made of white shells and pink coral. "This one is quite beautiful, and something about it reminds me of that necklace you are wearing."

Fehla had given her several gold pieces and, ignoring Catanya's protests that she'd been too generous, the queen had placed the bracelet on her wrist and held her hand out to admire it.

At the time, Catanya was so flattered and grateful to sell one of her bracelets that she hadn't thought twice about their encounter. But now that she replayed it in her mind, the entire interaction was charged with meaning.

Catanya ran her fingers along her neck where her mother's necklace used to hang. It was gone now, of course. It had been destroyed on the night of Cadyan's coronation. Diyah had explained that the necklace seemed to channel the energy passing through her and its force had destroyed the stone. But come to think of it, Catanya hadn't seen any shards. If the necklace had shattered, wouldn't it have left pieces behind?

She was picturing the rare gemstone, when she had another thought. She raised her hand to her head to touch the strand of hair she had concealed. Could it be a coincidence? Her hair seemed to shimmer with the same strange colourful pearliness as the gem she'd worn. But that was absurd. How could a gemstone channel powers? Had the queen known this when she'd given Catanya the stone? Could she have known everything that was going to happen?

Catanya was suddenly angry again. Had Fehla been planning this all along, knowing that her children would be obliged to become enemies? Had her mother ever even truly cared for her?

Catanya buried her face in her hands. She couldn't understand any of it. She had grown up believing that her mother was a simple woman who'd died in childbirth—a simple woman who loved her daughter with all her heart.

Lady Genna had always told her the same story. The same lie. "Your mother was young and fragile. She had no remaining family or connections when she arrived here, asking me to take you in. I think she knew she wouldn't survive the birth, and all she wanted was to leave you somewhere you'd be loved."

As a child, Catanya had romanticized versions of that story, comforted by the knowledge that her mother had loved her and, if she'd lived, would have raised Catanya, never abandoning her. She had never questioned it.

Never in her wildest dreams had Catanya imagined she was from such a complicated family, or that her mother had actually chosen to abandon her.

She didn't blame Genna for lying—she understood why the lies were necessary—but the truth still stung, even more given all the questions she still had.

"Catanya?" Jémys's asked. "Are you alright?"

She lifted her head from her hands. "Sorry," she said, rubbing her eyes. "I was lost in thought about my mother. There are so many things I wish I could ask her. But I can't." She heard the bitterness in her voice. Then she sighed and turned her gaze towards Jémys. "Tell me about your mother."

Jémys gave her a sad smile. "My mother left us when I was quite young. I hardly remember her. My aunt is the one who raised me."

"Oh, Jémys, I'm sorry," mumbled Catanya.

"Don't be," he replied, brushing away her concern. "My aunt was wonderful. I can't imagine a better mother."

"Still, no child should be abandoned by their parent," she said more aggressively than she'd intended. Jémys gave her a sympathetic look.

They sat in silence for a while, watching the flames. When the moon had fully risen, Catanya curled up beside the fire, and Jémys crossed to the opposite side to sleep.

Catanya lay there, gazing up at the stars shining above them. As she drifted off to sleep, she wondered where her mother was at that moment, and whether she was gazing at those same stars.

The next thing Catanya knew, she was being dragged to her feet by a pair of rough hands. It was dark. The fire had dimmed and, the air was full of loud, raucous voices and cackling laughter.

"Well, aren't you a pretty li'l thing?" The man clutching Catanya whispered into her ear. The smell of stale barkbeer and sweat made her cough.

"Oy, Drayk. Look wha' we 'ave 'ere!"

"What is it?"

"Gold. Lots of it." He rattled the satchel in his hand, and it jangled loudly.

"Put it with the rest."

"No! Don't touch it!" came Jémys's voice.

There was a scuffle and a grunt, followed by the dull thud of someone hitting ground. Catanya struggled against the man holding her captive. She looked around through the gang of outlaws, searching for Jémys. He was lying on his stomach near the fire with his arms pinned behind him, and his face was bloody and battered.

"Get off of him!" Catanya cried, and she struggled even harder.

"Calm down, sweet'eart, there's plen'y of other men you could 'ave."

The men cackled and hooted. Jémys struggled even harder to get free.

"That's enough."

A tall, dark-haired man came into view, the light of the feeble flames dancing unevenly on his face. He stood very straight and walked with an arrogant swagger. He seemed out of place among these shabby, uncouth men. His hair and clothes were neat, and he wore all black except for a dark crimson tunic, barely visible beneath his other layers of clothes and his cloak. He surveyed Catanya appraisingly, his head tilted to one side and a crooked grin playing on his face. His clear blue eyes twinkled under his thick, dark eyelashes.

"Well, hello there, gorgeous," he said. "What brings a lady such as yourself to a place like this?"

"None of your business, thief," she spat at him.

"Thief?" He laughed. "Yes, I suppose we are thieves, aren't we lads?" Hoots of agreement echoed through the group. "But I'll tell you what, we live in a dishonest world, so men like us, we're forced to live dishonest lives. But you mustn't feel sorry for us," he added sarcastically, smiling at Catanya.

"Drayk, what do you want to do with 'em?" called a wiry, dirty man standing beside the fire.

"I say we keep 'em both, I can think of lots to do with 'em," snickered the man holding Catanya.

The grin slid off Drayk's face and he shut his eyes tight in apparent frustration. "Shut up, you idiot!" he snapped. "Our orders are clear."

The man groaned. "Can't we 'ave a bit 'o fun?"

He started moving his hands deliberately down Catanya's front. She cried out, repulsed, and struggled to free herself. But before she could make a move, the man called Drayk had pulled out a blade and held it to the thief's throat.

"I said no." His voice was quiet, and his eyes were menacing.

The man gave a frustrated shout and pushed Catanya forward. She stumbled and almost fell, but Drayk caught her and lifted her up.

"Don't touch me!" she snapped, swatting at him.

He held his hands up in the air. "I wouldn't dream of it." The crooked grin had returned to his face, and he stared at her as he put the blade back in its sheath under his cloak. Then he turned and walked towards the pile of objects his crew had taken from them. He bent over and lifted Jémys's sword out of the mess.

"Fascinating. This is a nice blade. Made in Sidina, I think. Fitting of a knight. Tell me boy, are you a firkon?" He looked down at Jémys, who refused to respond. "No, I thought not," continued Drayk. "So tell me, how does a simple peasant boy lay his hands on such a high-quality sword?"

He lowered the blade to within an inch of Jémys's face. When Jémys still didn't respond, he twitched the sword, causing a small cut to appear on his cheek. "Come on, tell me what I want to know and I won't hurt you anymore. I'd rather not damage such a pretty face."

The gang guffawed and whistled as Drayk laughed.

Catanya glanced around, terrified. She was surrounded by outlaws. The nearest one was standing close enough to grab her, but nobody appeared to be watching her. They were fixated on Drayk and Jémys.

She needed to do something, and if she moved fast enough...

Catanya shut her eyes and took a deep breath. When she opened them again, she acted on impulse. She kicked the nearest outlaw in the shin as hard as she could. The man cried out and stumbled backwards. The others turned their attention on Catanya, but she dodged them and lunged at Drayk, grabbing him from behind.

He seemed surprised and he let the sword fall. He grasped at her arms and pulled Catanya off him, sending her flying to the ground.

She landed hard, coughing and spluttering. She could hear scuffles coming from behind her and she knew Jémys had freed himself and was fighting.

Catanya rolled onto her back and saw another outlaw bearing down on her. She scrambled backwards, fumbling with the blade strapped to her leg. Her hand was sweating and trembling as she gripped the handle and held it out defensively.

The outlaw laughed and kicked it out of her grasp. She cried out in pain, clutching her hand.

"Get up," he snarled. He bent down to grab her, but someone crashed into him from the side and the two people tumbled in a heap.

Catanya looked over to see Jémys. It seemed he'd kicked his opponent so hard, the man had flown backwards, hitting Catanya's attacker.

"Thanks," she breathed, climbing to her feet.

But Jémys didn't have time to respond. He was already fighting with another outlaw, and he hadn't noticed Drayk advancing on him, sword outstretched.

Terror shot through Catanya. She cried out incoherently and to her surprise, the dwindling fire beside Drayk blazed and expanded, catching his cloak on fire. Nobody else seemed to notice. But Drayk was distracted trying to remove his cloak and extinguish the flame. Catanya took advantage of this distraction to hit the sword out of his hand. He stared at her, his eyes wide in shock and then he fell to the ground—Jémys had struck him hard on the head and knocked him out.

Catanya surveyed the scene. All of Drayk's men were either unconscious or moaning on the ground, clutching wounds.

"Wow, you really are a good fighter," she said to Jémys. "I was useless with my blade." She examined her bruised hand, flexing her fingers. It hurt, but nothing was broken.

"No, you were great. You held your own without it." He glanced at the man lying by his feet. "Come on, we'd better tie them up and get moving."

The sun had started to rise as Catanya finished the last knot, tying the outlaws to the trees. Drayk had woken up, and he was eyeing her.

"I underestimated you," he whispered so only Catanya could hear.

She looked at him, their eyes meeting, and she was startled to see them still sparkling playfully at her. He seemed wholly unconcerned about his current predicament.

"I promise I won't make that mistake next time," he teased. "There's a lot more than meets the eye with you, isn't there?" He held Catanya's gaze, and it made her uncomfortable.

"I assure you, there won't be a next time," she said haughtily, acting tougher than she felt.

"I wouldn't count on that, gorgeous. Now I see there's something *special* about you." His eyes flashed knowingly. "I'll find you again. I can promise you that."

"Ready?" asked Jémys.

Catanya stood up, still staring at Drayk. Then she turned and said, "Ready."

"We'll meet again soon!" Drayk called after them, as they left the clearing. Catanya looked back to see him grinning widely. She was suddenly very uneasy.

8
———

## A LINE IS DRAWN

It was an unnaturally bleak and windy day, and the chill in the air carried a sense of foreboding despair. Even from the shelter of the castle courtyard, Fehla could hear the ocean crashing against the city's western walls, and taste the salt in the air.

It tasted bitter.

Fehla stood still, numbed from the cold and the sorrow. A group of servants carried her friend's lifeless and mangled body and tossed it unceremoniously onto a wooden cart before dragging it away to be burned.

The blood-stained scaffold would remain on display for days until the rain had washed it clean. It was meant as a grim reminder for the people, a reminder of their king's wrath.

As if they needed reminding.

A low rumble of thunder growled its displeasure in the distance, and Fehla wrenched her gaze away from the cart to scan the now dwindling crowd of spectators. She would never understand the attraction of a public execution.

She saw men and women of all ages leaving... children and families too. All these people had known Grante. He had been their physician. He'd saved them, healed them, and yet here they still were, watching his last moments with depraved fascination, as if his life had meant nothing to them.

Or perhaps it was just another distraction from their own pain.

Grante would have chosen to view it that way. He had never been one to judge or condemn another person for their actions. Somehow he had always managed to understand and to sympathize.

But Fehla wasn't like that. As she watched the spectators slinking back to their lives, she couldn't help feeling angry and resentful. These people had gathered to watch a good man die —one who'd devoted his life to service, helping them and caring for their families.

Another rumble of thunder echoed on the stone walls. It sounded much closer now. Fehla gazed at the sky as the first raindrops began to fall. It started slowly, but before long the gentle drizzle had evolved into a full-blown deluge of icy pellets.

But Fehla didn't move. She stood there, allowing the water to soak through her clothes, hoping it might wash away her grief or let her drown.

"My lady?"

Fehla looked down, startled to see a young attending girl, soaked from head to toe, wearing nothing but a thin work smock.

"My lady, we should go in," she urged, shivering in the freezing rain and wind.

The girl was thin and pitiful as she stared at her queen, eyes pleading to return to the castle. But Fehla didn't care. She wanted to be left alone in the rain. She deserved to suffer.

There was a sudden crack of thunder and the young girl jumped in fright.

Fehla closed her eyes in frustration. Then she sighed and

nodded, turning to follow the attendant up the stone steps and into the castle.

Once inside, Fehla dismissed the girl and stood in the hallway, listening to the storm rage outside. Then she started walking, drifting through the castle and taking no notice of the stares she attracted as she dripped all over the floors.

She didn't know where to go. Not wanting to return to her chambers yet, she continued to wander, allowing her legs to carry her forward, without knowing where they were taking her. When she began to recognize her surroundings, she came to a halt outside a familiar wooden door. There was a small carved sign posted beside it that read *Physician's Quarters.*

Instinct moved her hand towards the door, but then she stopped. She stood still, staring at that sign until she felt the muscles burn in her outstretched arm.

Nothing was in there for her anymore. Nothing and no one.

"My lady," came a voice from behind her, causing her to start.

Fehla turned to see Julyán striding down the corridor in her direction. He was still wearing his ceremonial attire and Fehla couldn't help but notice the faint red splatter across his front, barely discernable against the dark colour of his uniform. He *had* been standing very close.

"What do you want?" A sudden blast of hatred broke through her grief, returning some clarity to her mind.

She loathed the fírkon, they had always been a tool for oppression and a symbol of her husband's power. It infuriated her that now her son was using them the same way.

Once, perhaps, the fírkon had been a noble order, but not anymore. They were all corrupt now. As ruthless as their leader, and their king. Even the lone few who had struggled to keep their humanity were beginning to lose it. They all did in the end. The last one she knew with a meagre shred of decency was off with Slaedir, hunting her daughter like a wild animal. Fehla just had to hope that whatever loyalty he had to his queen would win out over everything else. She was counting on it.

"The king is planning a celebration feast and requires you to attend," said Julyán in his infuriatingly blank voice.

It took a moment for his words to register. "What?" she snapped, rounding on him. "A *celebration* feast?"

Julyán stared at her. "Traditionally the king holds a feast when a traitor is executed." He spoke as if by rote.

And suddenly Fehla was livid. Anger burned away her despondency, and she turned on her heel and strode off, leaving Julyán behind.

She bolted up the nearest staircase and stormed down the corridor towards her son's chambers. Then, ignoring the guards' protests, she burst through the door without knocking.

The door slammed behind her. She suppressed a shudder at the instant disquiet she associated with this chamber. It had once belonged to her late husband, but since his death and Cadyan's ensuing coronation, her son had taken it over as his own.

It was an enormous, lavish space, filled to bursting with bright-coloured furnishings and décor. An enormous stone fire-place stood at the centre of the room, framed by two grand armchairs. The massive four-poster bed was carved out of the finest cherry wood and draped in countless furs and pillows, while a matching table, trunk, and wardrobe sat atop an expensive burgundy damask rug, which covered nearly the entire floor.

But perhaps worst of all were the intricate tapestries that hung on the walls, each depicting another brutal battle from the Quiescence Wars in explicit and excruciating detail. The scenes of gory battlefields, the images of Maílater Caer vanquishing hordes of practitioners, and the pained expressions on those practitioners' faces as their Resonance was ripped from their souls.

Fehla had nothing but horrible memories staring at those tapestries. Memories of her own pain and fear, her own oppression. She tried not to look at the walls as she marched up to her son.

"A celebration feast?" she demanded.

Cadyan was standing on a small footstool in front of a mirror, while his valet handed him different coats to try. "Well, it is the custom, isn't it?" he asked, gesturing for the valet to give him one of the more elegant options.

"Grante was a good man," she said through gritted teeth.

Cadyan snorted before turning to stare at his mother. "There's no such thing." His voice was cold and detached. "Besides, maybe now you will think twice before betraying me in the future."

A hollow pit settled in Fehla's stomach. "You knew Grante your entire life. How could you?"

They'd had this argument countless times this week, and nothing she said seemed to make any difference.

Cadyan just smiled tauntingly and said nothing.

"Don't look at me like that," she snapped.

"Oho!" Cadyan laughed and jumped down off the stool with a swagger. "Well, Mother, you have only yourself to blame for what happened here today. What did you expect me to do? Really?"

Fehla's face flushed as the prickling sense of shame mixed with her anger. When she spoke next, she tried to keep her tone even and calm. "I have told you a hundred times, I wasn't hiding her from *you*, I was hiding her from your father."

"Right," said Cadyan, snapping his fingers. "That makes perfect sense, especially since Father has been dead for weeks now and you still didn't tell me." He curled his lip in contempt. "What? Did you think I'd never find out about her?"

Fehla clenched her teeth and closed her eyes tight in frustration. "Come now, Cadyan. Catanya is not your enemy. She's your sister. We're family."

"Family? Ha!" he scoffed. "We're not a family and we never were. We're a regime, Mother. A bloodline. The only thing that matters is succession. One must supplant the other to survive, but I won't be replaced. I won't! And certainly not by *her*. She has no right to claim my throne. I've waited too long to get here and I've earned it! I will not allow anyone to compromise what I've achieved."

Cadyan's words resonated in Fehla's memory. It sent a chill down her spine. "Spoken like your father's son," she said coolly, taking no pains to hide her disgust.

Cadyan's nostrils flared and his eyes flashed. For a second, it seemed like he wanted to hit her, but then his mouth curved into a wide grin and he laughed. "Oh, if only Father could see me now. He'd be so furious to see me on his throne... in his chambers..." Cadyan held his arms out and twirled around, gesturing at the room in apparent glee. "But I'm the king now. And I'm the king that Caerlon deserves, not *him*—not anybody else. I'll do whatever it takes to keep what is rightfully mine." He stopped spinning and stared at his mother. "Everyone knows I've killed for this throne once already, and I will do it again. As many times as I must."

Fehla's entire body stiffened. "Leave us," she snapped at the valet, biting back her anger. When he had bowed and left the room, she rounded on her son. "Stop that!" she half-whispered, half-shouted. "Stop encouraging those rumours. I know you didn't kill your father."

Rumours had been flying for weeks about the mysterious illness that resulted in the late king's death. The illness had come as if from nowhere, causing breathing troubles and abdominal discomfort until his body had seized, paralyzing him. He died in unimaginable agony, frozen inside of himself until he finally suffocated.

It was a gruesome death, and although she'd hated the man, at night the memory of it still haunted Fehla.

Early in his reign, Casréyan had been moderately well-liked, but as the years progressed and he developed increasingly unpredictable and malicious tendencies, the kingdom had come to despise him. As a result, very few people could claim to be sorry when he died—but speculation about his sudden illness had sparked a popular rumour that Cadyan had poisoned him to speed his accession to the throne.

It was a rumour that Cadyan himself delighted in propagating.

"How do you know I didn't kill him?" he asked. "Maybe I did kill him, Mother. How would you know? I believe we've established the fact that you and I don't always tell each other the truth."

"No," hissed Fehla, shaking her head. "I know you didn't do it!"

"You'll never know for sure," said Cadyan with mock pity. "And let's be honest. The man deserved it. To die in agony by his son's hand—I can't think of a more fitting punishment or reckoning." His voice had adopted a cold, nostalgic tone and there was a bright gleam in his eye. "After all the years I suffered at his hand, powerless and trapped... to watch him die that way—ooh." Cadyan suppressed a shudder of delight. "That was, quite simply, the greatest moment of my life."

Fehla was deeply disturbed by what her son had said. "Come, Cadyan, this isn't you." She was desperate to make him see reason.

"No, this *is* me, mother!" he snapped, hostile again as he stamped his foot like a petulant child. "You don't understand, do you? I'm not only *his* son, I'm yours too! *You* raised me. You're the one that turned me into this. So be proud, Mother. Be proud of my accomplishments or stay out of my way. Rest assured that I will remove everything and everyone who interferes with my plans—even you, if it comes to it."

He stood glaring at her rebelliously, waiting for her to respond.

But Fehla didn't know what to say. Cadyan's words had cut through her anger, melting it away and leaving her miserable once again.

Cadyan nodded. "That's what I thought." He swept past her out of the room.

As his footsteps echoed through the walls, an aching sorrow was once again building inside Fehla. She was beginning to think that her son was beyond her reach. What happened to the boy she remembered? The boy whose laugh used to warm her soul, not leave her frozen and hollow.

Despite all the pain and abuse he'd suffered, Fehla used to be able to see a softer side to her son. But not anymore. With every passing day he sounded more like his father. She could feel him slipping away.

Although she was certain that Cadyan had not murdered his father, that knowledge did nothing to comfort her anymore. After all, Cadyan hadn't even been king for a month and he'd already caused the deaths of untold numbers of people, including Grante.

Grante had been with Fehla since the beginning. When she'd first arrived in Caerlon as the new queen, young and naïve, Grante was one of the first people she met. He'd been with her through everything. The sleepless nights, the countless bruises and fractured ribs. How many times had she sat with him in his chambers, just to have someplace she felt safe? She had shared everything with him, all of her biggest fears and all of her darkest secrets. And he had never judged or criticized her for them, he had never thought less of her for her choices or her mistakes. Instead, he had helped her to carry her burdens. He'd risked everything to help her and her daughter, and he'd never asked for anything in return.

She couldn't believe he was gone. Grante hadn't only been her confidante, he had been her friend. And that friendship had cost him his life.

Fehla didn't know whether she wanted to scream or cry. Angry and grief-stricken, her guilt was threatening to overwhelm her. She stared at her surroundings, remembering all the painful memories she had in this room. She longed to undo them all. To go back and make different decisions—to change everything.

But there was nothing she could do. Grante was dead, her daughter was gone, and her son was transforming into something unrecognizable. There was no one left. Despite her best efforts, her family seemed cursed to repeat the same awful patterns for all eternity.

And everyone around them suffered for it.

But then Fehla remembered something. Maybe there was still someone left...

She deliberated briefly, wondering how best to proceed. Then she wrenched open the door, and strode down the corridor towards the opposite end of the castle. Her sodden clothes made her shiver, but she didn't care.

Rounding the corner, she hesitated when she saw a maid-servant coming in her direction carrying a pile of fresh linens and a small carafe of water.

"I'll take those," she said, holding out her hands.

The girl jumped and let out a faint squeak. She hadn't noticed Fehla and seemed surprised to find her in the west wing, so close to the servants' quarters, not to mention soaking wet and unkempt.

"I'm sure the king would appreciate a celebratory drink," suggested Fehla, not wanting to dawdle. "Perhaps you could go down to the storeroom and fetch him a bottle of spiced wine?"

"Of course, my lady," stammered the servant. Then she curtseyed and headed off down the hall.

Fehla cast around to make sure nobody saw her, then she hurried off towards the dungeons.

"My lady." The guards shot to their feet when she approached. "My lady, this is no place for you—"

"I'm here to see the prisoners from Faltir," she interrupted, giving the guard a steely look. "You will take me to them, now."

The men exchanged awkward glances. "Y-yes, my lady. Of course. Right this way."

One of them unlocked the gate, grabbed a torch, and led Fehla along a dank, narrow passage lined by barred cells.

Fehla's breath caught in her throat. In all her years at the castle, she'd thus far managed to avoid entering the dungeons, so she wasn't prepared for what lay within. The stench alone was enough to make her queasy, but the cold air and the prisoners' incoherent sobs were truly suffocating.

As she followed the guard deeper, she tried not to picture the hundreds—perhaps thousands—of people who had rotted to death in these filthy cages.

"Here they are." The guard stepped aside for Fehla.

"Very well, you may leave us now," she said. It was difficult to speak while straining to avoid inhaling the stench.

The guard wavered, looking uncomfortable. "My lady, these vermin can be dangerous. They go mad down here. I wouldn't feel right leaving you here alone."

"I told you to go," she commanded, and then, softening her tone, she added in her best simpering voice, "I shall call for you if I require any assistance."

"Alright," he agreed reluctantly. He used his torch to light another one in a nearby bracket and turned to leave. "I'll be just out here, then. If you need me."

"Thank you." She waited until he was gone before dropping the act. Then she peered through the bars at the young woman and girls sitting chained to the cell floor. "Hello?" she called.

The woman leaned forward so the torch on the wall illuminated her face. It shocked Fehla to see the bruises and cuts. She held her breath, struggling to push away the thought of her son torturing these people.

"What do you want?" asked the woman. Her voice sounded dry and pained.

"Here, I've brought you some linens and water."

The younger girls crept forward and Fehla could see that they were pale and dehydrated, with cuts and bruises on their faces. The sight of it brought back painful memories of Cadyan at that age.

"Here." She handed the linens through the bars. She needed to do something to help.

One of the girls moved to take them, but the young woman stopped her. "Don't touch them, girls. Don't trust her." She shot Fehla a look of disgust and mistrust.

Fehla was taken aback. But then she realized what they must think of her and she understood. "You can trust me, I swear. I've only come to help." She attempted to give them a reassuring smile.

The young woman scowled. "Help? Like you helped your daughter? Or like you helped us when they dragged us down here to be tortured?" she scoffed. "Go away."

Fehla hung her head in shame. "I won't deny that I—I've been... complicit in everything that's happening, but never... *never* for a moment did I want to hurt anyone, especially not my daughter. Nor, as I've come to discover, my daughter's dear friend." She gazed through the bars, longing for her to understand. "It's Diyah, isn't it? I overheard the firkon talking about you."

Diyah glared at her through the dark and nodded almost imperceptibly.

"Well, Diyah, you may call me Fehla."

Diyah continued to stare at her without speaking.

"I promise you, I have only come here to help. Please, take these." She held up the linens. "You could use them to make bandages. It looks like you need them. And this"—she lifted the carafe—"this is fresh, cold water for you, I swear." She pushed the items through the bars. As she pulled her hands back, her sleeve caught on the metal and she had to tear it free.

"What is that?" asked Diyah suddenly, leaning forward.

"What? This?" Fehla held out her wrist, pulling a pale pink and white bracelet of polished shells and stones from under her torn sleeve.

"I recognize that," said Diyah, inching forward and wincing as she moved. "Catanya made that. You kept it? After all these years?" She sounded surprised.

Fehla nodded. She rolled the bracelet over her wrist and thought back on the memory. As delighted as she'd been to finally meet her daughter, it had made every day since that moment infinitely more difficult. It was so much harder, knowing where Catanya lived and having to force herself to stay away.

"This bracelet has never left my wrist since the day I bought it," she declared, hearing the regret and sorrow behind her words. "And every single day I've looked at it and I've wondered about her."

Fehla's stomach lurched as she stared through the bars at the beaten and bloodied face of the young woman within.

"Is my daughter safe?" The words came tumbling out of her. She felt awful asking about Catanya, given how battered and vulnerable Diyah was. But she needed to know.

Diyah leaned back. Her demeanour had softened somewhat. "I don't know."

"But—" Fehla bit her lip. She didn't know how to ask this next question. She was afraid to make Diyah suspicious, but it was important. "Catanya... is she... I mean, does she really have —have *powers*?" she finished, staring at Diyah.

Diyah surveyed her, frowning. "I don't know," she said again.

Fehla grimaced and bowed her head. "I hope not."

Diyah looked at her in surprise. "Why? Those powers might be her only weapon. They might be her only defence against *him*." She had a slightly accusatory note in her voice, and her eyes had narrowed.

Fehla tensed her shoulders. "I despise magic," she explained, thinking of all the horrible things her husband had done with it. The things he'd done to *her* with it. "If I'd had my way, Cadyan never would have taken that elixir. I never wanted him to be like his father. I tried to shield him from it, to protect him—teach him compassion. But it seems all my efforts were in vain." She felt the weight of everything bearing down on her. "I suppose it was always inevitable."

Through years of worrying that Casréyan would discover his daughter, she had never considered the possibility that Cadyan would end up being her problem.

She rubbed her eyes. "I just hope Catanya is alright."

Diyah stared at her. "*Alright*?" she repeated hotly. "Catanya's entire life has been a lie and now it's gone—destroyed by your son—and she's on the run from soldiers who want to kill her. She's probably terrified. So of course she's not *alright*... none of us are." She lapsed into a bitter silence, turning her gaze towards the young girls in the cell beside her.

Diyah's severe tone caught Fehla off-guard, and she felt a little ashamed of herself.

"No, of course," Fehla mumbled.

"But Catanya is strong," continued Diyah in a defiant voice, though Fehla thought she detected a faint quaver. "I believe in her and I'm never going to give up hope... and you shouldn't either."

Fehla could feel the prickling of tears forming in her eyes, and she tried to blink them away. "Hope is all I've had to help me through these last twenty years."

Diyah frowned and eyed her sharply. "Well... your daughter helped me through them." She held Fehla's gaze for a moment, then she turned to the girls beside her and said, "Here girls, have some water. And Meya, help me rip these linens into bandages."

Fehla was pleased to hear Diyah speak so highly of Catanya. It comforted her to know that her daughter was strong, and that she had meaningful relationships in her life. It sounded like Catanya had grown up to become everything Fehla had hoped for and more.

If only Fehla could have given her son the same opportunity.

She twisted the bracelet on her wrist, feeling drained. "I can't stay long, or it will arouse suspicion." She glanced reflexively behind her.

When she turned her attention back to the cell, she saw Diyah watching her with her forehead creased. "What would he do if he discovered you'd been down here?" she asked.

Fehla half-shrugged, half-sighed. "I don't know, but I pray we never find out."

"But..." The line between Diyah's brows deepened. "You're his mother. Surely he wouldn't—" But she stopped short at the look on Fehla's face.

"I'm not sure there's anything he wouldn't do anymore." Fehla gripped the cell bar and closed her eyes. It pained her more than she'd ever admit to say this about her son. "No," she said, shaking her head. "I'm afraid the boy I knew is gone. Whoever that man is, I don't recognize him."

Diyah nodded and said nothing.

There was a brief silence as Fehla peered sidelong at her. There were so many questions she longed to ask, but she needed to approach this cautiously. She didn't want to push Diyah and risk losing her trust.

"I should go," she said, standing up straight. "I'll try to return soon and bring more water and some food."

Diyah cleared her throat awkwardly. "Thank you," she said with a small note of contrition.

"It is the least that I can do," said Fehla.

As she walked the corridors back towards her chambers, she knew she'd made the right decision. Diyah was important to Catanya.

If Fehla wanted to stand a chance of protecting the ones she loved, she needed to gather as much information as possible. At least Diyah could give her answers about her daughter.

Fehla had made several dangerous decisions in her life, the consequences of which she never could have foreseen. There was nothing she could do to change that now. All she could do was hope to control what happened next, and that meant she needed to stay one step ahead of everyone else.

9

———

# FINNUA

It was approaching sundown when Jémys and Catanya arrived in Finnua. They emerged from the forest atop a hill that sloped down towards the village nestled below. They could see the outlines of buildings set against the low-hanging sun like an elaborately wrought fire grate. A wide rolling meadow blanketed the hill, brimming with wildflowers that rustled in the gentle breeze.

On the far side of the field sat a modest manor house overlooking the village and surrounding farms. It bore signs of neglect, with crumbling garden walls and wild vines that snaked their way up the pinkish-grey stones towards the roof. Crooked green shutters hung off the windows, and the entire house seemed vaguely slanted to the left. It was less than half the size of Camlee Lodge, only one floor high and sitting quite low to the ground, and there was a modest lawn with a quaint rock garden and one long vegetable patch, which was wildly overgrown with weeds.

"It's a little worse for wear." Jémys shifted anxiously and looked from Catanya to the house.

"I think it's lovely," she said. Despite its rundown appear-

135

ance, the house appeared warm and inviting. Catanya was eager to be indoors again.

They walked across the meadow towards the house. As they stepped over the crumbling garden walls, the front door burst open and a young boy with bright blonde hair and round cheeks came running out to greet them.

"Jémys! Jémys! You're back!" cried the little boy as he ran.

"Oh, here's trouble," said Jémys, dropping his pack and bracing himself for impact.

When the boy jumped, Jémys caught him and lifted him up in the air, spinning him around, squeezing him, and returning him to the ground.

"You've gotten so big!" Jémys panted dramatically.

"Mother says I grew an inch last week!" said the boy with pride. "Soon I'll be taller than you!"

"I'm sure you will be." Jémys was grinning, his eyes bright with affection.

"Where have you been?" asked the boy, as he started nosing around Jémys's pack.

"Where have I been?" repeated Jémys, eyeing the boy. The corners of his mouth quirked up. "I've been all over... on an adventure!"

"An adventure?" The boy looked up eagerly.

"That's right. I've been travelling the kingdom, meeting strange people and facing dangers you couldn't imagine." Jémys winked at Catanya.

"Really?" squeaked the boy.

"Oh, yes."

The young boy was shaking his head in awe. Then he noticed Catanya and stopped. "Who are you?" he asked baldly.

Jémys laughed at the startled look on Catanya's face. "Catanya, this is Olly, and Olly—"

"Ollyán!" interrupted the boy.

"Oh, it's Ollyán now, is it? No, sorry, you'll always be Olly to me." With that, Jémys bent down and hoisted Olly over his shoulder like a sack of potatoes.

The boy squealed with laughter and kicked his feet helplessly in the air.

"Come on." Jémys motioned for Catanya to follow him towards the house.

Laughing, Catanya grabbed the pack off the ground and moved to join him. Then she noticed a woman standing in the doorway, beaming at them. Her long grey plaits were wound together in a neat bun and she was short and brawny, with broad shoulders and strong arms that spoke of years of hard labour. Underneath its many lines, her face bore a distinct softness and kindness that resembled her nephew so closely that there was no denying who she was.

"Hello, Aunt," said Jémys, bending down to kiss her on the cheek.

"Well, let me look at you." She put her hands on his arms and peered at his face. She was at least a foot shorter than him, and she had to crane her neck to see him. "You look tired, dear. And what happened here?" She indicated the fading bruises and cuts on his face.

"Oh, nothing." Jémys raised his fingers to his tender cheek. "A minor accident, but I'm fine." He brushed away her concern.

Her lips drew into a thin line like she knew he was lying, but she didn't press the matter. "Well, I'm so happy you're home safe. I worry..." Her voice sounded choked.

Jémys flipped Olly around and deposited him smoothly back onto the ground. Then he bent down and pulled his aunt into a warm embrace. "I'm happy to be home." He smiled. Then, pulling away, he added, "I'd like to introduce you to someone." He stepped aside to present Catanya, who was waiting a few feet away. "Catanya, this is my aunt Nelle."

"Catanya, a pleasure to meet you." Nelle held out her hand in greeting. "And how do you two know one another?" She frowned quizzically at Catanya and then cast her nephew a curious glance.

Catanya suddenly realized how strange she must look wearing Jémys's clothes. She fidgeted uncomfortably.

"We met in our travels in the woods," said Jémys. "Catanya's home is, well, gone..." He trailed off, eyeing Catanya. "So I offered to bring her here to stay with us for a while."

"Oh, of course, dear. You poor thing." Nelle took Catanya's hand and gave it a sympathetic pat. "Stay as long as you like."

"Thank you, that's very kind." She glanced nervously at Jémys, who was watching the exchange and beaming.

"Come in, come in. Let's get you something to eat." Nelle linked arms with Catanya and led the way into the house.

The entrance hall was narrow and dark, but it opened into a large, cozy sitting room with a sturdy fireplace in the middle and several worn but comfortable-looking chairs. At one end stood a short staircase, which led down a half-floor into the kitchen.

The kitchen was warm and bright, with several west-facing windows that looked out towards the vegetable patch and the village below. A second, smaller fireplace gave off the delicious smell of spices heating in a pot.

They sat down at the table while Nelle busied herself filling two bowls with generous portions of mutton stew.

Olly scrambled up onto the bench beside Jémys. "Where were you really?"

Jémys grinned as Nelle placed the bowl in front of him, and he grabbed his spoon. "I was up north building ships in Brigmun Bay."

"What! Really? Were they big ships?" asked Olly, leaning forward and causing the rickety table to shake.

"Enormous," said Jémys through a mouthful of piping hot stew. He swallowed with some difficulty and then smiled across the table at Catanya, his eyes watering. "Thirty, forty tons, some of them."

Olly whistled. "That's very big," he said like an expert.

Jémys chuckled. "Here," he stood up and grabbed his pack, "I brought you something."

"A present?" Olly sat up straight, eager and excited.

Jémys rustled in the bag and pulled out a small toy ship carved out of wood.

"It's a toy model of the biggest ship in the port, *The Murbanya*, it's called." Jémys handed the toy to Olly and sat back down at the table. "There was this old fellow who lived near the port. He was a shipwright his entire life, working on some of the grandest ships, including *The Murbanya* there. Well, unfortunately, the old man can't handle the hard labour anymore, so he sits by the docks carving models to sell as souvenirs and tokens for travellers."

"Ooh." Olly was turning the toy over in his chubby little hands and admiring it from every angle. "So did you see the real one?"

"I did, actually." Jémys nodded. "*The Murbanya* was just leaving when I arrived. But I was able to see it heading out to sea. It was very impressive."

Olly moved the boat through the air, imitating the sound of waves crashing against the hull. "Thank you," he said, with a wide smile.

"You're welcome."

Olly sat beside Jémys, asking endless questions about the different ships he'd seen and worked on. He wanted to know whether Jémys or Catanya had ever sailed on a ship as large as *The Murbanya,* and although neither of them had, he was confident they'd all get a chance quite soon. He chatted happily, leaving very little room for responses until they had all finished eating.

"Now, it's getting late." Jémys interrupted Olly before he

could ask yet another question about the top speeds of the biggest ships. "Why don't you take that toy and run on home to show your mum? You can come back tomorrow. We'll test it on the trough outside to see if it sails as well as the actual ship."

"Okay!" Olly squeaked as he jumped off the bench. "Bye!" He ran out the door.

"Bye!" they called after him.

Catanya chuckled. "He seems like a rambunctious boy."

"Oh, he is," Nelle said, laughing. "But he's a sweetheart. And he admires Jémys so much. He looks up to him like an older brother or father, and Jémys is so kind to him." She beamed at her nephew.

Jémys's cheeks flushed. "Olly's a good lad. I've always watched out for him. His father died not long after he was born, so it's just him and his mother, Ranya. She hasn't been well these last two years though. Between losing her husband and worrying about Olly's future... We help however we can, but there's not much we can do anymore." He exchanged a dark glance with Nelle.

"What is it?" asked Catanya.

"Well, Olly's the only child. The only son." Nelle had a distant look in her eyes. "With the new laws, he'll be taken away in a few years... he'll be taken to Caerlon."

Catanya felt sick. She had completely forgotten the new laws. "So he'll become a fírkon?" she asked, not wanting to believe it.

"Eventually." Jémys sounded dejected. "But he'll start as a page and train with one of the fírkon until he becomes a squire. Not long after that he'll compete in the tournament. He'll have to prove himself..." Jémys trailed off into a bitter silence.

Catanya didn't need Jémys to explain; she had heard the stories about the Maífírkon Tournament. A hollow feeling formed in her stomach, as she imagined Olly being forced to fight against countless soldiers with more experience and training.

She thought about the soldiers who'd attacked Camlee Lodge, and the untold horrors committed by the firkon every day. She couldn't bear to think about Olly becoming one of them.

Catanya was lost in her thoughts about Caerlon and she could barely hear the conversation going on beside her, until something Jémys said caught her attention.

"Between that and the reports of trouble brewing in the east—"

"Trouble in the east?" Catanya snapped back into the conversation. "Do you mean in Awnell?"

"It's just a rumour," said Jémys, standing up to clear the dishes. "They're saying that the people of Awnell are growing more bold. They're crossing uninvited into our land and causing trouble."

"What kind of trouble?"

"I don't know exactly, but I don't think it's a coincidence Caerlon is recruiting more soldiers now. I expect we'll be at war before long."

"Fools," grumbled Nelle. "You'd think they'd know better than to take on Caerlon. It never ends well. For anyone."

That was true. Everyone knew the stories about the Tirimsi Desert—an entire kingdom and its people reduced to sand and ash in what was now a barren wasteland. And the Ruins of Bratia still bore scorch marks along the remaining walls and foundations, from the battle that levelled the city.

"It won't end well this time either," said Jémys, sounding fatigued. "And it will be boys like Olly who pay the price."

"That's horrible," whispered Catanya. "Is there nothing you can do to prevent them from taking him?"

Nelle leaned forward, crossing her arms on the table.

"Ranya could take Olly and run, but they wouldn't get far on their own. No one ever does."

"And a life on the run? What kind of life is that?" Jémys added.

Catanya stared at her hands, thinking about her own situation. "No life at all," she muttered.

They all lapsed into silence.

Catanya was trying to picture Olly's future as a soldier. She didn't know anyone who'd become a firkon. There were no noble families with children in Faltir, and Caerlon had only recently expanded the levy to include commoners. King Casréyan had introduced the new rules towards the end of his reign. Catanya had hated him for it. She'd assumed it was his last-ditch effort to exert his control—yet another reason to loathe the man she now knew was her father. She even remembered hoping Cadyan might repeal the command when he took power.

But not anymore. Now she knew there was more to it. Caerlon was building an army.

She supposed that several of the boys she'd known in Faltir would end up being required to join the king's army, just like Olly. Every first-born son, whether noble or not, would now be taken to Caerlon.

Every first-born son.

Catanya furrowed her brow and started to ask, "Jé—"

"It's getting late," said Nelle without noticing that she had cut off Catanya. "You two must be exhausted. Come with me, Catanya, dear. I'll show you to your room."

They left the kitchen, crossing the sitting room towards a narrow corridor that stretched along the side of the house. There were several doors leading to different bedrooms and what appeared to be a modest study, cluttered with old books and various odd items. Nelle showed Catanya to one of the guestrooms at the northeast corner.

The bedroom was inviting, with a low ceiling and one round window that faced the meadow, and the forest beyond it. A plain mirror hung on the wall opposite the window, and the bed and wardrobe were carved from pale wood.

"I'm afraid it's quite small, but I hope you'll be comfortable here. I've brought in some blankets and a spare nightshirt. And I hung some old dresses in the wardrobe. Hopefully something fits. I'm sure you're eager for some proper clothes." Nelle gestured to the outfit Catanya was wearing.

Catanya smoothed down her wrinkled tunic and smiled. "Thank you," she said, privately thinking these were actually the most comfortable clothes she'd ever worn, loose and flexible for movement. "You've been very kind. And don't worry. I should only be here a couple of nights, I don't want to trespass—"

"Nonsense," Nelle interjected. "Stay as long as you want, dear. Jémys brought you here so we could help, didn't he?" She patted Catanya on the arm and nodded. "It's our pleasure to have you. Sleep well." Then she stepped out, closing the door behind her.

Catanya stared at the room, feeling reassured and comfortable—two feelings she hadn't experienced since before the coronation night. Then she changed into the nightshirt and climbed into the bed. It was soft and warm, and she snuggled under the covers, grateful not to be outside anymore. She was exhausted and her muscles ached from days of stumbling through the forest. Almost as soon as she laid her head down and closed her eyes, she fell into a deep sleep.

***

She dreamed of a large castle. It was perched on the edge of a cliff overlooking the western sea. As massive waves crashed against the rocks, the castle came alive. It writhed and contorted into strange shapes, turning dark as a man came striding out from within. She recognized him immediately. She had seen him once before, in another dream. But this time, he was different. He wasn't in pain like before. He wasn't vulnerable. Now he was shrouded in a terrible light and wearing a cruel, triumphant smile. She needed to run, to get away before he saw her. She turned and found herself surrounded by people all clad in gossamer linen clothes. Their faces were blurred and unrecognizable, and she felt guilty that she didn't recognize them. They were important, like friends from the past she had forgotten. The figure standing in the centre reached out towards Catanya, and now she could see it was Diyah.

Catanya took Diyah's hand and allowed her to lead her forward. A mountain materialized in the distance—larger and more impressive than any mountain she'd ever seen—and she turned to smile at Diyah, but she was gone. Catanya spun around and found herself suddenly and completely alone. As she returned her attention to the mountain, it crumbled before her, the trees ablaze, and all around her people were screaming. It was death. Endless, faceless death. The screaming grew louder until Catanya awoke with a jolt.

Staring up at the uneven stone ceiling, it took some seconds before she remembered where she was. It was just after daybreak and the pale morning light reflected off the mirror, giving the room a gentle blue tinge. Her heart was pounding and the back of her neck was drenched in sweat. She rubbed her eyes, trying to force the images of the dream out of her head, but they only seemed to burn brighter.

A few minutes later, Catanya heard murmuring voices outside her door, so she threw off her blankets and crossed to the wardrobe in the corner.

The dresses hanging inside were decades out of fashion and faded, but they felt well-made—likely Sidina craftwork from the days before Nelle's noble rank had been stripped. After trying on two different dresses, Catanya settled on a pale blue one with eyelet lace trim that more or less fit (although it was several inches too short), then she joined Nelle and Jémys in the kitchen. They exchanged their morning greetings over tea, as Nelle prepared the porridge. When it was ready, Catanya helped herself to a bowl and sat down at the table.

"Is there anything I can do to help you today?" Catanya asked, stirring her porridge and watching the steam rise. She was eager for a distraction to keep her mind off the haunting images in her dream.

"Oh, yes, actually," said Nelle. "I was hoping you and Jémys could walk into the village this morning. I have a list of items I need from the bake house, and the cooper should be done with those cider casks we ordered. Do you mind?"

"No, of course not. I'm happy to help." She smiled as she blew on her spoonful of porridge to cool it down.

"Oh, and Jémys, if you could tell the miller that we'll have twice as much as I originally estimated?"

"Of course, Aunt Nelle." After a few minutes of silence, Jémys looked sidelong at Catanya. "What happened to the tunic and breeches?"

Catanya laughed and shrugged.

Nelle gave a start and turned around to examine her. "Oh, yes, dear, that dress fits remarkably well, doesn't it? You know, I bought that the first time I went to Sidina. I was younger than you then. Oh, I thought I was so stylish." She chortled fondly and shook her head. "But I must admit, it looks much better on you."

"Thank you." Catanya's cheeks burned hot, and she fumbled with the sleeve. She always felt uncomfortable receiving compliments.

When Nelle turned away, Jémys leaned in and whispered, "She's not wrong, but personally I preferred the other outfit."

His mouth twisted into a cheeky grin and Catanya let out a soft chuckle.

After breakfast, Catanya and Jémys set off down the road towards the central village.

The village of Finnua comprised a few small streets that connected with the main road, which led out of town in either direction. Along the road were a handful of misshapen shops including a tall smokehouse and a tinker's shop that leaned towards its neighbour, the smithy. A bridge had been erected across the river. On the opposite bank sat the cooper's workshop and brewery. Perched on the riverbank was a large watermill, whose wide vertical wheel was rotated by the water rushing under it, and used to mill the flour and barley from the adjoining fields.

But the true pride of Finnua was the vast apple orchard in its centre. The orchard had been planted several generations before, and it housed countless flourishing trees. By early autumn, they were already ripe with a brilliant collection of fruits that dangled from the knotted and sprawling branches.

Catanya and Jémys walked down the street past the orchard. When they arrived outside the tinker's shop, the door opened and three women came out onto the street. The two ladies in front were stooped and grey with age, but the third was young, possibly five or six years younger than Catanya, just entering adulthood. Her face flushed a deep red when she caught sight of Jémys.

"Oh, Jémys! Dear me, when did you get back?" squawked one of the older ladies. She was a small, bony woman who moved with surprising vigour for her age.

"Hello, Evyain, it's nice to see you," said Jémys, adopting a patient, somewhat indulgent manner. "We only arrived last night." He gestured casually at Catanya.

"Oho, *we*?" Evyain exchanged a knowing smirk with her

companion, a heavy-set woman with a wide jaw and beady little eyes. "And who is this pretty young thing?"

Evyain and her friend giggled. But the younger woman glanced from Jémys to Catanya before awkwardly averting her gaze.

"Come now, Jémys, introduce us to your lovely wife," said the beady-eyed woman.

"My *what*?" spluttered Jémys.

The women giggled even harder.

"I always knew it would happen this way," declared Evyain. "You disappear for months at a time, all mysterious like. I knew one day you'd find a bride out there and bring her home with you. Only, it's a shame for our young ladies here." She nudged the younger girl by her side. "Disappointed hopes, isn't that right, Roslin?"

The girl blushed and stammered, "I d-don't know what you mean." She averted her eyes pointedly away from Jémys.

"A likely story," chortled the beady-eyed woman. "So, dear, what's your name?" She turned to address Catanya.

Catanya was startled, but the embarrassed look on Jémys's face made her laugh. "My name is—" She stopped herself.

"Yes, dear?"

Her insides twisted. When she'd told Jémys her name in the woods, she hadn't been thinking clearly, but now... She considered giving a fake name this time—but how would she explain that to Jémys? She hated lying. Maybe she could shorten her name and go by Catya or Tanya, or—

"Catanya?" Jémys spoke, "is everything alright?" He was staring at her, a crease between his brows.

Catanya's breath caught in her throat. She squeezed her eyes shut, silently berating herself for not thinking this through earlier. Sometimes with Jémys, she almost forgot why she was running.

"Ooh, Catanya? That's a nice name, isn't it?"

"It is indeed. I knew a *Calanya* once… or was it Nalanya?" Evyain shrugged and turned back to Catanya. "Well, where are you from then?"

"What does it matter? She lives here now, doesn't she, Evie? Honestly." The woman folded her arms in exasperation.

Catanya took a deep breath to calm her nerves. Maybe it was okay. Her name wasn't that unusual. And after all, Caerlon City was miles away, and Catanya was only planning to stay in Finnua for a few days. No one would remember her after she left.

"Well, I'm curious. We've got to make sure she's good enough for our Jémys, don't we?"

The two older women started giggling again.

"Oh, for crying out loud," muttered Jémys, looking frustrated and uncomfortable.

Despite her uneasiness, Catanya couldn't help chuckling at his discomposure.

"Ladies! Ladies!" Jémys shouted across their laughter. "We're not married. This is Catanya, my *friend*. We met in our travels and decided to travel together, that's all."

The ladies stood slack-jawed for a moment until Evyain's friend scrunched up her face. "Not married? Really? Why ever not?"

The laughter and chatter started again with force.

"Honestly, Jémys, are you quite alright? What's the matter with you? I mean, look at her!" She gestured to Catanya, whose cheeks burned hot again.

"No, it's alright. It's good," interjected the other lady, waving her hands to shush her friend. "Because he's saving himself for a good local girl, isn't that right, Rosy?"

The young girl blushed an even deeper red and muttered something about needing to get home, and then she rushed off down the lane, leaving behind the cackling women.

"Now seriously, Jémys, it's so good to have you back! Finnua isn't the same without you," said Evyain, as if nothing had happened. "You'll be coming to the Harvest Festival and the Apple Picking then, won't you?"

"Yes, of course. I wouldn't miss it!" Jémys looked relieved at the change of topic.

"Well, very good, we'll see you later then. You'll come by the house for supper one evening this week? Good. Waltin will be eager to see you! Come on, Evyain."

The two ladies strolled off down the street, moving slowly and chatting away.

Jémys turned to face Catanya, cringing apologetically. "I'm sorry. Those two have always been a bit meddlesome, but they're actually very nice... once they stop talking."

He laughed and gave a half shrug.

"No, don't apologize." She brushed away his comment. "I'm fine, I just feel sorry for the poor young girl with them."

"Oh, Roslin? Yes. She's a sweet girl. That woman Evyain is her neighbour. Evyain and her husband were never able to have children, so she's taken Roslin under her wing. Whether Roslin enjoys the attention is... ah... *unclear*."

"Roslin seems quite taken with you." Catanya shot Jémys an arch look.

Jémys chuckled and shook his head. He pulled open the door to the tinker's shop and the two of them stepped inside.

As the morning wore on and they continued their errands, it became clear to Catanya that Jémys was a favourite among all the villagers. Everyone they passed came to greet him, welcoming him home with a handshake or a pat on the back, and more than once offering congratulations on his marriage.

Catanya was enjoying herself watching Jémys struggle to explain the situation to everyone. It seemed everyone was eager for Jémys to marry and settle down in Finnua to start a family.

"How long are ye stayin' then, sonny?" asked the elderly cooper, when they stopped to check on the casks.

"I'm not sure," replied Jémys, while idly exploring the shop. He lifted an old, rusted hoop off the nearest worktable and held it in front of his face like a mirror. "It depends how long the money lasts, and how strong the harvest is."

"Aye, that's true."

"I'm worried that, after Caerlon takes its tariffs, the village won't have enough to survive the winter. I may have to find work again in a couple months." He exhaled and tossed the hoop back onto the table, before wandering over to examine the casks stacked against the far wall.

"It's a right shame, tha' is. These tariffs bein' so high, tha' a good lad such as yerself can't stay in yer home, but ye has to be constantly runnin' and takin' hard work. S'not right."

"I don't mind," said Jémys.

"'Course you don't. 'Cause yer a good lad who cares more 'bout everyone else than ye does yerself. Takin' on responsibilities that weren't never supposed to be yers. Yer a fine, fine lad. Yer father'd be proud."

"Thank you, that's very kind of you to say."

The cooper waved his hand in the air. "Well, it's the truth... anyway, sonny, the casks are nearly done. I'll deliver 'em meself at the end o' the week if that suits."

"That's perfect, thank you."

Jémys and Catanya exited the shop and headed down the lane towards the river. They paused on the bridge, leaning over the frame to watch the water rushing below.

Catanya was thinking about what Jémys had told the cooper. "Is it true that there won't be enough food to last through the winter, once Caerlon takes its share?" she asked, frowning and watching the watermill churn up sticks, leaves, and other debris.

Jémys sighed. "Yes, I'm afraid that's going to be the case." He raised his eyebrows and motioned for them to continue. Catanya followed him across the bridge, back into the village.

They lapsed into silence again and Catanya felt a familiar frustration building within her. How could the royal family—she tried not to think *my family*—be so oblivious to the damage they caused? Or was that the problem? Maybe they knew, but they just didn't care.

But how could any decent person not care?

Catanya found it hard to believe they were so cruelly selfish that they didn't notice or care about the suffering of other people—the suffering of *their* people.

When she and Jémys had finished their errands and were heading back up the street towards the manor house, Olly came running down the cross street towards them, carrying his toy boat.

"Jémys! Catanya! Guess what?" He came skidding to a halt in front of them, splattering dirt in every direction.

"What?" asked Catanya and Jémys in unison.

"I showed my new boat to Blaese down the street, and he said it's the best toy he's ever seen. He's going to ask his father if he can carve him one just like it!"

"Really? That's exciting," said Catanya.

"And then we're going to race them in the river!" Olly started yammering on about how well his boat would sail versus the one Blaese's father was going to build.

Jémys took Catanya's elbow and leaned in. "Listen, I'm going to duck into this last shop for a second. Why don't you and Olly head towards the manor? I'll join you in a few minutes."

Catanya nodded. "Come on, Olly." She held out her hand and he grabbed it. "Let's go to the house. You can tell me all about your boat while we walk."

"Okay!" Olly sounded delighted.

The two of them meandered up the street, stopping every so often to watch birds or examine interesting insects. All the while, Olly chattered happily. Catanya watched him, recalling her time with the girls at Camlee Lodge. Slowly, an unpleasant lump formed in her throat.

She had deeply loved those girls. They were so clever and full of energy, just like Olly. They had their entire lives ahead of them... But now...

An image flashed before Catanya's eyes. The image of a little girl running—a little girl cut down by a sword.

Alli.

Catanya stumbled and nearly tripped.

"Are you listening to me?" Olly's little voice broke through.

"O-of course I'm listening," she said, blinking tears away. She plastered a smile on her face. "Blaese is a faster runner, but you can jump higher. So how high can you jump, then?" She made herself focus on Olly, refusing to let her mind drift back to that night.

"Well, I don't know how high exactly, but it's definitely higher than Blaese because..."

When they arrived back at the house, Catanya went into the kitchen to give Nelle the parcels they had bought throughout the morning. Then she went back outside to meet Olly at the trough. As she was walking around the corner of the house, she heard Jémys calling her name. He hopped over the fence and strode over to her.

"I've got something for you," he said, beckoning for her to join him. He was carrying a leather-bound book and a lumpy roll of cloth.

"What is it?" she asked.

Jémys handed her the roll of cloth first. Something was wrapped inside, and it was fastened with a neat knot. She untied the bind and unrolled it to reveal a small collection of brushes, paints, charcoal, and reeds.

"I thought you might like to use this." He handed her the leather book. "You can draw or paint—whatever you like. And you can take it with you wherever you go."

"Oh, Jémys, this is too much! You shouldn't have," she protested, overwhelmed at the generosity. She tried to hand them back, but he refused to take them.

"Don't worry about it. It didn't cost me anything. The shop owner owed me a favour," he said.

"Really, I can't accept this." She felt guilty taking the gift after everything that Jémys had already done for her.

"Sure you can. And maybe you can teach Olly about it..." He cleared his throat and looked down at his feet. "And me too, maybe?" He smiled sheepishly. "I always wanted to learn, but we never had opportunities."

His sincerity swept away all further protests. "Of course." Catanya returned his smile and examined the gifts in her hands. She'd never be able to show him how precious these items were to her. "Thank you."

She ran her hand along the surface of the book to feel the soft leather. She honestly hadn't believed she'd be lucky enough to have art supplies again this soon, and she couldn't wait to crack the book open and start. Her drawings had always been an outlet for her and a way to calm her spirits and organize her thoughts. She'd never needed that outlet more than she did now.

"Don't mention it." Jémys cleared his throat and rocked back and forth on his feet, looking cheerful. "Now, where's Olly?" He cast around for a sign of the boy.

"He's around back waiting for us. I'll take these inside and I'll join you in a minute."

Jémys headed off around the side wall towards the backyard. Catanya watched him go, clutching the gifts in her hands and feeling suddenly overwhelmed with sadness.

She hadn't expected to be so comfortable in Finnua. She knew she couldn't stay long, but the thought of leaving terrified her. The village felt safe. It was filled with kind and wholesome people, and she couldn't bear the idea of setting off alone again.

She frowned as she walked towards the house. Sooner or later she would have to leave—it wasn't safe for her in Caerlon anymore. She knew that. Part of her knew the longer she stayed in Finnua, the harder it would be for her to leave, but she couldn't leave yet, not when she'd only just arrived.

"I'll just stay for a few days," she said to herself. "There's no harm in staying for a few days." As she laid her gifts on the table and turned to follow Jémys, she tried to ignore the nagging voice in her head telling her she was wrong.

**10**

---

# DEVOTION

The musty smell of old books and sage tea brought back memories of boredom and frustration. Cadyan had spent most of his youth cloistered away in this study, listening to the chaplain drone on about one obscure historical fact after another.

He had hated every minute of it, but now he found himself wishing he had paid closer attention.

It was early afternoon, but the chaplain insisted on keeping the curtains drawn, making the room darker and gloomier than ever. The walls were lined with rickety shelves, each packed to bursting with books of different shapes and sizes. A long oak table in the centre was barely visible underneath stacks of paper and precariously perched candlesticks.

The disarray made Cadyan uncomfortable. "Why have you called me here? What have you found?"

He was impatient to hear if the chaplain was making any progress interpreting the materials from Bratia. The ring on Cadyan's finger still felt unnatural, and he ran his thumb along the coarse metal, spinning it. He'd been wearing the ring for days and still didn't know what powers it held or how it worked.

He was beginning to worry this ring actually was a piece of scrap metal, and the true relic remained lost along with the others.

Cadyan held out his hand and examined the band. It was the most hideous thing he'd ever worn. Roughly hewn and primitive, and it irritated his skin terribly. But none of that would matter if he could learn its secrets.

"Well, my lord, I've compiled the pages from the crate and they seem to belong to two different tomes. The first appears to be an old recipe book of sorts. Its pages have badly degraded, but there is one recipe for a seasoned nut loaf I wouldn't mind trying." The old man held up the page, examining it with mild curiosity.

Cadyan closed his eyes in frustration. "That's not what I'm looking for," he said through gritted teeth. "What about the second tome, it was a journal, right?"

The chaplain stared at him blankly for a second before his mind caught up. "Oh, yes." He began rifling around on his desk for the more relevant pages. "Here it is." He lifted a thin stack of parchment that he'd re-bound with new thread. "The journal of one Yúlndiar, an accomplished young practitioner who travelled down from what is now the Diyune Marshes to pursue studies with Maílehr Illayan. Rather unfortunate timing as it turns out, since he arrived in Bratia only a few weeks before its destruction and well—we know how that turned out for him, don't we?"

Cadyan frowned. Then he remembered Bordlun telling him about the skeleton in the chamber.

"Right." He brushed away the image of Yúlndiar suffocating and desiccating in a tomb beneath the city. "So what does the journal say?"

"Oh, it says many things," mused the chaplain in his soporific voice.

"About the relics," snapped Cadyan, rolling his eyes. This

was the main reason he'd hated his lessons so much. The chaplain had a habit of getting distracted and taking the longest route to explain the simplest things.

"Oh, yes." The chaplain took the book back and began gingerly flipping through it. "Well, Yúlndiar begins his journal while he is still making his way to Bratia. He discusses his excitement and nervousness. He was hoping to return home eventually and use his powers to help rebuild the village—a terrible drought, you see? Ironic given that now the place is a marsh... Anyway, he arrives in Bratia, where he begins his studies with Illayan and meets several of his other students. He spends a great deal of time describing how distracted and troubled Illayan seems. And then... where is it?" He was turning the pages, searching for something particular. "Ah, here we go." He stopped somewhere in the middle and held the book out for Cadyan to read.

Cadyan took it from him and stared down at the scribbled words in Awnle. He felt a stab of frustration mixed with embarrassment. "I can't read this," he said, forcing a contemptuous scowl on his face. He hated being made to feel incompetent.

"What?" The chaplain took the book back, clicking his tongue disapprovingly. "You should have worked harder in your studies, my boy. You were always so clever but undisciplined. I always told you that—"

"You are trying my patience, old man," snarled Cadyan. "I am not your student anymore. I'm your king."

The flames in the candles nearby flickered ominously and the chaplain's face fell. His eyes darted back and forth and he fumbled with the pages. "O-of course, Your Majesty, forgive me."

Then he cleared his throat and read aloud, "*I learned the truth today. The truth about the items we have been tasked to protect. Maílehr Illayan brought them here to be guarded until the relocation.*

*"As I suspected, the rumours about the stone have been exaggerated. The oracle stone, as I've heard it called many times before, does not possess the power of prophecy. Maílehr Illayan says that is impossible. No, I'm told the stone opens the spirit to the past and connects it to the present, but I must admit I do not fully understand.*

*"The crown, however—that I do understand. Although I do not know that I believe... Naturally, it is the most guarded item, because none can resist the lure of immortality. Even I find myself drawn to its promise of time. But somehow Maílehr Illayan resists—refuses to wear it. Is this strength or fear? I do not know. But whatever the reason, I'm sure Maílehr Illayan is wise.*

*"The ring's power is the clearest of the three. Compulsion and persuasion are powerful tools. Maílehr Illayan told me the greatest power one can possess is the power to influence others, but I do not believe we were speaking of Resonance that day. Rather, of leadership."*

The chaplain finished reading and looked up at Cadyan intently. "There you have it, my lord. The stone, the crown, and the ring." His throat rasped, prompting him to take a deep sip of his putrid yellow tea.

But Cadyan was barely paying attention to him anymore. He was thinking about the words he had just heard. For countless generations, nobody was certain what the relics were or whether they truly existed, but here was the proof. Finally. Here were the details explaining it all.

The crown of immortality was the legend everyone knew. Cadyan wanted nothing more than to be the king who finally unearthed it—the king who reigned forever—and now his dream was within reach. The crown was close. He could feel it.

But what about the stone? Cadyan had never heard stories of an oracle stone, and the journal's description was vague and confusing. *It opens the spirit to the past and connects it to the present.* He didn't know what that meant, but he was burning with curiosity. And regardless of what this Yúlndiar claimed, an oracle stone surely had to carry the power of prophecy, didn't it? Perhaps Illayan had been lying to him. Or perhaps neither of them had discovered the stone's true potential.

Either way, Cadyan was going to find it and learn the truth. After all, immortality and prophecy were powers befitting a king.

And in the meantime he had the ring.

Cadyan lifted his hand to examine it once again. Suddenly it didn't seem so ugly. In fact, now he thought it might be the most exquisite ring he'd ever owned.

*Compulsion and persuasion.*

Did that mean what he thought it meant?

He rotated his hand so the candlelight illuminated the indentations on the metal where it had suffered centuries of wear and tear. He twisted it around, examining it from all angles as he sensed his power reaching into it and vice versa.

"My lord?" The chaplain was standing nearby, watching Cadyan with his eyebrows pinched in curiosity and mild concern.

Cadyan stared at him, feeling distanced from his surroundings. "What do you think?" He held out his hand so the chaplain could see the ring. "Do you think it works?"

The chaplain leaned forward for a closer look. "I must admit, I find it difficult to imagine how any object could possess the power this journal describes, but"—he reached out as if he were going to take Cadyan's hand, then hesitated—"may I?" he asked.

Cadyan nodded and allowed the chaplain to bring it closer to the light.

"Curious," he mused. He held his palm a few inches away from Cadyan and the ring. "Do you sense an energy coming off it?"

"Yes, but I wasn't sure if it was the ring's power or mine."

The chaplain shook his head and backed away. "Regardless,

I believe you should approach this ring with caution, Your Majesty."

"What? Why?"

Before the chaplain could respond, a servant rapped on the door and entered, carrying a fresh teapot and a tray full of food.

"Your Majesty," she breathed, startled to find him there. She struggled to curtsey under the weight of the tray and blushed. Then she shuffled forward and placed the items on the table, before turning to face Cadyan.

Ever since he'd become king, Cadyan had noticed a marked change in how the servants behaved around him. The courtesans had always been brazen, but now the servants all seemed to believe they could blush and flash their vapid smiles to catch his attention or win his favour. He'd seen this behaviour around his father for years and it irked him. Casréyan had loved the attention, and he'd often boasted to Slaedir of his easy pleasures, pressuring Cadyan to do the same and punishing him when he didn't.

Cadyan glanced down at the girl curiously.

She was a young, buxom thing, and he supposed she was pretty, but he didn't really know or care. And in all honesty, he had never understood the appeal. He always preferred to be left alone.

He had more important things to do than waste his time cavorting with servants (or anyone, for that matter). It annoyed him that these people considered themselves worthy of his attention, or thought they could manipulate him into dropping his guard.

Well, perhaps it was time he proved just how foolish that behaviour was.

"What's your name?" asked Cadyan, plastering a false smile on his face. If she insisted on simpering to gain his attention, then she might as well be useful to him.

"E-Eva, Your Majesty," she said, blushing as she curtseyed again.

"Well, Eva, I have a question for you." He held out his hand with a reassuring nod and waited for her to rest her palm on his. "Tell me, what are you willing to do to please your king?"

She blushed again, even deeper. "I would do anything for my sovereign."

Cadyan raised his eyebrows at her. "Anything? Are you sure?" He held her gaze and wrapped his fingers around her hand, squeezing it tight.

The girl's smiled faltered, but she didn't respond.

Cadyan turned his gaze away and examined the contents of the tray she'd placed on the table. "Would you take your own life?" he asked, lifting a knife off the tray and pointing it towards her.

All the colour drained from Eva's face in an instant. "Your Majesty?" She tried to lean away.

Cadyan nodded. "Ah, I see, so not really *anything*." He dropped the knife back onto the table. "How about this?" He lifted a nearby candle and held it out to her. "What if I said I wanted you to hold your skin above the candle flame until I tell you to stop?"

"Why?" blurted the chaplain, staring at the king with a horrified expression.

Cadyan shrugged. "Why not?" He looked back at Eva expectantly. When she didn't move, he pressed down on her knuckles, studying her eyes as his ring rubbed against her skin.

"Y-yes, Your Majesty." She spoke in an oddly strained voice as she reached for the candlestick.

Cadyan watched in awe as she lifted the candle out of his grasp and wavered before holding it up to her forearm. Slowly but surely, her skin began to burn, turning redder and redder until large welts appeared and the smell of sizzling flesh reached his nostrils. She whimpered and yelped, and he felt her hand jerk in his like she wanted to yank it away, but she couldn't.

"That'll do," he said, releasing his grasp. He was genuinely surprised she had done as he'd asked. He looked over at the chaplain, who was watching with his mouth agape, like he couldn't decide whether he was frightened or impressed.

"You can go." Cadyan dismissed the servant with a wave. She clutched her arm, dashing out of the room.

There was a heavy silence while Cadyan and the chaplain processed everything.

"Well, Chaplain," said Cadyan finally. "I believe we can safely say the relics do indeed work." His face split into a wide grin as he realized the implications of what he had just proven. If the ring worked, surely the crown would too.

"Yes, but... the power to force others to do as you please..." The chaplain's eyes widened and he blanched. "I'm not certain that power is as desirable as one might think. Much like immortality, this power could become its own curse."

"What do you mean?" Cadyan nearly laughed aloud at the absurdity.

"Well..." The chaplain rubbed his neck, averting his eyes. Then he sighed and turned to face his king. "I suppose we must ask ourselves what is more valuable, obedience or loyalty?"

Cadyan frowned. "What is the difference?"

The chaplain raised his eyebrows, but didn't respond.

---

Later that evening, as Cadyan paced back and forth in his throne room, preparing to open the doors for his first Royal Offering, he couldn't help but dwell on what the chaplain said.

Did Cadyan want his subjects to be loyal or simply obedient? Was one truly better than the other?

He groaned and threw himself down into his throne, tapping his fingers on the gilded arm impatiently.

Or perhaps he could still have both...

It was the first full moon since Cadyan had taken his throne. He had invited the people of Caerlon to present their requests at court and seek his favour. As people came from across his kingdom to beg for his help, he would have countless opportunities to test the ring's power and test the limits of his people's loyalty.

As the hour approached, the sound of voices outside grew louder, and Cadyan began to feel excited, and even a little nervous.

The door opened and a group of fírkon entered, led by Julyán.

"Your Majesty," he said, bowing. "The entrance hall has reached capacity. We are ready whenever you are."

Cadyan glanced around the room. All of the courtiers were there, spread out through the room so they could watch the show. But someone was missing.

"Where's my mother?" he asked, trying to keep the childish hurt out of his voice. This was his first big initiative as king. He had expected her to join him.

Another door slammed and Cadyan twisted around to see Fehla striding towards him from the rear entrance. She had a sombre and unenthusiastic air. It made him suddenly wish she hadn't bothered to come at all.

"Hello, Mother," he called, turning away from her as she took her seat in a chair behind the throne. "Finally deigned to make an appearance, have you? Very well, let's get this started, shall we? Let them in."

The guards opened the massive doors and allowed the crowd to enter the throne room. The people jockeyed and pushed, desperate to be first, but the fírkon blocked their passage up the aisle, forcing them to form a line. Shouts and cries of desperation reverberated off the pillars. Cadyan found the noise grating.

"Silence!" he called, and an instant stillness settled in the room. "You will maintain order, or the firkon will remove you from the palace with force."

He thought he sensed a collective shiver run through the crowd. The courtiers near the throne exchanged smirks.

Cadyan straightened in his seat. "Bring forth the first person."

He was pleased by the turnout. Over a hundred of his subjects had come to the castle with requests ranging from help with their crops to disputes with their neighbours. Cadyan could solve most of their problems with a simple wave of his hands, and they adored him for it. They showered him with gifts and praise.

The guards beckoned for a young, mousy woman to come forward next. She jumped and hurried along, stumbling as she reached the dais and knelt down.

"What's your name, then?" asked Cadyan with affected benevolence. "What would you ask your king to do for you?"

"Your Majesty, my name is Priya, I live in the southwest quarter near the western gate." She sounded strained and desperate. "It's my son. He's very ill. He needs help." Her eyes pleaded with Cadyan.

"Ill?" he repeated, trying to conceal his disappointment. "I see. And you want me to heal him, is that right?"

"I-I would be most grateful, Your Majesty." She bowed her head, wringing her hands.

Cadyan sneered as he gazed at the woman kneeling before him. She had bags under her eyes and her skin was sallow and loose. She looked exhausted and desperate, but he found it difficult to have sympathy for such a pathetic creature.

"And what would you give me in return as payment?" he asked.

"I-I don't have much, Your Majesty." She emptied a pouch with a handful of coins into her hand. "It's all I have." She gazed at him imploringly.

Cadyan sneered at the pitiful collection of money. Then he contorted his face into one of false sympathy. He leaned forward and closed her hand over the gold, taking her other hand in his.

"Your gold holds no value here. No, I have a better idea." He sensed the power of the ring vibrating. "I'll try my best to save your son, but once he is healed, he will work off your debt in the work camps."

The young woman blanched and stared at him, horrified. "W-what? But he's so young. He's only a boy."

Cadyan leaned closer to her. "This is the payment I require in return for my efforts to heal your son. If you truly want to save him, this is what you must promise me. Nothing can come without sacrifice." He gave her a benevolent nod and squeezed her hands.

"Y-yes, of course, Your Majesty. Nothing comes without sacrifice. This is the payment you require." She nodded mechanically, her eyes glazed. "Thank you."

"Very well, then. You may go. Someone will call on you shortly to see your son." Cadyan released his grip and leaned back in his chair, pleased with himself.

She stumbled to her feet. Her complexion was green and she shivered, following the guard out of the throne room.

Cadyan watched her go, then reclined in his throne, stretching. Servants were making rounds through the courtiers and firkon, handing out drinks. The noise level was mounting, but Cadyan didn't mind anymore. He took the drink offered to him and downed it before grabbing another.

"You see, Julyán." He angled in his seat to address the man standing behind his throne. "These Royal Offerings were a stroke of genius. Look at them." He gestured to the crowd of people waiting to be chosen. "They're desperate for my help. They will do anything for it. That is power unlike anything else."

Julyán nodded once and said nothing.

But from the corner came the soft sound of someone clearing her throat.

"What is it?" asked Cadyan, struggling to conceal his annoyance as he glared at his mother.

Fehla's gaze hardened. "You may be the most powerful man in Caerlon, but your magic cannot cure the sick and dying. The elixir does not bestow lasting healing powers. You know that."

"True," said Cadyan, smiling. "But *they* don't know that." He jerked his head back at the crowd behind him and laughed.

"We have no court physician anymore. You murdered Grante."

"*Executed*, mother. That traitor was executed for his crimes against the throne."

Fehla's nostrils flared. "You promised to help that woman's son. How do you plan on doing that without a healer?"

Cadyan let out a sharp laugh. "Oh, Mother. I only promised my *efforts* to save her son. I never promised that I would be successful." He laughed again at the haughty outrage on her face. "And besides, that's not the point. It doesn't matter if I help them or not, it matters how much they are willing to do for me." Cadyan breathed deeply, savouring the moment. "It's not loyalty or obedience. It is *devotion*, and it's beautiful."

"What is the matter with you?" spat Fehla, springing to her feet. "How can you sit on that throne, listening to the desperate pleas of your people, and feel nothing? That woman's son may very well die—"

"Then he will die," hissed Cadyan. "Now sit down and stop making a scene." He glanced around to make sure no one had noticed.

"You don't care?" Fehla took a step closer to her son. Julyán moved to block her path. "The boy I raised would care."

"Why should I care about one insignificant little brat? His life makes no difference to me." Cadyan turned back to examine the crowd waiting cramped between pillars at the end of the room. They were jostling to reach the front, where the firkon might choose them to approach. "None of their lives matter."

"You can't truly believe that?"

"Can't I?" snapped Cadyan, whipping his head back to glare at Fehla. "Look at them, Mother. What are they compared to us?"

Fehla looked outraged. "They are your people, your subjects. And you are responsible for them."

Cadyan rolled his eyes. "They are just peasants. And peasants die. It's what they do."

"Ugh! How can you sit there and repeat that vile nonsense your father used to tell you? I thought you knew better than that! I thought you'd try to *be* better than that. This is not the behaviour of a king."

He raised his chin in triumph. "That's the point," he said, sneering at her before turning back in his seat. He motioned to the guards to bring forth the next man. "You there, come forward," he called loud enough to cut through the noise.

The bedraggled man hurried down the aisle and knelt.

"I will give you whatever you want, but in return, I want you to prove to me your devotion." Cadyan pulled out a dagger from inside his coat, unsheathed it, and handed it to the beggar expectantly.

"My-my lord?"

"You heard me." Cadyan glanced back at his mother, whose face was pale with horror. He could sense everyone else in the room waiting with bated breath. Then he placed his hand on the man's shoulder, pressing the ring against his coat, and watched as comprehension dawned on him.

The man reached out and gripped the blade, turning it over in his gnarled fingers to examine it. Then, without hesitating, he stretched out his other hand and pierced it with the dagger, carving a long gash along his palm. As the blood trickled down his wrist, Cadyan smiled and twisted around to view his mother's face.

"You see, Mother. I am not their king," he whispered. "Why settle for mere royalty, when I'm capable of something greater?"

He turned back to address the man at his feet, whose hand dripped blood onto the polished floor. "Thank you for your show of faith. Now tell me, what is it you seek?"

After another hour, the crowd thinned and Cadyan, who had grown weary of hearing complaints, stood up and declared the Offering done for the evening.

"But have no fear, I will receive your requests next time." He smirked and sauntered out the rear door, accompanied by Julyán and Fehla, while his guards ushered the disappointed subjects out the front.

Cadyan stopped in the corridor outside the throne room and turned to speak to his mother. "Do you understand yet, Mother?" He surveyed her expectantly, but she didn't respond. "I am not their king. No. I am something much greater." He felt a sense of wild exhilaration. "I am their god and they worship me. They would do anything for me."

At first, Fehla just stared at him with disgust in her eyes. Then she reverted to her usual disapproving frown. "And what will you do when they realize you do not keep your promises?" she asked in a lecturing tone. "Or when all your subjects have bled their last drop. Then what will you do? Who will be left to worship you?" She gave him a hard look before turning and stalking off in the other direction, leaving Cadyan and Julyán behind.

Cadyan couldn't help feeling unsettled. "My mother is weak," he said, turning to Julyán and trying to sound confident. "She doesn't understand, and she has always feared these powers. One day she'll see how wrong she was."

"Yes, Your Majesty." Julyán inclined his head, but his eyes were still trained on Fehla, who was just rounding the corner out of sight. Julyán's eyes narrowed as he watched her disappear.

"What is it?" asked Cadyan.

Julyán's jaw set. "I don't know yet, but I will find out."

# MOMENTS AND RUMOURS

Though it had only been a few days since her arrival, Catanya was already starting to feel at home in Finnua. It surprised her to discover how easily she slid into the rhythm of life with Jémys and Nelle. During the day, she would help Nelle in the fields and gardens or run errands into the village, and in the evenings they would cook and clean, or she would draw while they sat by the fire talking.

Working in the fields was exhausting, but it felt familiar and satisfying to be making herself useful again. And as long as she kept busy, she didn't have time to dwell on the sadness or the fear that had been threatening to consume her since she had learned her true identity.

Though she had only intended to stay in Finnua for a few days while she gathered supplies for the rest of her journey, she found herself making excuses to stay longer. First it was because she needed to recuperate, then it was because Nelle needed help. Now she had convinced herself to stay until after the Harvest Festival a week later. In truth, Catanya couldn't bear the thought of leaving Finnua and travelling alone again.

She didn't think she could handle the fear. It was easier to pretend that this was her life, and that she was safe.

With each passing day, she became increasingly convinced that she actually was safe. She'd heard no news from Caerlon and she was starting to wonder if Cadyan had abandoned his search for her. Some days she even caught herself hoping it was true, so she could stay in Finnua forever.

Finnua was a small, isolated village. As a result, its people were a tight-knit group with a keen sense of community. The annual Apple Picking was an important part of the Harvest Festival and a central event in the village every year, which meant everybody had a role to play in its preparations.

From what Catanya understood, the custom had begun generations earlier, when the village had banded together to harvest the apples from the orchard to make cider. Over the years, it had grown into a larger community event with evenings full of music, food, and celebration, marking the end of summer and the beginning of harvest season.

In a clearing near the orchard stood a large cedar barn, where the wheat and barley were stored after harvest and before threshing. This barn was also where they would store the apples during the festival, and the casks of cider as they distilled.

Jémys and Catanya had been working hard to restore the barn and create space for the new crop. It was a lot of work, since the barn had been neglected for several months and no one had bothered to stop the birds nesting inside and creating a mess. Its musty smell of stale barley mixed with sun-baked cedar and cinnamon made for an unusual aroma that was somehow both appealing and nauseating at the same time.

Years of spilled cider had made the floor permanently sticky. The squelching sound of their boots as they walked across the floor was a great source of amusement to Olly, who

—despite desperately wanting to be useful—usually ended up causing a great many distractions and delays.

One especially scorching afternoon, Jémys and Catanya decided to take a break in the fresh air until the barn cooled down. Sweaty and exhausted, they sought refuge in the shade beneath the apple trees, enjoying the cooling breeze. Catanya sat perched on an old horse cart, sketching—she'd been drawing every chance she got since Jémys had given her the book, and it was already half-full—while Jémys stood a few feet away talking with Olly.

"Now here." Jémys snatched up two long sticks from the ground and handed one to Olly. "Hold it out towards me. Keep your wrist straight. Good. Now bend your knees a bit. No, not that much."

Catanya chuckled and Jémys flashed her a grin, as Olly repositioned himself.

"Okay, Jémys, I'm ready!" called Olly with excited impatience.

"Not yet. First, let me see your footwork."

Olly, with his wooden sword out in front of him, took two steps forward and lunged.

"Good, but don't forget your eye contact."

"Okay, okay." Olly repositioned himself again. Then he demonstrated his lunge a second time, working hard to keep eye contact with Jémys.

"Good! Alright." Jémys lifted his own stick and held it out like a sword. "Now try to disarm me... if you can."

Olly attempted to hit the stick out of Jémys's hand, but Jémys was too quick for him. Olly lost his footing and stumbled, just as Jémys spun his stick around, sending Olly's flying off in the opposite direction.

Catanya laughed out loud as Olly, bewildered, looked around for a sign of his sword.

"Good effort," called Jémys, struggling to stay serious. "But it all starts with the footing. Grab your stick and practice your footing over there for a bit while I watch."

Jémys leaned against the cart where Catanya sat, while Olly scrambled after his stick.

"What are you drawing, then?" asked Jémys. He was still holding his stick, but he took off his real sword—which he insisted on carrying at all times—and laid it down on the cart behind them.

"Oh, a little of this, a little of that," replied Catanya, smiling at him.

Jémys craned his neck to see the page, but she snatched it out of view. "It's not done yet." She gave him a look of playful indignation.

"Oh, I see." Jémys grinned and turned to watch Olly again.

After a while, Catanya closed her sketchbook and set it on the cart behind her. She hopped down to stand beside Jémys. She had been observing him all afternoon with increasing interest. Now as he stood there nonchalantly, with his sleeves rolled up over his elbows, watching Olly scampering beneath the trees, Catanya saw the deep, loving pride written on his face.

Growing up an orphan, she had always been especially observant of other families and parents. She recognized the same fatherly love in Jémys that she'd seen in countless parents before.

"You really care about him," she said. "And you're so good with him."

"He's a good lad." Jémys brushed his sweaty hair out of his face before turning to Catanya. "Olly's father was one of my closest friends as a boy. He saw me through a lot of tough times, and I promised him I would watch out for Olly if anything ever happened to him."

"How did he die?" asked Catanya, seeing the sadness in Jémys's eyes.

"It was an accident. He was hunting in the woods and his horse fell... you would have liked him, though. He was very charming, full of life and energy just like his son..." Jémys trailed off.

Catanya studied Olly playing between the trees and tried to picture what his father might have been like. She imagined a young Jémys running around with him, carefree like Olly, and she felt a swell of affection.

"I'm sure he would be grateful for everything you're doing," she said, reaching out to rest her hand on Jémys's arm. Her fingers prickled where they touched his warm, sundrenched skin.

Jémys stared down at her hand and paused before taking a slow step forward and raising his eyes to meet hers. He was very close to her now, and he was studying her face.

Catanya's heart pounded. She held her breath. Before she knew it, she had raised her free hand to his face and pulled herself up to his height. She felt his hand on her waist and Jémys was leaning in when—

"Jémys, look!" Olly came running over to show them his progress. "What are you doing?" he asked when he saw them standing together.

"Nothing." Jémys took a quick step back, letting go of Catanya. His face was flushed, and he cast her an awkward glance. "What did you want to show us?" he asked Olly.

Catanya had trouble focusing on Olly's demonstration, but when he had finished, she cheered along with Jémys before saying, "Well, we should probably get back to work now, don't you think?" She glanced at Jémys, who was standing still, looking somewhat dazed, and then she headed back to the cart to collect herself. Her heart was still racing and her face felt very hot.

"Yes, she's right," came Jémys's voice from behind her. "Come on, Olly. We still have loads of work to finish."

As she gathered up her things, Catanya noticed Jémys's sword lying in the cart. She leaned in to grab it for him. As soon as her fingers touched the cold steel hilt, her vision started to blur, and she became dizzy.

"Good, but don't lose your eye contact," she heard someone say. She spun around expecting to see Jémys, but suddenly the surrounding trees showed signs of early spring. Olly and Jémys were nowhere to be seen. The man beside her was a good seven or ten years older than Jémys, with darker skin and shorter hair. He didn't seem to see her.

"Well done, son," he cried and Catanya noticed a boy standing off to the side, holding a stick. He appeared to be twelve or thirteen, with a thick crop of dark, wavy hair and unusually bright green eyes. He was grinning from ear to ear as his father showed him how to fight.

"One day this sword will be yours," said the father, holding out his blade so it glistened in the sunlight. "And you'll need to know how to use it."

"I will, Father!" shouted the boy. "I will be the best fighter in the entire kingdom." He brandished his training sword cockily and lunged forward, only to be blocked by his father.

"No." The father's face was suddenly stern. "You should not aspire to that, my son. Being the best fighter means nothing without honour and integrity. You must strive to be a good man before everything else. Promise me you'll do that."

"But I thought—"

"Promise me," he insisted, eyes boring into the boy.

The boy looked confused and nervous, but he nodded. "I promise, Father."

"Very well." The father's posture softened, and he smiled. "I'm so proud of you, my boy."

A fog blurred the edges of Catanya's vision once more, as the autumn colours bled back into the trees.

"Hey, wait for me!" called a new little voice.

Before she could see who it was, Catanya found herself back in the orchard beside Jémys and Olly.

"Well, hurry along then, Olly." Jémys was standing next to Catanya, eyeing her with a crease in his forehead. "Are you alright?"

"I-I'm not sure..." She cast around, searching for a sign of the father and his son, but there was nothing. "Did you see that just now?" she whispered, leaning in.

"See what?" Jémys glanced around, bewildered. "Are you sure you're alright? I mean... you're not regretting..." He cleared his throat and rubbed his neck.

But Catanya was barely listening. "No, I'm fine," she muttered, patting his arm and trying to force a reassuring smile onto her face, despite her uneasiness.

She had no idea what had just happened. She certainly wasn't fine, but she didn't want Jémys to worry.

The three of them left the orchard and returned to the barn. Olly chattered happily all the while, making any further conversation impossible.

---

Catanya and Jémys spent the rest of the day toiling in the sweltering barn. They worked separately, Catanya inside the barn cleaning and Jémys outside repairing the walls. Olly had quickly grown bored and run off under the pretext of asking the cooper how many casks he'd have this year. He hadn't returned in over an hour. But Catanya was grateful for the solitude, since it gave her time to think about everything that had happened earlier.

She had resigned herself to recurring nightmares, but this was different. She'd been fully awake, and the vision had seemed more concrete. It was closer to a memory than a dream, but a memory she'd never experienced herself.

*It could have been Jémys's memory,* she thought. *And that was Jémys's father.*

But how could that be? How could she be seeing visions of other people's memories?

"Ugh!" Catanya took her frustration out on an enormous pile of mulched hay and barley, as she shovelled it into a wheelbarrow by the door. She couldn't stand facing all these strange experiences with no means of understanding them.

She squeezed her eyes shut, trying to think.

*Maybe it was connected to the sword,* she thought. The vision had come as soon as she'd touched it. The sword might hold magical properties... or maybe this was another power she couldn't control.

Catanya sighed and wiped sweat off her brow, then she leaned on her shovel. As she replayed the vision in her mind, her frustration melted away.

If the vision really had shown Jémys and his father, then she was grateful to have seen it. Jémys's father had seemed so loving and wholesome. No wonder Jémys spoke so highly of him.

His father's only wish was that his son should grow into an honourable man.

Catanya felt a swell of happiness as she thought about Jémys and realized his father had gotten what he wanted. Jémys was a good man, possibly the best she'd ever met. She allowed her mind to drift back to the moment before Olly had interrupted them.

She genuinely liked Jémys. When she thought about kissing him, there was a fluttering in her stomach she had never experienced so strongly before. Catanya wasn't inexperienced. Growing up in Faltir, one or two boys had caught her eye, but nothing like this. Never such a powerful attraction.

However, for all she longed to be with Jémys, she knew she shouldn't. For his safety she needed to keep her distance. They could never have a normal life together, and sooner or later, she needed to leave Finnua.

Catanya had never imagined herself longing to lead a simple village life, but then again, she'd never met anyone like Jémys before. Maybe she wasn't yearning for a simple life exactly, but rather a life together with Jémys.

*If only Diyah were here,* thought Catanya. *She would know. She always knew me better than I did myself.*

With a pang of grief and guilt, Catanya thought about her friend and how much their friendship had cost her. She couldn't let that happen to Jémys too.

The sun was setting when Olly finally returned to announce that the cooper would have ten new barrels ready for the festival. Catanya and Jémys were finishing their work and Olly already had his mind on supper.

"Maybe Nelle will have more roasted venison," he said, as they made their way along the street towards the manor house. "And I bet there will be fresh-baked bread." He started walking faster at the thought of it.

Jémys and Catanya watched in silence as he scampered up the street ahead of them.

Catanya felt awkward. She was trying to think of a topic to break the silence, when Jémys said, "So ten casks. And we have five left that should be fully matured for drinking. I hope you like cider." He peered sidelong at her.

"I do like cider." She smiled, grateful to have something to talk about. "Who makes it? Do you do it?" she asked a bit more enthusiastically than she might have done under different circumstances.

"Me? No. It's usually Nelle and the miller who make it, and

the rest of us help where we can. We always have piles of apples left, so be prepared to join in the baking."

"I never had the patience for baking. Genna said I was hopeless in the kitchen." She laughed at the memory.

"Genna?" Jémys looked at her quizzically.

"Oh... um..." Catanya bit her lip. Until now, she'd taken care not to reveal anything that might connect her with Faltir, but she was so comfortable with Jémys that she'd momentarily forgotten. She considered lying now, but as she stared at his face, the truth came tumbling out of her. "Lady Genna... she was my guardian." Her voice cracked. "She ran the orphanage where I grew up, raising me like her own. She was like a mother to me, but I suppose she's... she's gone now."

Jémys paused before responding. "I'm sorry," he said.

Catanya cleared her throat and tried to force a smile. "It's okay. I know I was lucky to have her, but..."

"But it doesn't make losing her any easier," said Jémys, with an understanding nod.

When they arrived back at the manor, Nelle informed them that there was indeed fresh bread, but the remaining venison had been used to make cabbage venison stew.

"Do you need me to go hunting again tomorrow, Aunt?" asked Jémys, leaning against the doorframe.

"Tomorrow or the next day would be fine, I think. Now sit, sit. You must be famished."

"I am!" cried Olly, as he settled himself into a seat at the table. "Starving!"

"Oh, is that so? You worked up an appetite, then?"

Jémys snorted. "Oh, yes, he worked very hard. For all of five minutes before he ran off."

"Yeah, where did you get to?" asked Catanya, as Nelle placed a bowl on the table for her. She helped herself to a serving of warm bread. "You were gone an awfully long time.

We thought you must have gotten lost." It was difficult to conceal her amusement.

"Well, I ran to the cooper's shop straight away, but when I got there, he was standing outside whispering with old man Waltin."

"Is that so?" Nelle gave Jémys a knowing look, obviously endeavouring to keep her face serious. "And I suppose you behaved like the good boy you are, and you didn't listen in to their conversation at all?" she asked with a definite smirk.

"Well, I tried," said Olly defensively. "But they were speaking so loud, I—"

"Whispering loudly? How strange," Jémys muttered under his breath, flashing Catanya a wide grin.

Catanya laughed and shook her head. "So are you going to tell us what you overheard?"

"Yeah, but you'll never believe it! So Waltin was telling him all about his journey."

"What journey?" Nelle glanced from Olly to Jémys curiously.

Jémys swallowed his mouthful of stew and nodded. "Waltin just returned from Sidina," he said, reaching across the table to snatch a chunk of bread. "I guess, his cousin lives there, and he needed Waltin to help sort family affairs after the uncle died." Jémys shrugged and ripped a piece of bread off with his teeth.

"Exactly," said Olly matter-of-factly. "But the rumours are all over Sidina." He paused for dramatic effect.

"What rumours?" asked Nelle, her lips twitching like she was fighting back a laugh as she turned around to stir the remaining stew.

"About the Lost Princess of Caerlon."

Catanya had just taken a large mouthful of hot broth, and she choked in surprise. Jémys and Nelle laughed.

"This sounds like the sort of nonsense that Waltin would

dream up," said Nelle. "Are you alright, Catanya?" Her forehead crinkled.

"Yes," Catanya spluttered, taking a sip of water. "Yes, I'm fine." She looked at Olly and tried to force a chuckle. "Total nonsense," she said, but she couldn't help noticing her voice sounded several pitches higher than usual. Her heart was racing and her stomach had clenched, causing her to lose her appetite.

"It's not nonsense!" shouted Olly indignantly. "Waltin says the king has sent out soldiers searching for her." He spoke louder to carry over the sound of Jémys and Nelle laughing. "He says the king had a twin sister, and they sent her to live far away from Caerlon, but now the king knows and he's hunting for her."

"Really?" said Nelle, amused. "Well, I pity the poor thing if that's true. She won't last long if the king is chasing her."

Catanya laughed nervously, feeling hot around the neck.

"She might!" cried Olly. "Because apparently—and this is the best part—they say she has powers too!"

Nobody responded right away. Catanya watched in horror as Jémys and Nelle registered this information and seemed not to dismiss it.

"When you say, 'she has powers too'?" Jémys raised his eyebrows and glanced from Olly to Nelle.

"Well, that's why the king is hunting her, because she has powers just like his and she's going to use them to overthrow him!"

Jémys and Nelle stared at each other for a moment. Then Nelle pursed her lips and raised her eyebrows. "That would certainly be something. If it were true, of course."

"It is true! Waltin said—"

"Oh, come now, Olly, you know better than to believe everything you hear from the village old-timers. Every other thing Waltin says is fiction." Jémys laughed and shook his head.

"So... so you don't think it's true?"

Jémys peered down at him with pity in his eyes. "I think it seems very unlikely." He spoke in a slow, calm voice, and rested his hand on Olly's shoulder.

Olly looked crestfallen. He slumped down into his seat, jabbing his bread into his stew. Nelle and Jémys exchanged affectionate looks.

"What about the Apple Picking, Olly, dear?" asked Nelle kindly. "It's going to be a great celebration this year. Aren't you excited about that?"

"Yeah, I am," said Olly, although he sounded deflated.

The rest of the dinner conversation revolved around the upcoming festival. Catanya was glad for the change of subject, but she couldn't help feeling anxious about the rumours in Sidina. Nelle and Jémys might not believe them, but if stories about Catanya were spreading, it would be difficult for her to stay hidden much longer.

When they finished eating, Jémys left to walk Olly home in the dark, and Catanya helped Nelle tidy up after the meal. After they'd cleared everything, Nelle boiled some water for tea and the two of them sat by the fire, sipping from their cups, each lost in their own thoughts.

Catanya's mind jumped between thoughts about her growing feelings for Jémys and about what Olly had said. The overwhelming sense of guilt she had for wanting to stay in Finnua was eating at her. She couldn't let what happened in Faltir happen in Finnua. But she couldn't leave either —not yet.

"Are you alright, dear?" asked Nelle after a while. "You hardly said anything all night."

"Hmm?" It took a few seconds for her words to break

through. "Oh, yes. Yes, I'm fine. I'm just a little tired. It's been a long day."

Nelle nodded, and they lapsed back into silence. But a few minutes later, Nelle spoke again. "I'm very glad you've come to stay with us, Catanya. It's been ages since this house has felt so full." She smiled and took a sip from her tea. "When my brother was still alive, this place was bursting with energy." She was staring at the wall, transfixed, as though lost in a memory.

Catanya waited for her to continue, but she didn't. "You must miss him terribly," she said, placing her cup on the table between them.

"I do." Nelle wrenched her gaze from the wall and turned watery eyes towards Catanya. "He was caring and clever... and the kindest man I ever knew. An ideal brother and a perfect father. He took care of everyone... just like Jémys does now."

"He sounds wonderful." Catanya thought about the man she'd seen in the vision. She could picture it so clearly: the house filled with their entire family, and how happy they must have been. "I wish I had a brother like that," she said, and it surprised her to hear the note of resentment in her voice.

Nelle sighed and nodded. "Jémys was so young when his father died. We honestly never talked about it. It was all... too much. And Jémys doesn't even know the worst of it..." She trailed off, lost in her thoughts.

"Why, what's the worst of it?" asked Catanya.

Nelle averted her eyes, "Oh, nothing, sorry." She smoothed the front of her shawl and took a deep breath. "I'm just glad Jémys has you now."

"Me?" Catanya stiffened.

Nelle tilted her head slightly. "Yes, I mean he has you to talk to," she said.

"Oh, of course." Catanya laughed in relief.

Nelle furrowed her brow at her. Then she continued with a knowing gleam in her eye, "You two have a unique bond, don't you?" The corners of her mouth twitched as she watched Catanya fidget.

Catanya cleared her throat and looked away. "Yes, I suppose... good friends."

She smiled lamely, as the front door opened and Jémys traipsed into the house, looking windswept and tired. He unfastened his cloak and draped it across the table, before slumping down into the seat next to Catanya and shutting his eyes.

When he opened them again, he glanced at her and frowned. "What? Why are you staring at me?"

"Oh, no, no reason." Catanya grinned and averted her gaze. For a second, Jémys had reminded her of Diyah—the dramatic way Diyah used to collapse after a busy day—and it filled her with nostalgia and affection.

It was difficult to think about Diyah without grief marring the memories. But for a brief moment, Catanya could imagine her friend was there with her.

After a short while, Nelle excused herself and headed off to sleep, leaving Catanya and Jémys alone. Catanya pulled out her sketchbook to finish a picture she'd started earlier.

"Are you ever going to let me see your drawings?" asked Jémys, straightening in his seat, his eyes bright with curiosity.

Catanya laughed. "Oh, okay."

She handed the book to him reticently, then sat awkwardly watching him as he flipped open the cover and turned the pages, pausing to examine each drawing with interest.

"These are remarkable." He spoke in an awed voice. "This picture of Olly, especially. It looks exactly like him." He grinned as he turned the next few pages. "And who's this?" He held the book to show her the image.

"Oh, that's my friend..." Catanya's chest tightened and she took a deep breath. "Her name was Diyah."

"Diyah?" he repeated. "That's a lovely name. And she looks kind... you've given her a warm air."

Catanya silently remarked how nice it was that Jémys saw more than just her beauty. Diyah would have appreciated that.

"So, was she at the orphanage with you?" he asked.

Catanya nodded. "Diyah was like my sister and I—" She broke off, fighting back tears. "I miss her terribly," she blurted, unable to hold it back any longer.

Jémys took her hand and squeezed it. "I'm sorry. I know how hard that must be. But maybe she's not... I mean... maybe you'll find each other again." He was trying to sound reassuring.

Catanya smiled sadly and looked down at his hand holding hers. It was comforting. Sitting there, she could almost believe he was right.

Jémys cleared his throat and removed his hand to start turning pages again. "Hold on." He paused on a page partway through the book. "I know this man..."

"Hmm?" Catanya leaned over to see which picture he had open.

He turned the book sideways, squinting at the image as though trying to remember. Then he stared at her, his eyebrows raised in disbelief. "This is that thief from the forest, isn't it?"

"Oh, yes, it is." She frowned at the image, remembering their encounter in the woods.

"Why are you drawing that thief?" asked Jémys, sounding cross.

Catanya rubbed her neck, thinking. "I don't know. I was trying to remember what he looked like. There was something strange about him. I can't explain it, but the way he spoke to me —what he said. It made me uneasy..." She trailed off, remembering the gleam in his eyes when he'd watched her leave.

*There's something special about you.*

His words rang in her head and she couldn't shake the impression he had known her secret.

She realized Jémys was staring at her, and she felt her face redden. "Anyway... Drawing someone often helps me sort out how I feel about them. Or at least it helps me relax." She shrugged.

Jémys smiled and then peered back down at the book. "So tell me, with nearly a dozen sketches of me in your book, what feelings are you sorting out there? Do I make you uneasy too?"

Catanya felt hot around the neck. "No. No feelings. You're just a good subject to sketch."

Jémys laughed as he closed the book and handed it back to her, his eyes twinkling above his crinkled cheeks. "You've got a natural talent. That's for sure."

"Thank you," she mumbled. She was embarrassed, but she was having trouble tearing her eyes away from his face.

"Well," said Jémys a short while later, "I think I'll follow Nelle's lead and turn in for the night." He stood up and stretched. "I'll see you in the morning."

When Catanya was alone again, she opened the book and flipped to a blank page. Pencil in hand, she set to work on a new sketch—something only she could bring to life. Something she needed to see, but she'd never have the chance.

Two faces smiling and laughing together, beaming up at her.

Diyah and Jémys.

## 12

# AN UNEXPECTED OFFER

Diyah wasn't sure how long she'd been imprisoned in the city. It was horribly dark, and the dungeon air grew denser and more acrid each day. She could hear the scuttling of rats on the floor and a distant sound of dripping water. The meagre light that filtered in through the window was barely enough to register the days passing, and during overcast periods, the light was utterly non-existent.

She estimated at least three weeks had passed since she stood on that beach with Catanya, making plans to leave together—although it seemed like a lifetime ago. And as each passing minute stretched into hours, she felt that memory pulling farther away from her.

Day by day, the isolation and fear took root in her heart, chipping away at any hope she maintained. Neither Cadyan nor any firkon had returned to interrogate her again, and she wondered if maybe she and the girls had been forgotten.

Or worse, maybe this was the end—maybe neglect was their intended execution.

Death by isolation and deprivation was, in Diyah's mind,

one of the worst ways to die. If it hadn't been for Fehla, she might have longed for her death sooner rather than later.

Diyah had been prepared to hate Fehla, to hate the woman who had abandoned her friend and set them all on this miserable course. So it surprised her to discover how sympathetic the queen actually was. She hadn't expected Fehla to be so kind or so generous, nor to see glimpses of Catanya in her expressions and mannerisms.

Until now, Diyah had never considered how much Fehla suffered. She had never considered the type of fear that could drive someone to give up their child, nor the sheer strength it would take to do it.

After her first visit, Diyah had expected never to see Fehla again. But Fehla had been true to her word and, although her visits were scarce, each time she came, she brought food and water, and a small renewal of hope.

"I'm so sorry this is happening to you," she groaned, as she leaned against the bars to talk to Diyah. She had just given them a small bundle of fruits and dried meat, along with another carafe of water.

Diyah's body was weak and the wounds on her back were still sore, but she held onto the bars to keep herself upright.

"It's not your fault," she muttered, giving Fehla a thin smile.

Fehla sniffed and adjusted the cuff of her dress, but didn't respond.

Diyah turned her attention towards Meya and Hahney, who were slowly making their way through their portions of food. It was taking all the energy they had just to chew, and it pained Diyah to watch them struggling. They had always been such lively and animated girls, but now they were nothing more than broken shells of their former selves.

None more so than Gréys. She was lying on the floor, drenched in sweat, and her face was pale and drawn.

"Is she alright?" asked Fehla quietly.

Gréys opened her mouth to respond, but she started coughing uncontrollably.

"Shh, it's okay, don't talk."

Diyah tried to smile reassuringly, but she had trouble concealing her worry. With every passing day, the fever strengthened its hold on Gréys. Diyah feared she wouldn't last much longer.

"She's very sick," Diyah whispered to Fehla.

"Is there anything I can bring you to help her?"

Diyah had tried everything she could to help Gréys. She had tried every remedy in her Heiltúir satchel, but without proper tools and a steady supply of clean water, there was never much hope it would work.

"I don't think there's anything we can do," she whispered. "She's too young. Her body can't fight it off. She needs fresh air and sun, she needs to get out of here." Diyah pressed her forehead against the cold metal bars and squeezed her eyes tight.

She wasn't afraid to die, but the thought of having to stand by, helpless, and watch as Gréys, Meya, and Hahney wasted away—to have to spend her final moments watching them suffer in miserable agony, knowing that she couldn't change their fates—was worse than any torture she could imagine.

Diyah opened her eyes and noticed Gréys was shivering again. She crossed the cell—the chain around her ankle clanging as it rattled against the cold stone floor—and sat down, pulling Gréys close to keep her warm. The movement aggravated her wounded back, but she clenched her teeth and fought through the pain.

"Have you heard any news?" she asked, trying to change the subject, but she doubted Fehla's response would offer much comfort.

"Nothing." Fehla jabbed at the nearest bar with her foot.

"Slaedir hasn't returned yet, which means he hasn't found her. And that's a good thing. I know that's a good thing, but..." She trailed off, biting her lip.

"I know," said Diyah. "The uncertainty is almost worse. I just want to know she's okay. It would make all this," she gestured helplessly at her surroundings, "more bearable."

"And you really have no idea where she could be?" asked Fehla.

Diyah shook her head dismally. "No, I honestly don't know. I wish I did."

Catanya had never left Faltir before and Diyah couldn't help but worry about her, lost somewhere in the woods all alone. This wasn't how it was supposed to happen. Diyah had intended to join Catanya when she left Faltir. They were supposed to be together...

Diyah sighed and looked at the girls sitting beside her. Despite everything, she knew she'd made the right choice. Catanya would find a way to survive. She knew it in her bones. But these girls still needed her help, and she was determined to protect them, whatever the cost.

Diyah glanced up to find Fehla watching her, her face clouded with sadness. "You're a very good person, Diyah. You make me feel quite ashamed of myself."

Diyah frowned in confusion.

Fehla shrugged. "I have never been selfless," she said. "No, everything I've ever done has been motivated by fear, not bravery."

"I'm not brave," said Diyah with a snort. "I've just learned to be stoic." She smiled dismally at Meya and Hahney, who were listening to the conversation with mild interest. They were so wan and fragile, but Diyah thought perhaps their colour had improved after eating something.

"Well, I think I had better go," said Fehla, straightening up again. "But I'll return in a few days. I may not hold much influence over my son anymore, but I can still do this." She exhaled heavily.

"Well, well, well…" drawled a voice from the shadows.

Fehla spun around and the girls recoiled as Cadyan and Julyán stepped out of the darkness into view.

"Feeding the vermin, are we, Mother?" His lips curled in revulsion as he stopped in front of the cell to sneer at Diyah and the others. "I didn't want to believe it when Julyán told me."

"Have you been following me?" spat Fehla, shooting Julyán a look of deepest contempt.

Julyán met her gaze with one of utmost indifference. "Yes," he said flatly, crossing the passage to stare down at Diyah.

Diyah watched him, her eyes narrowed and her body tensed for a fight, but he made no move to open the cell door. He just stared at her, his jaw set and his face unreadable.

"Julyán knows where his loyalties lie, Mother." Cadyan spoke in a simpering drawl that made Diyah's skin crawl. "But I'm afraid the same cannot be said for you." He tilted his head, eyes narrowed with disapproval.

Fehla looked like she wanted to slap him. "Oh, please! This has nothing to do with loyalty," she retorted. "This is about decency! There is no call for chaining people in cells, torturing them, and starving them to death!"

"I disagree." Cadyan knelt down so he was eye to eye with Diyah. "I find it… rather entertaining." He smiled tauntingly as he stood up again.

"*Entertaining*?" Diyah winced at the pain in her back, as she rose to her feet so she was level with him again. "You find it entertaining to watch young children wasting away in a cage?"

Cadyan's eyes flashed, and he held her gaze in silence for a moment. "Well, it *was* entertaining, but I've grown quite bored now, actually." He turned his back on Diyah. "Julyán, I think it's time to put an end to this farce, don't you? Kill them all."

There were cries and shouts as Diyah attempted to shield the three girls, and Fehla threw herself in front of the cell door to block Julyán's path.

"Move," commanded Cadyan.

"No." Fehla stood stiff and unflinching as she stared at him.

Cadyan's eyes flashed in the light of the nearby torch. "I said *move*," he commanded again even louder. He placed his hand on his mother's shoulder.

Fehla's posture softened abruptly, almost as if she was struggling with her own resolve. She took two stiff steps forward and turned. Cadyan smiled, lifting his hand off her. But as soon as he let go, Fehla screwed up her face in anger and swatted his outstretched arm away.

"And I said, no!" she repeated, returning to her position in front of the cell.

Cadyan's face fell, and he seemed surprised. He shook his hand out like he was trying to cast something off. "Interesting." He eyed his mother with a furrowed brow.

Mother and son stood glaring at each other in tense silence, and then Cadyan exhaled heavily. With a dangerous glint in his eye, he spoke in a disconcertingly cool voice, "Very well."

He swept his hand through the air, and Fehla went flying across the room where she landed hard against the opposite wall, crashing her head on the stone. She tried to stand, but she seemed to be trapped by an invisible force holding her down.

"Release me!"

"No," said Cadyan without feeling, as he turned his attention towards Julyán. "Well, get on with it." He gestured towards Diyah.

But this time it was Julyán who didn't move. He was standing with one hand on the cell door, frowning.

"What are you waiting for?" snapped Cadyan.

"My lord, I've had a thought." He glanced from Diyah back to his king. "This woman, my lord, she is one of the Heiltúir. Quite possibly the last." He paused in contemplation, but when Cadyan made an impatient gesture, he continued, "It occurs to me that Caerlon is in need of a healer. Think about that woman at the Offering. How many others will ask for similar help? You need a healer and you have one right here." He shrugged. "You could live ten lifetimes and never meet another Heiltúir. Consider it, my lord. To have one of the ancient healers at your court... It would be a significant advantage."

He let the suggestion dangle in the air. There was a pause as Cadyan considered his options.

But before he could respond, Diyah interrupted his contemplation. "No, you can forget it," she declared. "I will never help you. I won't disgrace the Heiltúir by using our knowledge in service of someone like you."

Outrage and arrogance stretched across Cadyan's face. "You don't have any other choice," he spat, sounding menacing again. Then he turned back to Julyán. "Very well. Take the woman, kill the rest."

Julyán moved to open the cell door.

"No!" Horror flooded through Diyah. She spread her arms wide and backed away from the door to protect the girls, who were quivering and crying behind her. "Alright! Alright!" she shouted.

She didn't have a choice. They were going to drag her out, kicking and screaming, but maybe she could use this situation to her advantage. "I'll help you," she said, forcing herself to sound calm and controlled. "I'll do whatever you want. But only if you let them go." She gave Cadyan a hard look as she stood shielding the girls from Julyán.

Cadyan's lip curled into a sneer. "You are in no position to be making demands," he hissed.

"Maybe not," said Diyah, hardly daring to believe her nerve.

"But if you release them, I will work for you willingly. I won't cause any trouble and I won't resist." She held her breath, waiting and hoping that this would be enough.

"My lord," Julyán spoke in a quiet voice, barely loud enough for anyone but Cadyan to hear. "It couldn't hurt to maintain a certain... *leverage*. To motivate her." He shrugged and looked at Diyah, who was glaring at him, brimming with hatred and disgust. "The healer will undoubtedly be more cooperative."

Diyah's chest tightened as she understood what Julyán was saying. Cadyan seemed to register Julyán's words. "Fine," he muttered, walking towards the cell door. "I'll let them go, but you, *healer*, will remain here as my physician and you will do everything you are told without question. And if you step out of line, I will not hesitate to kill them. Understood?"

Diyah nodded stiffly.

"And Julyán, I want you to keep a close eye on her. If you ever see her trying to escape or doing anything other than what I've instructed her to do, you will kill her on sight."

"Yes, Your Majesty." Julyán inclined his head, looking completely indifferent.

"Good. Then take her to the physician's quarters and make sure she's ready to start tomorrow. And find someplace to send those brats. Somewhere close where we can keep an eye on them. Find some farmer or spinster and tell them I rescued the urchins from a terrible disaster. Or some other such nonsense." He waved his hands impatiently.

"Yes, Your Majesty," Julyán said once again.

"As for you, Mother." Cadyan walked over to where she lay trapped on the floor. He knelt down to stare at her, and Fehla struggled against her invisible barricade. "You're lucky this time I'm in a forgiving mood, but don't expect the same mercy again. Now stand up." He reached down and yanked her to her feet. "And get out of my sight." He shoved her forward so she stumbled into the wall.

She glowered at him as she straightened out her dress and shawl, then she turned and marched towards the exit. She made fleeting eye contact with Diyah before continuing along the passage out of the dungeons.

Diyah watched her go, moderately dazed and confused. She couldn't believe what had just happened.

"Now, Julyán, I trust you have everything under control." Cadyan appeared strained. He was clutching his right hand with his left, twisting the ring on his finger absentmindedly. "I have somewhere to be." He turned on his heel and followed his mother.

There was silence while Diyah and Julyán stood staring at each other. Julyán's expression was difficult to read.

"Come," he said imperiously, unlatching the cell. The door swung open, and he strode inside to where she stood chained to the floor. Then he knelt to unlock the shackles.

Diyah stared down at him for a moment, torn between fear and curiosity.

"Why?" she asked. "Why did you save us?" She studied him through narrowed eyes, her distrust growing with every passing second.

He glanced up at her and shook his dark hair out of his face, before standing up abruptly. "We need a healer," he grunted.

"But—"

"Let's go," he cut her off and moved towards the door, beckoning for her to follow him.

Diyah looked down and was surprised to find her leg free of its chain. She was free to go, but she couldn't move. She stood rooted to the floor as if her chains were still holding her in place.

"Let's go," he repeated.

When she still didn't move, he crossed back into the cell and grabbed her by the arm to drag her out.

"Wait." She yanked her arm out of his grasp, wincing as she felt her wounds twist and reopen. "Just..." She glanced back at Meya, Gréys, and Hahney. "Let me say goodbye first."

He frowned at her. "Make it quick," he said.

Diyah didn't want to give him time to change his mind. She turned around quickly and knelt down beside the girls. Their tiny faces were pale with fear. "Okay, I need you to be brave now. Everything is going to be okay. You'll be released from here soon."

"Diyah, I don't want to leave you," said Meya, shivering as she reached out to take Diyah's hand.

"I know, but you have to. It's better this way."

"What will happen to you?" asked Hahney, sounding hopeless.

Diyah faltered as she struggled to steady herself. "Me? Oh, I'll be fine," she reassured them, straining to keep her voice even. "Don't worry about me." She forced a smile onto her face.

"And what about Catanya?" whispered Meya.

"Don't worry about her either. She's strong, she'll make it through this no matter what." At this, Diyah thought she noticed Julyán tilt his head in interest. "Now, come here," she continued hurriedly, reaching out and hugging Meya and Hahney. She closed her eyes, ignoring the searing pain she felt inside and out. Then she turned her attention to Gréys. "You're going to be fine. Once you're out of here, you'll be right as rain." She bent down and kissed her on the forehead.

"Will we ever see you again?" asked Gréys, coughing on the dank air.

Diyah's eyes burned, and she felt the tears coming, so she smiled at them one last time. "Of course. We'll see each other very soon."

Then, before they could see her cry, she turned her back and walked towards Julyán. She attempted to avert her eyes as she joined him, but he was watching her so closely that she knew he must have seen. She cleared her throat and tried to force the tears back, as she followed him out of the dungeons and away from the last three remaining members of her Camlee Lodge family.

## 13

## A FESTIVAL

Catanya ran, stumbling over her own feet. Faceless soldiers were pursuing her and her only weapon was a fragile stick she had grabbed off the forest floor. The harder she tried to run, the faster the soldiers gained on her. And then she fell, tumbling down a steep, never-ending hill until finally she crashed into the mossy earth at the bottom. Everything was calm. She was safe. A community had gathered around her and someone was helping her to her feet. But who was it?

Catanya awoke with a start. She sat in bed trying to remember how the dream had ended, but with every waking second it seemed to slip farther away.

In the dream, a group had gathered underneath a canopy tent somewhere deep in the forest, but the scene was unusual. The trees appeared ancient and gnarled, and the people were strangers to her. She hadn't recognized any of them except—

"That man!" she said aloud.

She was sure of it. It was the thief from the woods. But why was she dreaming about him? What was he doing there? She groaned and pressed her hands against her eyes, as she swung her legs around the side of the bed to reach the floor.

She squeezed the bedpost and stood up, blinking bright spots out of her vision. "Get a grip on yourself, Catanya. It was only a dream." She crossed the room to the wardrobe and began rifling through its contents.

She was eager to find Jémys. He always managed to take her mind off whatever was troubling her. In fact, she was starting to think that nothing in her life made sense anymore, except for him.

It was a beautiful, crisp morning. Catanya headed out to the garden, where she found Nelle. A gentle mist hung in the air and somewhere nearby, a mourning dove cooed.

"Good morning," she said, yawning as she knelt beside Nelle on the edge of the cabbage patch. "Where's Jémys?" She looked around, disappointed not to see him.

"Oh, you just missed him. He's off hunting, but he should be back before noon." She turned to face Catanya. "Oh, dear, you look a bit drawn. Are you ill?"

"No, I just had a restless night. I'm fine." She stifled another yawn as she waved away Nelle's concern. "What do you need me to do today?"

Nelle gave her an appraising look, and then seemed to accept Catanya's assurances she was fine. "Well, I could use your help in the garden this morning to speed things along. Afterward, we can head to the orchard and start setting everything up for the festival tomorrow. Here." She handed Catanya a basket. "You work from that side and we'll meet in the middle."

The vegetable garden was expansive. Besides the voluminous cabbage patch at one end, there were rows upon rows of beans, onions, potatoes, and carrots, all ripening in time for the harvest. The far end of the garden fence was overgrown by a thick row of raspberry bushes, which still held a few fruits. The wildflowers from the nearby meadow had spread, popping up between the plants and giving the garden a vibrant and untamed quality.

They worked all morning, pruning, harvesting, and weeding, until the sun had risen high in the sky and the mist had disappeared. It was almost midday when Jémys returned from his hunt with a brace of rabbits and three plump pheasants.

"Oh, this is perfect, dear." Nelle took the game from her nephew and laid it gingerly on the kitchen table.

"I'll go out again in a couple days and see if I can catch us another deer," he said offhand, as he grabbed a carrot off the table and started eating it. "Maybe I'll take Olly with me... show him how it's done."

"That sounds like a splendid idea," said Nelle, swiping feathers off the vegetables. "Catanya, dear? Could you run to the edge of the forest and try to gather some fresh herbs for me? There should be plenty of sage and chives along the treeline. Oh, and some lavender would be nice."

"Sure," said Catanya, standing up and grabbing an empty basket off the table.

"Jémys, why don't you go with her?" added Nelle, with a casual tone. "You can show her where to look." She smiled at Catanya.

Catanya felt her cheeks flush.

Jémys nodded and finished his carrot, before following Catanya out the door.

They left the house, crossed the garden into the meadow, and climbed the hill towards the trees. A gentle breeze rustled through the air, carrying with it the sweet earthy smell of the forest.

Neither of them spoke as they searched the area for Nelle's herbs. The silence stretched on and Catanya struggled to find something to break the tension. Once or twice she opened her mouth to speak, then closed it again and turned away.

Finally she settled on an easy topic. "I used to do this with my friend Diyah... herb picking," she added, answering the question on his face. "Diyah's father was a healer—one of the last Heiltúir in fact—and he passed that knowledge on to her before he died."

"Really?" Jémys looked interested. "My father taught me about the Heiltúir," he said, with a hint of reverence in his voice. "I think we met one once when I was a young boy. I vaguely remember it. We were touring the Tarus Valley on our way to Murina."

"Murina?" said Catanya eagerly. "That's where Diyah was born."

If Jémys had been to Murina as a boy, then maybe the Heiltúir he'd met had actually been Diyah's father.

"We never made it to Murina, though. I don't know why." Jémys frowned, trying to think back on the memory. "I heard shortly after that the town was destroyed by some sort of plague..."

Catanya's heart fell. "It was," she said. "That's when Diyah came to live with us at the orphanage."

"Such a shame," mumbled Jémys, shaking his head. "But if she's one of the Heiltúir, she must be an incredible healer."

Catanya smiled fondly. "Yes, she was... she was the best."

Jémys was observing Catanya closely. He seemed to understand what she was feeling without her having to say it. "We've never had a healer here in Finnua," he continued after a while. "We just do the best we can, and I'm afraid it's not always enough." He sighed and stared off into the trees. "A few years ago, a terrible sickness swept across central Caerlon, hitting Finnua, and a lot of good people died. Children..." He exhaled heavily, shaking his head. "I should have done something."

"What could you have done?" asked Catanya, surprised by his harsh tone.

"I don't know... I should have found a healer." He kicked a

stone at a nearby tree trunk. "It all happened so fast, and I was so helpless. But these people"—he gestured back towards the village—"I feel like they are my responsibility, you know? They rely on me and when I let them down—"

"You didn't let them down," interjected Catanya. "These people adore you. Things like that—they can't be helped. Even a Heiltúir can't cure every illness." She thought back on the evenings she'd spent listening to Diyah talk about her work. "Some illnesses are so bad that they can't be cured. Diyah used to tell me that death wasn't something to fear. She used to say that everyone dies, and how could something inevitable be bad? She used to make it all sound so peaceful."

Jémys took a deep breath. "I know you're right, I'm just... tired. I've been struggling to keep this village alive for as long as I can remember, and it keeps getting more and more difficult. No matter what I do, it doesn't make a difference. The taxes continue to climb every year, our people get sick or they starve, and now—"

He broke off and turned away, shaking his head. Catanya walked over to him and put her hand gently on his arm.

"I understand," she said. "It's not easy knowing that everyone is depending on you. You feel cut off from them. Isolated and alone."

Jémys nodded and looked at her. "I did feel alone," he said. "But ever since I met you, I don't know..." He cast around for the right words. "I guess I never realized how much I needed someone... somebody I can share things with. Thank you..." He trailed off, searching her face. "I like having you here," he added in a low voice.

Catanya gazed out across the meadow, down the hill towards the village. Then, taking a deep breath, she said, "I like being here with you." She turned to face him. His bright green eyes shone in the sunlight as she moved towards him and slid her hand down his arm, lacing her fingers through his.

Jémys reached out and placed his other hand on her face, bringing it up to meet his. Their lips met, and they stood pressed firmly against each other, not daring to move. Then they both exhaled heavily and surrendered into each other's arms. She moved her hands up around his neck and pulled him in closer, as he gripped her tight and pressed his body against hers. She curled her fingers through his hair, never wanting to let him go. Her head spun. His arms were the only things keeping her from falling apart.

Too soon, it was over. They broke apart and stared at each other without speaking. Then Jémys grinned sheepishly and lowered his hands.

He cleared his throat. "Perhaps now is not the best time."

"No." Her voice sounded breathy, as she straightened out her dress. "Perhaps not. We should get back to the manor. I'm sure Nelle is waiting for us."

Jémys bent down to pick up the basket full of herbs. "But"—he looked up at her and grinned—"it was nice."

Catanya laughed and beamed back at him. "Yes, it was."

They spent the remainder of the day making final arrangements for the Apple Picking and Harvest Festival. A great deal of work remained and, without opportunities for privacy, Catanya and Jémys contented themselves with stealing glances and smiles, or occasional brushes of the hand as they passed each other.

Catanya was happier than she'd been in ages. She had never felt this strongly about anyone, and she was so filled with joy and excitement, it was getting easier for her to forget her worries. She was light and carefree. It didn't matter who she was, it mattered who she could become as long as she and Jémys were together.

The day of the festival arrived and the entire village gathered together beneath the trees in the orchard. There were people everywhere, picking apples and weaving baskets, while the children ran back and forth from the barn, squealing and laughing. Ladders had been erected to reach the higher branches, and the elderly villagers sat nearby doling out instructions to everyone else.

Catanya spent the morning sitting with Olly's mother, Ranya. Together, they wove baskets and laughed as they watched Olly scampering around with his friend Blaese. The boys shadowed Jémys, asking inordinate questions and begging for him to hoist them up so they could reach the highest apples.

Around midday, Nelle cracked open the old casks of cider and the baker arrived with a cart full of pies and assorted foods for everyone. The energy in the air was one of cheer and amity as everyone worked together and celebrated.

Catanya recognized Evyain and her friend sitting beneath the largest tree, talking to anyone who passed, their cheeks growing pinker and pinker as their cider cups emptied and refilled several times. Catanya smiled to herself, and gave them a wide berth, not wanting to find herself trapped this early in the day. She'd circle back later to say hello.

As the day progressed and the cider barrels emptied, the noise and merriness increased. Fewer and fewer people were picking apples, and eventually the singing and dancing won out completely.

Catanya laughed heartily at the sight of Nelle dancing with Olly, wincing as he trod on her feet. She observed the older couples in the village dancing together, their eyes full of love and tenderness.

As the burnt-orange sunset deepened into night, lanterns were brought out to line the rows of trees. The effect was magical as they cast their warm glow around the orchard, dancing and flickering in the gentle breeze.

Catanya noticed Roslin standing awkwardly to the side, looking self-conscious and nervous as she eyed Jémys, who was laughing and chatting with a group of people nearby.

Catanya lifted two ciders off the nearest cart before walking over to join her.

"You look lovely this evening, Roslin," she said, smiling warmly as she handed her the cider.

"Oh, no." Roslin blushed. "Not as nice as you." She raised her hand to her hair. "I tried to do my hair like yours, but I don't think I managed it."

"I think you look perfect," Catanya reassured her, examining the slightly messy braid.

Roslin beamed at her and took a sip from her cider, watching the festivities.

Catanya surveyed the orchard and realized there weren't many other young people in Finnua. She supposed Roslin must be lonely without anyone to talk to or laugh with.

"You know," ventured Catanya after a while. "I've never been a good dancer." She laughed as she watched the couples spinning nearby. "I've always been a bit ashamed of it, actually." She grinned sheepishly at Roslin.

"Yes, but Jémys says you're a wonderful artist. He says you draw and paint better than anyone he's ever met, and Jémys has travelled all over and met all kinds of people. If he says you're the best, you really must be." Roslin's eyes were wide with admiration. "I can't do anything like that. I've never been very talented."

"Well," said Catanya thoughtfully. "I could teach you if you want to learn."

Roslin gaped at her. "Oh, I would love that!"

"Then it's settled." Catanya smiled as Roslin's face brightened. "I'll come by after the harvest and we can do some drawing together."

A few minutes later, Jémys appeared at Catanya's side. He took her hand, leading her out to dance. As she went with him, she threw a joking look of dread in Roslin's direction and saw her laugh. Then she turned her attention back towards Jémys.

He placed one hand on the small of her back and held her tightly in his arms as they danced under the trees. It was true that Catanya never considered herself a skilled dancer, but tonight with Jémys, she felt like she could do anything.

When no one was looking, he craned his neck down and pressed his lips softly against her neck and up towards her chin. She shut her eyes and squeezed his arm with her hand. She wanted to be alone with him, she wanted to kiss him and taste his lips against hers.

He pressed his cheek against her head and inhaled deeply, smelling her hair.

It was well past midnight when people started trickling away. Those who remained were helping carry sacks of apples to the barn or wheeling carts and barrels towards the mill.

"Where did Olly run off to?" asked Jémys, as he helped Catanya load the last cart. "Ranya asked me to bring him home."

"I think I saw him heading towards the barn a little while back. I'll go check."

Catanya hurried off in the direction of the barn, while Jémys stayed behind to finish loading.

"Olly?" she called, as she pushed open the barn door with a creak. "Are you in here?" She was scanning the barn when she spotted him curled up asleep in the hay on top of the rafters. She chuckled to herself and stood watching him until Jémys came in, pulling the cart.

"Did you find him?"

"Shh." She pointed to the rafters and grinned. "He must be so tired."

Jémys laughed quietly and moved to stand next to Catanya near the door. "You know, I think this might be the most successful festival we've had yet," he whispered, wrapping his arms around her waist and pulling her into his body. "And it looks like the rest of our harvest will be strong too. Even after the royal delegation takes their share, we should have plenty to carry us through the winter."

But cold reality had just crashed over Catanya. "The royal delegation... I almost forgot. When do you think they'll arrive?" she asked, backing away from him a little.

Jémys let his hands fall to his sides. "Not for another month, I imagine. That's when they usually arrive. Why? What's the matter?" he asked, frowning and looking a little self-conscious.

"What? Oh, nothing." She met his gaze again with a strained smile.

Jémys glanced around to make sure they were alone. Then his face broke into a wide grin. He grabbed her hand and twirled her around into his arms.

She couldn't help but laugh as he held her, swaying in the moonlight. Then he tilted his head and brought his lips down to hers. They stood there, kissing under the stars until—

"Ew!" cried Olly.

The two of them broke apart, laughing.

"What are you doing?" he squealed down at them from the rafters. "Only old married people do that."

"Oh, sorry, we didn't know," said Jémys, his voice thick with irony.

Catanya laughed. "Right. It's a good thing you're here to teach us these things, Olly."

Jémys gave Catanya an amused look. "I'm going to make one last round to see if we missed anything." He walked past Catanya, kissing her cheek as he left.

She sighed and watched him go, feeling a strange mixture of longing and guilt.

"Olly, why don't you come down now?" She turned her attention to the boy in the rafters. "It's very late, we should take you home."

"I could just stay here though. I like it up here!" he called, as he started hopping around on the beams.

Catanya had to hold back a giggle. "Oh, do you?" She nodded exaggeratedly. "Will you like it quite so much when the coyotes come searching for their midnight snack?" she asked, eyeing him slyly.

"Coyotes?" Olly stopped dead in his tracks.

"Oh, yes. Coyotes love cider, didn't you know that?" She acted nonchalant as she watched his reaction.

"No..." He seemed to give it a great deal of thought, and then he said, "Okay, I've decided I should probably go home. I'm coming down."

Catanya giggled as she peered up at Olly to see the serious frown on his face. "Okay, I think you're right. That sounds like a good plan."

Everything that happened next seemed to occur in the blink of an eye. As Olly stepped across the beam towards the ladder, the rafter underneath him gave way. He went crashing headfirst towards the floor. Catanya reacted in a heartbeat. She threw out her hands and felt her skin burn, as an invisible force seemed to slow Olly down and guide him towards the ground, where he landed gracefully and without injury. Just as she was lowering her hands, another beam broke apart from the rafters and swung dangerously over him. As she cried out in alarm, the beam shattered into a fine dust that floated gently down on top of them both.

They stayed motionless, coated in wood dust and staring at each other for several seconds before Olly stood up. "Whoa!" he gasped. "How did you do that?"

"Do what?" Catanya's pulse was racing. She hid her hands behind her back and tried to make her face appear normal.

"You just made that beam explode, and you made me fly!" Olly squealed as he came running over to her.

"Shh!" Catanya was panicking now, and she cast around to make sure nobody else was nearby. "Olly, be quiet."

"You can do magic!" he cried again.

"Shh, please. I'm begging you, don't tell anyone. No one can know, do you understand me?"

"Why not?" He stared at her, his eyes wide with wonder.

"Because it's not... I can't..." Her brain seemed to have stopped working. "Because it's not safe."

"Not safe, but you just saved me?" Olly looked confused. Then his jaw dropped and he gaped at Catanya. "You're her?" he asked in awe.

"What?" spluttered Catanya, flabbergasted.

"You!" Then recollecting himself, he whispered, "You're the king's sister, aren't you?"

Catanya groaned in defeat and slumped down on to the floor next to Olly.

"Promise me you won't tell anyone." She grabbed his hands, her eyes boring into his. "You don't understand how dangerous this is."

"Okay, okay." He nodded. "I can keep a secret. I'm an excellent secret-keeper." He puffed out his chest proudly. Then his forehead puckered, and he looked at her. "But if you're the princess, what are you doing here? I thought you were supposed to be fighting the king?"

Catanya grimaced and rubbed her forehead. "You don't understand. These powers... they're not a gift, they're a curse. I'm not a hero, Olly. I'm just trying to stay alive."

"But... you could stop him." There was a slight accusatory look in his eye as he stared at her, bewildered.

"No." She shook her head, heartbroken by the hurt and

confusion on his face. "No, I'm sorry, but I can't stop him. Where would I even start? I have no clue how these powers work. I can't control them."

Olly's face brightened. "I can help you," he said confidently. "Now that I know your secret, I can help you practice."

"Practice?" she repeated disbelievingly.

"Yeah. My mother always tells me that if I want to improve at something, I just need to focus on my goals and practice hard. So that's what you need to do." His voice was matter-of-fact and confident, as if mastering her magic was the simplest thing imaginable.

"I don't know..." Catanya didn't like the sound of it at all. It was bad enough that Olly had discovered the truth, but now he wanted her to start using her powers more. "This is dangerous, Olly, what if you get hurt? I don't think it's a good idea."

"Well, I do." Olly jumped to his feet and shook the dust out of his hair. "Don't worry." His eyes shone as he held out his pudgy little hand for hers. "I believe in you."

**14**

———

## IN THE MEADOW

"**P**lease!"

"I said no, Olly."

"Oh, come on!"

Catanya was standing at the kitchen table peeling potatoes. Olly sat across from her, his face scrunched in an obstinate pout.

"It's not safe, I told you. Now will you please just drop it?" She turned around and tossed the potatoes into a large pot.

For days, Olly had been pestering her to practice her magic. He was adamant in his belief that she should fight for control of Caerlon, and all she needed to do was learn to use her powers.

"I will not drop it."

"Shh! Please, Olly." She looked at him, wide-eyed. "Keep your voice down."

"I don't understand why we can't tell Jémys and Nelle," he said, frowning.

Catanya sighed. "I've already explained this to you. We can't tell anyone. This isn't safe. You should forget about it too. Just let it go."

"But why don't you want to use your powers?"

"I never wanted these powers, Olly!" She was losing her temper now. "They're dangerous and it's not like I can—" She broke off and began hacking at the potato in her hand.

"What?"

She shoved the hair out of her face. "There's nothing I can do, Olly. This dream of yours where I take over Caerlon and save everyone... it's just a fantasy." She snatched a fresh potato off the table and started peeling. "We should focus on the harvest, that's what really matters."

"But..." He looked disappointed and frightened. "If you won't save us, what are we going to do?"

Catanya felt a pang of guilt. "I'm sorry, Olly, but there's nothing I can do."

For a few minutes, neither of them spoke. Then Olly jumped down off his chair and shouted, "But I don't want to join the firkon!"

Catanya looked over to see his eyes filling with tears. Then Olly ran out of the kitchen, nearly colliding with Jémys, who was coming in carrying a large stack of firewood.

"What's going on?" He dropped the wood beside the stove and glanced back at the spot where Olly had disappeared.

Catanya didn't answer. She was thinking about everything Olly had just said, feeling ashamed of herself for not understanding sooner. She should have realized why this was so important to him.

"Should I go talk to him?" asked Jémys.

"No, let me." She put the knife down and wiped her hands on her apron, before removing it and leaving the kitchen.

After a few minutes searching, she found Olly sitting in a tree behind the house, his eyes puffy and red. He didn't look up as Catanya approached, instead he started pulling leaves off the branches and shredding them in his hands.

"Look, Olly," said Catanya, leaning against the tree. "You

have to understand how new this is to me, and how frightened I am." She glanced at him and shrugged. "Until recently, I thought I was an orphan. And now suddenly I've got an entire family I've never met and these powers I can't control. And now you want me to fight and become some sort of saviour. It's a lot to take."

Olly sniffed feebly but said nothing.

Catanya exhaled heavily. "But I think you're right," she said, shaking her head and silently hoping this wasn't a mistake. "These powers aren't going anywhere. Maybe I should at least be learning how to control them."

"Really?" Olly straightened up on his perch and peered down at her.

"Yes." She sighed, working hard to suppress the smile that was twitching at her lips in response to his brightened mood. She needed him to understand how serious this was. "Listen, I can't promise anything, and I don't want you to get your hopes up, okay? I said I'm willing to try. But only small things. Nothing dangerous. And you can't be a part of it." She raised her voice, ignoring his protests. "I'm sorry, but no. I don't know how dangerous this will be, and I won't risk your safety."

"But once you figure it out, then you'll show me right?" he asked.

Catanya surveyed him. She could feel the smile breaking through her defenses. "Oh, alright." She laughed, shaking her head.

Olly's face cracked into a wide grin and he jumped down from the tree.

"What are you going to start with?" Then, not waiting for an answer, he said, "I think you should start trying to make objects fly. That's how you protected me, right? So you already know how to do it."

Catanya laughed to herself and rubbed her forehead.

"Start with something light, like a feather and then move to bigger objects—" He broke off, frowning, and gaped at her. "How did you get your powers?" he asked. Then his eyes lit up with excitement. "Ooh, did you find the lost mountain? Did you find Túir-Avlea?"

Catanya couldn't help laughing at the absurdity. "Túir-Avlea? Olly, there's no such place. That's just a legend, a story told to children to give them hope."

"Then how?"

"Well... I don't know, but I promise you Túir-Avlea is just a story."

"But you have powers," he insisted. "So maybe the lost mountain exists too. I bet if you—"

Catanya cleared her throat and shook her head warningly. Jémys was coming out of the house.

"Well, someone seems to be in better spirits now," he called, jogging to join them.

"Oh, I don't know, I think he might need more help cheering up. I expect a nice dip in the trough should do the trick," Catanya suggested, flashing Jémys a playful grin. "What do you think?"

Jémys grinned back at her. "I think that is an excellent idea. You get his arms, I'll get his legs."

"No!" squealed Olly as he dodged out of the way.

"Oh, come on, it'll make you feel better," said Jémys, chasing him in circles around the tree.

Catanya laughed heartily as she joined in the pursuit.

"You'll never catch me," called Olly in his shrill little voice. They chased him around the yard until he clambered back up the tree and beyond their reach.

Catanya and Jémys stopped, panting and laughing.

"Ha! I told you," cried Olly, sticking his tongue out at them.

Nelle poked her head through the window and called for Olly to come help her inside. As he clambered back down the tree and sprinted off towards the house, Catanya and Jémys moved to lean against the tree and catch their breath.

"What?" asked Catanya.

Jémys had been studying her, his eyes bright with an odd gleam.

"Nothing," he said, grinning from ear to ear. "I was just thinking..."

"Thinking about what?" she asked, as her head began to fog. Whenever he smiled like that, she found it distracting. She raised her hand up to his face and traced her thumb across the indentations on his cheek. His happiness was so hard to resist.

He smiled even wider before leaning in and kissing her lightly on the lips. His lips were soft and warm, and when he tried to pull away, Catanya instinctively pulled him in closer to her. He responded with passion as he pressed her back against the tree. The warmth of his arms enveloped her, and she was lost in him.

Jémys paused. Pulling his lips off hers, he spoke in a low breathy voice, "I was thinking how grateful I am that I met you. It was a stroke of luck, us finding each other in the woods, and I'm so happy we did."

Then he kissed her again.

But Catanya was uneasy. It was as though the weight of her secret had crashed down between them.

"Wait, Jémys. I need to tell you something," she said, gently pushing him away.

"What is it?" He gazed into her face, unsuspecting.

"Well..."

She fidgeted and felt her heart racing. She didn't know why she was so scared. Jémys cared about her, didn't he? He'd understand...

"I don't know how to tell you this, but I'm not... I mean I'm—"

"Jémys, Catanya, could you come help me for a second?" It was Nelle calling from the house.

Jémys smiled and shrugged. "Don't worry, we can find time to talk later. Come on." He took her hand and led the way back to the house.

<hr>

Although the festival had officially ended, a lot of harvesting work still needed to be done. They spent the better part of the next several days either toiling away in the gardens or in the kitchen preparing various crops for storage. And in addition to their individual gardens, every able body in Finnua took shifts reaping the barley and wheat from the two fields on the edge of town. They then transported the grain across the river to the mill for processing.

It was tremendously exhausting work, and it kept Jémys and Catanya both so occupied that they were never alone together for more than five minutes.

With each passing day, Catanya felt increasingly guilty about the lies she was telling. It was getting harder and harder to justify keeping the truth from Jémys, especially now that Olly had figured it out.

She knew she needed to tell Jémys before she got any further entwined in his life, but the thought of telling him terrified her.

They had been living inside a perfect dream these past few weeks and she was scared that by admitting the truth, the dream would end. She wasn't sure she was ready to face reality just yet. Especially not since the truth meant she couldn't stay in Finnua. As much as she wished otherwise, she knew she needed to leave, and she had already delayed her departure for far too long. But she wasn't ready to leave. She needed more time.

Then something happened that wrenched her back to harsh reality sooner than expected.

Late one afternoon, as she and Jémys were finishing up at the mill, she overheard a conversation between two workers who had joined them in the wheat fields that day.

"Did you hear what happened in Linlon?" asked one man. "They say the whole place was ransacked. Houses turned inside out, valuables stolen... it's a wonder no one was injured."

Catanya felt suddenly cold. Somewhere in the back of her mind, she remembered hearing about Linlon. It was one of the ancient lake towns, and, if memory served, it wasn't very far from Finnua.

"Ransacked by who?" asked the other man.

"No one knows." The first man tossed his bundle of wheat off the cart so it landed atop the growing pile outside the mill. "But apparently it wasn't the royal delegation, because they only just reached Sidina a few days back. They couldn't have reached Linlon that fast."

The conversation dwindled when the miller emerged to thank them for their hard work.

Jémys had been inside, making arrangements for the next day. When he came outside, he smiled and took Catanya's hand. "Let's go home," he said, pressing her hand against his lips.

*Home.*

Catanya was deeply unsettled as she walked along the main street, hand in hand with Jémys.

"How far is Linlon?" she asked, rubbing a sore knot out of her shoulder. Her entire body ached from the days of hard labour, and now her tension was building again.

Jémys furrowed his brow as he thought about his answer. "Three days' ride, maybe two if the weather is fair. Why?"

Catanya shrugged. "No reason." But a familiar sense of dread was creeping back into her heart.

Cadyan was closing in on her. There was no question about it. She couldn't stay in Finnua any longer. She knew she needed to leave, but what should she tell Jémys? The idea of leaving him nearly brought her to tears, and she didn't think she'd be strong enough to say goodbye.

But it had to be goodbye. She could never ask him to come with her.

No, it was better if she went alone. She could content herself with the knowledge that Jémys was safe in Finnua—much safer without her in his life anymore.

Catanya spent the remainder of the afternoon and evening preparing her departure. She couldn't waste any more time, she needed to leave tonight.

After careful consideration, she decided it was best to slip away under the cover of darkness without saying goodbye. She told herself that the less Jémys knew, the safer he'd be. And this way, she wouldn't have to shatter the perfect dream. She could carry the memories of her time in Finnua like a torch, using them to light whatever dark times lay ahead.

With a rush of sadness and a pang of guilt, she realized her plan to leave tonight meant she wouldn't have another chance to see Olly, or explain to him why she had to go. She knew how important it was to him that she learn to use her magic, and a big part of her felt like she was letting him down. But Olly was a child. He didn't understand how dangerous this situation was.

Catanya rounded up everything she needed for the journey. She tried to pack light, but it was difficult to know how long she'd be travelling or what dangers might lie ahead. She grabbed a thick cloak, and she filled an old bag with some food, a canteen, and her few spare possessions, including the hunting knife Jémys had given her, and the sketchbook.

As she held the sketchbook in her hands, she flipped open the cover and turned to a page featuring an image of Jémys, Nelle, and Olly all beaming out at her. She blinked, and a tear slipped out from under her eyelid. It landed on the page above the image and dripped down, smearing some of the lead marks.

Catanya took a shaky breath and shut the book, sliding it into the bag along with the other items. At least this time she was bringing her sketches with her, a reminder of these people she cherished. She'd carry them with her forever.

That night, as she sat with Nelle and Jémys eating dinner, she felt nervous. She had trouble focusing on the conversation, and every few minutes, her eyes darted to the window, watching the sun inch closer to the horizon, as she waited for her opportunity to sneak away.

"Are you alright, dear?" asked Nelle. "You're awfully quiet."

"What? Oh, yes. I'm just tired." Catanya couldn't bring herself to make eye contact. She watched Nelle slicing portions of pie and wondered if they'd ever see each other again. She felt a lump rising in her throat. "I want to thank you," she blurted.

Nelle paused mid-slice and looked up, surprised. "Thank me? Whatever for?"

Catanya lifted her shoulder in a half shrug. "For everything you've done for me," she said. "You've been so kind and I—" She broke off, chewing her bottom lip. "Well, I'll never forget how generous you've been."

Jémys and Nelle exchanged confused but flattered glances, then Jémys grinned. "Are you sure you're alright?"

Catanya gave a feeble laugh and nodded. She took the slice of pie Nelle handed her and didn't speak again.

She retired early and sat awake in her room, waiting and listening. When she was sure Jémys and Nelle had both fallen asleep, she grabbed her belongings and moved towards the door, but something held her back. She stood with her arm outstretched, listening to the muffled sounds of the autumn evening, unable to move.

"What are you doing?" she whispered, trying to shake some

sense into herself. But her heart was pounding louder and louder, drowning out the thoughts in her head.

She didn't know how long she stood like that, but eventually her pulse began to slow. When she could think clearly again, she shut her eyes and focused on her breathing.

"You have to do this." She spoke calmly as she wrapped her fingers around the door handle.

Before she could change her mind, Catanya pried open the door and slipped out of her room towards the kitchen. As she unlatched the back door, it revolted with a noisy creak that echoed through the silent house. Catanya froze, praying no one had heard. Then she crept through the opening and into the chilly night air.

The sky was full of stars that sparkled and pierced the darkness, illuminating the world below. Catanya climbed over the garden wall and crossed the meadow towards the edge of the forest. Taking a deep breath, she turned to have one last look at the manor, trying not to imagine how Jémys would react when he awoke tomorrow and realized she'd left.

But to her surprise, she saw Jémys hurrying out the door towards her.

"Catanya!"

Her heart pounded as she watched him hop over the garden wall and continue towards her. She needed to leave. Speaking to Jémys would only make it harder for her. She tried to turn away, to keep moving, but Jémys ran to reach her.

"Wait." He grabbed her arm and spun her around to face him. "What are you doing? Where are you going?"

She couldn't look at him. She struggled to pull her arm out of his grasp. "I-I have to go. I can't stay here." Her pulse raced faster, and she couldn't think of a way to explain without telling him the truth. But the truth was dangerous. "I have to leave. I'm sorry, but it's safer this way."

Jémys frowned. "What are you talking about? Safe from

what?" He sounded confused and hurt. She attempted to turn away again, but he crossed ahead of her and blocked her path. "What are you running from?" he asked. He had his hands on her arms and he searched her face, eyes gleaming in the starlight.

"Look." She averted her gaze and brushed his hands off. "It'll be better for everyone if you let me go. Just forget that you met me."

He grimaced and buried his hands in his hair. "What are you talking about?"

Catanya sighed. Jémys wasn't going to let her leave without a reason.

She shrugged, trying to feign indifference, and braced herself to say what was necessary. "I don't belong here. Not in Finnua, not with you." Her voice sounded false and unnaturally high, so she cleared her throat and took a few steadying breaths. "I've already stayed too long."

Jémys's eyes were glossy and pained. "Please, stay." He wrapped his hands around hers. "Please."

Catanya squeezed her eyes shut. When she opened them again, she shifted her gaze to meet his and held it, unflinching. "I don't want to," she said with all the strength she could muster. She pulled her shaky hands out of his grasp and turned to leave.

Her entire body trembled as she crossed through the meadow towards the forest. She nearly tripped as she hurried forward, willing herself to keep moving without turning back.

But before she could reach the tree line, Jémys called after her in a calm but defiant voice, "I don't believe you."

She stopped dead in her tracks, still facing the trees. She could hear Jémys taking slow, measured steps towards her.

"I don't believe you," he said again. "I know you're scared, and I know there's something you're not telling me. You've lost everyone you've ever loved and you're terrified to let me in.

You're afraid you'll lose me too, I understand. I'm scared too, but that's no reason not to try. You won't lose me, I promise. Come on, Catanya. Don't run away from me, please." He stood just behind her and spoke softly, "I don't want to lose you either. Not when we've only just begun... please, Catanya. Whatever you're scared will happen, we'll figure it out together. Please. I love you." He paused before resting his hand on her arm. "I love you," he said again, his voice shaky with emotion.

His words echoed inside her head. Tears trickled down her face as she turned around to face him, her resolve to leave weakening with every second. She reached forward and kissed him hard on the mouth. Jémys reacted quickly, wrapping his arms around her and drawing her into a tight embrace. They stood like that, locked together under the stars, until Catanya pulled away, wiping her eyes.

She looked at him and said, "I love you too." Then she laughed shakily, feeling her fear and tension melt away.

Jémys's face lit up with joy. He locked his lips around hers again, momentarily lifting her off the ground. When they pulled apart this time, his eyes drifted over her face with a twinkle that made her ache, pushing aside every concern she had. She dropped her travel bag.

They'd figure everything else out later, but right now—

She pressed her lips against his again, moving them gently at first, but then the kissing became more urgent. She parted his lips and instinctively slid her hands down his chest to the laces on the front of his tunic. Jémys paused, but then he moved his hands to meet hers as they untied the laces and pulled the tunic over his head. She unfastened her cloak and tossed it on the ground, as Jémys loosened her bodice and pulled her dress away from her body.

The air was cold on her skin, but Jémys's body warmed her as he pulled her tight. His rough hands were gentle as they glided down her back and gripped her waist. She ran her hands over his chest and felt the strength of his arms holding her close as he kissed her neck.

She'd never been in love before. It surprised her how different everything felt because of it. Her passion for him was so intense that every touch, every kiss was stronger than any she'd experienced before.

She pressed herself against him harder, trying to show him she wanted more. She wanted all of him. They shed their remaining clothes and sank to the ground. Jémys's long, wavy hair fell in his face as he ran his lips down her chest towards her stomach. Catanya twisted her fingers through his hair and brought his face back up to meet hers. She felt his fingers grip her legs as she wrapped them around his waist. And then their eyes met and Catanya exhaled as he pushed himself inside her.

They lay there motionless for a moment, breathing each other in, until Catanya's lips found his and she urged him to continue. Grasping at his shoulders, she held her breath as he moved above her, trembling and sweating.

She wanted to call out, to laugh and cry, and exclaim her passion to the stars. Her soul was aching and her skin was on fire, and sooner than expected, she felt her body tighten. She arched her back and squeezed his arms, as a wave of release coursed through her, and she laughed.

Jémys's eyes gleamed. She grinned at him, pulling his face down to hers. They shared a long, tender kiss. Then she buried her face in his neck as he started moving again, slowly at first and then faster and faster. Jémys pulled away from her and moaned as his body shuddered.

Catanya laughed again and propped herself up on her elbow, watching as he rolled onto his back and smiled. He wrapped his arm around her, drawing her close and kissing her once more. Then he pulled Catanya's discarded cloak over them to keep warm.

They lay pressed together, gazing up at the stars until they both fell asleep, and for one blissful moment, nothing else mattered.

But then Catanya awoke with a start. She was disoriented. She couldn't tell what had woken her. Then she heard someone scream—a high, blood-curdling scream coming from the village. She twisted around to find the source and was met with a horrible vision. The entire village was in flames.

15

# PAIN AND WRATH

Catanya and Jémys scrambled to their feet and pulled their clothes on, before racing back across the field towards the house. Below in the village, they could see people running in every direction, pursued by menacing figures on horseback. Rows of houses were ablaze and everywhere, people were screaming.

A small group of riders broke away and raced up the lane towards the manor house.

"No!" called Jémys, but Catanya grabbed him and pulled him down and out of sight.

"Shh. We need to be careful," she whispered. "Let's go in around back."

Keeping as low as possible, they ran along the wall towards the back door, where they stopped to listen. They could hear banging and shouting as the men broke the front door and crashed into the house.

"What is the meaning of this?" came Nelle's voice from inside. "You!" Her tone was accusatory, and Catanya thought she must have recognized one of her attackers.

"Search those rooms," commanded a rough voice. "Bring out anyone fit enough to work."

"How dare you—"

There was a dull thud and a cry of pain. One of the soldiers had hit Nelle.

"Have you seen this woman?" he shouted. There was a rustle of parchment and another thud. "Tell me!"

Jémys was livid. He made a motion as though he were about to storm the house, but Catanya held out her arm to stop him.

"Just wait," she mouthed.

"I don't know what you're talking about," cried Nelle.

Jémys gave Catanya an inquiring look, but Catanya shook her head and moved in closer to the door to listen.

"There's no one here, sir," came a second man's voice.

There was a heavy crash followed by a shout of frustration.

"Maífírkon, sir?"

"Very well. Take anything valuable. Round up the ten strongest villagers and put them with the rest. We cannot return to the king empty-handed," said the maífírkon. Then Catanya and Jémys listened as he stomped out of the house, leaving his men behind to ransack it.

"How dare you?" shouted Nelle again. "You think you can just take whatever you want? Hurt whoever you want? Well, I'm sick of it! Where is my nephew? What have you done to him?"

Catanya eyed Jémys and saw a deep, dark pain etched on his face.

The commotion inside sounded like Nelle was putting up a fight. Then, before Catanya could stop him, Jémys burst through the door. He was unarmed, but he had the element of surprise as he launched himself at the man attacking his aunt and wrestled the sword out of his hand. Then in one swift movement, he brought the sword through the air, cutting the man down. As the soldier fell, his two companions sprang forward to engage Jémys.

The entire world seemed to slow as Catanya watched what happened next. Jémys disarmed one man and knocked him to the ground. Then he thrust the sword out towards the man's neck, ready to strike, but the other soldier broke free from the scuffle and yanked Nelle off the floor, holding a knife against her throat.

Everyone froze, staring at each other and not daring to move.

"Think carefully, sonny," said the firkon, as he pressed the tip of his blade against Nelle's neck.

"Alright." Jémys's eyes were wide as he backed away slowly, releasing the man from the floor, so he could jump to his feet. "Alright, just don't hurt her," said Jémys, dropping the sword to the ground with a clang.

The man holding Nelle sneered. "Sentimental fool... kill him." He nodded the instruction towards his partner.

"No!" cried Nelle and Catanya in unison.

As Nelle grappled with her captor, Catanya jumped forward. She clawed at the other man's hand, trying to wrestle the fallen sword out of his grasp. He elbowed her in the ribs and she cried out. Blinking away tears of pain, she stomped on his foot and shoved him so he stumbled and lost his balance. Taking advantage of his instability, Catanya kicked him in the chest.

With a sickening crack, he smashed his head against the stone mantle and slumped down in a heap, his neck twisted at a strange angle.

Surprised at herself, Catanya just stared at his motionless body, watching as blood began to seep from his fractured skull.

For a moment, nobody moved, and then the man holding Nelle called out in anger. Nelle twisted and struggled to escape, but he plunged his blade through her ribs, yanked it back out, and pushed her away before turning and dashing out of the house.

Nelle stumbled forward a few steps and then collapsed into Jémys's arms.

"No... no, no, no, no." Jémys stammered as he tried to hold Nelle upright. "No, no! Hold on, Aunt, hold on."

Nelle reached up to touch her nephew's face and smiled thinly. "It's okay," she said in a weak voice. Blood was streaming from the wound on her side and she was fading quickly. She struggled to keep her eyes open.

Jémys cast a frightened look at Catanya. "Help me. What do I do?"

"I—"

But Catanya didn't know what to say. She moved forward and placed her hand on Jémys's shoulder.

Nelle's eyes slid in and out of focus. "Find him," she whispered, finally locking her gaze on Jémys.

Catanya frowned. It surprised her to hear Nelle encouraging Jémys to seek revenge.

"Find him. Promise me you'll find him." Her eyes glistened as she put her hand on her nephew's face.

Jémys sobbed and closed his eyes. "I promise." Tears were pouring down his face as he lowered his aunt to the floor. "I love you."

Nelle smiled. "I love you too. Both of you."

And then, with one final shudder, she was gone.

Jémys clutched at his aunt's lifeless body, rocking back and forth and weeping.

Catanya was hollow. She couldn't believe Nelle was dead. They hadn't known each other long, but in their short time together, Catanya had grown to care for her deeply. To love her like family too. And now her affection was soured by guilt.

"I have to leave," she said, pulling herself out of her numbness.

Jémys turned his tear-streaked face towards her, but before he could respond, they heard screaming outside.

Jémys's face contorted in anger. He laid his aunt down with care, and stood up, snatching his sword off the table. "We have to help them." He marched out of the house.

Catanya gave a heavy sigh and followed him.

Great clouds of billowing smoke were rising from the village centre, and a blinding orange light contrasted calamitously with the darkness of the night.

The entire orchard was on fire, ablaze with a canopy of flames that traced the outlines of the trees and stretched up towards the sky in a towering inferno. The sound was deafening and the heat overwhelming, as the firestorm raged and the flames soared through the air, latching onto anything and everything in their path.

People were running in every direction in mass panic.

Catanya and Jémys choked on the smoke as they struggled to wend their way through the chaos. They could see the firkon dragging people from their homes and striking them down as they attempted to escape.

"Get off me!"

Roslin was struggling against a massive firkon who held her by the neck. She stomped down hard on his foot and he released her.

"Oh, you're a feisty one," he taunted, advancing on her. "Royal or not, I think I'll have a turn with you right now." He grabbed her and pinned her to the ground, but Jémys seized him and swung him off. Then Jémys struck him hard, and the man fell to the ground, unconscious, blood trickling from the wound on his head.

Catanya reached down for Roslin, who was straightening out her dress.

"Thank you," she said, as Catanya pulled her to her feet. "What's going on? Why are the firkon attacking us?"

Jémys's mouth set in a hard line. "I don't know, but listen, Rosy, you need to hide." He sounded frantic and worried. "Go up to the manor house. They've already searched it, so you should be safe there."

Roslin nodded, then turned and started running up the street.

Jémys turned to face Catanya. He opened his mouth to say something, but just then a high-pitched voice screamed her name.

They spun around to see Olly, silhouetted against the flames, running as fast as he could.

"Catanya, they know!" he cried as he raced towards them.

Terror flooded through Catanya as she remembered the night in Faltir. She couldn't let it happen again.

Catanya and Jémys started running to meet Olly, but before they could close the gap, three riders appeared behind him.

"Seize the boy," called the rider in front.

Jémys let out a strangled cry. "Don't touch him!"

"Catanya, Jémys, help me!" shouted Olly, as he tried desperately to outrun the soldiers.

One soldier twisted in his saddle and Catanya recognized the man from Faltir, the firkon she had narrowly escaped in the forest. "Wait, that's her!" he cried. "We found her! Forget the boy, seize that woman!"

"No!" Olly stopped running and turned around, trying to block their path. But he was too small.

"Olly, don't—" The anguish in Jémys's voice was piercing, and he ran even faster.

Catanya raced to keep up with him.

They weren't going to make it.

The man's horse reared up and kicked Olly hard in the face. Olly hit the ground and before he could move, the firkon brought his horse down upon him. Olly cried out in pain and the man sneered as he drew his sword and drove it through the little broken body.

"NO!" screamed Catanya and Jémys in unison.

Cold, blind fury shot through Catanya like the sword that killed her friend. The ground beneath her feet trembled as tears of rage filled her eyes. She screamed a high, raw battle cry. Her eyes burned gold as the power she had been ignoring and repressing took hold of her, encasing her in a brilliant light.

She read the fear in their eyes, as the stars darkened and the wind howled uncontrollably around them. Shards of wood, stone, and glass whirled around her in a tempest of debris, and the flames behind the firkon swelled to even wilder heights. She advanced on them, sending wave upon wave of rubble careening towards them. The horses reared up in fear and sent their riders crashing to the ground. She watched, enjoying the sight of the men fleeing for safety from her violence. She delighted in bringing them pain. They deserved it.

They deserved to die.

"Catanya?" called a voice over the noise. It sounded distant, and it echoed in the wild storm around her. She turned to see Jémys watching her, a look of horror in his eyes. She stared at him for a moment, not registering what was happening. Then she let go.

The storm stopped immediately. Catanya glanced down at her hands in surprise. The firkon were lying scattered on the ground, bloodied and unconscious. The nearest firkon groaned and moved. Before he could stand up, Catanya grabbed Jémys by the hand and ran.

They ran across the fields towards the forest and plunged into the tree cover.

"Catanya, what—"

"I'll explain later, right now we need to run."

"Catanya." He was pointing at her. "Your hair."

"What?" She reached up and pulled her hair across her eyes to see it. Where once her hair had been black, now there were large strands of iridescent colour interwoven throughout.

"Never mind that now. Come on," she said, dropping the

strands. "We need to put as much distance as possible between us and those soldiers."

<hr>

They ran through the forest all night. They ran for ages without stopping until the darkness had ebbed and a fine mist hung in the pale morning air.

"Okay, stop!" shouted Jémys, grinding to a halt and doubling over to catch his breath. "Stop. We've gone far enough. We need to talk."

Catanya stopped beside him, panting and clutching at a stitch in her side. For several minutes, neither of them said anything.

"Jémys, I—" she started, but broke off. She didn't know how to begin. She was devastated and overwhelmed, and she couldn't bear to imagine how Jémys must be feeling. His entire life, everything he loved, had been ripped apart and shattered, and there was nothing she could say to change that.

"What was all that back there?" He stared at her with apprehension on his face. "Who are you?" There was an almost accusatory wariness in his eyes.

"I'm-I'm, well..." She didn't know how to say it. She cast around helplessly, looking for some way to explain it.

"You have magic." It wasn't really a question. Jémys's voice was calm, but it sounded strained and higher than usual, as he eyed her sharply.

Catanya turned her gaze to meet his and braced herself. "Yes," she said, grimacing.

He nodded mechanically. "Then it's true. Everything Olly said is true." He had a far-off look that gave him a slightly mad appearance. "You're the king's sister."

Catanya felt sick as she studied his face. "Yes... I'm so sorry, I wanted to tell you, but—"

"You're a royal?" He was shaking now and he seemed to be struggling to process everything. He ran his hands through his hair and clenched his fists around it. "You're a royal," he repeated. His tone had shifted so that now Catanya heard a definite note of disapproval in it. "You're the king's sister and he sent his firkon to find you. That's why you were on the run when we met, and that's why they raided Finnua. They were looking for you."

Catanya closed her eyes and sighed. "Yes."

Jémys nodded again, obviously struggling to contain his emotions. "So this was all because of you. The village, Nelle, Olly—"

His voice cracked, and he stopped, blinking tears out of his eyes.

Catanya moved forward instinctively and laid her hand on his arm, but he pulled it out of her grasp.

"Don't." His eyes were reproving as he backed away from her. "Please don't touch me." He stared at her as if it were his first time truly seeing her. "You lied to me," he spoke in a hard whisper. "And now everyone I love is dead!"

"I'm sorry," she groaned. "Please believe me. I never meant for this to happen. I never wanted any of this."

"Believe you?" He laughed a little hysterically. "Why should I believe anything you say?" He was shaking his head. "You've been lying to me since the beginning. And now look at you. Look at your hair!" He pointed at her, his expression panicky. "You know they say that's how *he* looks. They say the *magic*"— he jerked reflexively as he said it—"they say it did that to him too."

A shiver went down Catanya's spine. She seized her hair and started frantically weaving it into tight braids. "Jémys, I—"

"I can't believe this!" His voice was getting louder. "You're a royal. You're one of them."

"That's not true." Catanya's eyes started filling with tears.

She couldn't bear to hear him say that, and the hostility in his eyes made her ache. "Jémys, I'm still me. And I love you." She tried to take his hand again. "I love you," she repeated. "That's why I wanted to leave. I thought if I left, everyone would be safe, but..." She trailed off, unable to continue.

Jémys groaned and buried his face in his hands. "I should have let you go, I shouldn't have stopped you." He was rambling, as he rubbed his face and backed away from her even farther, wearing a mingled look of fear and betrayal. "I should never have brought you to Finnua with me. Maybe then, they might still be alive."

Catanya felt her insides twist. "Jémys, please," she pleaded. "I don't know what to do. Tell me what you need me to do."

Pain and sadness clouded his features as Jémys cast around, at a loss for words. There was a long, heavy pause before he spoke again. When he finally did, it relieved Catanya to hear him sounding somewhat calmer.

"I don't understand how this could happen. How can you be his sister? How can you even have these powers?"

Catanya frowned. "I-I don't fully understand it myself. I never knew the truth until a couple months ago. Then suddenly I had a mother and a brother and these powers..." She held her hands up, examining them uneasily.

Despite everything that had just happened, she still had trouble believing it. She didn't know how she'd received these powers, nor how she'd managed to use them.

"You should have seen yourself back there." Jémys's tone was dark, and he shivered at the memory. "I've never seen anything that terrifying before."

The thought of it scared Catanya too. She had never felt so out of control in her life, and she couldn't believe the blinding anger and violence she'd experienced. In one night, she had already caused so much damage. She'd killed one man, and she felt sure she would have killed them all if Jémys hadn't stopped her.

Never before had she relished the idea of causing someone pain. It scared her to think she'd changed. Because even now, there was a small part of her that wished she'd done it—she wished she had killed them all.

"Jémys..." Catanya fidgeted nervously. "I never wanted these powers. I never wanted to hurt anyone." She needed him to believe that she wasn't like the rest of her family.

Jémys breathed heavily and looked at her. "That doesn't change anything, Catanya. People are already getting hurt, people are dead."

They stared at each other for a while, feeling the distance between them growing.

"I don't expect you to forgive me," said Catanya in a small voice.

Jémys just nodded and said nothing.

"So where do we go from here?" she asked.

# INTERLUDE

## CADYAN

# THE CESSION

Cadyan was agitated. After pacing back and forth outside the chamber for almost ten minutes, he still hadn't mustered enough courage to go inside. He wasn't sure what to expect when he did.

It baffled him that his mother had been in there all night. How did she do it? How did she play the role of concerned, loving queen when she hated the man more than anyone?

Cadyan had never been as adept at concealing his emotions. As a child he had believed—as he suspected most children do—that he loved his father and his father loved him. But that was a child's fantasy. Several years had passed since he'd dropped all pretence of affection for the man.

It was too exhausting to pretend.

But how was he supposed to behave now? What was he supposed to do when the man he hated died?

Cadyan stopped pacing and stared at the door. He knew he needed to go inside. He needed to witness it, to know it was finally over. But he still found himself unable to move.

Cadyan groaned and rubbed his face in frustration. *The man is on his deathbed, so why am I still so scared?* He hated feeling like this. Weak. He'd spent his entire childhood cowering from that man, overpowered by fear and dread, and he'd promised himself it was over.

*You're a grown man now, and you will look your father in the eye before he dies.*

Cadyan took a deep breath, placed his hand on the door, and pushed it open.

The room was dark. The shutters were closed and the fire had burned down, leaving mere embers glowing behind the grate. The few candles scattered around flickered their feeble lights without penetrating the gloom.

The macabre ambiance lent an air of self-important gravitas to the situation. Cadyan almost let out a snort as he thought to himself that even on his deathbed, Casréyan was an arrogant ass.

Rolling his eyes, Cadyan closed the door behind him and crossed over to the chair by the fire, where his mother sat slumped. He thought from her posture that she was sleeping, but as he approached, he realized her eyes were open.

"Mother? Have you been here this whole time?"

Fehla sat up straighter in her chair, rubbing her tired eyes as she looked up at her son. "I needed to be here," she mumbled. "But I didn't think you'd come..."

Cadyan shrugged. "I almost didn't. But like you said, I needed to be here." He grabbed the iron and stoked the fire before sitting in the chair opposite her.

Fehla nodded and turned her attention towards the bed in the corner. Cadyan could hear the irregular rustling of blankets and the faint murmur of continuous spluttering and gasping, but he stared resolutely at the fire, watching it flicker back to life.

"Grante says any minute now." Fehla spoke in a low, shaky voice. Anyone who didn't know her might have mistaken her tone for sadness, but Cadyan knew better.

"Good," he said, finally turning his gaze towards the man in the bed.

King Casréyan wasn't a large man, but the shadowy outline of his contorted body seemed bulky beneath the mountain of covers. It was as though the servants had attempted to conceal his grotesque form, but they'd only made it more obvious.

Even Cadyan had to admit the scene was hard to watch.

He turned his gaze back to his mother's face. She was half in shadow, but for a brief moment he thought he detected a smile. Then he blinked, and it was gone.

"Are you alright?" he asked.

Fehla pursed her lips. "Yes... and no," she replied. Then she reached out, taking his hand in hers and squeezing it gently.

Cadyan didn't need her to explain, he understood completely. "I've been dreaming about this for longer than I can remember," he said.

Fehla's brow creased, and she tilted her head. "I'm sorry," she said, and she sounded sad.

Cadyan was taken aback. He stared at her.

Fehla squeezed her eyes shut. "It cannot be good that we've spent our lives wishing for the death of another." She let go of his hand and leaned back in her chair, rubbing her forehead, and looking older than Cadyan had ever seen her. "I'm sorry you were made to feel that way. I'm sorry for a lot of things."

They sat together in silence, each lost in their own thoughts as they listened to the sounds coming from the bed in the corner.

Cadyan knew his father was in agonizing pain, and a small part of him wanted to feel sympathy, to care. But he couldn't. Instead, he felt something darker and more twisted. Cadyan suppressed a shudder as he tried not to let those feelings overwhelm him.

He never wanted to be like that, like *him*.

"Things will be better now, Mother." Cadyan endeavoured

to sound reassuring. "We will finally be free from him. And when I am king, I'll do things differently."

Fehla smiled at him, but it didn't quite reach her eyes. Cadyan's heart sank.

"You don't believe in me," he grumbled. It wasn't the first time he'd suspected his mother of doubting him and his ability to rule. He had always hoped he was imagining it, but here they were on the brink of getting everything they'd ever wanted, and she still wasn't happy.

"No, no." Fehla waved her hand. "Of course I believe in you, son. It's just..." She inhaled and stood up, walking towards the window where the pale light of dawn was barely visible through the slats of the shutters. "I wish you didn't have to do this. I wish you could lead a normal life."

"Normal?" Cadyan grimaced. "What, you mean you wish we were commoners?" He couldn't understand why anyone would wish for that. From everything he'd seen, commoners led dismal, pitiful lives. Why would he choose that when he was destined for greatness?

"No, not commoners. But—" She whirled around to face him, her eyes alight with a fervour he'd never seen before. "What if you didn't drink the elixir? What if you just let its power go?"

Cadyan gaped at her. "What? Why would you even suggest such a ridiculous idea? The King of Caerlon always takes the elixir."

"Yes, but what if you didn't? You don't need it, Cadyan." Her voice sounded strained and urgent.

"Yes, I do," he said. He'd spent his entire life dreaming about that elixir. He would not walk away from it now.

Fehla sighed resignedly. "You're so young," she mumbled. "Trust me when I tell you the things you want when you're young don't always turn out for the best. There's still so much you don't understand." She gave him an indulgent, almost pitying smile and Cadyan felt a stab of annoyance. He despised being pitied. All his life, everywhere he went, people pitied him. But he was the prince. It wasn't supposed to be like that.

"I understand plenty," he muttered. After today, no one would dare pity him again.

Fehla seemed to realize she'd upset him, so she walked back over to where he sat and placed her hand on his shoulder. "I just want you to be happy, son. And I see little happiness in Caerlon anymore."

Before Cadyan could respond, a gentle knock sounded, and a servant entered, accompanied by the physician.

"Ah, Grante," said Cadyan, grateful for the interruption. "You've returned." He adopted a solemn demeanour, and stood up, walking over to join the physician. "How is he?"

Grante moved over to the bed and Cadyan followed, somewhat reluctantly.

Up close, he could see the pain and fear etched on his father's face. Casréyan's bloodshot eyes gazed forward imploringly, as his body continued to seize in uncontrollable fits.

Grante lifted a heavy satchel and placed it on a table by the bed. He bustled around for a few minutes, mixing a putrid brown tonic that steamed as he lifted it and attempted to tip its contents into the king's mouth.

"Drink, Your Majesty, it will alleviate some of your pain."

Cadyan felt a flash of pettiness as he privately hoped the tonic wouldn't work. He chanced another glance at his mother, wondering if she was hoping the same. But she had her back facing him and stood gazing into the fire.

Grante struggled to pry open the king's mouth and pour in some tonic, but Casréyan spluttered and the liquid dribbled down his chin, staining his bed clothes.

Grante sighed and wiped the remaining tonic away. "I'm afraid there's nothing more I can do." He turned to face Cadyan. "You should send for the chaplain now."

Cadyan was temporarily stunned. He stared down at his father and watched as outrage and frustration mixed in with the pain. The king could still understand everything that was happening, but he was trapped, frozen and powerless.

Cadyan felt a warped smirk form on his face, as he continued to stare at the man he loathed. He had to fight the sudden urge to laugh.

This was too perfect.

Clearing his throat, he struggled to keep his voice even as he instructed the servant to fetch the chaplain.

"Thank you, Grante," he said, wrenching his gaze away from his father's face. "I know you did everything you could." He could hear the badly contained sarcasm beneath his words, but he didn't care.

"Of course, Your Highness." Grante sounded strained, and as he repacked his satchel, he avoided making eye contact.

"What is it?" asked Cadyan. "Speak your mind, Grante."

Fehla stepped away from the fire, curious.

Grante cleared his throat. "Well." He fumbled with the clasps on his satchel. "It's just that this illness, it's unlike anything I have ever seen before."

Cadyan waited for him to continue, but when Grante didn't elaborate, he jerked his head. "And?"

Grante exhaled heavily and turned to face him, still not making eye contact. "And... well, I don't believe it is an illness, my lord."

"What do you mean?" asked Fehla. Grante gave her a meaningful look.

Comprehension was dawning on Cadyan now. Ignoring the silent exchange between the other two, he glanced back at his father's contorted form.

"Poison," he said. Someone had poisoned his father, poisoned the king. "Who could have done this?"

He sensed movement around him and looked up to see

Grante, his mother, the chaplain, and the servant all standing around, staring at him. It surprised him to see them all. He hadn't heard the others arrive. He frowned as they traded nervous glances and awkwardly avoided his gaze.

Suddenly Cadyan understood, and once again he had to fight the urge to laugh.

They thought *he* had done it. They thought he had poisoned his father. Cadyan turned his attention back towards his father and saw the same conclusion written on his face.

Cadyan did not try to conceal his delight anymore. "Well, why not?" he whispered so only his father could hear. "What was the poison?" He addressed the room at large, not taking his eyes off Casréyan. The expression of betrayal and fear was too delightful. He'd never seen those emotions on his father's face before and he wanted to remember it.

Grante cleared his throat again. "I'm afraid that whatever poison was used is not something I recognize." He walked up to stand beside Cadyan once more. "But whatever it was, I'd say it was chosen because of this effect." He gestured towards the king. "Someone wanted him to die painfully." Grante shuddered, grabbed his satchel off the table, and walked away from the bed.

Fehla inched forward to stand next to her son. The king's eyes darted towards her face and for a moment Cadyan thought his father seemed surprised.

"Well, Mother, I suppose we need to find whoever did this, don't we?" Cadyan was smiling outright now, as he waited for her to look at him, but she didn't move. She was staring transfixed at her husband, with a haunted look in her eyes.

"Mother?" Cadyan frowned as he reached out and touched her shoulder. She gave a little start and turned abruptly, walking away from the bed to reclaim her position next to the fire.

And then, without warning, Casréyan seized. He convulsed

uncontrollably, spluttering and gasping. It sounded as though his lungs had finally succumbed to the paralysis. He was flailing and spasming in ways that looked excruciating, and even Cadyan had trouble watching.

"It's time," said Grante. He was standing next to Fehla by the fire and surveying her closely.

"Very well," wheezed the chaplain. He was carrying a dagger and a wooden chest about the size of a small book that was adorned with golden inlay and violet gemstones. He walked over to Cadyan and placed the items on the bedside table. "You know what to do." He inclined his head and backed away.

Cadyan's pulse quickened and his breathing felt shallow and weak, but he nodded. He did know what to do.

Trying his best to ignore his father's spluttering, he reached forward to unlock the chest. He was surprised to find his hands trembling. He didn't know if it was fear or excitement that he felt. The lid swung open to reveal a small glass vial nestled in a velvet cushion. The vial was nearly empty, but a small amount of dull yellowish liquid had settled at the bottom.

Cadyan lifted the vial out carefully and held it up to the nearest candle. He twirled it around, examining every angle. It was such a modest, inconsequential object, and anyone who didn't know better would probably discard it as unimportant.

But it was the single most important item in all of Caerlon.

"Well, Father." Cadyan spoke quietly as he uncorked the vial and slid the dagger off the table. "The time has finally come."

He paused, bracing himself before he closed his fist around the blade and pulled, carving a long gash into his palm. It hurt, but Cadyan didn't mind. He was accustomed to pain far worse than this. As the blood trickled down his wrist, he tossed the dagger back onto the table and held the vial out to collect the first glistening drop.

The blood connected with the yellow liquid and rested on top without sinking, almost as if the liquid was resisting it. Then slowly the fluids began to swirl and sizzle, letting off a delicate steam. The red and yellow gradually mixed until the vial's entire contents glowed like polished copper.

The first step was complete. He'd marked himself as its next master, the only one who could claim its power. He should have done it years ago to protect the family legacy, but Casréyan had never allowed that.

Of course, Casréyan had never intended to die.

Cadyan leaned over the bed once again, watching the man writhing beneath him. "I hate you." His voice was colder and crueller than he'd ever heard it before, and it gave him a strange sense of strength. "I hate you more than anything in this world and it gives me true pleasure to know that this"—he gestured towards his father's contorted form—"this is how you will die. Pathetic, tormented, and undignified. While everything you ever wanted is taken from you."

Cadyan laughed a mirthless laugh. "Your precious throne is mine. And your elixir... well..."

He smiled triumphantly as he waved the vial above his father's face.

The king gave a great heave and his entire body seized.

"I hope the stories are true, you know?" whispered Cadyan, ignoring his father's convulsions. "I hope your spirit remains trapped forever in eternal torment, forced to sustain the power you craved so much. *My* power now."

Casréyan gave a loud shuddering gasp, and Cadyan leaned in closer so he could observe his father's last moments. "Enjoy death, Father."

And finally, Casréyan lay still.

There was a long silence as everybody waited, watching.

Then a low rumbling began to resonate throughout the

room as Casréyan's body gave off a faint glow that grew brighter with each passing second.

*This is it*, thought Cadyan, as he held up the vial.

A powerful wind filled the room, billowing and gusting in every direction as though it couldn't escape.

Cadyan held the vial even higher and felt as the wind, which seemed trapped and confused, slowly oriented itself in his direction.

It was like standing at the centre of a squall. Cadyan struggled to stay upright and keep his hands around the vial, as the wind billowed and buffeted him on its way towards the glass. His ears were deafened by the sound and his eyes stung from the force.

Then his palms began to burn, as the vial filled up before his very eyes. He forced himself to ignore the pain and keep his grip on the glass. He could smell his flesh burning. His muscles shook as he fought the instinct to let go.

As the liquid reached the top and turned a brilliant golden colour, the wind slowly died down.

And then, as abruptly as it had started, it stopped, leaving an aching silence that was almost worse than the squall.

Cadyan stood still, shaking in pain and exhaustion. His hands were raw as he peeled them from the glass and jammed the stopper into the vial, before laying it back in the chest.

He was trembling from head to toe. He examined his hands to find them blistered and caked in blood. But he didn't care.

"Your Highness?"

Cadyan turned to see the others observing him nervously.

"I'm fine." It surprised him how eerily calm he felt.

"Give me your hands." Grante rushed forward and began bustling around for bandages. "These burns are bad, and this gash... I'm afraid you're going to scar."

"No, I won't. The elixir will heal them," muttered Cadyan. He wasn't paying attention to what Grante was doing. Instead, he stared across the room at his mother, who was watching him with tears in her eyes.

"What is it?" he asked, feeling distant from himself and from her. He couldn't make sense of her expression. Was it fear? Relief?

Fehla's face went blank and she turned to leave.

Cadyan felt disappointed as he watched her go.

Somewhere nearby, the chaplain cleared his throat. "Your Highness?" he prompted. "Shall I return the elixir to the strongroom?"

Cadyan stared at him, a little dazed. "Y-yes." He shook his head, trying to clear it. "Yes, take it to the strongroom. I will announce the king's passing later today. We'll have the customary two-week mourning period. Set my coronation for a fortnight tomorrow. On the full moon."

Cadyan suppressed a shiver. A full moon. He liked the imagery of that.

"Of course, Your Highness." The chaplain collected the elixir and held it reverently as he shuffled towards the exit. But then he stopped and turned to face Cadyan. He cleared his throat and spoke in a steady voice. "I mean, Your *Majesty*. The king is dead, long live the king." Then he stooped into a low bow and left.

# PART II

16

## SLAEDIR RETURNS

"Good morning, Priya." Diyah walked through the open door into the cramped stone house. "How is he today?"

"Slept the whole night. I think he's breathin' better too. And his cheeks have got some colour."

Diyah crossed to the corner, where a small boy lay sleeping in a bed. She placed her hand on his forehead, then turned to smile at Priya. "Yes, his fever has broken. A few more days' bed rest and he should be back on his feet. Just make sure he drinks this tincture every morning for a week." She handed the mother a small bottle of grey liquid. "It will help him ward off another bout of this illness."

"Oh, thank you, miss. Thank you. You have been a blessing. How can I ever repay you?"

"Oh, no, that's not necessary," said Diyah, but Priya seemed not to hear her.

"And you, sir!" Priya indicated Julyán, who was looming in the doorway, watching the scene. "Thank you, sir. You've been so kind."

Diyah cleared her throat and shot Julyán a look of deepest loathing. Julyán eyed her briefly before he turned to Priya. "I do only as the king commands."

"The king! Bless him. He truly cares for his people, doesn't he?" She beamed at Diyah.

"Yes, he's so... *magnanimous.*" The words were sour in Diyah's mouth, but she knew better than to disparage Cadyan in front of Julyán.

Julyán just watched her, his countenance as inscrutable as ever, but Diyah thought she detected a hint of amusement.

Diyah had been visiting Priya and her son for over a week, trying to cure him of his near-fatal illness. Throughout every visit, Julyán had never left her side. Cadyan didn't trust her and he had tasked Julyán with watching her every move. When he wasn't following her on her house calls, he was standing guard outside her chambers. It was like having a second shadow, but one who reported everything she did to her enemy.

Diyah remained every bit the prisoner she had been since first setting foot in Caerlon. The only difference was that now her captors expected her to work for them.

But Cadyan had been true to his word—he'd released the girls from the dungeon—and knowing they were safe made everything Diyah had to endure worthwhile. And although she would never admit it, she was grateful to be working again, even if it was on Cadyan's behalf. Diyah needed to help people, she needed to make a difference. It didn't matter if these people thought Cadyan was to thank for it, it mattered that Diyah was making their lives a little easier.

In addition to Priya's son, Diyah had already helped half a dozen other children who were suffering from a similar illness. She had also helped an aging cobbler ease his chalkstones, a fisherman cure his dropsy, and had offered a remedy for a young woman's chronic headache. Instead of dwelling on her situation, Diyah tried to focus on all the good she was doing.

She only really had two options. She could stay in Caerlon working forever as the court physician (or at least until Cadyan decided to kill her), or else she could try to flee and risk being killed, not to mention the ever-looming threat against the girls.

And any attempt to flee meant escaping Julyán first, which wouldn't be easy. His constant presence grated on Diyah's nerves. He barely spoke a word, and when he did, it was always cold and unfeeling. She never would have believed it possible that she could meet someone she loathed as much as Cadyan.

That being said, she knew Julyán had been the one to secure her release. If it hadn't been for him, she'd still be trapped, rotting in that cell, or dead.

She couldn't figure him out. On one hand, he'd killed Lady Genna and everyone else at Camlee Lodge without hesitating, but on the other hand...

"Why did you do it?" she asked, as they returned to the castle later that afternoon. "Why did you convince him to spare me?"

"We needed a healer," he said tonelessly.

"Right," she echoed his blankness. She should have known better than to expect a different response.

Julyán looked at her appraisingly. "The Heiltúir are all but gone. Good healers are rare in these parts. Not many people choose such a life."

"What, a life of morality and compassion? I can well imagine."

"Indeed. Few people would willingly sacrifice their own happiness for the welfare of others."

"What happiness?" She stopped in her tracks. "What happiness? Tell me. Do you honestly believe these people are happy?" She gestured back at the lower districts, where hundreds of people lived in poverty and squalor.

"No, you misunderstand me." He stopped and turned to face her. "What I mean to say is that few people would choose to spend their lives fighting to keep others alive. Struggling against the inevitability of death is a burden we all must bear. And to do so on someone else's behalf is irrational." He started walking again.

Diyah was surprised. This was the longest she'd ever heard Julyán talk, and she needed a minute to wade through everything. "So you don't care who lives and who dies?" she called after him.

"Everyone dies," he responded. "A healer merely gambles with the timing."

"So you think this is pointless then?" With every passing moment, she was growing surer of his character.

"I think it is a thankless pursuit, undertaken only by a rare few."

Diyah didn't know what to make of this statement. She was about to retort, when she heard hooves pounding behind her. A dozen men on horseback were racing along the street towards the castle.

"Julyán!" It was Slaedir calling to them from atop his horse as he slowed beside them. "So the king has you taking strolls with pretty girls, while I am sent to risk my neck for the good of the kingdom." He jumped off his horse and landed hard on the ground.

The stable boy came hurrying out to collect the reins, as Slaedir advanced on Julyán and Diyah. "Do you have any idea what we've endured while you've been here trifling with this wench? And what is she doing here, anyway? Does the king know you've been dallying with his prisoners? Do we all get a turn?" He leered as he tried to grab Diyah, but she slapped away his hand.

"I do as I'm ordered by the king," said Julyán once again. "And if I recall, the king gave you some orders too. Though it seems you haven't been very successful." He glanced around at the soldiers who were dismounting their horses, looking exhausted and disappointed. "Don't tell me you let her escape again?"

Slaedir merely grunted as he turned and traipsed up the steps into the castle. The remaining soldiers followed.

"Come." Julyán beckoned for Diyah to hurry and they climbed up the steps behind the soldiers.

"Tell the king his maífírkon has returned," Slaedir ordered a guard outside the throne room. The guard disappeared and returned a moment later to show them into the room.

"I'm sure there's no need for you to follow," Slaedir sneered at Julyán.

"Actually, sir, the king has requested that Master Julyán be present with him. A-and the healer girl," the guard stammered, gesturing towards Diyah.

"What?" Slaedir sounded incensed.

Julyán smirked and pushed Diyah into the throne room. Slaedir and his soldiers followed. As Diyah walked past them, she noticed that several of them were sporting injuries ranging from cuts and bruises to broken bones.

They proceeded down the aisle towards the dais where Cadyan stood alone with his hands on the throne, looking displeased.

"What happened?" He spoke in a dangerously quiet voice.

"My lord, we searched several villages and we've brought you countless treasures. Gold and silver, we brought everything we could find and—"

"Where is she?" Cadyan cut him off. "Why have you returned without her?"

The men behind Slaedir were shuffling nervously.

"Well, my lord. We did find her, but once again... I'm afraid she evaded our capture." Slaedir looked at his king apologetically.

Relief washed over Diyah. She smiled to herself as she thought of Catanya, still out there somewhere.

"How can that be possible?" hissed Cadyan.

"Well, sir. It is as we suspected. She does indeed have magic the same as yours. And she has grown stronger. She overpowered us. We barely escaped with our lives."

"And why should I care about your lives?" Cadyan glared at Slaedir.

A tense silence filled the room until one of the other firkon spoke. "She had help, my lord. There was a man with her."

The other men murmured and nodded.

"He was a skilled fighter, he killed two of our party. Well, one. She killed the second."

"What village was this?" interjected Julyán.

"I believe it's called Finnua. Well, it *was* called Finnua, there's not much left of it anymore."

Julyán only nodded. His face was as impassive as ever. "Were there any survivors?"

"Not many. After the girl escaped, we cleaned up the mess. Niral took a few to the dungeons to await transport. But we killed the rest," said Slaedir, with a gratified, almost reminiscent, tone.

Diyah felt sick looking at him, so she turned her gaze to Julyán. For a brief moment, she could have sworn his face bore an expression of disgust, but then she blinked and it had resumed its usual stony state.

"And how *exactly* did this upstart overpower you?" asked Cadyan.

The men all exchanged apprehensive looks.

"Well, it's hard to explain," muttered the man who had spoken earlier. "She sort of unleashed this blast of energy. It was chaos. We couldn't see anything, there was debris flying everywhere. And fire. Everywhere the fire threatened to engulf us. We couldn't escape. And the horses were crazed. They threw us off and bolted. By the time we corralled them, the girl had disappeared."

"It's true, my lord," said Slaedir. "It was unlike anything I've ever seen."

"Is that so?" Cadyan's voice was dangerously quiet again. "Unlike anything you've ever seen. So you believe she is more powerful than I am?"

"What?" Slaedir looked terrified. "No, my lord!"

"You are beginning to think she is too powerful to be stopped?"

"N-no," Slaedir stammered, backing away.

Cadyan raised his hand and the dagger fastened to Slaedir's belt flew out of its sheath and sliced through the air. Slaedir gasped in pain and raised his hand to touch the deep gash on his face.

"Once again, I find myself disappointed," spat Cadyan, slicing his hand through the air again. Then he brandished his other hand and an invisible force knocked Slaedir to the ground.

"You have failed a second time to capture the girl." He stepped forward, eyes glowing gold, and watched as Slaedir began writhing in agony, screaming.

Everyone stood, transfixed by the scene playing out in front of them.

"I am forced to wonder if perhaps you are not up to the task," snapped Cadyan as he waved his hand and sent Slaedir flying across the room, where he collided hard with one of the pillars. "Perhaps you are no longer fit to be *maífírkon*." He punctuated the last word with another wave of his hand and Slaedir was sent careening in the opposite direction.

Cadyan's nostrils flared. He threw Slaedir back and forth across the room, until he stopped abruptly and Slaedir crumpled to the floor.

"But I suppose this is my fault." Cadyan's tone was suddenly ruminative. "After all, if you want something done properly..." He kicked Slaedir, who went sliding across the floor and landed at Diyah's feet.

Diyah recoiled.

"You have another patient," declared Cadyan. Then he turned to address Julyán. "See to it she heals him quickly. Tomorrow we ride." He dismissed the remaining fírkon. "It's time I had a chat with my *dear* sister."

With that, Cadyan marched out of the room, leaving Diyah, Julyán, and Slaedir behind in awkward silence.

"Ugh, here." Diyah knelt down and used her smock to wipe blood off Slaedir's face. "Can you stand?" she asked.

"Of course I can stand," snapped Slaedir, pushing her away. "I am the Maífírkon of Caerlon. I don't need your help. What business is it of yours, anyway?"

"She is Caerlon's new healer," said Julyán.

"What?" Slaedir stared from Diyah to Julyán, then his face cracked into a painful-looking grin. "You mean to tell me that the king has started employing his prisoners?" He threw his head back and cackled with laughter. "This nag is our healer? Well, in that case, perhaps I do need her healing touch." He took a step towards Diyah, who backed away.

"The man you spoke of," interrupted Julyán, ignoring Slaedir's advances on Diyah.

"What of him?" Slaedir was still staring hungrily at Diyah.

"Who was he? Had you seen him before?"

"How should I know?" he retorted. "He seemed real cozy with her though, if you catch my drift. Seemed like they'd known each other *intimately* for a while." Slaedir cackled again. "But what does it matter?"

"You idiot," breathed Julyán with an irritable edge.

Slaedir glared at him. "What did you call me?" he growled. "I'm still your maífírkon, boy."

"Well, then, act like one! Use your head. If we figure out who the man was, it may help us predict where they'll go next."

"I bet *she* knows." Slaedir jerked his head towards Diyah. "I bet this was all part of the plan. She got herself caught so her friend could run off and be with him. I bet she knows who he is and I bet I can make her tell us too." He snatched at Diyah, but she slapped his hand away again. "Come on, love. One night with me and I'll have you calling out all kinds of names." He smirked at Julyán, who just stared blankly back at him. Slaedir laughed. "Oh, come on Julyán, live a little. You can't tell me you don't want a taste."

Slaedir attempted to grab Diyah again and pull her in, but Diyah smacked him hard in the face and sent blood from his wounds spattering across Julyán's vest. "Don't you dare touch me," she said. "Back off before I give you a real scar to worry about."

"What did you say to me?" He leaned in menacingly, but Diyah held her ground. "I'm going to make your life miserable, you hear me. I will haunt your every step and break you down until you're begging me to take you."

"You are a despicable, desperate snake. You are *pathetic*." She spat the last word at him.

"Careful now. Do you know who you're talking to?"

"Yes, I know exactly. I'm talking to a worthless, pitiful worm. Your king has just made a fool of you in front of your fírkon, so you're looking for a way to make yourself seem relevant, or maintain your delusion of authority. But a truly powerful man doesn't find strength by making others feel weak. A man of real power is strong within himself, but you'll never be that. You will always be this." She gestured at his bruised and bloodied body with a look of disdain on her face. "*Pathetic*," she repeated, enunciating every syllable.

Slaedir's face contorted in rage. "You think you can speak to me like that? You stupid little bitch, I'll show you who's powerful." He reached out to grab her again, but this time Julyán blocked him.

"What are you doing?" Slaedir glared at him.

"Leave it," said Julyán, sounding bored.

"What business is it of yours? What do you care?"

"We don't have time for this. You heard the king. We ride at dawn. Come." He beckoned to Diyah. "I'll take you back to your chambers." He grabbed her arm and steered her away from Slaedir and towards the door.

They walked in silence down the corridors through the eastern wing. Diyah was lost in her own thoughts until Julyán came to an abrupt stop. She looked up and saw a burly firkon walking towards them.

"Niral." Julyán extended his hand in greeting.

"Julyán." Niral gripped his arm briefly. "You missed out on a good one, my boy. Mind you, I expect you enjoyed your time alone here." He jerked his head in Diyah's direction and let out a long whistle.

Diyah rolled her eyes and turned her attention away from the two men as they started discussing arrangements for the following morning.

It took a while before she realized she could hear hushed voices coming from the door beside her. She chanced a glance at Julyán to make sure he wasn't watching, then she leaned in closer and strained her ears, trying to listen.

"I'm sorry, my queen. By the time I arrived in Linlon, the town had been ransacked. No one knows where he went. And no sign of the map."

"Ransacked? Was it Verratrí?"

"I believe so."

"Curse it all," grumbled Fehla. "That's just what we need." There was a short pause before she continued. "Well, I'll just have to think of something else."

When the man spoke next, he sounded timid and apologetic. "My lady, I'm sorry, but I don't think I can... Slaedir, he noticed my absence. I can't risk it again."

"What?" Fehla sounded alarmed.

"I'm sorry, I know my father promised you, but..."

"It's okay, I understand. You've done enough. I won't ask you—"

The rest of the conversation was drowned out by the sound of Niral laughing.

Diyah looked back towards them in time to see Niral leaving. Julyán tightened his grip on her arm and pushed her forwards once again.

"He seems lovely," said Diyah with scorn, pretending she had been listening.

Julyán didn't respond, but Diyah thought she noticed a slight tension in his jaw.

When they reached the physician's quarters, Julyán held the door open for Diyah, but before he could close it, she whipped around to face him. "If you're leaving, who will guard me night and day to ensure I don't escape?"

Julyán still didn't reply.

"Because I will, you know? Escape. No matter how long it takes me, I will get out of here, I promise you."

Julyán seemed to measure her up. "I have no doubt," he said in his usual blank voice. "But I'd be careful if I were you. I know three little girls who will pay the price for your actions."

Then he closed the door with a bang, and Diyah gave an involuntary start. All of her calm and composure vanished in an instant.

Julyán was the only person who knew where to find Meya, Gréys, and Hahney. He was the one who'd arranged their release. If Diyah planned to escape, she needed to make certain they were safe from him first.

Somehow.

But based on what she'd just overheard, there was at least one firkon still loyal to Fehla, so maybe that meant he'd be willing to help her too. She just needed to figure out who he was.

# 17

# A PROMISE IS KEPT

Jémys had barely said a word to Catanya for days, as they climbed vaguely northeastward through the forest, with no sense of a final destination. They stopped to rest in shifts, with one person keeping watch while the other slept, and even then, Catanya could only get a few brief words from him before he reverted to stony silence.

She didn't blame him for being angry, of course. He had every right to hate her. She had lied about who she was and that lie had gotten his entire family and village killed. No, she didn't mind his anger. Catanya was angry with herself too—furious for being so naïve and believing she could stay hidden. She knew Jémys would never forgive her, and she honestly didn't think he should. She would certainly never forgive herself.

But there was something else in Jémys's silence that did make Catanya uneasy. It took her a while to figure it out, but she saw it in the distance he left between them and the wariness he wore on his face. Jémys didn't trust her anymore. Not only did he not trust her, he was afraid of her.

Whenever it was her turn to keep watch, she would replay their argument in her head over and over.

*You're a royal?* She could still hear the disgust in his voice. *You're a royal. You're one of them.*

His words haunted her. Catanya didn't know who she was anymore, and it was tormenting her. She tried to remember who she'd been before all this happened—before she knew her ancestry. Before magic. She wished she could wake up from this nightmare and find herself back in Camlee Lodge, surrounded by people she loved.

Catanya sighed and looked at Jémys, who was sleeping, propped against a tree nearby. She reminded herself that if none of this had happened, she wouldn't have met Jémys, and as much as she longed to undo everything and go back, she couldn't fathom her life without him. It was a cruel twist of fate that the worst aspect of her life had led her to one of the best. And now everything was in turmoil again.

But even as she sat in the dark, questioning her identity, she knew one thing for sure: she loved him. And that made everything so much harder.

Catanya watched Jémys sleep while running through all her happy memories of their time together. Those memories seemed distant now, like scenes from a story she'd seen in a dream. She knew she loved him. She loved him more than she had ever loved anyone, but as she watched him sleep, she knew they'd never be what they were before. Even if he could bring himself to forgive her, their relationship would never return to what it was.

Catanya's eyes burned. She tore her gaze away from Jémys to stare at the sky. It was an uncommonly clear night. Through the canopy she could see thousands of stars twinkling above, as though taunting her and her anguish.

She heard rustling behind her and turned to see Jémys sitting up and rubbing his neck.

"How long was I asleep?" he asked.

"A few hours."

Jémys nodded and, shivering, started rubbing his arms.

In their haste to leave, he hadn't brought any travel supplies with him. All they had were the swords and the handful of items Catanya had packed for her journey before Jémys caught her in the meadow.

"Here." Catanya unfastened her cloak and handed it to him.

"No, I'm fine," he protested.

"You're not fine, you're only wearing a thin tunic. Just take it." She, at least, was wearing a thick cotton dress and long-sleeved bodice.

Jémys took the cloak from her. "Won't you be cold?"

Catanya shrugged. "I'll survive for the time being." She pulled her sleeves down tighter around her arms. This dress had been in perfect condition a few days ago, but as with everything else she owned, it was torn and filthy now. And there were several burn marks where stray sparks from the flames in Finnua had singed it.

Jémys wrapped himself up in the cloak, while Catanya began rummaging through her pack for some food.

"It's not much," she mumbled, handing him a chunk of bread. "I think we should decide where we're heading so we can plan how much to ration."

Jémys chewed on the stale bread. "Where were you planning to go that night, before... well..."

Catanya fidgeted. "I didn't have a firm plan, I just knew I needed to leave. I had thought I might be safe in Awnell."

"Safe." Jémys repeated the word blankly. "Right. Well, I suppose Awnell makes as much sense as anything. But we've been going the wrong direction. We'll need to cross the river and turn south towards the ocean if we want to reach the road leading to the city."

Catanya hesitated, and then she cleared her throat. "We? So

does that mean you want to come with me?" After everything that had happened, she'd assumed Jémys would be eager to rid himself of her. She had been on edge for days, waiting for him to announce he was leaving.

"I have nowhere else to go, do I?" Jémys stood up and brushed the crumbs off of his pants. "Come on, we may as well keep moving."

They walked for another day, eventually meeting up with the river heading south. Catanya felt nervous retracing their steps towards Finnua. What if the fírkon had regrouped and followed them into the trees? Would she be able to fight them off again? Catanya shuddered at the memory of that night. She wasn't sure what scared her more, the fírkon or her magic.

The weather grew bleaker and bleaker, and around midday a fog rolled in that gave the forest a grim sense of foreboding. As they continued walking, Catanya felt a prickling on the back of her neck, almost like someone was watching them. She tried to tell herself it was only her fear playing tricks, but she couldn't help casting around from time to time to check that no one was following them.

The sooner she and Jémys crossed the river into the eastern limits of Caerlon, the better.

Eventually the river narrowed. The water level was low enough that several large, slippery rocks protruded above the surface.

"I think we should cross now," said Catanya. The sky was overcast and the air had a frosty nip. She didn't relish the idea of braving the water, but this might be the best opportunity they'd have. "Maybe we can use the rocks as stepping stones."

Jémys merely nodded.

Together they trudged down to the river's edge. The water

rushed and frothed, filling the air with icy spray. Catanya shivered as she watched Jémys step gingerly onto the nearest rock. He teetered, getting his balance and then launched himself to the next, where he crouched low, using his hands to stabilize himself.

Catanya followed him. The rocks were uneven and jagged under her feet. More than once she nearly skidded and plummeted into the rapids below. She was panting and sweating despite the cold spray that clung to her clothes, dampening them, and she was anxious to get off the river and onto land again.

Without thinking, she sprang onto the next stone and crashed into Jémys, who had stopped. They staggered precariously and both nearly fell. Jémys grabbed hold of her and yanked her towards him.

"Ah, sorry!" she panted, clutching his arms. "Why did you stop?"

He tightened his grip and waited until they were both steady before responding, "I don't think I can make the next jump." He pointed to the nearest stone. It was at least a dozen feet away, and almost entirely submerged in water. Even if they could cross the distance, they'd most likely slip on the landing.

Catanya groaned and looked down at the water. Despite the rapid current, the water was clear, and she could see fish swimming back and forth. "It's shallower here. I can see the bottom…"

She glanced up at his face and saw the resignation forming on it. Jémys took a deep breath and nodded, but he didn't move.

Catanya ran her hands down his arms and leaned into his body, thinking about the last time they'd been this close together. Jémys suddenly let go of her, shuffling his feet awkwardly.

"Right. Sorry." She dropped her hands and felt her face flush. Then she lowered herself into a seated position, where she unlaced her shoes and stuffed them into her already full travel bag.

"There's no room for anything else," she said apologetically.

"It's fine," muttered Jémys.

Catanya tightened the bag's strap so it sat high on her back. Then she bunched up her skirts as far as she could and crept forward on the rock. She swung her legs off the edge, stifling a gasp as the frigid water enveloped her skin.

"It'll be easier if we don't think about it," she said, clenching her teeth. Then she shoved herself off the stone and into the river.

The icy water rose above her waist, drenching her skirts. The violent current tugged at her, but she planted her feet firmly on the riverbed and held her ground.

A sharp intake of breath behind her told her Jémys had followed. Shivering, she craned her neck back to see him. He had taken off his cloak, boots, and sword, and he was struggling to hold them above the water line.

"Okay," he said, "let's get this over with." He stepped forward, bracing his body against the weight of the current.

They made their way through the water with some difficulty, moving slowly and clutching at the sparse stones for support. When they reached the eastern bank and hauled themselves out, they had a few minor cuts and scrapes, but were otherwise unscathed.

"Sh-should we make a fire?" asked Catanya, trembling as she struggled to pull her shoes back on. She squeezed the excess water out of her skirts and stood up. Her dress felt heavy and it clung to her legs uncomfortably, but at least the travel bag was dry.

"I think we should keep walking until sundown. The air isn't too cold. As long as we keep moving, we should be fine." Jémys strapped his sword back onto his waist and rubbed his arms. "Here." He handed her the cloak. "My clothes will dry faster than yours." Then without waiting for a response, he stepped forward into the trees.

Catanya threw the cloak over her shoulders and followed. She was too tired to argue. They walked the rest of the day in miserable silence. The air was barely warmer than the water, but the wind blew with enough force that their drenched clothes slowly began to dry.

Catanya was exhausted. It had been more than a day since she'd last slept, and lately her nights were plagued by incessant dreams. She either dreamed about the events in Finnua, replaying the horrible scenes over and over, or she dreamed of soldiers chasing her into a clearing where she was surrounded by faceless people in linen robes. She couldn't shake the feeling that these dreams meant something and she was supposed to recognize these faceless people.

As the sun began to set, Catanya and Jémys finally stopped to make camp. Jémys took the first watch and Catanya curled up near the fire to sleep. Her clothes were almost dry, but she was trembling from fatigue and cold. She wanted to be as close to the warmth as possible.

For a brief moment, she considered asking Jémys to lie with her, but then she thought better of it. She doubted he wanted to be near her.

*At least the chances of running into fírkon on this side of the river are much slimmer,* she thought, grasping at anything that might give her comfort.

Catanya was just drifting into an uncomfortable sleep when she found herself being wrenched awake.

"What's happening?" she blurted out, trying to pull herself free from whatever was holding her.

"Catanya!"

The fear in Jémys's voice sent a shiver down her spine. She couldn't see who was holding her, and she tried desperately to tear herself free. Then something hard struck her head and everything went black.

---

"Where do you want 'em?"

"Tie the man up and guard him. Bring the woman to my tent."

Catanya could hear men cackling and hooting all around her. Her heart started to race. Someone grunted nearby and she knew Jémys had been thrown onto the ground. *He's alive,* she thought, feeling relieved. She kept her eyes closed and pretended to be unconscious while someone carried her away. She could hear Jémys protesting incoherently and knew he must be gagged.

The sound of Jémys and the other men grew fainter as whoever was carrying her moved farther away. Then suddenly and unceremoniously, she was hurled onto the ground. Working very hard to stay limp, she allowed her hands to be tied around what felt like a tree trunk.

"Leave us," came a cool voice. It sounded familiar. A pit formed in her stomach as she remembered why.

"Aye, sir. Enjoy." The second man snickered as he scampered away.

There was a brief silence and then: "You can stop pretending now. I know you're not really asleep."

Catanya begrudgingly opened her eyes to stare at the man she'd left tied to a tree in the forest.

"I love a good reversal of fortunes, don't you?" he said. "I told you that you hadn't seen the last of me, didn't I?" He chuckled to himself and crouched down so he was level with her. "Catanya, huh? Well, that's a mouthful, isn't it? Ever thought of just going by Tanya? Or Catya?"

"No," she lied.

"Interesting, I'd have thought someone like you would do anything to conceal her true identity." He held her gaze without blinking.

"I'm not sure what you mean." Catanya braced her back against the tree and pushed herself into a standing position so she was staring down at him.

"Mmm, I thought you might say that," he mused, looking up at her from his crouching position. Then he sprang to his feet. "Well, me, I think I'll be calling you Catya. I like how it rolls off the tongue. Catya." He repeated it a few more times, smiling as though enjoying the way it sounded coming out of his mouth.

"And what makes you think you'll be calling me anything, *Drayk*?"

Drayk grinned widely. "So you *do* remember me, excellent. I was worried we'd have to start over, which would have been so tedious."

Drayk crossed the tent to sit in a chair across from her. Catanya surveyed her surroundings. She was inside a large, makeshift canopy that had been erected using the nearby trees as posts. The fabric walls flapped lightly in the breeze and a small, improvised desk sat in one corner beside what appeared to be a bed. The entire tent was lined with furs and other draperies, and there were several candles and lamps on the desk, giving it a warm glow.

"Do you like it?" asked Drayk, eyeing her for a reaction. "It's my little home away from home, as it were."

Catanya said nothing. Instead, she just stared at Drayk.

Drayk smirked, apparently unfazed by her silence. "You're quite the artist," he announced, lifting her sketchbook off the table and waving it through the air. "I take it you drew these. They're really very good." He flipped through the pages. "But who's this?" He held open the book to show her the picture of himself and grinned from ear to ear.

Catanya rolled her eyes. Drayk laughed.

"No, no, I know. It's an excellent likeness. Very handsome." He gave another arrogant smirk and continued turning the pages. "Lots of pictures of your friend out there... but then there's this one." He held up the picture of Cadyan she'd drawn after one of her many nightmares. "I found this one very interesting. Tell me, have you met this man before?"

Catanya glanced at the picture and attempted to keep her face impassive.

"Have *you*?" she responded serenely. Drayk was trying to bait her. She would not let him gain the advantage.

Drayk seemed to surmise as much, because he laughed jovially and tossed her book onto the desk. "So tell me, Catya." He winked at her. "What brings you to this part of the forest?"

"Oh, just passing through," she said, adopting his casual tone while trying to mask her fear. Her heart pounded and her eyes darted around the tent, trying to find an escape.

"Passing through from where?"

"Nowhere."

She tugged at the ropes on her arms and felt them tighten unpleasantly. Even if she could escape the tent, how would she get past the other bandits outside, let alone rescue Jémys?

"Where are you headed?" Drayk asked.

She looked back at Drayk and smiled disdainfully. "Nowhere," she said again.

Drayk grinned even wider. "I see. So you're on the road to nowhere from nowhere. Sounds like a truly *riveting* adventure." He stood up and swaggered forward, placing his hand on the tree beside her head. Then, leaning in, he whispered, "Come now, why not try telling the truth?"

His face was inches away from hers and he grinned provocatively. His eyes were a piercing blue, and they sparkled beneath his dark eyebrows as he scanned her face.

Catanya struggled to suppress a shudder. "So, is this it, then?" she asked, acting braver than she felt.

"Is this what?" he asked, still gazing at her desirously.

"Is this where you force yourself on me?" She tried to sound strong and defiant, like she wasn't scared out of her mind.

Drayk frowned and leaned back. "Excuse me?"

"Oh, please." She was shocked at how shrill her voice sounded. She was panicking. "Why else would you bring me to your tent, if not for privacy?"

"Mmm." He tilted his head to the side, pursed his lips, and asked, "Is that what you want?" He raised one eyebrow, a crooked smile on his face.

"What?" Catanya was struggling hard to stay calm, but her voice was getting higher and higher. "No! Of course I don't want that. Why would that be what I want?"

"Mmm." He leaned in closer to smell her neck. "Are you sure?" he taunted. He made eye contact with her and lingered briefly, before standing up straight. "Honestly, what do you take me for?" He sounded genuinely offended. "No, darling, believe me, I can find plenty of *willing* partners. And, as gorgeous as you are, it's actually something else I want from you." He backed away and stood with his hands clasped behind his back.

His sudden shift surprised Catanya. "Something else?" she asked, eyes narrowing.

"Oh, yes." He began pacing back and forth. "You see, it's rare that someone outmatches me in a fight. I want to know how you did it. Well"—he stopped and looked at her—"no, that's not true. I know how you did it. But you're going to prove me right. There's something special about you, and I want you to show me."

"I don't understand." Catanya kept a close eye on him as he paced back and forth. "Show you what?"

"Don't play dumb with me."

Catanya raised her shoulders, trying to look innocent. "I'm not playing anything. I have no idea what you're talking about."

Drayk sighed and closed his eyes in apparent frustration. "You, Catya, have magic." When he opened his eyes again, they gleamed manically.

Catanya forced a derisive laugh. "That is absurd," she declared, trying to feign amusement, but her laugh sounded artificial and shrill.

"Is it?" Drayk raised his eyebrows expectantly. "So all those weeks ago when we met in the forest, when I had you in my grasp, and flames surged as if from nowhere, catching my coat on fire and distracting me just long enough for you to escape... that *wasn't* magic? That's just what fires do?" His tone was glib and he was smiling.

Catanya shrugged again.

"Oh, no, I don't think so." He shook his finger at her.

"Whatever you think you saw, I can assure you that you are mistaken. I suggest you accept what happened and move on with your life."

Drayk grinned at her. He was clearly enjoying himself. "What I saw was a golden flash in your eyes at precisely the moment my coat caught fire. Can you explain that?" He was walking towards her in slow measured steps.

"A trick of the light, I'm sure. My eyes are grey."

"I noticed," he said casually, moving closer still and lowering his voice to a mock whisper. "Hence my surprise when they turned bright gold. You see, in my experience, eyes tend to stay one colour."

Catanya tried to force another derisive laugh.

Drayk stared at her coldly. "I have seen enough in this world to recognize magic when I encounter it. And you, my dear, have magic... Perhaps you just need a little motivation." He smiled menacingly. "Len!" he called. "Bring the man."

"What are you doing?" asked Catanya.

"Motivating you." Drayk turned his back on her and walked away.

The man named Len appeared in the tent, dragging Jémys by the back of his shirt. He threw him on the ground at Drayk's feet.

"Thank you," said Drayk, as Len left the tent. Drayk dragged Jémys over to the chair and tied him down in it. "Now, love." He looked at Catanya again. "You have two choices. One, you let your friend here endure unimaginable pain, or two, you prove me right and I let him go."

"I don't know what you expect from me!" she shouted. "You're deluded!"

Drayk grinned widely. "It has been said before."

Then he pulled back his arm and struck Jémys hard in the face.

"Stop it!" shouted Catanya. She started wrestling with the ties on her wrists, trying to free herself. But the more she struggled, the tighter the binds became, until they were slicing into her skin and causing her hands to go numb.

"Show me what I want to see," Drayk said.

"I-I don't know how," stammered Catanya.

Drayk sighed. "Still not ready to tell the truth? Have it your way then." He struck Jémys again, sending blood spraying onto the ground.

"I *am* telling you the truth! I don't know!" shrieked Catanya, helpless and angry.

Drayk hit Jémys again, leaving a gash on his left cheek. "I don't believe you." He pulled out his sword and began heating the tip in the oil lamp flame on his desk. Turning to look at Jémys, he asked, "Have you ever experienced the pain of a scalding sword being driven through your flesh? No? Well, let me tell you, it does not feel good." He smiled at Catanya through his lashes.

"Stop! Please, stop. Why are you doing this?"

"I've already told you. I need to know I'm right." He lifted the sword out of the flame, and it burned bright. "Now, where to start, where to start…" Drayk clicked his tongue as he waved the sword over Jémys.

Jémys's eyes were wide with terror, as Drayk pressed the hot metal against the inside of his leg. The gag muffled Jémys's cries, but the sound still pierced Catanya's soul.

"STOP!" she cried and at that moment, a powerful gust pushed past her, hurling Drayk away from Jémys. He stumbled and crashed against the desk, dropping his sword so the hot metal singed a hole through the fur rug.

There was a pause before Drayk started laughing and whirled around to gaze triumphantly at Catanya. He stamped his foot on the ground and let out a whoop of enthusiasm.

"That's more like it," he exclaimed, crossing the tent to face her again. "Now, I want to hear you say it." He wagged his finger next to his ear.

Catanya glanced helplessly at Jémys before turning her eyes towards Drayk. "It's true," she muttered. "I have magic."

"I knew it." Drayk clapped his hands in the air and bent down to pick up his sword, returning it to its sheath.

"Now what?" Defeat sapped Catanya's energy and she slumped against her bonds. "What more do you want from me?"

Drayk sauntered towards her, his eyes gleaming covetously. "That'll be all for now," he said. "But we'll have another little talk soon."

He laughed in triumph as he swept out of the tent, leaving Catanya and Jémys alone.

18

# BOUND

"Jémys, can you get your hands free?"

"No, can you?"

"No."

Catanya and Jémys were tied up shoulder to shoulder, strapped against a tree a few feet from where their captors lay sleeping. The rough tree bark scraped against Catanya's hands, turning the skin raw, and her back ached from being pressed against the trunk for hours.

By Catanya's estimation, it had been three days since the outlaws had captured them. Three days since Drayk had forced her to use her powers. Since then, nothing had happened. In fact, she had scarcely seen Drayk since that first night and she was beginning to wonder what he was doing. What was he waiting for?

"I don't understand. Why don't you just—I don't know—use some sort of magic to get us out of here?" hissed Jémys as he struggled with his binds.

He was still furious with Catanya and he obviously disapproved of her magic, but apparently their current problems had taken precedence over his feelings. At this point, he seemed open to anything that might help them escape.

"I wish I could. I've been trying. But I don't really know how to control it," said Catanya.

"Well, you sure seemed to know what you were doing in Finnua," he retorted with poorly concealed bitterness.

"I was distraught and emotional. I completely lost control, and I nearly killed everyone."

It stung to hear him speaking about her powers with such a derisive tone when every time she thought about them, she felt sick with grief and pain. Every time she closed her eyes, she heard their screams and saw their faces. She never wanted that to happen again.

Jémys exhaled heavily. "So you need to lose control in order to control it. *Perfect.*"

Catanya rolled her eyes. They had gone three days without food, and the hunger was wearing on them. As angry as Jémys was with her, she knew he'd never be this rude under normal circumstances.

"Tell me, what's the *point* of having powers if you don't even know how to use them?" he snapped.

"I don't know! Okay?" blurted Catanya a little louder than she had intended. After three days of starvation, even she was having trouble keeping her emotions in check. "Look"—she lowered her voice with effort—"it's not like I asked for this, remember? I have no idea what I'm doing, and it terrifies me. I don't even know where to *begin* learning how to control them. And I can't exactly ask my brother for help," she added darkly

"Oy!" One of the men threw his canteen at them. It ricocheted off the tree an inch from Jémys's head. "Shut up! We're trying to sleep, here."

The fire was burning low, and the night was growing colder. The outlaws had spent the last three evenings drinking and gambling, while Drayk remained secluded in his tent. With each passing night, they'd become more unpredictable and unruly. It seemed the longer these outlaws stayed in one place, the more rambunctious they became.

They appeared to have unlimited supplies of barkbeer, and they drank from sunup to sundown, occasionally taking breaks to sleep or set traps for animals. Every night the gambling escalated, causing altercations that only ended when someone had a black eye and everyone else was laughing.

On this particular night, after an especially intense scuffle, the mood had been reaching an uneasy peak when someone tossed a small, round pouch on the fire, eliciting delighted whoops and laughs from the group. The effects had been nearly instantaneous. The smoke had taken on a vivid green colour, and the fumes had turned noxious.

"Is that what I think it is?" asked Catanya.

Jémys nodded, coughing on the fumes in the air.

It was a delirium pouch—a potent combination of herbs and drugs that, when burned together, created an intoxicating and hallucinogenic effect. They were incredibly rare because of how difficult they were to make, and if the blend was off by even a little bit, the pouch would be lethal. A few years ago, a rash of delirium deaths had led Caerlon to ban them altogether.

Catanya had never seen one before, but she remembered Diyah talking about them and explaining how dangerous they were.

Fortunately, she and Jémys had been sitting far enough away that the fumes mostly dissipated before reaching them. But the outlaws had become utterly inebriated. They'd lumbered around, laughing and cheering, singing tuneless songs at the top of their lungs and telling outlandish stories. Eventually, two of them had snuck off into the woods, giggling, and the others had fallen asleep where they sat.

Catanya and Jémys had remained silent throughout it all,

suspecting that the less attention they drew to themselves the better. Diyah had warned Catanya that people under delirium's influence could be erratic and dangerous. Catanya had no desire to learn what that meant.

After the outlaws had fallen asleep, she and Jémys tried everything they could to break free from their binds, to no avail. After a while, Catanya thought she could feel blood trickling down her wrist, and she stopped struggling. Whatever it was about these binds, it seemed like the harder they struggled, the worse it got.

Her head was pounding and she was nauseated. She suspected the fumes from the pouch had affected her more than she'd initially thought.

"Oh, it's no use," she muttered, slumping back in resignation. Jémys sighed and did the same.

After a while, she slipped into an uneasy sleep against the tree. She could feel the warmth of Jémys's body next to hers, and though they weren't exactly on good terms at the moment, it reassured her to know he was there.

<hr>

Shortly before dawn, she awoke with a start. She was drenched in a clammy sweat and she might have been sick if it weren't for the fact that she hadn't eaten in days.

Her dreams had been filled with feverish, distorted visions of her time in Finnua, and it took her a minute to remember where she was now. She heard murmuring nearby and she froze, pretending to sleep as she listened.

"She needs to know what happened in Linlon. We should report back."

"We will, Len, I just have a few things I need to finish here first."

She recognized Drayk's voice, so she opened her eyes a sliver and turned her head to watch the exchange.

"With the girl?"

Catanya's head was still foggy, but she thought she detected a hint of jealousy in Len's voice.

"Oh, don't do that, don't make this personal, Len." Drayk tried to reach out and touch him, but Len backed away.

"I'm not making this personal," Len retorted in an angry whisper. "I'm concerned. The others are getting impatient and we're tired of the half-truths and empty promises."

Drayk snorted and muttered something under his breath.

There was a bristling pause as Len glared at him.

"Fine," he said through gritted teeth, obviously annoyed by whatever Drayk had said. "If that's what you think of me, then I'm done."

"Oh, lighten up," replied Drayk, trying to brush away the tension.

"No!" snapped Len. "No. I never should have gotten involved with you. Rey was right. You're not worth the pain, and I—" Len broke off and looked away, his body language tense like he was trying to hold back his emotions. "I'll see this last one through, but after that I'm gone," he continued in a cooler, more measured tone. "I can't take this anymore. So will you please give the order? We need to be moving on." With that, Len stormed off, leaving Drayk standing alone, with a sour look on his face.

Drayk groaned and kicked a stone, which skittered and disappeared into the underbrush nearby. He was standing tall and rigid, with his back facing Catanya. He pressed his hand against his forehead and then raked it through his hair.

Suddenly, he turned around and shouted, "Up! Get up, lads. We're leaving." He stomped through the camp, prodding his unconscious men with his feet.

"Leavin'?" asked one man groggily. "Goin' where?"

"Where do you think, idiot?" snapped Drayk. He spared Len a quick glance and shrugged as he continued making his way through the group.

Len nodded, looking relieved.

"Where are Tuln and Caal?" Drayk asked.

"Woods," grunted one of the others. "S'tedious just sittin' around doin' nothin' all the time. Gotta make merry however we can."

Drayk rolled his eyes. "Someone go fetch them." Then he examined Catanya and Jémys. "And get the prisoners something to eat. We can't have them fainting along the way."

There were grumbles and groans as the outlaws roused themselves and started gathering their supplies. They loaded what they could carry into a series of packs, and dismantled Drayk's tent, before tossing everything they weren't bringing into the fire.

Len came over to where Catanya and Jémys sat roped to the tree, and began loosening the binds around their wrists.

"Where are you taking us?" asked Catanya.

Len just shook his head and yanked her arms around to bind them in front of her. He did the same with Jémys, then stuffed two meagre bowls of porridge into their grasps. "Eat," he grunted before walking away.

The porridge was cold and mealy, but Catanya was so hungry she didn't care. She wolfed down the food and continued watching the movement around her.

There were six outlaws in total: Drayk and Len, and the other four seemed to be called Fin, Caal, Tuln, and Hil. To Catanya's surprise, Drayk actually seemed to be the youngest of the lot. The other five were significantly older, and except for Len, they didn't seem to have much respect for their leader. They followed his orders grudgingly, and more than once Catanya caught them exchanging disgruntled looks behind Drayk's back.

But despite their feelings towards Drayk, they seemed to have a renewed enthusiasm as they prepared to start moving again.

When everything was packed and ready to go, the one named Hil came to untie the binds around Catanya and Jémys's feet. It wasn't until Hil stood directly in front of them that Catanya realized he wasn't a man at all. Hil was actually a short, brawny woman with a nasty scar on her cheek that gave her a gnarled appearance.

"You're a woman," breathed Catanya in surprise.

"Yeah, so are you." She yanked Catanya to her feet. "What of it?"

Catanya was surprised a woman had joined this gang and equally surprised these men accepted her. But they didn't appear to have any problem with Hil.

The only thing they obviously disliked was Drayk.

"Curious," muttered Catanya, exchanging glances with Jémys as he was yanked to his feet beside her.

It wasn't an easy walk, especially given the restraints on their hands and the pounding aches in their heads. Drayk seemed determined to keep moving. They clambered through the woods at an unreasonably fast pace. Catanya lost count of the number of times she tripped.

"Ugh, cut it out, will ye?" shouted Fin, when she stumbled once again and knocked into him.

"Oh, I'm sorry," she snapped, her voice dripping with disdain. "Is my captivity inconvenient for you?"

Jémys snorted and Fin looked outraged, but before he could do anything, Drayk called from the front, "Leave it!"

Fin glared at his leader. But then he deflated and strode off, putting some distance between himself and Catanya.

They carried on like this for several days, only stopping to camp overnight. After the novelty of travelling had worn off, resentment returned amongst the gang, stronger than before.

Catanya was curious to know how Drayk had become the group's leader when they obviously didn't respect him. She'd heard stories of outlaws as a child, but they were always romanticized tales of renegades and fugitives. In every story, the leaders had been heroes, beloved by their followers. They were stories of outcasts, united for a common purpose with a sense of community and honour.

But this group didn't fit that description at all. There was no common ideal or shared purpose. They were a group of individuals, working together for some reason Catanya didn't understand.

Yet somehow they seemed to move in synchronization, like they had rehearsed their steps a thousand times before. They were certainly rowdy and belligerent, but they were also surprisingly disciplined and organized in their movements, almost as if they had trained together.

Almost like soldiers.

What kind of soldiers would be traipsing through the woods, stealing, kidnapping, and carousing? And where were they taking her now?

One night, three of the gang members had grouped together on the edge of the camp, drinking and muttering under their breath.

"Expects us to jus' do whatever he says," grumbled the man called Fin.

"Aye, 'e's always been 'er favourite," replied Caal. "And I think we know why, eh?"

They all laughed and grunted.

"Pretty boy Drayk," Fin scoffed. There were incoherent grumbles from the others. "'E may be pretty, on'y he ain't even that smart."

"Yeah. What's she going to want with these two, anyway?" Tuln gestured towards Jémys and Catanya.

"Got me," said Caal. "Must be part of the mission."

"I don't know. Maybe there's somethin' special about 'em," said Fin. He glanced back at Jémys and Catanya and grinned. "Speakin' o' pretty..."

The other two guffawed.

"Yeah, I suppose she'll have some fun with them."

The three bandits separated and spread out to sleep, and Catanya turned to Jémys. "Who do you think '*she*' is?" she whispered.

"I have no idea," said Jémys darkly. "But it doesn't sound like they're very happy with Drayk, does it?"

Catanya bit her lip and grimaced. "No, it doesn't. And frankly, I'm not sure if that's good or bad for us."

They exchanged worried looks, and Catanya knew Jémys was thinking the same thing she was. As bad as their current situation was, if Drayk lost control, there was no telling how much worse it would get.

"Catanya," said Jémys in a serious voice. "We need to get out of here."

"I know."

That night, as everyone slept, Catanya turned her mind towards escape.

*If you can reduce an entire village to ruins, you can certainly loosen a set of ropes,* she thought bitterly.

She squeezed her eyes shut and strained to focus all her energy on the braided fibres around her wrists. She imagined them loosening, unwinding, fraying, disappearing.

But nothing happened.

Her frustration was taking control. She forced herself to take a deep breath and relax. Getting upset would not help.

So she tried again. Closing her eyes, she focused her attention on the areas of her wrists where the ropes chafed. The pain in her skin made it easy to do so. She imagined the sensation of relief it would be to have the ropes slip away, to have the cool breeze soothe her aching skin, to stand up and stretch her sore muscles.

In her mind, the image formed like a sketch on a page. She could see her own wrists, bound and trussed together, and she could sense the power she needed to free them. It was right there, at the tip of her fingers, itching to be used.

Then in a flash, the image was gone, replaced by a wall of flames as they engulfed Finnua. She almost cried out in pain as she saw Olly's terrified face and Nelle's dead body. The images were as vivid as the day they had happened, and she could feel the intoxicating thrill of the power as it had coursed through her body, taking control. She was filled with a terrible wrath and anguish and she wanted to hurt everyone.

*No*, said a voice in her head.

Her mind cleared. Every bit of energy she had disappeared in an instant, leaving her body trembling from the sudden drain. She was exhausted and miserable, and she could feel the tears pooling under her eyelids.

*I can't control it*, she thought miserably. *This is all my fault.*

She craned her neck to look at Jémys and realized he had fallen asleep, slumped against the tree beside her. Even though he was sleeping, she thought he still looked sad. It was as though the burden of everything he had lost was permanently etched onto his face.

His chest gently rose and fell as he breathed, and the light of the dying flames flickered across his face, highlighting all the bruises from where Drayk had beaten him.

She leaned forward, trying to see the spot on his leg where Drayk had burned him, but it was too dark and her binding was too tight.

She held her breath momentarily, fighting back her anger and remorse.

After everything that Jémys had endured, he didn't deserve this too. He deserved to be free, leading a peaceful, happy life somewhere far away from her and the destruction that followed her. She owed it to him to give him a chance. She owed it to him not to give up.

With that thought, she closed her eyes and refocused her attention on the ropes. No matter how much it scared her, she needed to keep trying.

# 19

# A MOTHER'S REGRET

It was late in the evening and Diyah was sitting alone in her chambers in the dark.

The physician's quarters were surprisingly large. They included a modest bedchamber and a wide-open workroom with a small table and a long workbench. A massive set of cupboards covered the wall behind the bench, overflowing with tinctures, salves, ointments, and powders. Several rickety bookcases leaned beside it, each packed with large tomes detailing different illnesses and healing practices.

On the opposite wall stood a plain but serviceable fireplace with several iron stands and pots for cooking and heating medicines. In the corner, standing against the wall beside the window, was a small cot she could bring out for patients whenever necessary.

It was a much better space than Diyah would have imagined, but it didn't change how she felt about her situation.

Cadyan had departed the city over a week ago and there was no news of his progress. With each passing day, Diyah's anxiety grew worse. She was terrified for Catanya and powerless to help.

When she'd learned that Cadyan, Slaedir, and Julyán would be leaving the castle, along with a handful of other fírkon, she had hoped her supervision might relax. But she was wrong. Now that Julyán wasn't there to watch her, the entire castle seemed tasked with the responsibility instead. Her every move was scrutinized, and she spent every waking minute in the company of one palace guard or another. Even now, alone in her chambers, her solitude was just an illusion. Outside the door stood two guards, listening.

*I'm going to die here*, she thought. *I'm going to spend the rest of my life as a prisoner.* She stood up and moved to stand by the window. As she gazed at the stars above and felt the chilly draught on her face, she tried to force her mind away from her own sorrows.

She thought about her patients—the people in the city who needed her help. Every day she met more people suffering and struggling to survive. Even if she could escape, how could she leave them all with no help? Not to mention what would happen to Meya, Gréys, and Hahney, wherever they were.

Besides, even if she escaped, where would she go? She couldn't return to Faltir and she had no idea where Catanya was. There was nothing she could do to help her friend, but she *could* help the people living in this city. She could give them hope for a better future.

"Catanya will save us," she said to herself for the hundredth time. She had been saying it ever since she had arrived in Caerlon, and it helped her to keep going. As long as Catanya was alive, Diyah had hope. She had a reason to keep fighting every day.

It scared Diyah to think about Cadyan out there searching for Catanya. His powers were strong and he was even more ruthless than Diyah had imagined. She hoped that wherever Catanya was, she was learning to use her powers, so she'd be ready when the time came.

*Catanya is strong,* she thought. *If there's one thing I believe in, it's her.*

As Diyah lay in bed that night, her thoughts wandered back to the night Slaedir had returned from his search. She remembered what he'd said about the man helping Catanya.

*He was a skilled fighter. He killed two of our party.*

Diyah was curious about him. She had no idea who he was or how Catanya had met him.

*He seemed real cozy with her though, if you catch my drift. Seemed like they'd known each other intimately for a while.*

She shuddered at the memory of Slaedir's slimy tone, but she couldn't help wondering if there was truth in his words. She liked the idea that wherever Catanya was, she wasn't alone, and maybe the man with her was someone who cared about her—someone who would help her.

Diyah smiled as she remembered the days she'd spent with Catanya laughing about the boys in Faltir. They both hated the pressure to settle down, but after Catanya came of age, she'd tested out a couple different relationships. In the end though, she had always lost interest. So whoever this man was now, if he'd managed to capture Catanya's attention and her trust, he must be a rare individual.

That thought offered her a slight sense of peace.

---

Diyah spent the next few days trying to keep busy so that she wouldn't dwell on her own misery or drown in the fear she felt for her friend. She threw herself into her work, preparing various balms and remedies and making extra rounds through the poor district and the west barracks, where a recent bout of sweating sickness had taken hold.

At first she'd thought treating the firkon would be difficult —they were the enemy after all—but the longer she spent visiting the barracks, the more she realized that, with Slaedir gone, the firkon were surprisingly bearable. For the most part, they were polite and grateful for her aid. Only a rare few seemed innately villainous.

Then Diyah remembered that these men had all been normal boys once, like the ones she'd known growing up in Faltir. None of them had chosen this life, they were all born into it or taken from villages throughout the kingdom. They were as trapped as she was.

Living cooped up in such close quarters meant illnesses spread through their ranks like wildfire. This particular bout of sweating sickness was a nasty one. It was even seeping into the palace. Diyah had already treated one maidservant with it and now the chaplain was laid up in bed. Given his old age, Diyah worried his recovery might be slow.

She was doing her best to keep the casualties to a minimum, but it was a challenge. The illness seemed to spread faster than she could mix the tonics.

One afternoon, as she worked frantically in her chambers, someone knocked on her door.

"Ugh, I'm busy! What do you want?" she snapped. Guards had been interrupting her all day.

"Diyah?" called a gentle voice. "It's Fehla."

Diyah nearly dropped the bowl in her hand. She stared at the door, surprised. Then she set the bowl carefully on the table and crossed the room, wiping her hands on her smock.

"I'm sorry." She opened the door to find Fehla standing outside, eyes wide in mild curiosity. "I assumed it was one of these idiots." She indicated the guards looming on either side of the entrance. "Come in." She stood back to let Fehla pass, ignoring the guards' glowers as she closed the door again. "What can I do for you?" She walked back over to her worktable.

Fehla didn't respond immediately. She crossed the room and lifted a vial off the table, looking at its contents curiously.

"Fascinating," she said in a hushed tone. "How did you learn to do this?" She moved along the table, admiring the different concoctions.

"My father taught me. And I was born with a certain natural talent, I suppose."

"So it's true then." Awe spread over Fehla's face. "You really are one of the Heiltúir?"

Diyah had never truly believed she'd earned the right to call herself a Heiltúir. Her father had died before she could complete her formal training with him. But she couldn't deny her heritage, or her instincts. The Heiltúir were born to be healers. It was in her blood.

"I do what I can." Diyah shrugged and turned to rummage through the cupboard, searching for fresh yarrow. She had to stand on her tiptoes to reach the far corners of the top shelf. As her fingers brushed against the springy flowers, something clanged behind them.

Curious, she put her foot on the table and climbed up to see. A small vial lay tucked in the corner of the shelf. The wax seal around the cork was broken. The vial was half-full of a sickly green substance that resembled the scummy surface of a bog.

"What is this?" she wondered aloud, jumping down and turning to face Fehla. "I've never seen anything like it before."

Fehla glanced at the vial. "I wouldn't know." Then, changing the subject, she asked, "But tell me, how are you doing? I'm sorry I didn't come earlier, but I wasn't sure I should. I don't want to get you in trouble." She gave Diyah an apologetic look.

Diyah gave a dismissive wave. "I'm sure it's fine. Besides, what harm can I do locked up in this castle under constant supervision?" She shook her head dismally. "It's nice to have the company, to be honest."

Diyah turned the green vial around in her hand, examining it. She was about to uncork it and smell its contents when Fehla asked, "Can I do anything to help?"

Diyah glanced up. Fehla's face had brightened at the idea.

"Maybe." Diyah placed the vial on a lower shelf. Having an untrained assistant might make her job harder, but she was eager for the opportunity to get closer to Fehla. "Do you have experience with healing?" she asked.

Fehla had lifted one of Diyah's metal instruments off the table and was inspecting it curiously. "Ah, no. Not much," she admitted, putting the instrument back down. "But I used to visit Grante here occasionally to help him with the patients. Before he died..."

A sudden sadness washed over Diyah. She'd heard about Grante's execution. By all accounts, it had been a gruesome affair. She'd been trying hard not to picture it. "I wish I'd known Grante better," she said. "I only met him briefly, but he seemed like a kind, honourable man."

She felt guilty taking over his quarters and his patients, like she was stealing from his corpse before it was cold.

"He was," said Fehla sadly. "Loyal and selfless. And he paid the ultimate price for that loyalty. He died for helping me conceal Catanya."

Diyah paused before saying, "So did Genna."

They stood staring at one another across the table, both suffering under the weight of their losses. Diyah still had trouble accepting everything that had happened and her mind was bursting with questions for Fehla.

"I have to ask," she said, unable to stop herself. "Why did you do it? Why did you separate them?"

Fehla clutched the table as though bracing herself. "It was the only way to keep her safe. Casréyan would have killed her, you know? Without hesitating, he would have killed her. He barely wanted one heir, let alone two. I needed to protect her... I just wish I could have protected Cadyan too."

Diyah felt lost for words. Fehla seemed to interpret the silence correctly. "You can't understand why anyone would marry a man like Casréyan, can you?"

Diyah rubbed her neck awkwardly. "Well, no," she confessed, with an apologetic half-shrug. "Were you in love with him?" She struggled to keep the scepticism out of her voice.

Fehla smiled meekly. "I thought I was." She stared at her hands. "Or maybe I believed I could convince myself to love him given time... Casréyan could be very charming when he needed to be. He had all of Mórceá convinced he was righteous and fair. And a young, inexperienced woman like me, chosen by the King of Caerlon himself... Well, I'm sure you can under-stand how it felt."

Diyah nodded understandingly. But privately she thought if she'd been in Fehla's position, she would have known better than to trust someone like Casréyan. "How did you meet?" she asked.

"We met during the Midwinter Carnival in Awnell, actually. I lived at the castle there."

"Really?" Diyah was surprised to hear it. "So does that mean Queen Ayr is your sister? I thought Ayr only had one sister... and didn't she die years ago?"

"Oh, no, Ayr and I are not related." She seemed oddly disturbed by the idea. "No. I do have a sister actually, but not Ayr. My sister and I were King Ayln's wards."

Diyah wiped her hands on a cloth and began untying her apron. "His wards? So... your parents?"

"They died when we were quite young. As did yours, I believe?"

Diyah nodded and crossed the room to open a cupboard

behind the table. She pulled out a bottle of auburn liquor and two glasses. "I told them I needed it for healing." She smiled as she handed a glass to Fehla. "So you were raised at the palace of Awnell. How did you end up marrying Casréyan?"

Fehla took a long time to answer. She swirled her glass around in her hand and took a sip, closing her eyes as if relishing the taste. "I loved the King and Queen of Awnell, almost as if they were my own parents, and I wanted desperately to please them. So when they told me that Casréyan wanted to marry me and that our marriage could bring about peace between the two kingdoms, I believed them. I convinced myself I wanted to marry Casréyan. Convinced myself that I loved him and he loved me and that our union would save lives... I should have known better."

"How could you have known?" asked Diyah.

Fehla had a vague, strained look in her eyes. "Have you ever been in love, Diyah?"

Diyah was taken aback by the question. "No. I can't say that I have," she said, shrugging. She couldn't see how that was relevant.

"Well, when you do fall in love, you'll understand then."

Diyah resisted the urge to roll her eyes.

"Real love feels different. I should have known I could never have that with Casréyan. That is one of my biggest regrets, you know? Marrying him. I was too weak to follow my heart, and look what's become of it."

"This isn't your fault," said Diyah.

Fehla gave her a grateful pat on the arm and walked over to the window. She gazed out at the kingdom below. "You know, when he was a baby, Cadyan was the sweetest thing. He used to have this laugh." She smiled as she thought about it. "It was like music—the most beautiful music imaginable. He was so full of love and affection, that boy." A shadow fell over her face. "But now..." Her voice shook.

"What happened?" asked Diyah. "What happened to turn him into what he is now?"

"I'd like to say it was all because of Casréyan, but Cadyan has only gotten worse since his father died. He's becoming something I hardly recognize—something vicious and twisted... How is it possible that he can be that boy who was so full of joy?"

"I don't know what to say," mumbled Diyah. "I can't imagine..." She shuddered to think what Catanya would have become if she hadn't left Caerlon as a baby. Would she be just as damaged as her brother? Or would she be dead?

"It was naïve, I guess. I had hoped that once Casréyan was gone, my son and I could move forward, move on. I even thought maybe we could find Catanya together... be a family." She brushed a loose strand of hair out of her eyes.

"You saved Catanya," said Diyah. "You were right to send her away. She was better off removed from all this."

"I know that," muttered Fehla. "But what about my son? How am I supposed to help him now?"

It was hard for Diyah to talk about Cadyan this way. To talk about helping him when all she wanted was to stop him. "I don't know," she admitted. "I'm sorry to say it, but I think he might be beyond your help at this point. Think about everything he's done. He killed his own father for the throne. That kind of thing leaves a mark you can't—"

"No one can prove he did that," interrupted Fehla.

Diyah gave her a compassionate smile. It wouldn't serve anything to contradict Fehla when she was already so upset.

Fehla sighed heavily. "But even if he didn't kill his father, he has killed countless other people, hasn't he?"

Diyah gave her a commiserating glance, but she was saved from having to respond when someone hammered on the door. It opened to reveal one of the guards.

"What?" Diyah snapped. "Can't you see I'm busy?" The

guard eyed them suspiciously before closing the door without saying a word. "Ugh, I mean honestly. Do they have to check on me every five minutes? What do they think I'm doing in here?"

Fehla laughed and walked back over to the table. "Well, how can I help you? I'm tired of sitting around waiting for Cadyan and his men to return. I need to do something or I'll go mad."

Diyah looked around for something to give Fehla. "Here." She handed her a jar of valerian root. "I need to replenish my stock of sleeping tonics. Can you cut this up and soak it in boiling water?"

"That sounds easy enough." Fehla smiled as she took the jar and opened it.

They worked together in silence. Diyah was trying to think of a way to ask about the conversation she'd overheard between Fehla and the mystery firkon. She wanted to ask who he was and whether he was trustworthy, but she wasn't sure Fehla would be willing to discuss it.

Before she could settle on a casual way to broach the subject, Fehla broke the silence. "Tell me, Diyah, you were born in Murina, weren't you?"

"Yes, I was." Diyah was surprised by the question. "Why do you ask?"

"Oh, I'm just curious." Fehla averted her gaze as she began pouring the valerian root tea into separate vials. "Did you ever get to visit Linlon, by any chance? It's supposed to be breathtaking. They say during the spring, birds of every size and colour overrun the entire town. Apparently they flock from all across the kingdom, attracted by plants in the lake."

Diyah stopped working for a moment. "No, I never saw it. I've heard it's wonderful though," she said, eyeing Fehla. What was it about Linlon that held such an interest for her? She hoped Fehla would venture some details about her interest in the place, but when she didn't say anything, Diyah pressed on.

"Linlon isn't far from Finnua is it? Perhaps the firkon passed through there recently?"

"Mmm." Fehla nodded. "No—I mean yes, it's not far." She placed the pot back on the table and sighed. "Well, I should probably leave before the guards decide we're plotting something in here." She laughed and shook her head.

Diyah felt the sting of disappointment, but she nodded.

Fehla began tidying up and before she left, she turned to Diyah. "If it's alright with you, I'd like to visit again soon. Perhaps you could show me how your medicines are made and..." She trailed off, looking nervous. "And if you're willing, I'd love to hear some stories about my daughter. I think it would help me feel better to learn about her life."

Diyah smiled warmly. "Of course."

She was happy to have the company, especially if it meant Fehla might open up to her. The queen clearly had secrets. Diyah couldn't blame her for keeping them, given everything she had been through, but if Fehla was working on a plan to either help Catanya or stop Cadyan, Diyah wanted to be part of it.

**20**

---

## A BETRAYAL

I t had been days since the outlaws had left their camp and still Catanya hadn't managed to free herself from her binds. She couldn't understand what was wrong. It was as if something was blocking her from accessing her magic and no matter what she tried, she couldn't get around it. She was running out of time.

The longer they remained on the move, the more disgruntled the outlaws seemed to become. Catanya had noticed a shift in their displeasure. Where once they had blamed Drayk for their circumstances, now they also seemed to blame her and Jémys.

Once or twice she overheard them making snide remarks about what they would do to her and Jémys if they got the chance, and she realized Drayk was the only reason these things hadn't already happened.

With each passing day, she was growing more frightened and desperate to escape. Jémys had given up hoping she'd be able to use her magic to get them out of this and had set his mind on more tangible methods. He had started tracking the different outlaws' behaviours, looking for vulnerabilities and opportunities to take advantage of them.

Catanya worried he was growing reckless. He had a habit of saying "What have I got to lose?" whenever she mentioned her concerns, and this scared her almost more than anything else.

After yet another day stumbling through the woods, the group's energy changed. They seemed more cheerful, more animated.

"What's going on?" Catanya asked Hil, who was walking beside her, holding her ropes.

"We're close to the Drowning Dragon," she said. Her excitement was palpable.

"Yeah, I say we stop in for a pint," cheered the man holding Jémys's ropes.

The group shouted its assent, and even Drayk seemed excited about the prospect of drinks and a change of scenery.

When they'd finished making camp for the night, everyone disappeared in search of the traveller's pub, leaving only two behind to watch Catanya and Jémys.

Catanya waited until Len and Caal had settled for the evening, then she turned towards Jémys. "What do you think?" she asked in the quietest whisper she could manage.

"I think it's now or never," he replied. "Caal carries a blade strapped inside his boot. I just need to make him angry."

"What? No—"

But before she could stop him, Jémys had called over to Caal.

"Hey, moron! Yeah, that's right, you. Have you always been the pathetic reject of the group or is it a recent development?"

Catanya was taken aback. She'd never heard Jémys say anything so rude, and she found it unsettling.

"Sod off," grumbled Caal.

Jémys laughed tauntingly. "Because your friend there, Len,

is it? I reckon he's only here to watch you and make sure you don't do something stupid. Am I right?"

"I'm warnin' you, kid." Caal flushed an angry red colour.

Catanya gazed from him back to Jémys and read the reckless determination in his eyes.

"Oh, yeah?" he asked. "What are you going to do? You're the runt of the group, it's obvious. I bet you can't even throw a punch."

"You want to bet?" Caal sprang to his feet, fists clenched at his sides.

"Caal, leave it," said Len in a bored voice. He was watching the exchange with weary disinterest.

"Don' tell me what to do. I ain't leavin' nothin'. Jus' 'cause you been sleepin' with Drayk doesn't mean yer above me."

Catanya and Jémys exchanged quick looks of surprise, but Len just smiled and shrugged, which seemed to make Caal even angrier.

"Firs' it's weeks of sittin' around, then we get to the Drownin' Dragon and *he* tells me I gotta stay here," snarled Caal. "I deserve a little fun, don' I?"

Len scratched his chin, as Caal walked towards Jémys, doing his best to appear intimidating.

"Jémys," Catanya cautioned as she watched the man approaching them and realized how burly he was.

"It's our only chance," muttered Jémys so only she could hear. "Come on, you lumbering troll!"

Caal's face contorted in rage and he swung his fist, striking Jémys in the face.

"No!" cried Catanya, and in an instant the ropes around her arms had slackened. For a moment she sat stunned.

"Come on," called Jémys, spitting blood on the ground. "Is that the best you've got? Why don't you remove these ropes and we'll have a proper fight?"

Caal sneered and moved in for another hit.

"Stop!" she shouted, forcing herself to stay still. "Stop, please. We'll be quiet, I promise."

Jémys shot Catanya an enquiring glance, but she just lifted her eyebrows. "You don't need to do this." She caught Jémys's eye, who nodded to show he understood.

Caal grumbled some inarticulate insult about how Jémys should keep his mouth shut if he wanted to keep it, before lumbering back over to the fire and sitting down.

Catanya waited for a while before daring to move. When the outlaws had let their guards down again, she pulled the ropes off her wrists, taking care not to make any obvious movements. Jémys looked at her, wide-eyed, but she shook her head warningly.

Caal sat by the fire nearby, while Len was leaning against a tree, facing the opposite direction. If she moved quickly, she could take them by surprise.

She stood up as quietly as she could and crept forward to where Caal was reclining beside the fire. Lifting a rock off the forest floor, she smashed him on the head. He keeled over, unconscious.

"What?" Len turned towards the commotion, drawing his sword from his belt. In his moment of hesitation, Catanya charged him, disarming him and knocking him to the ground.

She held the blade to his throat. "Get up slowly."

Len got to his feet, careful not to take his eyes off Catanya's sword.

"Now, untie him." She indicated Jémys.

Len moved begrudgingly over to where Jémys sat tied to the tree and knelt down to untie his ropes.

"Well, it's about time," drawled a voice behind Catanya.

She spun around to see Drayk standing nonchalantly behind the fire, holding his sword in one hand and a bottle of sourwood rum in the other.

"Thank you, Len, you can go."

Catanya glanced at Len, who gave her a triumphant smirk as he headed off through the forest towards the pub.

Drayk walked to stand next to Caal's unconscious frame. He clicked his tongue and prodded the man with his foot.

"Poor fool. I must say, I didn't think you'd knock him out cold." Drayk took a swig from his bottle and leaned over to examine Caal. "Oh well, I never liked him. And it serves him right... *ass*." Drayk kicked him again a little harder.

"I don't understand." Catanya eyed Drayk suspiciously. "You wanted me to escape?"

"Well." He took another swig and walked towards her. "I assumed you would try. And I was eager to see how you'd do it. Tell me, how did you get the ropes off?"

He gave her a playful grin. Catanya just stared at him without saying a word.

"I thought as much," he said, nodding. "You see, those ropes are made of Heirla jute. Strongest material around and nothing gets out of a choke knot when it's properly tied." He tilted his head. "Come, walk with me." He returned his sword to its scabbard and motioned towards the forest. When Catanya didn't move, he sighed. "You can fight me if you want, but you won't get very far before my men find you again. We know these woods better than anyone."

Caal moaned softly. He was waking up.

"Oy!" Drayk kicked him again. "Get up, you oaf. Watch him." He jerked his thumb towards Jémys.

Jémys and Catanya exchanged meaningful glances. Jémys nodded almost imperceptibly and Catanya lowered her sword.

"Walk with you," she repeated blankly, looking back at Drayk, who smiled serenely. She couldn't explain why, but she felt compelled to join him. "Alright..." she agreed, taking a wary step forward.

Drayk held out the bottle for her. She took it from him and

hesitated before raising it to her lips and letting the liquid burn down her throat.

"Good, isn't it?" he said, taking the bottle back.

Catanya choked and spluttered. She had never had sourwood rum before. It tasted strange, like fermented earth and honey. She wasn't sure she liked the taste, but it seemed to warm her from the inside. She didn't mind that sensation.

They walked together a few paces before Drayk spoke. "So tell me, Catya—"

"Don't call me that," she said more forcefully than she'd expected.

"So tell me, Catya," he repeated.

Catanya exhaled irritably.

"With talents such as yours, I'm curious what exactly you plan to do?"

"Other than getting away from you?"

Drayk grinned. "Surely you've thought about it. You've considered the possibilities for someone like you."

"What possibilities?" blurted Catanya. Then, recollecting herself, she lapsed into silence.

Drayk eyed her with his head tilted. "Interesting. So you feel trapped then? Trapped by the powers you never wanted. Am I right?"

Catanya stared at him, surprised by his perceptiveness.

Drayk nodded pensively, and then, halting, he spun around to face Catanya. "Who are you?" he asked.

"What do you mean?" She was thrown off by the bluntness and tried to deflect his question.

"I mean"—he thrust the bottle into her hand and reached inside his jacket to pull out a piece of parchment—"who are you?"

He unfolded the parchment to reveal an image on the other side. Catanya stared at the drawing of a young woman—a young woman whose face bore a striking resemblance to hers.

Drayk pointed at the words written on the bottom.

*Wanted alive. 10,000 gold pieces.*

"By order of the King of Caerlon himself," said Drayk in mock reverence. "One of my men found this at the Drowning Dragon. They were posted everywhere last week, so says the barman."

"Really?" Catanya kept her tone light, while attempting to ignore the pounding in her chest.

"Yes, really." Drayk gave her a calculating look. "So tell me, why is the King of Caerlon searching for you?"

"What? You think—"

"Don't insult me." Drayk's tone was harsher now. "I know this is you."

"Do you?" Catanya tried to sound sceptical, but she was having trouble keeping the panic out of her voice.

"Yes. And let me tell you what else I know. For weeks, rumours have been flying about a second heir to Caerlon's throne. A sister with powers to rival her brother's, so they say."

"I-is that so?" Catanya edged away from him.

"Oh, yes," said Drayk, following her. "At first I didn't believe it, of course. I thought it was complete nonsense. But imagine my surprise to find you—a young woman roughly the same age as the *dear* king, not to mention bearing an uncanny resemblance—running through the woods like some sort of fugitive. And with untamed magical powers no less."

Drayk let out a low whistle and smiled triumphantly.

He was standing mere inches away from her now and was searching her face avidly. "You're her, aren't you?" he whispered.

It was the second time someone had said this to Catanya. But when Olly had said it, his voice was full of wonder. Drayk's voice was full of something else. Triumph and passion, and she didn't like how he was gazing at her with mixed awe and longing. She wanted to back away from him, but instead she stood rooted to the spot, frozen.

Slowly, as though transfixed, he raised his hand to stroke the strands of her hair that had changed colour. "Remarkable," he whispered.

Still unable to move, Catanya's mind went blank. Then a memory came to her, a memory of the dream she'd had weeks ago. The dream where she'd found sanctuary with a group of people in the forest, and this man... This man had been there with her, he'd helped her. And at the time, she'd felt safe, but now...

Catanya's instincts were confused. She couldn't make sense of what she was feeling. Finally recollecting herself, she took a step back from Drayk, pulling her hair out of his grasp.

Drayk shook his head as though trying to clear away a fog. "My apologies," he mumbled. He opened his mouth again to speak, but before he could say two words, they heard a commotion coming from the camp. Angry hollers and the sound of bottles smashing.

Drayk looked at Catanya with one eyebrow raised, then drew his sword and headed back towards the site. Catanya hesitated before following.

"Oy, where is she, boy?" shouted someone at the camp.

Catanya and Drayk arrived to find the entire gang returned from the pub and surrounding Jémys like a pack of drunken wolves.

One man hit Jémys in the stomach just as Drayk called, "Oy, what are you lot doing?" and marched boldly into the centre of camp. "Fin? What is this?"

"Look at this, Drayk." Fin handed him a poster identical to the one Drayk had shown Catanya. "She's worth ten thousand pieces."

"I—" began Catanya, but she stopped when she saw the warning look on Drayk's face.

Drayk took the parchment and stared at it momentarily, before letting out a bark of laughter. "Lads, please, this could be anyone," he said, brandishing the parchment and laughing even harder.

"Anyone, my ass!" cried Fin. "It's 'er, alright! And she'll fetch us a pretty penny in Caerlon."

He made a move towards Catanya, but Drayk stepped in front of him to block his path.

There was a pause as everyone turned their gaze towards him.

"Wha's the matter with you, Drayk? Let's take 'er to Cadyan!"

The rest of the group shouted in agreement.

"Lads, please." Drayk held up his hands. "Even if it is her—and I'm not convinced—would you honestly trust the king to pay? If you take her to Cadyan, he will kill you all."

Murmurs ran through the group and a couple of them exchanged sceptical glances.

"And think about it. If the king is this desperate to locate someone, that someone is probably pretty important, don't you think? And since when are we interested in helping Caerlon?"

"Since he's offering us a load of gold to do it!" cried Tuln.

"Yeah!" the others shouted in unison.

"Aye, I'm sick of living on nothing!"

"We want what's ours. This mission has been nothing but disappointment after disappointment."

"Yeah!" The shouts were getting louder.

"It's not happening." Drayk cut through the noise. "No."

Catanya stood behind Drayk, staring at him in shock.

"*No?*" taunted Fin, mimicking him. The others laughed. "You kno' wha', Drayk, I'm gettin' pretty tired of takin' orders from you."

More murmurs of assent ran through the group.

"I was there, you kno', lads! I was there when Lia pulled this wretch ou' o' the filth and decided to keep 'im instead of killin' 'im. Should've known righ' then, she'd lost it. I knew he'd never really be one of us!"

Fin marched up to Drayk and stopped mere inches away. Drayk stayed perfectly still.

"Time was, Lia used to be a lil' more selective who she let lead a crew. But not anymore, 'pparently. No. You're no Verratrí. You're still the same arrogant shit you've always been."

He spat at Drayk's feet.

The other men sniggered and leered.

"I see," said Drayk, casually wiping his boots in the grass. "So am I to understand that you will be betraying Lia tonight, betraying your people in favour of the King of Caerlon?"

"Betraying Lia? Oh, *betraying Lia*? Tha's cute," said Fin, laughing.

Drayk seemed remarkably calm despite the fact that he was surrounded by a pack of angry, drunk outlaws. "I'm just wondering how best to explain why I had to kill you all," he said.

Everyone stood gawking at Drayk.

"What? You think you can beat us all on your own?" asked Tuln.

Drayk shrugged and smirked mockingly.

Fin laughed and glanced back at his comrades before suddenly sending his fist speeding through the air at Drayk's head. But Drayk ducked and slashed out with his sword. Fin tripped in his effort to dodge the blade and toppled over. In the short time it took for the group to realize what was happening, Drayk managed to spin around, knocking two others to the ground in one quick, fluid motion.

Pandemonium broke out. Shouts and cries of anger rang through the air as the outlaws converged on Drayk. Tuln broke away from the pack and ran towards Catanya. Without thinking, she smashed the bottle of sourwood rum over his head and kicked him hard in the chest. He crashed to the ground.

"Stop this!" cried Len, as he attempted to block Fin from hitting Drayk.

"Get out of the way, Len." When Len still didn't move, Fin barred his teeth like an angry wolf. "Fine," he growled. "You always were a useless lackey." He plunged his sword straight through Len's chest and yanked it out again with brutal indifference.

"Len!" cried Drayk. He ran forward to catch him, but Fin blocked his passage. Their swords clanged as they connected, spattering Len's blood into the air, and across Drayk's face.

"Someone grab her!" shouted Fin, narrowly avoiding Drayk's next attack.

Caal, who was standing behind them, turned and began advancing on Catanya.

Catanya stood frozen. She still held Len's sword, but she didn't really know how to fight.

Drayk cried out in pain as Fin flung him into the tree where Jémys remained helplessly tied up.

"Untie me," said Jémys.

Drayk raised his blade. Wincing, he cut through the ropes in one swift movement. Jémys sprang to his feet. Fin tried to grab him, but Jémys was too fast. He dodged Fin and lunged forward, tackling Caal to the ground. Then he lifted a rock and smashed it into Caal's head.

"Second time's the charm," panted Jémys. "Come on." He stood up and grabbed Catanya's hand, trying to run.

"Wait." She dug her heels into the ground.

"What? Let's go!" he urged, tugging on her arm.

"We can't leave him."

She gestured to Drayk, who was still slumped against the tree where Fin was looming over him, baring his teeth in a cruel, menacing grin.

"You can't be serious," protested Jémys, aghast.

Catanya ignored him and ran to help Drayk.

"I've been waitin' a long time to do this," said Fin, as he raised his sword high to strike.

"Keep waiting," shouted Catanya. She smashed him hard on the head with the hilt of her sword. He collapsed. She held out her hand for Drayk, who took it, looking surprised.

He winced as she pulled him to his feet, and then he let go of her hand to wipe the spattered blood off his face with his sleeve. He glanced down at Fin momentarily, his face twisted with anger. Then his eyes travelled over the unconscious bodies of his gang, finally resting on Len. Catanya couldn't read his expression... Was it sadness? Regret? Guilt?

Fin twitched and groaned on the ground. He was waking up. Tuln and Hil were stirring now too.

"Come on!" Catanya yanked Drayk forward.

Jémys had found his sword among the mess and was fastening it to his belt when Catanya and Drayk ran over to join him.

"Now can we go?" Jémys said.

"Wait." She had just seen her pack lying on the ground along with two others. She grabbed all three and swung them over her shoulder. "Okay, let's go." She led the way into the forest.

**21**

---

# UNCOMFORTABLE ALLIES

I t was well into the morning before Catanya, Drayk, and Jémys finally slowed their pace. They stopped to rest in a small clearing and Jémys threw himself down on a log, trying to catch his breath. Drayk leaned against a tree with his eyes closed, clutching his left arm in his hand, and Catanya rummaged through the packs, taking inventory of everything they had.

"Here." She tossed a spare cloak over to Jémys, who grabbed it mid-air.

"Thanks," he panted, swinging the cloak around his shoulders. "What else is there?"

"Some bread and cheese, one blanket, a bit of rope." She was pulling the items out and laying them on the ground. "A canteen and a handful of gold"—she jangled a small purse full of coins and shrugged—"it's more than we had before."

With a pang, Catanya realized she'd lost her sketchbook. She hadn't seen it since the night Drayk had it, and it wasn't in any of the packs. With a heavy sigh, she started repacking the items. She knew she ought to be grateful they'd even managed to grab these items, but her sketchbook was important to her and not just because it was a gift from Jémys. The images in it had been a source of comfort, and drawing had always helped calm her nerves.

Jémys groaned and pressed his palms against his forehead. "I can't believe this." He sounded just as worn and downcast as she felt.

Drayk laughed shakily, and Catanya glanced up to see him sliding down the tree. He looked pale and weak.

"Something's wrong." She crossed over to stand next to him. "What is it?"

"My arm," he mumbled, sliding another few inches down the tree.

"Let me see." She pulled his hand away, and he flinched as she touched his shoulder. "I think it's out of place."

"Hmm, I thought it felt different." He tried to crack a winning smile, but winced instead and slid even farther down the tree. "Not to worry, love," he mumbled. "I've never been one for conformity. Shoulder should be able to do whatever it wants." He attempted to push himself up, but the exertion almost caused him to collapse.

"Oh, shut up," said Catanya, carefully pushing him into a seated position. "You're not making any sense."

"Maybe you're not making any sense," muttered Drayk. He was struggling to keep his eyes focused on her face. "Stand still, would you?"

"I'm not moving."

"Nonsense."

It alarmed Catanya to hear him slurring his words, and she watched as he slid onto the ground, muttering incoherently.

"Come and help me," she called to Jémys. "We need to push his shoulder back in place."

But Jémys didn't move. "Why should we help him? He kidnapped and tortured us. Why not simply leave him to rot?" He was staring at Drayk with obvious distaste.

"You don't mean that," said Catanya, turning away from him.

"Don't I?"

"No, you don't!" she shouted, feeling cross. "I know you, and you'd never leave someone to die in the woods. Especially not someone who just risked his life to save you."

"He didn't do it to save me."

"What?" spat Catanya.

"He didn't risk his life to save *me*. He risked his life to save *you*."

There was a long, tense silence as Jémys and Catanya glared at one another.

"Fine," she snapped. "Don't help me, I'll do it myself."

She crouched down beside Drayk and pushed him flat on his back, with his arm out to the side. She had never reset someone's shoulder before, but she remembered seeing Diyah do it once. So she grabbed Drayk's arm and pulled it out to the side, then she placed her hand carefully on his shoulder and guided his arm up over his head. A sickening popping sound told her she'd done it. Drayk cried out in pain and sat bolt upright.

"A little warning next time?" he protested, clutching his arm and glowering.

"Don't be a child," said Catanya, sitting down next to him. "Here." She handed him the canteen. "Drink it. And try not to use your arm for the next few days."

Drayk took the canteen and drank deeply. He was still pale and clammy, but he seemed more alert, more lucid.

Catanya laid her head against the tree and closed her eyes, exhaling as she stretched her legs out. She was exhausted, everything hurt, and she longed to forget the last several hours.

"Thank you," said Drayk.

Catanya opened her eyes again and stared at him. Then she nodded and brought her knees up to her chest.

"Why did you protect me?" she asked. "You could do a lot with ten thousand gold pieces. Why not take me to Caerlon?"

Drayk sighed and looked away from her. "I have my reasons," he said mysteriously.

Catanya gave him a hard look. He just laughed.

"Alright, let's just say, I'm not a great supporter of your dear brother. Maybe I'm not all that eager to help him out." He took another sip of the canteen and swallowed heavily. "And I don't trade in human beings." He scowled as though remembering something painful.

"Who's Lia?" asked Catanya.

Drayk frowned. "Nobody." He adopted a forced calm tone. "Don't worry about it." He reached up with his right hand and, grimacing, pulled himself into a standing position. "We should make a plan," he announced, changing the subject. He closed his eyes, and Catanya thought he was fighting the urge to faint.

Jémys scoffed. "A plan?" he repeated. "We're not your gang. We don't need you to order us around."

Drayk opened his eyes and glared over at Jémys. "Well, if I know my *gang*"—he pronounced the word scathingly—"they won't give up. They'll find us. I suggest we get as far away as we can. Hold on." He looked at Catanya, alarm in his face. "You two were already running, weren't you?"

Neither Catanya nor Jémys said anything, but Drayk seemed to interpret their silence correctly. He swore loudly. "If Cadyan's men are on your trail, there's no time to waste. Trust me, the fírkon move fast."

"And where do you suggest we go?" asked Jémys, closing his eyes in frustration.

Drayk was silent for a moment. Then a dark shadow crossed his face. "I know a place. It's a sort of safe house, I suppose. I've used it before. We can lie low there for a while until we decide our next move."

"*We?*" repeated Jémys, glaring at him. Catanya had never

seen him stare at someone with such loathing. It was discon-
certing.

"What's your problem?" asked Drayk, stepping forward so
he was directly in front of Jémys.

"So many to choose from." Jémys rolled his eyes. "YOU!
You're my problem!" he shouted, suddenly livid, as he sprang to
his feet. "What makes you think you'll be coming with us?"

Drayk just laughed in his face. Despite his weakened state,
he could still match Jémys's animosity. "Oh, get over it already,
will you?"

"Get over it? Get *over* it?" Jémys let out an incredulous
laugh. "Who do you think you are? What gives you the right to
expect anything from us?"

"How about the fact that I just saved your skin?"

"Oh, right, you saved us from the situation we were only in
thanks to you!"

"Stop it!" shouted Catanya. She ran to stand between them,
putting one hand on each of their chests and pushing them
back. Drayk backed off, wincing, but Jémys stood unmoved.
"Stop it. This arguing isn't helping."

"I don't trust him," spat Jémys.

"Neither do I!" Catanya looked over at Drayk, but he just
shrugged it off. "Neither do I," she repeated. "But we stick
together, for now."

"Why?" Jémys sounded exasperated. "He's a liability. And
he's injured. He'll only slow us down."

"Injured or not, I bet I can still beat you," replied Drayk
with a smirk on his face.

Jémys took an angry step forward, but Catanya blocked
him.

"Stop it! Like it or not, we're in this together. Trust is a
luxury we do not have," she said coolly. "We don't have to like
one another, but we do need to cooperate if we plan to stay
alive."

Jémys was fuming, but Drayk seemed to find the situation amusing.

"Can you be civil?" asked Catanya, looking from one to the other.

"Anything you say, Catya, love." Drayk winked at her and grinned.

Jémys jerked his shoulders irritably, but seemed to deflate somewhat. He nodded.

Catanya lowered her hands. "Good. Now, this safe house of yours, Drayk, where is it?"

"A few days south of here roughly... on the outskirts of Glorna," he added, seeing the question in her eyes. "By the ocean."

"Okay..."

Catanya tried to think it through logically. Glorna was on the route towards Awnell and it would be good to have somewhere to stop and plan their next steps.

"Okay. We head there to start."

"Great," said Drayk, wearing a triumphant expression. "Follow me." And he led the way onward, his movements still laboured from the pain in his arm.

Seeing the disapproval on Jémys's face, Catanya pulled him aside. "Look, I don't like it either. I don't trust him. Not for a second. But we need somewhere we can safely regroup, and it's the only plan we've got."

Jémys sighed and nodded, but then he clenched his jaw. "Don't let your guard down," he whispered. "There's something he's not telling us."

<hr>

That night, they stopped to rest by a small stream. Catanya had insisted that Drayk and Jémys take the first shift sleeping while she kept watch. Drayk needed the sleep, and she was eager for some peace and quiet.

She sat for a while, propped against a log, listening to the stream trickle nearby and the wind rustle through the trees, as autumn leaves drifted to the ground. The air was crisp, so she pulled her cloak tighter around her arms to keep warm, and watched the shadows of the trees flicker in the moonlight.

She allowed her mind to drift, but she found it difficult to stop herself from dwelling on all the horrible things that had happened these past few months. Now that she had the peace and quiet she'd wanted, her thoughts were screaming at her. She pressed her thumbs firmly against her temples, trying to knead away the soreness. When that didn't work, she decided she needed a distraction.

She opened her bag, seized her canteen, and carried it over to the stream. After she refilled it, she rinsed her hands and splashed the water over her face. It was cold and bracing as it ran through her fingers and spattered on the front of her dress.

Reinvigorated, she perched on the bank, listening to an owl hooting nearby. For a moment she wished she could be that owl. Free to soar above the earth, unburdened and unafraid.

She sat perfectly still, listening, until a small shadow crossed the sky and she knew the owl was gone. With a heavy sigh, she took a sip from her canteen and listened to the other forest sounds, trying not to be afraid.

A little while later, she heard soft movements behind her and twisted to see Jémys coming to sit beside her.

"Are you alright?" he asked gently.

"I'm fine," she said, staring off into the distance. "Are you?" She turned to face him. They hadn't really talked since they'd left Finnua, and she was desperate to know what he was feeling, but she was afraid to ask. "How's your burn?" she said finally, settling on something a little easier.

Jémys shrugged and looked down at the spot where Drayk's sword had burned a hole through his clothes and seared his leg. "It doesn't hurt anymore," he said.

They sat together for several minutes, watching the stream and not saying anything.

Then Jémys sighed heavily. "Why didn't you just tell me?" he asked, sounding dejected. "If you had trusted me, maybe—" He broke off, shaking his head.

Catanya didn't need to ask what he meant. She rubbed her forehead wearily. "I wanted to tell you, but I didn't know how," she replied, fully aware how empty her response was. "Of course I trusted you—I still do. I was just afraid of how you'd react. You have to understand, Jémys, I don't want to be this person. I don't want any of this. And if *I* can't accept it, how could I expect you to accept it?"

Jémys nodded and squinted off into the distance, but he stayed silent. Catanya had the sense he was holding himself back from saying something that might hurt her.

She stared down at her feet, feeling disheartened and miserable.

But then she felt Jémys's hand take hers and her heart lifted. She looked up at him, gladdened. His eyes were still fixed pointedly in the opposite direction, but they shone in the darkness.

Catanya wanted to cry. She wanted to embrace him and tell him how sorry she was, how wretched and terrified she felt. But she contented herself with looking at him.

She understood. He hadn't forgiven her, but he still cared. And for now, that was enough.

They sat together in silence for a while. Catanya could have stayed like that forever, but eventually Jémys spoke, breaking the spell. "You must be tired," he said. "Why don't you go rest? I'll keep watch."

"Okay." Catanya withdrew her hand and stood up.

She walked away from the stream, back towards the area where Drayk lay fast asleep, and sat down on the soft forest floor, watching him curiously for a moment. She envied his apparent ability to disregard everything that had happened, to tune everything out and make light of the situation.

As she laid her head down on the forest floor, she thought bitterly to herself that at least someone could sleep soundly. She closed her eyes, dreading another night full of tormented dreams.

As usual, she slept poorly, and when she awoke again, she could hear birds chirping and hushed voices nearby.

"You don't need to worry, mate. I'm on your side now."

"I am not your mate. And I don't care. I don't trust you and I never will."

Jémys and Drayk were a few feet away, bickering. Catanya didn't want to get pulled into their argument, so she lay still, pretending to sleep.

"Fine by me. I don't need your trust. It's not *your* trust that matters, now is it?" retorted Drayk.

"You're awfully confident, considering only hours ago you heard her say she didn't trust you either." Jémys sounded irritable and tense.

"How do you imagine I've gotten through life if not by embracing my overconfidence?"

Even with her eyes closed, she could tell by his glib tone that Drayk was grinning.

"I assumed by living dishonourably and only caring about yourself," said Jémys.

"I do whatever is necessary to survive. Surely even you can understand that."

Catanya could feel the frustration bubbling up inside her. She had hoped that Jémys and Drayk would at least try to be civil. Of course, Jémys had every right to be angry—to hate

Drayk. But Catanya was tired, and she had no intention of playing peacekeeper for this entire journey.

"When it comes down to it, you'll betray us to save your own skin. I'll bet on that," said Jémys.

Drayk let out a short laugh. "Never bet with a dishonourable man. That's a bet you're not likely to win."

"Just know this," muttered Jémys, and the threatening tone of his voice was clear. "When you cross us, and you *will* cross us, I will not hesitate to kill you."

"Ooh, should I be scared?" asked Drayk.

"Your overconfidence will be your undoing. Mark my words."

"Consider them marked." There was a hint of irony in Drayk's voice.

"You think we need you, but we don't," snapped Jémys. "The only reason you're here is because Catanya feels sorry for you. Because you're hurt and she would never leave you to die in the woods. But sooner or later, she'll remember what kind of man you are and she'll realize that we don't need you."

"Strong words coming from you."

"What exactly is that supposed to mean?"

"You think she needs *you*?" Drayk laughed, evidently enjoying the reaction he'd provoked. "No, the truth is that she doesn't need either of us. And when she realizes that, where do you think that'll leave us?"

There was a short pause. Catanya sensed their eyes on her.

"Trust me, mate. I've met plenty of powerful people in my life, and none of them even come close to her. I look forward to the day she realizes that."

"So do I."

"Do you?" Drayk sounded sceptical. "Now who's overconfident?"

Catanya didn't want to hear any more of their sniping, so

she stretched theatrically and sat up. "What time is it?" she asked.

"It's not late. The sun only just came up." Jémys stood up quickly and walked away from Drayk.

"Good, we should keep moving." Catanya rubbed her eyes as she climbed to her feet, and walked past Jémys to stand in front of Drayk. "How's your shoulder?"

"Fine."

"Let me see." She crouched down next to him and motioned for him to take off his coat and vest. As she pulled back his tunic to see his shoulder, she noticed several scars on his back and a large burn mark across his chest just above his ribs. She looked up at him searchingly, but Drayk pulled his shirt back up over his shoulder, averting his eyes.

"See, it's fine." He snatched up his clothes. "Shall we go?"

Catanya paused, momentarily lost in thought. Then she collected herself and said, "Yes, let's go."

22

—

## LORD ZADÍLAR

The afternoon sun hung low in the sky, signalling that the day was already nearing its end. The days were getting shorter, which always made Diyah miserable. She had never forgotten the warmth and sunshine of her home in Murina. Farther south, they didn't lose as much daylight as the northern cities in winter, and at this time of year she always found herself pining for her home.

Diyah put down her tools and moved to stand in the narrow patch of sunlight that still streamed through her window. The warmth of it prickled her skin and she imagined herself standing in her family's garden, back in Murina.

She had been a little over six years old when she'd left her home to live at Camlee Lodge, but she still remembered the soft sand under her toes, the flush greenery of the olive and stone pine trees, and the sweet, flowery smell in the air.

She wondered how much of her home was still there. The plague that killed her parents had decimated the town, but maybe others survived, maybe Murina had recovered.

It had always struck Diyah as odd that she remembered the town so clearly but struggled to remember the people. She could still remember her mother's face, her smile and her laugh; she could remember feeling loved and safe, but that was all. Just a collection of images and impressions, but nothing more concrete. She knew she'd loved her mother, and they were happy together, but there were no other memories for her to hold on to.

It was like that with everyone in Murina, every person she had ever known there, except her father.

Diyah remembered everything about him. Perhaps it was because she'd spent the most time with him, or because he was a Heiltúir like her and they'd shared a different type of connection. She didn't know why, but she remembered every conversation they'd ever had and every story he'd ever told her. When she closed her eyes, she could relive the days she spent watching him work and learning from him.

He taught her to read at a very young age and they used to sit together for hours, looking through books and talking about them. Even after she went to Camlee Lodge, she continued to learn quickly, devouring every book in Genna's library and enquiring about the world outside. She had never questioned it until she started helping Genna teach the younger girls and realized how strange she really was.

Even Catanya—who was a couple of years older and quite clever herself—had never managed to keep up with Diyah.

Diyah wasn't sure if she was just unusual or if this was another part of her Heiltúir ancestry she didn't fully understand. With her father gone, there was no one left for her to ask.

She often wondered what became of his books. The townspeople had probably burned them along with everything else that had been exposed to the infection. Her father had tried desperately to explain that it was an unnecessary precaution, but people were frightened. They weren't healers, they didn't understand the way illnesses spread. It was easy to see how superstition took control.

Diyah ran her fingers through her hair and drifted back to her worktable, trying to turn her mind to more present matters.

Work had been steady lately—a few broken bones and a bout of wheezing cough—it was nothing she couldn't handle. But as the weather grew colder, an influx of illnesses would hit the city, and she wanted to prepare a supply of remedies now so they'd be ready when she needed them.

Besides, the more she worked, the less she dwelled on the things she couldn't control.

So Diyah worked, slicing, mincing, and grinding as many ingredients as she could find to make her medicines. She made a list of what she needed, with approximate quantities based on her projections of the most likely illnesses. The list included sleeping draughts, pain-relief tonics, and a special disinfectant salve her father had taught her about years ago.

The salve was the trickiest concoction to mix. She needed to heat an exact amount of balsam to the perfect temperature before blending in a combination of oils and bringing it to a jellylike consistency. Then she'd add the ground spices and herbs.

As the mixture reached the correct temperature, it always gave off a putrid smell, and after several batches, Diyah was growing nauseated. Her face was covered in sweat from the constant heat, and her hair had matted unpleasantly against her neck.

She was scooping the remaining salve out of the mixing bowl and into a sealable container, when someone knocked on her door.

Diyah looked up, startled to find the sun had set. The room was dark, except the fire burning behind the grate. She had been so focused on her work that she hadn't noticed the hours passing.

"Come in," she called. Fehla had promised to visit with a bottle of spiced wine, and Diyah was looking forward to having the company. She put her bowl down and began lighting the candles on her worktable.

The door opened and Diyah was surprised to hear the sound of laughter. She turned to see a man standing outside her door, surrounded by a group of firkon. They were talking in loud, jubilant voices, like they'd spent the day drinking together.

"Well, gentlemen, as delightful as this afternoon has been, I'm afraid I must attend to my business now." The man inclined his head, smiling widely at the firkon.

The surrounding men all grumbled resignedly.

"Aye, it's good to see you though, Zad, come back soon, eh?"

"Depend upon it," the man replied, waving them off, before turning to waltz into the physician's quarters.

Diyah was thrown off guard. She had never seen this man before, but he was obviously someone important. He was dressed in a smart, spotless outfit, with a high-collared coat and a blue silk undershirt. His neatly threaded hair was ashy with hints of black still visible, and his boyish face was lined in a way that suggested he had done a great deal of smiling in his life.

"Can I help you?" she asked tetchily, standing up straighter. Anyone who could mingle so happily with firkon was not someone she was keen to meet.

"Forgive the late intrusion," he spoke in a smooth voice that had a glib undertone. "I'm afraid the lads were rather reluctant to let me go."

He chuckled affectionately and Diyah felt a stab of annoyance.

"I was told I could find you here." He crossed the room with surprisingly spry steps for a man his age, and extended his hand in greeting. "Lord Zadílar, at your service. I'm delighted to meet you at last."

Diyah hesitated. She wiped her hand on her smock before

taking his, somewhat reluctantly. "At last?" she asked, raising her eyebrows.

Zadílar smiled deliberately. "Oh, yes." He pressed her hand to his lips in an old-fashioned sign of deference that took Diyah by surprise. "I heard Caerlon had a new healer, but I never dreamed it would be one so young, nor so pretty, if you don't mind me saying." His eyes twinkled as he released her hand and leaned over the cluttered worktable. "So what have you been mixing today?" He spoke as though he were just making pleasant conversation with an old friend.

Diyah was disoriented. "A disinfectant salve," she replied, wary and uncomfortable. Normally she prided herself on her ability to read people, but this man was strange, he seemed oddly artificial.

"Is that so?" He sounded impressed. "Splendid, simply splendid!" He looked up at her, beaming. "And how do you like your new post, eh? Court physician of Caerlon. You must be pleased."

Diyah resisted the urge to snort. *Pleased*, she thought. That was hardly the word for it.

Zadílar was watching her with a smirk, as though he knew exactly what she was thinking. "It is a great honour to serve our young king, isn't it?" His mouth twisted into a wider grin, as he eyed Diyah with amusement.

"If you say so," she retorted, realizing too late that it probably wasn't wise.

Zadílar laughed out loud. "Oh, my dear, you ought to be careful. Opinions like that could get you killed."

Diyah frowned, suddenly irate and defiant. "Is that a warning or a threat?" she asked.

Zadílar smiled from ear to ear. "Both, and neither, I should say."

Diyah stared at him. He was either teasing her or testing her, and she didn't want to play along.

Zadílar laughed again. "Forgive me, my dear. I like to provoke, it's one of my bad habits... or so I'm told." He chuckled. "You're quite right to object. But as I'm sure you can attest, sometimes us clever folks need a little sport to keep our minds sharp, keep us entertained. You understand, of course." He inclined his head towards her. "You're exactly what I imagined. A very bright young woman, that much is obvious, and I suspect you're a very gifted healer."

Diyah shifted uneasily, unsure how to respond. "So you've heard about me?" She was surprised to think news of her had spread so fast.

"Oh, I keep up with the rumours." He gave a benign nod and turned to examine the books on the shelf. "And when rumours of a Heiltúir in Caerlon reach my ears, I pay attention."

Diyah was shocked. She could understand how rumours of a court physician might spread, but hardly anybody knew her heritage, and the Heiltúir had all but faded into legend. So how did this man know?

"Forgive me," she said a little coolly, "but I'm still not sure who you are, Lord Za—"

"Zadílar," he finished, nodding. "But of course a name is just a name, isn't it?" He chuckled, turning around to face her again. "Who I am is the Lord Steward of Sidina. At your service, my dear." He inclined his head.

Comprehension dawned on Diyah. She *had* heard of him before. Everyone had.

Sidina was the second largest city in Caerlon, and he was the steward who controlled it. He managed the city on behalf of the king, and in return he received a substantial income. Zadílar had never married and the rumours were that he spent his considerable wealth on frivolous entertainment and recreation. His older brother had died after one year of service in the firkon. Zadílar was only twelve years old when he'd assumed control of the city.

Sidina had once been its own kingdom, but during the Quiescence Wars, its king had chosen to surrender rather than see his subjects suffer the way those in Bratia had. He relinquished his throne and made a deal with Maílater Caer to ensure his people's safety under the new regime.

The land around Sidina held the biggest iron deposits in the kingdom. Many of its workers specialized in crafting the greatest weapons and armour known to man. It was said that even the king's magic couldn't craft finer metal, and every piece of armour outfitted for the firkon came from Sidina.

Miners had carved the city into the earth over years of working the land. It's red-soil chasms rippled outwards, encircling the central city with layers of valleys and plateaus. Some of the smaller basins had filled with water, sprouting new life and decorating the land with sparkling pools and hot springs.

Diyah had always thought it sounded like a decadent place. It was a favourite retreat for the royal family and the wealthiest members of court. Thanks in large part to the grand welcome they received from Zadílar.

"Oh." Diyah shifted again. "Well... it's... it's nice to meet you." She felt awkward, trying not to dislike him just because of his title. "My name is Diyah and, as you said, I'm the court healer so... is there something I can help you with?" It had been a long day. She was tired and looking forward to a quiet evening with Fehla.

"Diyah?" repeated Zadílar, his eyes twinkling again. "Now *there* is a name." He chuckled again and rocked back and forth on his heels, contemplating her with a serene smile. "Right, I won't sport with you any longer," he continued, seeing her expression. "My apologies." He inclined his head once again. "I have come here today to seek your expertise. There is a sickness sweeping through my city and I'm afraid our healers are struggling."

"A sickness?" Diyah's curiosity was piqued by the hint of genuine concern she detected. "Describe it to me." She began loading her jars of salve into a small crate, as she listened to Zadílar's description.

"We've had several deaths already and haven't been able to stop the spread. It starts with extreme fatigue, then difficulty breathing and pain. Eventually they develop a deep cough and are no longer able to eat or drink."

Diyah lifted the crate off her table and carried it over to an empty shelf. "Hmm." She crouched down next to one of the cabinets, searching for the right jar.

From Zadílar's description, this sickness sounded like the same lung and throat inflammation she had treated in Mellot Cove a few years ago.

"Here it is." She pulled a large pot of a sticky brown substance off the shelf and carried it back to the table, where she ladled a generous amount into another, smaller container. "Take this," she said, handing it to him. "Mix a pea-sized amount with a full pot of water and heat it into vapour. It will ease the breathing troubles and pain. I'll give you a list of herbs for your healer to blend in order to treat the stomach issues. I would send some with you, but it needs to be made fresh."

Diyah pulled a loose piece of parchment from a pile on the table and began scratching down the list of ingredients for the stomach tonic. "They should drink this mixture twice a day until the illness is completely gone." She blew on the parchment to dry the ink before handing it to him.

Zadílar glanced down at the sheet and smiled. "I thank you." He tucked it into one of his coat pockets.

Diyah nodded. Now that he had his remedy, she assumed he'd be on his way. But instead, he continued to stand there, watching her with a shrewd look on his face.

"I am sorry," he said finally. For the first time since his arrival, he seemed serious.

Diyah was taken aback. "Sorry about what?"

Zadílar gestured around the room. "There are many who might dream of holding this post, but it's not an enviable position, is it? And we both know you weren't given a choice."

Diyah was stunned. "How did you—"

Zadílar waved away her comment. "Oh, please. The official story might suggest you accepted this post owing to your loyalty to Caerlon, but I've been around long enough to know which stories are true and which stories are absolute hogwash. You're a prisoner here, aren't you?"

Diyah eyed him cautiously before nodding.

"I suspected as much," said Zadílar. "That's what everyone else will never understand. What it's like to have the illusion of freedom, the illusion of control. It's almost worse somehow, isn't it? And for you..." His eyebrows creased pityingly. "This is going to be very difficult. *A Heiltúir is first and foremost honest.*" He recited the words from the ancient Heiltúir oath.

Diyah gaped at him. "How do you know that? Are you a Heiltúir too?" She had never met another Heiltúir, not since her father. And until now, she'd never realized how badly she longed to know she wasn't alone.

Zadílar gave her a sad smile. "No, my dear, I'm afraid I am just a man. However, I am familiar with Heiltúir beliefs, and I'm sorry to say that if you want to survive, you may be obliged to do things you never would have considered."

"What do you mean?" asked Diyah. Now she was beginning to feel nervous.

"Honesty is not your friend. You must be calculating and vigilant." Zadílar sighed and walked around the worktable so he was standing in front of Diyah. He lowered his voice to a whisper and continued, "I came here with two intentions today. To seek your help, but also to offer you mine. You're in a dangerous position, Diyah. There are forces at play here we don't fully understand, and there's no telling how everything will unfold. Change is coming, but until then, we wait. Keep your priorities clear, but never let them see, never let them know what you're thinking."

He took her hands in his and squeezed. Diyah's head raced as she struggled to keep up with his sudden and intense candour.

"I'm afraid it is not within my power to help you escape, it's too great a risk. But there will always be a place for you in Sidina, my dear. In fact, I'm working now to build a hospital of sorts, a sanctuary where we can train other healers... perhaps one day..." He rubbed his chin. "In the meantime, if ever you need anything, you can count upon my friendship. I made a promise long ago and—"

The sound of someone knocking on the door cut him off. He dropped her hands and circled quickly back around the worktable, just as the door opened to reveal Fehla.

She stopped dead when she saw who was in there.

"Zadílar." She pronounced his name with coolness. "I didn't know you were in the city."

"*Queen* Fehla," he declared, overemphasizing her title and stooping into an exaggerated bow. He had reverted to his original facetious manner, with no sign that anything more serious had happened. "I wasn't aware you needed to be kept apprised of my activity, I'll be sure to have my valet inform you of my movements in the future. Do you prefer written updates or oral accounts? Or perhaps I should commission a group of players." He grinned, but Fehla just rolled her eyes, stepped into the room, and closed the door.

"Why are you here?" she asked in a brusque, snappish tone.

"Why are any of us here, my dear? You cannot expect me to know the answer to such a question." He was smiling even wider now, enjoying the jest.

Fehla scowled. "Well, Cadyan is away, so it seems you've wasted a trip."

"Is he now? How silly of me! You'd think I would have checked before making the journey, but alas, here I am. Perfectly on time to miss the king." Zadílar snapped his fingers in mock disappointment and winked at Diyah when Fehla wasn't looking.

"Very well," said Fehla, her mouth drawn in a thin line. "If you haven't come to meet my son, then why are you here? I can't imagine anyone here actually sent for you."

Zadílar rocked back and forth on his heels again. "Oh, I fancied a change of scenery. You know how it is... Besides, I couldn't miss out on the opportunity to welcome your new healer. What a stroke of luck! A Heiltúir showing up just when poor Grante became... well... *indisposed.*"

Fehla's face flushed. "Grante was my friend."

Zadílar clicked his tongue disapprovingly. "That's a shame, isn't it? But I always told him he was foolish to trust you. Alas, he refused to heed my advice and now look where we are. But" —he spread his arms in a gesture of mock resignation—"what's done is done. At least now, we have the delightful Diyah to brighten up this dismal place. Isn't that right?"

He winked at Diyah again. Fehla's face burned bright red as she glared at him, hatred in her eyes.

"We all make decisions we have to live with, don't we, Fehla?" he continued. "And from what I hear, *several* of your decisions are coming back to haunt you, aren't they?"

Fehla stared at him, stony-faced.

"I'll take that as a yes." He grinned and shook his head. "Fehla, Fehla, Fehla," he drawled, collecting the jar off the table and walking to stand next to her. "I always knew you were a short-sighted fool, but I never thought you were stupid. Apparently I was wrong." He turned back to face Diyah. "Thank you again, my dear, and remember what I said, will you?"

He nodded, eyes twinkling, and cast Fehla a scornful look, before sweeping out of the room and leaving a stunned silence in his wake.

Fehla let out a loud huff, and joined Diyah beside the worktable.

"What was all that about?" Diyah's head was reeling as she tried to make sense of everything Zadílar had said.

Fehla's expression hardened. "*That* was just an ongoing quarrel between two people who've hated each other since the moment they met." Fehla pursed her lips. "He is honestly the most pompous and impertinent man I have ever known, lording his superiority over others and acting like he knows everything. He is a slimy, untrustworthy disease of a man!" She slammed the wine bottle onto the table. "What did he say to you before I arrived? He delights in making mischief and tormenting people."

Diyah turned around to collect glasses off the shelf behind her, hiding her face from view. "Oh, he came to get a remedy for an illness in Sidina," she said. She still wasn't sure how she felt about Zadílar, and she doubted Fehla would be open to hearing different perspectives.

"Well, let's hope that's all he wanted," said Fehla darkly.

Diyah handed the glasses to her.

Diyah had come to trust Fehla, but she had to admit that Fehla's judgement hadn't always been sound. She had made several poor decisions in her life, and this Lord Zadílar seemed like the sort of person who planned his moves well in advance. It was no wonder they didn't get along.

Zadílar was obviously an astute man who could use his charm to disarm people, giving him the advantage in most situations. So why had he let his guard down with Diyah? His offer of friendship had seemed sincere. And despite her first impression, Diyah felt inclined to trust him.

There was something else too, something Diyah couldn't

quite place. A sense of familiarity, like she'd met him once before and couldn't remember.

Whatever it was, Diyah couldn't deny that his words had resonated with her.

*Keep your priorities clear, but never let them see, never let them know what you're thinking.*

She had never excelled at concealing her emotions. But she knew he was right. If she was going to survive, she needed to keep herself in check. It wasn't going to be easy.

**23**

———

## COTTAGES AND DREAMS

The wind tugged at Catanya's skirt and cloak as she stumbled across the slimy rocks. A dense mist hung in the air, lending an eerie loneliness to the weather-beaten cottage ahead. It was perched on a shallow bluff overlooking the ocean, where massive waves rose and crashed against the shore, threatening to tear the building down.

"This is what you call a safe house?" called Jémys from behind her. Intense winds were gusting so loudly that he nearly had to scream to make himself heard.

"What's the matter? Afraid of a little water?" called Drayk, smiling back at them.

The look of apprehension mixed with defiance on Jémys's face made Catanya wonder if maybe he actually was nervous.

"What is this place?" she asked, quickening her pace to match Drayk's. In her haste, she lost her footing and stumbled. Drayk caught her just before she hit the ground. He paused for a moment, looking into her face and wincing faintly from the pain in his shoulder. Then he hoisted her up so that she stood pressed against him.

"Thanks," she said, stepping away from him.

"Don't mention it." His hand was still on Catanya's waist and his eyes twinkled as they drifted across her face.

"I'm fine now," she said emphatically. His gaze was making her uncomfortable.

"Of course." He dropped his hand, looking a little stunned, and smiling sheepishly.

"So..." Catanya glanced at Jémys, who frowned as he caught up. "What is this place?" she asked Drayk again.

"It's just an old sea cottage. It has been abandoned for years."

"How did you learn about it?" Catanya peered around, taking in the isolated surroundings. She found it hard to believe anyone could have ever lived here.

"I've known about it for ages."

"Well." Jémys clapped Drayk on the shoulder and smirked at the sight of him wincing. "Let's hope *it's* not rotten inside and out." He gave Drayk a snide glance as he brushed past him to walk with Catanya.

When they reached the front door, Drayk grimaced as he pushed it open and it creaked painfully on its hinges. Inside, the building was dark and gloomy. It contained only two cramped rooms. The first held a meagre stone fireplace in one corner, accompanied by a stack of uneven firewood, and a long rickety table with three mismatched chairs. The second room held a narrow, soggy-looking bed and an assortment of torn parchment and broken trinkets on the floor. One wall was charred and blackened as if it had been scorched in a fire.

"So... how long do we plan to stay here," asked Jémys in a whisper, as he followed Catanya into the second room. He looked just as unsettled as she felt.

Catanya shivered. "I don't know... hopefully just a few days. We need to decide where we're going next, and it'll be nice to be inside at least." She tried to convince herself it was true, but part of her thought this place might be worse than the forest.

She glanced at Drayk, who was still standing near the entrance, surveying his surroundings with disdain. The dark shadow had returned to his features, giving him an oddly unhinged appearance.

"Drayk?" she asked hesitantly.

"Hmm?" He seemed to pull himself out of some reverie. "Right." He clapped his hands together with a return of his usual bravado, and marched across the room, yanking the table forward a few feet. He knelt down and used his dagger to pry up a section of the floorboards to reveal an assortment of items beneath. Then he pulled out a good-sized sack of gold, an axe, several blankets and swords, a handful of candles, a long ornate spear, and what appeared to be a fishing net.

"Here." He tossed the net to Jémys. "I trust you know how to fish."

It was late by the time the smell of roasting fish and the sound of crackling wood filled the cottage.

As Catanya ate, she remembered the last time she'd been this close to the ocean. It was before she had left Faltir. Before she had lost so much, and before she'd become a fugitive. She enjoyed being near the ocean again. It felt like home to her. Her eyes tingled as she thought back over her favourite memories on the beach in Faltir. But those memories belonged to someone else now.

"What is it?" asked Jémys.

Catanya was surprised to see him studying her face. "Nothing," she lied, blinking the tears out of her eyes.

Drayk was lounging against the wall, watching the exchange with mild interest. Catanya caught his eye momentarily before standing up.

"I'm just tired," she said. "I think I'll try to get some sleep."

"Take the bed." Drayk gestured to the other room and tossed his remaining fish bones into the fire. "I'll keep watch tonight," he added, staring into the flames.

"Thank you." Catanya yawned and walked over to the door.

"Wait." Jémys jumped up to meet her. He frowned and lowered his voice, "Don't tell me you actually trust him."

Catanya sighed. "I don't know, Jémys. I'm tired. And he got us this far, didn't he? What reason would he have to betray us now?"

Jémys glanced back at Drayk. "Men like him don't need a reason."

"Jémys," Catanya reproached him patiently, "I really don't think we need to worry about him."

Jémys stared at her in disbelief. "How can you say that? After everything he's done?"

Catanya frowned. "I don't know." She had been thinking a lot about her conversation with Drayk in the woods, and the way he'd reacted when his gang had suggested they take her to Caerlon. "I guess... I think he's on our side."

"But how can you be sure?"

Catanya didn't know how to explain it. It was a sense she had about Drayk similar to how she had intuitively trusted Jémys when she first met him. Or Diyah. She didn't exactly trust Drayk, but she knew that, for now at least, he was their ally.

"Look, if you can't trust him, can you at least trust me?" She ran her hands down Jémys's arms and searched his eyes. "You trust me, don't you?" She gently pulled him towards the room with her. "Please come stay with me tonight. I don't want to be alone."

Jémys closed his eyes and took a few steps forward before stopping. He stared down at her, eyes tight with pain. "I did trust you, Catanya. And look what happened." Then he stepped away and strode back to the fire. "We'll both keep watch tonight. Someone has to keep an eye on you," he said, shooting Drayk a scowl.

Drayk just snorted and shook his head. But as Catanya left

the room, feeling miserable and disheartened, she thought she heard him mutter under his breath, "You're a fool."

---

Catanya slept unevenly that night. The bed was cold and damp, and her mind raced with all the thoughts and worries that plagued her during the daytime. She found herself in a state between dreaming and wakefulness, and she had the sense that someone was with her.

She could sense a presence, but she couldn't see anyone.

Then she heard it—a voice coming from somewhere deep in the darkness saying, "It's high time we met, don't you agree? *Sister*." Then suddenly she was surrounded by death. There were bodies strewn all around her in heaps of broken limbs and pools of blood. Lady Genna...

"No..." Catanya moaned.

Diyah...

"No!"

Alli, Meya, Gréys...

"No, stop it!"

Nelle and Olly...

Hot tears streamed down Catanya's face, as she spun around, desperate to escape the horror of the bodies lying at her feet.

Then someone laughed a high, callous laugh. She turned to see the man standing beside her. She saw the face that resembled hers so closely, the same steely eyes and thin nose, the same high cheekbones and dark eyebrows... but he was wearing an expression she didn't recognize, an expression of cruel amusement and triumph.

"Well done, sister," he said, giving her a proud smile. "Now let's go home." He held out his hand for her. As she lifted her own, she realized it was covered in blood.

Catanya bolted upright. Her heart was racing frantically and she was shivering, drenched in sweat. She could tell from the pale light outside that it was near dawn. Soft voices murmured behind the door, and it comforted her to know Jémys and Drayk were nearby.

She swung her legs off the bed and sat for a few minutes, waiting for her heart to steady and trying not to dwell on her nightmare. With her face buried in her hands, she moaned, struggling to force the images of her dead loved ones out of her mind.

She opened her eyes and cast around for a distraction. Her eyes landed on the pile of torn parchment beside the bed, and she bent down to grab the nearest piece, turning it over to reveal a crude drawing of a boy on the other side. It reminded her of the drawings the young girls at the lodge used to show her when she tried to teach them.

Smiling at the memory, she grabbed the remaining parchments and laid them on the bed to examine them. She found several drawings of the same little boy. The most detailed one, which had obviously taken the child quite some time, was torn along one edge. Part of the drawing was missing, so she rifled through the remaining parchment until she found several smaller pieces and laid them together, trying to reform the picture.

The complete drawing depicted a woman smiling and holding the little boy's hand. As Catanya stared at the innocent picture, she felt overcome with sadness.

Without warning, the edges of her vision blurred and a stream of images flashed before her eyes. She couldn't make sense of anything she was seeing, and it happened so fast it made her dizzy. She gripped the edge of the bed, trying to focus on something—anything.

Somewhere in the distance she heard the faint sound of a child crying. It wasn't the dramatic cry of a child throwing a fit; it was the quiet sobbing of a child who just couldn't stop.

Catanya's heart ached, and as she yearned to help the child, her vision became clear.

A young boy of six or seven was crouching, huddled in the corner of the room, and sobbing uncontrollably into his knees. In his hand, he clutched the torn-up drawing of the boy and his mother.

Catanya stood up and walked towards him, hoping to comfort him. As he came into clearer focus, she had to stifle a cry. Along his arm and one side of his face were the purple and green outlines of bruises, all at different stages of healing.

She was reaching out to touch him, when the door banged open and a figure appeared, silhouetted in the frame like a furious shadow.

"Get up, you worthless shit!" shouted the woman.

Before the boy could react, she lifted a clay pot off a nearby shelf and hurled it at him. The pot cracked in half as it struck his head and crashed to the floor.

The boy yelped and jumped up, clutching his bleeding forehead.

"Now look what you did! Useless, ungrateful brat!" She turned on her heel and stormed away.

Catanya's eyes began to blur again. She struggled to hold on to the vision, but it faded fast. The last thing she saw was the awful heartbreak in the boy's brilliant blue eyes, as tears streamed silently down his cheeks.

Catanya blinked. She was back in the present, shaking with emotion and still holding the torn pieces of paper. She peered down at them. They were charred around the edges, with faint smudges as though tears had bled through the pencil marks. She stared at the image of that little boy, feeling a tight, aching sensation build in her chest.

This was Drayk's childhood home.

She examined the dreary walls and remnants of a previous life, trying to imagine a boy Drayk growing up here. Catanya wanted to cry. She couldn't stop seeing the little boy, weeping all alone with no one to listen.

She stared helplessly at the pictures in her hand. Being an orphan didn't seem so bad now that she thought about it. She felt sick, as she remembered the burns and scars on Drayk's body. What kind of mother would do that to their child?

Then she recalled what Fin had said the night they'd fought in the woods. *I was there when Lia pulled this wretch ou' o' the filth and decided to keep 'im instead of killin' 'im.*

Is this what he was talking about? Had this Lia person found Drayk here and saved him? Saved him from an abusive mother?

Catanya couldn't imagine being raised by an abusive parent. She thought about Lady Genna and how wonderful she had been.

*I'm so lucky my mother sent me to Faltir,* she thought. Then with a pang she realized that her mother had only done that to save her—to save her from growing up with a father like Casréyan.

For the first time, Catanya felt something akin to gratitude for the mother who'd abandoned her. Gratitude for the mother who'd given her daughter away, sparing her a life of torment, like the one this beautiful little boy had known.

She looked down at the paper and experienced a second pang as she remembered her brother—her brother, who had not been spared that torment, but had grown up surrounded by it.

Catanya didn't know what to feel. She thought she might burst from the pressure building inside. She wanted to cry and curse the Natures, or drain every ounce of sadness and guilt from her soul.

There was a faint knock, and Jémys spoke, "Catanya, are you awake?"

"Yes." She hastily folded the bits of parchment and tucked them in her pocket, just as Jémys pushed open the door. "Yes, I'm awake," she breathed.

"I thought you might like something to eat," he said.

"Yes, I'm famished." She managed a grateful smile and followed him out of the room.

---

As they ate that morning, Catanya had trouble focusing on anything they discussed. Her mind kept wandering back to the pictures in her pocket or to the castle in Caerlon, where she imagined Casréyan abusing his son.

More than once, she caught herself staring at Drayk across the table, lost in thought. She wanted to reach out and comfort him. But he wasn't that little boy anymore, and whatever his childhood had been, that didn't change the fact that he'd done some truly horrible things as an adult.

Nevertheless, she couldn't help but feel differently towards him. She thought she saw a glimmer of that sweet boy peeking out from under his haughty grin, and she detected something in his eyes, like a deep emptiness and a longing to fill that void.

"Catanya, are you listening?" Jémys's voice took a while to reach her.

"Hmm?" she asked, turning to face him. "Sorry, what were you saying?"

"What's going on with you this morning?" Jémys looked from Catanya to Drayk, his face set in a suspicious frown.

"Me? Oh, no-nothing. I just didn't sleep very well." Catanya stifled a yawn.

Jémys eyed her and nodded. Then he leaned in and asked, "More nightmares?"

"What?" Catanya gaped at him in shock. She didn't think anyone had noticed.

Jémys gave her a sympathetic look and opened his mouth to respond.

"Well, whatever we decide," Drayk spoke over him. "We should do it soon. My men won't be far behind us." The corners of his mouth twitched, as he laced his fingers behind his head and leaned back, balancing on only two chair legs.

"You say that like it's something you're proud of," said Jémys.

Drayk smirked. "Well, what can I say? My men are exceptional trackers. Only the best can do what we do, you know? And only the best of the best can be their leader," he added, winking at Catanya.

"Is this all a big game to you?" snapped Jémys.

Drayk laughed, his eyes twinkling in the light of the early morning sun.

"This isn't a game. This is serious and—"

"Listen, mate, you need to lighten up. You only get one life, so you may as well try to enjoy it."

"Well, excuse me if I don't find it enjoyable to be hunted far and wide by legions of corrupt soldiers and outlaws."

"Well, that's your problem, isn't it?" Drayk leaned forward, slamming his chair back down on all four legs. "Me, I happen to love a challenge." His smirk didn't falter as he turned from Jémys to Catanya. "Don't you, Catya?" He stared at her intensely for a moment before continuing, "I say let them come, I'd welcome a chance for revenge on those lads."

"And if they capture Catanya and take her to Caerlon, that's fine by you?"

Drayk just continued smirking.

"I think you'd better figure out whose side you're on," spat Jémys, standing up and walking over to the fire. He muttered something about getting fresh air, snatched his cloak off the back of his chair, and marched out of the cottage.

Drayk chuckled to himself, as he tilted his chair back once again. "He's wound up awfully tight, isn't he? I can think of a few ways to help him unwind..." He clicked his tongue suggestively.

Catanya ignored Drayk's last comment. "Jémys has been through a lot," she said, staring at his empty seat.

Drayk snorted. "Haven't we all?"

Catanya surveyed him, as he pulled out a small dagger from inside his vest and started twirling it absentmindedly in his hand. After a while, his eyes glazed over as he stared, transfixed, at the wall, his features clouded by revulsion.

"This was your home, wasn't it?" asked Catanya.

Drayk looked at her, his face blank. "It was never a home."

"I found these." She pulled out the pictures from inside her pocket, unfolded them and slid them across the table.

Drayk glanced at them.

"They're yours, aren't they? You lived here with your mother?"

Drayk said nothing.

"What happened?" she pressed gently.

Drayk sighed as he contemplated her. "Listen, Catya, I am who I am. Don't go seeking an explanation. There's no soft side to me and searching for one is a waste of your time."

"But—"

"I'm sorry to disappoint you, love, but what you see is what you get. I'm just an outlaw. A greedy, shameless rake." He winked at her again. "Nothing more."

"You weren't always like this." She pushed the pictures forward insistently.

Drayk's face contorted into a pained half-smile, half-scowl. "There's no going back." He brushed them away again. "You should know that better than anyone." Then he moved to stand in front of the fire with his back towards her.

Catanya took the pieces of parchment off the table, folded them, and put them back in her pocket, ignoring the sting of disappointment.

**24**

---

# THE DROWNING DRAGON

adyan jumped down off his horse and stood for a moment examining the shabby building in front of him. A large, crooked sign hung above the door that read *The Drowning Dragon Inn and Tavern*. The air was thick with the stench of urine and stale barkbeer. He could hear loud voices and laughter inside the inn, and he thought, with a cringe of revulsion, that this would be a terrible spot to spend an evening.

"So this is the tavern?" he asked, raising his eyebrows at Julyán, who had just jumped down from his horse to stand beside his king.

"Yes, Your Majesty," said Julyán. "If she passed through this area, someone in that tavern will know. I guarantee it."

"How can you be sure?" asked Slaedir. He tossed his reins to another firkon and strode over to join them.

"Because it's the only tavern for miles. Everyone ends up here eventually."

"It's disgusting." Cadyan stared at the building with disdain and revulsion. "How long would it have taken her to walk here from that village—what's it called?"

"Finnua," replied Julyán mechanically. "Maybe four days. Three, if she didn't make many stops."

Ten days had passed since Cadyan and his men left Caerlon City, and Cadyan was growing more and more impatient. He was determined to find his sister and put an end to the rumours sweeping through his kingdom—to remind his people that *he* was their only rightful leader.

"Let's go inside then," he said. "Slaedir, Julyán, with me. The rest of you wait here." He marched forward and pushed open the door.

Inside, the tavern was dank and dusty. There was a large bar on one end where a grumpy-looking barman stood, polishing glasses and mumbling to himself. The common room was full of assorted tables where groups of drunken men sat noisily talking and singing. Several lewdly dressed women drifted between the tables, flirting and inviting the men to follow them upstairs.

Everyone in the inn turned to stare at the entrance. Gradually the chatter subsided, replaced by a tense, frightened silence. The barman dropped the glass he was holding. It shattered on the floor, sending shards of glass in every direction.

Cadyan strode into the room, followed closely by Slaedir and Julyán. Slaedir swept a tankard off the nearest table and downed it in one swig.

"Y-your Majesty," stammered the barman, dropping into a hasty bow. "It's an honour. Can I get you something to drink?" He began bustling around, and in his agitation he knocked over a pitcher of haymead, splashing its contents along the bar.

"No." Cadyan's voice was cold. It cut through the silence like ice. He looked around the room, taking no pains to hide his contempt. "I seek information."

"Information, Your Majesty? What information?"

Cadyan crossed the room and snatched a poster off the wall. He brandished the image of Catanya. "I have reason to believe this woman passed through these parts less than a week ago. She is a dangerous fugitive and she poses a threat to all of you. Any information you provide that leads to her capture will be generously compensated."

Julyán cleared his throat quietly.

"I'm sorry, my king, I ain't never seen that woman." The barman kept his head low as he fidgeted. "Honest," he added, seeing the dangerous look on Cadyan's face. "I'm 'ere every day and I ain't never seen her, I swear."

"I see." Cadyan turned to address the room. "What about the rest of you?"

The people stared helplessly at each other, murmuring and shaking their heads. Cadyan's disappointment was turning to anger as he glared at the sea of useless faces. But then someone spoke.

"We migh' 'ave seen her. S'hard to be sure."

Cadyan twisted around to see who'd spoken and saw a group of men sitting cramped at a corner table.

"What happened to your face?" asked Julyán, sneering.

The man bore several cuts and a large bruise that extended towards his cheek on one side of his head. Cadyan looked at the other group members. Several of them also sported bloody gashes and bruises.

"Got in a spot o' trouble," said the man. "It happens 'round these parts, eh lads?"

The group snickered.

"You've seen her then?" Slaedir cut through the chatter.

The man shrugged mulishly, and Cadyan felt his frustration rising.

"Was she travelling with a man?" asked Julyán.

"She migh' 'ave been..." The drunkard trailed off coyly.

Cadyan pressed his fingers into his temple and exhaled. "You're trying my patience," he said. Anger bubbled inside him and his skin began to itch. He welcomed the sensation, stretching his powers out towards the man. They connected and he wrenched, watching as the man began to wheeze and splutter. The candles lining the walls flickered and died. Cadyan felt a sharp thrill course through his body, as his voice reverberated in the darkness. "Tell me what you know, now. Or I will kill everyone in this room, slowly and painfully." He released his hold and the man slumped onto the table, panting. The candles flickered back on. Everyone in the room sat petrified.

"Alrigh', we saw her," gasped the man, clutching at his throat. "An' wha's more, I've a fair guess where the three o' them'll be headed next."

"Three?" Cadyan glanced at Slaedir, who blinked in surprise.

The man grinned crookedly, rubbing his neck. "Aye. An' I'll take you there... s'long as I get my reward." He smirked at Cadyan and rapped his knuckle on the nearest poster.

*10,000 gold pieces.*

The corners of Cadyan's mouth twitched. He couldn't help but admire the nerve of the man. "Tell me something." He ran his finger through the dust on the table in front of him and flicked it into the air. "These men sitting with you, are you their leader?"

The man glanced around the table. "I s'ppose I am, now. Yeah." He puffed his chest out, brimming with pride.

"Yes? Excellent, then I propose a counteroffer." Cadyan's lips curled into a predatory smile. "You will take me to the girl and her friends, and in return, I won't kill you the way I killed all your men." Cadyan stared at him, eyebrows raised, waiting.

"What?" blurted the man stupidly, casting around and laughing. "Wha' d'you mean 'killed my men'?"

Cadyan continued to smile as he held the man's gaze. As if on cue, his companions around the table started twitching and crying in pain. Blood poured from their eyes, ears, and mouths.

Their veins bulged through their skin, swelling as they struggled to contain their fluid. There was a loud screech, as dozens of stools scraped across the floor. Everyone scrambled towards the exit, shouting in terror. With a flick of his wrist, Cadyan barricaded the door.

"No, you will stay. You will witness what happens to those who defy their king."

Slaedir laughed at the chaos, while Julyán lounged against the bar, looking bored, as usual.

When it was over, the drunkard stood surrounded by bodies in a pool of blood that swirled together like some nightmarish concoction.

Cadyan stared down at his handiwork, calm and satisfied. His anger disappeared as rapidly as it had come.

"Shall we?" he asked nonchalantly, gesturing for the man to lead the way.

25

---

## A SHIP AT SEA

Catanya had hoped that, given time, Jémys might learn to trust Drayk—or if not trust him, at least tolerate him. But if anything, Jémys seemed to hate Drayk more with every passing minute. And the more he protested Drayk's presence, the more Drayk appeared to be enjoying himself. He seemed to find the entire situation amusing, and Catanya suspected that he liked prodding Jémys to get a rise out of him.

Catanya had no trouble understanding why Jémys disliked Drayk; after all, Drayk represented the exact opposite of everything Jémys respected and valued. By all appearances, Drayk was a man without honour, loyalty, or decency. But Catanya was beginning to suspect his behaviour was just a veneer—a flashy display he used to distract people, hiding his true feelings and desires.

Catanya's softening attitude towards Drayk did nothing to repair the rift between her and Jémys. She knew no amount of time would heal the wounds from the losses Jémys had suffered in Finnua, nor would it change the fact that those losses were her fault. She didn't know what to hope for anymore. Part of her hoped Jémys still loved her and wanted to stay by her side no matter what happened, but another part of her hoped he might decide to leave, to move somewhere far away from her where he could be safe. Because even if he could forgive her, they'd never be able to forget.

It was early in the morning on their third day at the cottage. Catanya huddled in a blanket by the fire, trying to keep warm. A damp chill had hung in the air all night, seeping into her bones and freezing her from the inside out. Drayk was asleep in the other room and Jémys had gone outside in search of firewood, although there was already a sizeable stack beside the hearth.

Catanya suspected Jémys was avoiding her, or at least avoiding being alone with her. As much as he hated Drayk, she supposed it was easier for Jémys when Drayk was around. It was easier for him to hate Drayk than to hate her.

The cottage door creaked open and Jémys entered, carrying a small pile of wood and an axe. He tipped the wood onto the already heaping stack, laid the axe against the wall, and slumped into the chair beside Catanya.

"It's not much warmer in here than outside," he said, leaning forward to warm his hands by the fire. "I don't suppose your magic gives you power to control the weather?" he added in a strained effort at levity.

"I-I don't know." Catanya stared at her hands. "To be honest, I've been too afraid to try anything."

"Right." Jémys looked sidelong at her. "So-so you weren't using it then? Back in Finnua before... well, you know..."

"No, I only used it once. To save Olly." She remembered that night in the barn before everything went so wrong. "He was playing in the rafters and he fell. I panicked and I threw my hands out. It was instinct, I suppose. And he just floated to the ground without a scratch."

"Really? How did you explain that to him?"

Catanya didn't respond. Instead she turned her gaze back to her hands, thinking about all the mistakes she had made.

"I see," said Jémys, interpreting her silence. "So Olly knew." He nodded, turning his eyes away to hide the bitterness. "That's why he was trying to reach you, to tell you to run. He wanted to protect you, that's why he... he—" Jémys broke off and stared resolutely at the wall. He looked wan and despondent. Thick stubble lined his jaw and dark circles dulled his normally vibrant eyes.

Catanya didn't know what to say or do. She wanted to comfort him, but she wasn't sure he wanted her sympathy right now.

"He didn't deserve that," said Jémys. "Olly was just a little boy, he was innocent. He didn't deserve—" He broke off again. "I was supposed to protect him—to protect all of them..."

Tears welled in Catanya's eyes as she listened to Jémys's heartbroken voice.

"How am I supposed to live with this? How do I go on, when I know they're all gone? I'm so empty, Catanya. I've never felt this way before. So cold and heavy like nothing matters anymore."

It pained her to hear how hopeless and downtrodden he sounded. In the time she'd known him, he had always been so full of joy, so full of light.

"I understand," said Catanya. "I've been feeling that way for months. Ever since I lost my home... but then I met you and everything changed." She willed him to understand. "You made me happy again. I felt safe and loved—that's why I stayed. I didn't want to lose you. Not when I'd only just found you, not when I'd already lost so much. But now..." She bowed her head and picked at a sliver of wood on the chair. "I'm going to lose you anyway, aren't I? I wish I could do something to make this better."

Jémys laughed flatly. "Me too."

Catanya watched him, longing for him to look at her. "I love you," she breathed, brushing away the loose strands that had fallen across her face. "I think I always will, even if you don't... if you can't love me anymore."

Jémys finally turned to face her. His emerald eyes were glistening and wet. "I love you too," he admitted. "More than I ever thought possible."

Catanya exhaled in relief. She laid her hand on his face, tracing her thumb across his cheek—across the lines that used to crease when he smiled.

He closed his eyes at her touch and breathed deep. When he opened them again, they were pained, and he lifted her hand off his face.

"But every time I look at you now, I see them." He stared at her, eyes tight with sorrow. "I see them all, screaming, running... dying. Everyone. My aunt, my village... Olly." His voice cracked and he stared down at her hand in his. "I feel betrayed and I'm... I'm angry," he said, wearing an apologetic expression. "I love you and I don't want to blame you, but I-I can't help it. I don't know how to move past this, I'm sorry."

Catanya nodded. His words stung, but she couldn't fault him for feeling them. "You don't have to stay, you know. You could leave. I wouldn't blame you for it." She tried to keep her face impassive, to show him she meant it.

Jémys furrowed his brow and shook his head. "I can't leave."

"Why not?" She worked hard not to get her hopes up.

Jémys smiled wryly. "Because I still love you," he said. "And I can't lose another person I love either." He lifted her hand and pressed his lips against her wrist.

Catanya saw the pain written on his face.

"I just need you to give me some time." He stood up, letting her hand fall lightly onto her lap, and he walked out the door without turning back.

Catanya watched him go, feeling ruffled and anxious. He needed time. But how much time? From the expression on his face, Catanya wasn't sure he'd ever be ready. She wanted desperately to regain the closeness they'd had and to be together, but if he couldn't forgive her, their relationship would always be strained.

As she sat there alone, wallowing in pity, she wondered—and she hated herself for thinking it—if she would really be able to live like that. Could she really live with someone who blamed her as much as she blamed herself, someone who could never forgive her? She was already suffocating under the weight of her own guilt. She didn't think she could stand any more of it.

"Why are you trying so hard to please him?" came Drayk's voice from behind her.

She twisted around to see him lounging in the doorframe, observing her. "How long have you been there?" she asked.

He shrugged. "Not long. So tell me, why are you grovelling?"

"I don't grovel," said Catanya acidly, turning away from him again.

"No, I wouldn't have thought so, but..." He broke off, shaking his head. He strode across the room and flipped Jémys's chair around, sliding down into it with his arms resting on its back. "So why is he angry with you?"

Catanya just glowered at him.

"Oh, come on, Catya. I think I can recognize the signs. I know why he hates *me*, but why does he hate you?"

"He doesn't hate me," she retorted.

"Right." Drayk was eyeing her with one eyebrow raised.

"He doesn't hate me. He's just hurt."

"I see," said Drayk sceptically.

Catanya exhaled and crossed her arms. "It's not something I'd expect you to understand."

"Oho!" Drayk clutched at his heart mockingly. "Ouch, princess."

"Don't call me that!" she snapped as she stood up and walked away from him towards the fire.

"Don't call you what? *Princess*? But that's what you are, aren't you?"

Catanya stared determinedly at the fire and pretended she couldn't hear him. The bright orange flames flickered and glowed as the smoke rose up the chimney and disappeared. The wood crackled and the heat wafted out towards her.

"I hate to break it to you, love." Drayk stood up and crossed over to join her by the mantle. "But you are a princess," he whispered, with a taunting smile. "Sooner or later you'll need to come to terms with that. Whether *he* wants you to or not." He gestured at the closed door and gave her a smug look.

"You think that's what this is about?" she scoffed. "What? You think Jémys is upset because he doesn't want me to be royal?" She laughed in his face.

"Isn't he?" asked Drayk.

"No!"

"Oh, okay." Drayk's voice dripped with sarcasm. "So you mean to tell me that no part of your squabble is because of your ancestry or your destiny?"

"*Destiny*?" Catanya couldn't believe she'd allowed herself to get sucked into this with him, but Drayk had hit a nerve. "What are you even talking about?" she spat, trying to sound scornful, but she could see the self-satisfied smirk forming on his face.

"Come now, love. You must have realized it by now." His tone was glib, as if he found her indignation amusing.

"Realized what?"

Drayk was laughing now. The sound of it, plus the smugness on his face, infuriated her. Catanya had to resist the urge to smack him.

"Look." She tossed her hair out of her face and squared her

shoulders. "I don't expect you to understand. How could you? By your own admission, you've never cared about anybody but yourself. So how could you possibly appreciate what it's like to hurt somebody you love? To have to live with the guilt of causing them unimaginable pain and sorrow? It's unbearable, okay? And I have to try to make amends. I have to." She lapsed into a stony silence.

"You're wasting your time," said Drayk, and all hint of humour had left his voice. "People can't be pleased. Not really. It's human nature to be selfish, to be greedy and unsatisfied. You shouldn't waste your time pretending you're different. Forget about what *he* wants for a second. Focus on what you want. That's the only way you're going to survive."

"Well, you would say that, wouldn't you?" replied Catanya coolly.

"And why not? Why should we spend our lives trying to please other people—people who will never be grateful or satisfied? All we'll gain from that is more misery and regret. No, I learned long ago that the key to happiness lies in being selfish. The only person who matters in your life is you."

Catanya rounded on him. "Can you honestly tell me your life has been happy?"

Drayk opened his mouth to retort, but before he could speak, Jémys came bursting through the door in a panic.

"There's a ship out there," he said, gesturing towards the water.

"What?" Catanya asked.

Drayk swore loudly and ran to stare out the window. "It's too late," he groaned. "They'll have seen the smoke from the fire." He swore again and made a move like he wanted to hit the wall, but restrained himself. "I didn't think they'd be coming back this way so soon! Last I heard, they were in Sidina." He groaned again and brushed the hair out of his face. "This means they've been to Awnell..."

"Who are they?" Catanya joined him by the window.

Just offshore, cutting through the ocean with ease, was a massive three-mast carrack with a full square rigging and a high rounded stern. The stem was raked steeply against the water, and the ship bore a large figurehead of a vicious, grotesque serpent that was altogether too lifelike.

"Marauders," whispered Drayk. "Smugglers. They travel between Caerlon, Sidina, and Awnell, trading in secrets and stolen goods... among other things," he added with a dark shadow on his face. "They're lawless, and they answer to no one."

"And Caerlon just allows that?" Jémys said.

"Caerlon finds them useful," said Drayk, sneering. "As does Awnell... unfortunately."

"What do you mean?"

Drayk raised his eyebrows. "It's easy to make yourself useful when you have no loyalties or morals. Those smugglers are willing to do anything for the right price."

"And you think they'll be coming here?" Catanya was trying not to panic. "Could they even dock here? Isn't it too shallow?"

"Don't worry, they're not coming here. They're heading west."

"Then why does it matter that they saw the smoke," asked Jémys, frowning as he struggled to follow Drayk's logic.

Drayk sighed. "They'll know I was here," he said vaguely. Then he made a strange gesture as though he were suppressing a shudder. "They'll stop at the Ruins of Bratia on their route back to Caerlon." He screwed his face up in disgust.

Catanya and Jémys exchanged confused looks. "So what? The Ruins are just an old landmark, aren't they?" asked Catanya.

"Yeah, maybe once they were," he said in an ominous tone. Then he caught sight of their faces and he frowned. "You really don't know?"

Jémys and Catanya shook their heads.

"The entire area around Bratia has been transformed into one massive work camp. For generations, thousands of people have been enslaved, toiling and dying in endless pursuit of the supposed Relics of Illayan. Your family"—he gave Catanya a significant nod—"is obsessed with finding them, and Cadyan has ordered his firkon to increase the output... They've been abducting people from all over the kingdom and shipping them off in droves."

"What?" said Catanya, aghast. "How is it possible we haven't heard about this?" She couldn't believe something so horrific could happen without the kingdom knowing.

"Until now, they've been fairly quiet about it. Only taking criminals, vagrants, people without family or connections... But something—or someone—has made Cadyan impatient." He looked at Catanya meaningfully.

She felt sick as she watched Drayk cross away from the window and start pacing in front of the fire. *A camp full of enslaved workers.* She tried not to let her imagination picture it. Drayk's reaction spoke volumes.

Catanya hadn't believed her family could be any worse, but this was a new level of despicable. She had always imagined the Ruins of Bratia as a mystical, awe-inspiring place. She'd heard stories of the city's grandeur and its importance in the days before the Quiescence Wars. The Ruins were supposed to be a beacon of an ancient age, not a slave camp. And the Relics of Illayan were just supposed to be a story. What kind of king would enslave his people in pursuit of a mere legend?

Drayk was muttering to himself, looking more agitated than Catanya had ever seen him. He seemed to be weighing options in his head, and then suddenly he stopped.

"We can't stay in Caerlon anymore, we've already lingered here too long." His voice sounded unusually flat. "We should cross into Awnell now." He pressed his fingers into his brow line as though bracing himself.

Catanya was surprised to hear him say it. They'd discussed the possibility of going to Awnell, but, until now, Drayk hadn't seemed overly enthused about the idea. "That was my original plan..." She trailed off uncertainly, looking at Drayk. "I mean, *they're* not hunting me, are they? There's no price on my head once I'm outside Caerlon. We should be safe in Awnell, right?"

"Don't underestimate Queen Ayr." Drayk started pacing again. "Her Verratrí move quickly. She likely already knows about you."

"Verratrí? I've heard that word before," said Jémys, frowning.

Catanya tried to think back over earlier conversations. "That's right, Fin said it. Actually, he said *you* were a Verratrí?" She gave Drayk a sharp look.

"I am—I mean, I was."

"What exactly is a Verratrí?" asked Jémys, with a definite edge to his voice.

"We were. My crew and I—at least before they went rogue and chose to help Caerlon," he said with bitterness. "We worked for the Queen of Awnell."

"What?" Catanya was shocked. "What kind of work?"

"Spying on Caerlon primarily." Drayk shrugged. "We weren't mere outlaws and thieves. I mean, that's what we wanted everyone to think, but we had specific orders. We were tasked to retrieve information and assets that might be useful for Awnell and its queen."

"Useful how?" asked Catanya warily.

"Anything. Any information she could use to undermine Cadyan and Caerlon."

Jémys scoffed. "And what kind of information would—" He stopped short and stared at Catanya, comprehension dawning on him. "That's why you captured us." He spoke quietly, his eyes narrowing as he glared at Drayk. "You were planning to take us to her?"

"Yes."

"To do what?" asked Catanya.

Drayk stared resolutely at her. "Knowing Ayr... to fight."

"Fight?" Catanya echoed the word, feeling numb.

"You're talking about starting a war with Caerlon," said Jémys, breaking through Catanya's sudden daze.

Now it was Drayk's turn to scoff. "*Starting* a war? Not starting, *finishing*. The war never ended! I guarantee you that Ayr is already planning her attack. Mark my words, she'll be marching on Caerlon before the year is out."

"Then she'll die," said Jémys, and Catanya couldn't help but agree. Everyone knew it was madness to take on Caerlon.

"Not necessarily." Drayk rested his gaze on Catanya.

Catanya felt hot around the ears. Why did everyone seem to think it was her mission to overthrow Cadyan? *I just want to be free*, she thought bitterly. She turned away from Drayk and Jémys to stare out the window, watching the outline of the ship as it sailed farther away.

"If Ayr knows about you, she will want you to fight," said Drayk.

"I can't," protested Catanya, losing her cool. "I can't fight, I'm not a warrior." She stared at them both pleadingly. "I am no match for *him*!"

Jémys was eyeing her with a mixture of fear and sympathy, but Drayk threw his hands up in exasperation.

"Fine," he said, shaking his head. "If you don't want Ayr to find us, we'll have to pass through the city undetected and reach the mountains, somehow. We can't take the main road though, she has scouts all over."

"Then how?" asked Jémys.

Drayk paused before answering. "We'll go by boat. I keep a small skiff hidden near here. We can take it straight into the coast of Awnell. If we go during the night, we might make it through unseen... if we're lucky."

"I don't know..." Jémys sounded nervous.

"Well, it's the best chance we have." Drayk looked at Catanya for support.

Catanya took a deep breath and nodded. Then she turned to walk away, but Drayk called after her.

"Catya," he said, eyes boring into hers. "The only way you will ever truly be safe, is if you learn to control those powers. Whether you like it or not, there *will* be a fight in your future. The sooner you accept that, the greater your chance at survival."

**26**

---

# THE CONFRONTATION

atanya stood on the shore, looking out at the grey, choppy waters and listening to the waves crash at her feet. The ocean spray was cold on her face and the wind whipped through her hair. She inhaled the salty sea air and closed her eyes, allowing the breeze to envelop her and imagining what it would be like to fly. She imagined herself weightless and soaring out over the ocean to watch the waves from above as they rushed towards land.

Catanya felt her feet lift off the ground and for one mesmerizing moment she knew she was floating. Then her eyes snapped open and she lost control, stumbling back down to the ground.

With her feet planted firmly on the rocky shore, Catanya tried to process what had happened.

"I was floating," she whispered to herself in awe. "I wonder..." She closed her eyes and imagined it happening again. She attempted to jump into the air and leave the ground behind, but nothing happened. She tried again. And again and—

"What are you doing?"

It was Drayk. He had come out of the cottage and was standing nearby, watching her, his mouth twisted in amusement.

"Nothing." Her face burned hot, and she kept her eyes trained on the water, listening to Drayk's footsteps on the rocks as he moved to stand beside her.

"Nothing?" he repeated, with one eyebrow raised.

Catanya's mouth curved into a smile.

"Right. Well, it'll be dark soon. We should go over the plan again before we leave tonight."

"Okay." Catanya nodded.

But neither of them moved. They stood staring out at the ocean, entranced by the sound and movement of the waves, lost in their own thoughts.

"Come on," said Drayk after a while. He seemed to have pulled himself out of his trance and was turning towards the cottage.

"Wait." Catanya grabbed his arm. "Do you see that?"

"See what?"

"Out there." She pointed towards the centre of the horizon. "I can just make it out. It's far off, but I think it's an island." She was surprised to hear herself speaking in hushed tones.

Drayk squinted in the direction she was pointing. "I can't see anything but water."

"No, I'm sure of it." Catanya brushed away his response. "There's an island out there and I think... is that a mountain?"

"I can't see it." Drayk stepped forward to look. "Where?"

"Right there." She pointed ahead again. "You-you don't see it?" Her voice faltered.

Drayk shook his head and glanced at Catanya, brows knitted in mild concern.

"Hmm." Catanya bit her lip.

She stared back out at the water as the fog rolled in thick like smoke, obscuring the horizon. Then she looked at Drayk, shrugged, and walked back towards the cottage, leaving him behind, squinting out at the water.

---

The sun was setting, the fire in the cottage struggled to warm the room, and the light of the last remaining candles danced eerily on the walls as Catanya, Jémys, and Drayk made their final arrangements. A nervous energy buzzed in the air while they talked through their plan one last time.

"We should arrive in the night tomorrow," said Drayk.

"One full day out at sea... In a small fishing skiff with only four oars." Jémys's anxiety was palpable. His eyes were wide and glazed as he gave a stiff nod.

"She's steady as a rock," declared Drayk, clapping him on the back. "Don't worry, mate, she'll get us there. Besides, if something goes wrong, I'm sure your princess here can save us." He winked at Catanya and looked pointedly at Jémys.

Jémys closed his eyes in irritation, and Drayk grinned, obviously enjoying himself.

"So," Drayk addressed Catanya, "unless we want to wait for your dear, sweet brother to find us, this is our only plan."

Catanya's heart sank when she glanced at Jémys and saw the pain and frustration on his face. She could sense Drayk smiling at her and knew he was delighting in the reaction he'd caused by mentioning her connection to Cadyan. Provoking Jémys seemed to be one of his favourite pastimes.

The rest of the evening dragged by as they waited for the cover of darkness to start their journey. Catanya had been hoping for an opportunity to speak with Jémys in private, and as the twilight darkened into night, she finally had her chance.

Drayk had gone to load the boat with what little supplies they had, leaving Catanya and Jémys alone in the cottage.

Jémys was standing by the window with his back to her, and

she walked over to join him. She had something to say, and it wouldn't be easy.

"Jémys, we need to talk." He turned towards her slowly, and she had to take a deep breath to steady herself. "I'm not expecting you to forgive me or trust me after everything that's happened... but this is my life," she gestured around the dreary cottage. "I realize now that my life will always be like this."

"You don't know that," said Jémys, trying to sound reassuring.

"Yes, I do." She couldn't let him distract her from saying what needed to be said. "I can't go back to who I was. Whatever future I might have had before all this... it's gone now. I'll always be running, fighting, struggling..." She trailed off, trying to find the right words.

"What?"

Catanya sighed. "It's hard enough as it is. But looking at you and seeing the pain in your eyes... seeing the affection we've lost. I-I can't—" She averted her eyes.

"What are you saying?" he asked warily.

Catanya took another deep breath, trying to maintain control. "I'm saying that I can't do this anymore. The pain is too much... I've lost everyone I've ever loved, and if I'm going to lose you too, I'd rather do it sooner than later."

She gave Jémys a steely look. He seemed surprised. "Lose me?" he repeated, frowning and shaking his head in confusion.

"I know you said you needed time. But I'm sorry, I need to know... will you ever be able to move past what's happened?"

She forced herself to face him directly. He hung his head and rubbed his neck without responding. He tried to turn away, but she grabbed his arm to stop him.

"I need to know," she repeated more sternly. "Please. I can't change who I am or what has happened because of me. I don't know what the future holds, but it won't be easy or safe and I understand if you can't accept it"—the words caught in her throat—"but I just need to know."

"Catanya..." Jémys was avoiding her gaze. "I don't know what you want me to say. I just don't know if I can trust you again."

Catanya's heart sank. "Well..." She rubbed her forehead. "Then I think maybe we should go our separate ways now. My life will only get more difficult, more dangerous. At least if you leave now... at least maybe you'll be safe... You can start again. Rebuild."

Jémys frowned and shook his head. "Is that really what you want? You want me to leave?" He sounded hurt.

"No. It's not what I want at all!" She met his eyes with hers and worked hard to remain calm. "You know what I want."

They continued staring at each other, the space between them growing tenser with each passing second. Catanya took a step forward to close the gap and laced her fingers through his. She raised herself on her toes and was about to kiss him when the door swung open. Drayk strolled into the cottage.

He stopped dead in his tracks when he saw the two of them, and then his face broke into a knowing grin. "Don't mind me," he said, leaning against the doorframe as if he intended to watch.

"Unbelievable," muttered Jémys, pulling away from Catanya.

"She is, isn't she?" rejoined Drayk. He wore a wide smirk on his face as he looked at her pointedly.

Catanya's cheeks burned.

"What's the matter with you?" Jémys rounded on Drayk. "What? Do you enjoy fuelling other people's torment?"

"Sometimes," said Drayk with a gleam in his eye, which only made Jémys angrier.

"Why are we even trusting you?" Jémys advanced towards

him. "You're a liar and a cheat. We can't believe anything you say."

"True. But trust is overrated, anyway." Drayk shrugged.

"Well, I can't live like this!" shouted Jémys. "I can't put my life in the hands of someone I don't trust." He turned around to face Catanya.

There was a long pause, as Jémys's words hung in the air and their meaning slowly sank in.

"Well then, I have my answer," said Catanya in a quiet voice.

They all stood, not daring to move, until Drayk exhaled a slow whistle and laughed.

A flash of rage shot across Jémys's face. He spun his fist around and hit Drayk hard in the face before storming past him through the open door.

"Jémys!" shouted Catanya in shock. She ran after him, but he had already disappeared into the darkness. She felt light-headed, and she gripped the doorframe, trying to ignore the devastating feeling of pain and betrayal. "A-are you alright?" she asked, turning to look at Drayk. Her hand shook as she reached up to touch his injured jaw. It wasn't broken, but his lip had been split. He turned his head to spit blood onto the stones outside.

"I've had worse." He dabbed his lip with his thumb.

"Serves you right," said Catanya bitterly as she lowered her hand, but Drayk grabbed it and held it fast.

"Are *you* alright?" His earnest tone caught her off guard, and he followed her gaze out the door.

Catanya thought about lying and saying she was fine, but she was tired of pretending. She shook her head. "Maybe he'll be back," she said.

"Maybe." But Drayk sounded unconvinced. "We can stay for another hour or two, but then we should leave."

Catanya nodded and closed the door to block out the cold air. She walked over and curled up in a chair by the fire, exhausted. Resting her head on her knees, she shut her eyes, allowing the tears to pour out of her.

---

The next thing she knew, she was being shaken awake by Drayk.

"We have to go. NOW."

"What is it?" asked Catanya, rubbing her eyes as she stood up.

"Riders. I saw at least ten of them." He gestured towards the door. "Fírkon. They were coming out of the forest when—" Drayk raised his hand and craned his neck to listen.

Catanya could hear it too, the unmistakable sound of hooves hitting the ground.

The two of them stood frozen in place, listening to the sound grow louder as the horses approached the cottage.

"Only ten?" whispered Catanya. "I don't understand, last time there were dozens."

Just then the dying fire blazed behind the grate, sending clouds of smoke and ash billowing into the room. A wild wind engulfed the cottage, roaring and wailing through the cracks in the wood so that the walls quaked and the shutters flew off their hinges.

"Tell me you're doing that," called Drayk over the noise.

Catanya stared at him wide-eyed and watched the dread spread over his face.

They both stood paralyzed in fear as they heard the horses come to a stop outside the cottage and the distinct sound of feet hitting the rocks.

There was a brief pause when everything fell silent, and then—

"I know you're in there!" called a voice from outside. A voice she recognized from her nightmares. "I think it's time we met face to face, don't you? Why don't you come on out and we'll have a nice, friendly chat?"

Catanya looked at Drayk. His eyes were wide and he clenched his fists, backing away from the door to stand next to her. He drew his sword.

"No?" called Cadyan in a mocking tone. "So be it."

Without warning, the door ripped off its hinges and flew into the cottage. It crashed against Drayk and sent him hurtling to the ground.

"Drayk!" Catanya rushed over to help him, dragging him out from beneath the splintered wood. He scrambled to his feet, unharmed except for a few minor cuts.

The entire building lurched. The floor quaked beneath them, shaking the walls and hurling the room into chaos. Catanya could barely stay on her feet. An ominous cracking sound rent the air as particles of dust rained down. She glanced at the ceiling in time to see it cleave in half. She grabbed Drayk and hauled him under the table, as the rafters splintered and collapsed.

The cottage was filled with falling debris. Catanya scrambled to her feet, choking on the dust. She could hear shouting voices, but she couldn't understand what they were saying. The wooden floorboards creaked and fractured beneath her feet, scraping her legs as they gave way, sinking into the foundation. She struggled to stay upright on what remained of the floor. She could feel Drayk's arm around her, and she used his weight to steady herself.

Almost as suddenly as it started, everything stopped. Catanya opened her eyes to see that she and Drayk were huddled beside the window, surrounded by a mass of rubble blocking their path to the door. Moonlight shone through the gaping hole in the ceiling, illuminating the dusty air. Catanya coughed, blinking grit out of her eyes.

Footsteps crunched on the debris nearby, and panic flooded her as she looked around for an escape.

"Here," said Drayk.

He kicked the remaining glass out of the window frame and hoisted her up through the opening and onto the ground outside. Then, turning briefly to look behind him, he climbed through and landed beside her.

"Come on." He grabbed her hand and pulled her around the side of the house, down the slippery rocks towards the shoreline.

Catanya tried to wrench her hand away, but Drayk tightened his grip and refused to let go.

"What about Jémys? He's out there somewhere, what if they find him?"

"It's not Jémys that Cadyan wants. It's you," said Drayk. "Jémys will be fine."

Catanya was about to protest again when someone behind them shouted, "O'er here, she's gettin' away!"

Catanya glanced over her shoulder to see who'd spoken. Even by the light of the moon she recognized his face.

"Fin," snarled Drayk, his voice full of loathing. "Oh, I knew I should have killed him. Cowardly traitor."

Drayk brandished his sword and made a move back up towards Fin, but before he had taken two steps, the ground shook again. There was a resounding crash as the remaining cottage walls crumbled to the ground in ruins.

Catanya yanked Drayk forward. The two of them hurtled down the steep incline towards the beach, where a small boat lay waiting for them. Fin followed close behind. As they landed on the rocky shore, Drayk raised his sword and crossed in front of Catanya to fight. Just as Fin reached them, he halted. His eyes were popping in fear and he clutched at his throat, choking and gasping as he fell to his knees.

"You promised," he spluttered.

A high, cruel laugh echoed through the air, as Cadyan came striding down the incline to meet them, accompanied by five of his firkon. "No, I said I wouldn't kill you the way I killed your men."

Then Cadyan drew his sword and plunged it through Fin's heart.

"I forget sometimes," said Cadyan calmly, "how satisfying it is to do that without using magic." He yanked his sword out of Fin's chest, wiped it on the dead man's cloak, and returned it safely to its sheath.

The sky was clear and the wind died down, so Catanya and Drayk stood facing Cadyan in an almost unnatural calm. The moonlight shone off the grey rocks at their feet, giving everything a ghostly pale appearance—nothing more so than Cadyan himself, whose ethereal hair and jagged features gave him the look of a corpse.

"So." Cadyan clapped his hands together and smiled. "You are my sister. We meet at last." He held up his hand to signal that his firkon should stay back, and he strolled up to her.

Catanya stood still, not daring to move or to speak. She gazed at the face she knew only from her nightmares. She stared at him, taking in the similarities of his features to her own. Until this moment, part of her had never truly believed she had a brother, but standing opposite him now, seeing the same nose and cheeks, she knew it was true. Even his eyes bore similarities, though he had a coldness in his gaze that Catanya hoped had never been in hers.

"It is odd," Cadyan frowned and tilted his head, "to be meeting the sister I never knew I had. Tell me, how long have you known?" he asked conversationally. "How long have you known about me?"

Catanya hesitated briefly then responded in a stiff voice, "Not long."

"No... I thought not," said Cadyan. Then he leaned forward

and glanced at her hair. "I see you haven't been using your powers. Well... not much." He pointed at the streak of colour.

Catanya raised her hand to her head. She could sense Drayk shifting behind her as though readying for a fight.

"Why not?" asked Cadyan, surveying her with incredulity. "Why not use the gift you've been given?"

"It's not a gift," retorted Catanya. Then, seeing the surprise on Cadyan's face, she continued, "It isn't a gift. I never wanted these powers, I still don't want them."

Cadyan's face cracked into a sceptical grin. "Come now, there's no need to lie. We are family, after all. You can tell me the truth."

"I *am* telling you the truth."

Cadyan cocked his head to the side and narrowed his eyes. "No. I don't think so." He spoke so low he was barely audible. "I think you've been lying to everyone, even yourself. You must have felt the intoxicating thrill of it, the strength it gives you... You can't resist it forever. Trust me. You should let it in, let it take control, and accept who you are."

"And who is it you think I am?" she asked, backing away slowly.

"You are my sister. You belong in Caerlon with me." He took a step forward, a manic glint in his eyes. "Imagine if we worked together. There's never been two of us before... Imagine if we combined our powers. We could be unstoppable."

Catanya's mind was racing. "To what end?" she asked, horrified. "What is it exactly that you want?"

Cadyan gave her an appraising look. "Everything," he replied.

Revolted, Catanya took another step back, shaking her head in disbelief.

Cadyan clicked his tongue disapprovingly. "There's no need to fear it, sister. We were born for this."

"No. No, I don't believe that."

"Believe it."

"No!" she shouted, glaring at him.

Cadyan stared at her. There was a long pause before Catanya spoke again. "This isn't right, surely you can see that," she pleaded, gesturing around at the ruined cottage and Fin's broken body. But the look on Cadyan's face told her he was beyond reason.

"Stand with your king," he commanded. "Come with me to Caerlon. Let me show you what it means to be part of this family." He held out his hand, smiling.

Catanya hardly dared to breathe. For a brief moment she imagined herself going with him, she imagined herself in Caerlon with a mother and a brother, and an entire kingdom at her feet.

But then she thought about Bratia, about people enslaved in camps and people starving throughout the kingdom. She remembered Olly's broken body, and Nelle's lifeless face. She remembered the terror at Camlee Lodge and the chaos in Finnua. And pain. Too much pain.

"I know what it means," she said quietly, pulling herself out of the fantasy. "I won't be part of a family like that."

Cadyan sighed and lowered his hand. "Very well. I tried to be generous. I gave you a chance, but I must say, I expect this will be cleaner in the end."

The wind was picking up again, sending rocks, mist, and sand flying in every direction. Catanya struggled to muster some strength to fight back, to channel something—anything. But she didn't know how. It was like grasping at emptiness.

Drayk grabbed her hand and she turned to see him struggling to stay upright against the wind's force. He was gasping and clutching at his throat like he couldn't breathe. His eyes bulged and the veins on his face pushed through his skin in a grotesque purplish mask.

Catanya wanted to help him, but an agonizing tightness

squeezed against her chest like a tourniquet. She looked up to see Cadyan's eyes glowing gold. Her lungs burned and bright spots formed on the edges of her vision. She gasped on the hollow air and knew she was dying.

"It is a shame that our poor mother never got the chance to meet her daughter," called Cadyan over the howling noise. "The daughter she loved so much, she sent her away to keep her safe. Oh, how well that worked out in the end..." He cackled as he moved forward, bearing down on her.

He threw his hands forward so Catanya and Drayk soared backwards, crashing into the hard, rocky ground. He repeated the gesture again and again. He hurled them back so they tumbled and flipped, finally collapsing into a heap.

Catanya grasped blindly at her magic, desperate for something to help her. She strained to force Cadyan's power back at him but nothing happened. With every passing second, her vision blurred more. She tried to stand, but her legs shuddered beneath her.

"It's no use," shouted Cadyan. "You're too weak. Your magic is undisciplined. But I've spent years learning about Resonance —years preparing to wield my powers. You can't fight me."

He sent another blast of energy at her so she toppled backwards, colliding with the side of the boat and sliding onto the damp ground.

Then everything stopped.

Catanya and Drayk lurched forward, wheezing and breathing great gulps of air. As she spluttered and choked, waiting for her strength to return, Catanya noticed a spear lying a few inches away. It had fallen out of the boat. She reached out towards it, but then a shadow loomed above, and Cadyan knelt beside her.

"Last chance, sister." He gripped her shoulder with his hand and smiled as if resisting the urge to laugh. "Come with me to Caerlon."

Catanya felt a shudder run through her shoulder and into her spine. It was painful and numbing at the same time, and it branched out through her bones, reverberating and echoing inside her.

She couldn't think clearly anymore. Her mind was going blank, her own panicked thoughts replaced by the image of her and Cadyan, ruling Caerlon together through pain and bloodshed.

"No," she moaned, trying to force the image away. She could feel her will to resist slipping.

Her pain and sadness were gone. It was so much easier to give in.

*We're brother and sister.* Cadyan's voice was inside her head, calm and persuasive.

He was right. She could join him now and everything would be fine. They'd be together and they'd be happy. She had found her place, finally.

*Come with me,* he called to her. *You and me, we're family.*

These words resonated somewhere deep within Catanya, and a new image formed in her mind, brighter and stronger than everything else.

Diyah.

A blast of golden light erupted around Catanya and the numbing pain shot out of her, as Cadyan wrenched his hand away, stumbling back.

He straightened up and whirled around, glaring at her and clutching his hand as if it had been burned. In his anger, the wind began to rage again.

Catanya wasted no time. She snatched the spear off the ground and sprang to her feet, swinging it through the air as hard as she could. It smashed against Cadyan's head and sent him flying to the ground.

The wind stopped at once. Still holding the spear, Catanya stood motionless, staring at her brother's unconscious outline, hardly daring to believe it. She turned towards Drayk and laughed nervously at the disbelief on his face.

All at once, cries and shouts filled the air as the five firkon who had stood watching launched across the beach towards them. The air was full of swords. Drayk fended off three firkon, while Catanya blocked the attacks of two others as best she could using the spear.

Catanya was out-matched and out-numbered, and her mind was clouded with panic. She managed to knock one firkon down and watched Drayk do the same with two others.

"We need to get out of here!" she shouted as she struggled to block further attacks. She glanced helplessly at the boat behind her, wishing she could get it out into the water.

As if on cue, the water level around them began to rise. The rocks grew slippery and treacherous, causing several firkon to trip and fall into the rising tide.

"Come on!" Drayk grabbed her hand as he disarmed another firkon and kicked him back several feet. Profiting from the momentary distraction, Drayk spun around and pushed the boat out into the water. Catanya jumped into the front and snatched up a set of oars.

Several firkon were getting back up and one of them was dragging Cadyan out of the water towards safety. The tide was rising fast. When Drayk jumped into the boat after her, they were already beyond the reach of the remaining firkon.

"What about Jémys?" asked Catanya as Drayk grabbed the oars at the stern and began rowing with frantic energy.

"We can't wait. Cadyan won't be out for long. We have to go now." When Catanya didn't answer, he added, "Jémys is gone, Catya. He left. With any luck, he's far away from here already. If we stay, we stay to die. Let's go, please!"

Catanya spared one last look at the demolished cottage. Then she nodded and plunged her oars into the water.

They rowed madly, trying to put as much distance between

themselves and the shoreline as possible. They watched as the man they'd seen dragging Cadyan to shore turned to stare at them and seemed to debate whether to swim after them or to tend to his injured king. It was dark, but Catanya would have recognized his face anywhere. It was the same firkon who had chased her from Faltir months ago, the same man who'd trampled an innocent boy to death before her eyes.

Fury coursed through Catanya as she relived those moments, remembering everything that man had taken from her. She wanted to turn back—to make him suffer.

Drayk seemed to read her mind. He twisted around in his seat to face her. "We can't go back."

"I know," she said through gritted teeth. But for the first time in her life, she imagined herself fighting. She imagined herself getting justice for everyone she had lost. Breathing hard from rowing, she hoped against all hope that Jémys wasn't the latest addition to that growing list of people she longed to avenge.

"Jémys is fine," said Drayk. "I'm sure of it."

Catanya just nodded, desperately hoping he was right.

# EPILOGUE

CADYAN

# THE CAPTIVE

Cadyan opened his eyes with a start and found Slaedir leaning over him, his unkempt and grizzled face illuminated by the moonlight.

"My lord, are you alright?" Slaedir grabbed his arms to help him stand.

"I'm fine," spat Cadyan, pushing him away. "She merely caught me by surprise. A mistake I won't make again." He cringed, rubbing the side of his head, which was swelling painfully underneath a long cut. "Where is she?" A prickling sense of shame crept over him. He hated feeling vulnerable. He was the single most powerful man in Caerlon; nothing should make him feel weak anymore.

Slaedir hesitated before answering. "Gone, Your Majesty. She and the dark-haired man... they escaped by boat."

"What?" Cadyan straightened up, shaking the grit out of his cloak. "Why didn't you stop her?" His shame gave way to violent anger in a heartbeat, and he glared at Slaedir.

"M-my lord?" Slaedir stared at him like he'd lost his mind, which only fuelled Cadyan's anger more.

"That upstart bitch attacked your king and you just let her

escape? You useless, ungrateful—" Cadyan let out an inarticulate cry of anger and, forgetting his magic momentarily, slammed his fist into Slaedir's face.

Pain surged along his arm. It felt like it might shatter into pieces. Slaedir stumbled back, spitting blood, and Cadyan clutched his aching arm, gazing down at it. His hand smarted and the skin on his palm was tender.

Then he remembered what had happened—the burst of light and the energy forcing him away...

How was she able to repel him? Why hadn't the ring worked?

He held his hand up to the moonlight, examining the rough iron band. It was difficult to tell, given all the dents on the ring already, but he thought he noticed a faint crack forming on one side. He stroked the mark with his thumb and felt a strange scratching sensation against his skin, like something was inside and trying to escape.

In a flash of panic, he shook his arm out, wincing at the pain and weakness of his muscles, and pushed the ring from his mind. He turned towards the dark ocean, fuming as he watched the waves crashing against the rocks.

The boat was nowhere to be seen.

"Perfect," he spat. "Just perfect." As much as he'd prefer to blame Slaedir, he knew this wasn't the maífirkon's fault. Cadyan had let his guard down, allowing his sister to escape. He should have known better.

Cadyan stalked back towards the rocky incline, stopping when he reached the dead drunkard who'd led them here from the tavern. He prodded the man with his foot, admiring his handiwork and thinking, *At least something good came from this misadventure.*

Now there was one less drunkard sullying his kingdom.

He turned to leave, but he paused when he noticed something sticking out of the man's cloak. Curious, he knelt down to pick it up. It was a tattered old book full of drawings.

"Interesting." He flipped through the pages and realized whose book it was.

"That man," said Slaedir, pointing at one drawing. "That's the man we caught. Julyán's watching him now." He jerked his head up the bluff.

"You caught someone? Why didn't you tell me?" Cadyan resisted the urge to hit Slaedir again. "Show me," he commanded, snapping the book shut.

Slaedir led the way up the incline, around the demolished cottage, and back to the forest, where the fírkon gathered, waiting for their king. Julyán was standing with his arms crossed, looking contemptuously down at the bloodied, unconscious man at his feet.

"Has he said anything?" asked Slaedir.

"No. I found him in the rubble on the other side of the cottage. Looks like he was trying to get into the building when it collapsed."

"And you're sure he's the one from the drawing." Cadyan glanced from Slaedir back to the sketchbook. "He was with her in that village?"

Before Slaedir could respond, the unconscious man shifted and opened his eyes. His gaze rested on Julyán and he lifted his head, a look of shock and disbelief on his face.

"JJ?" he mumbled, eyes sliding in and out of focus.

"What was that?" Slaedir lifted his foot and kicked the man in the chest. The man wheezed and rolled over onto his side. Slaedir frowned at Julyán suspiciously.

"That drunken idiot who led us here, did he tell us this man's name?" asked Cadyan.

"Jémys," responded Julyán.

Jémys rolled in the dirt, mumbling incoherently as he drifted in and out of consciousness.

"I'm not in the mood for the insane ramblings of a half-dead farmer," said Cadyan. His head was pounding, and he was disappointed and angry. He curled his lip and turned his attention back to the sketchbook. He flipped through the pages, scowling at the pictures until he landed on a page halfway through, and received a jolt.

His own face stared up at him from the page.

He rotated the book to examine the image from a different angle, startled by how accurate and detailed it was. The sight of it made him uneasy, and he couldn't explain why. He felt strangely empty, almost sad. He ran his fingers over the pencil marks, trying to imagine his sister drawing it. Before he knew it, a white-hot rage had consumed him once again.

"So she spent her youth learning to draw. While I... I..."

"My lord?" Slaedir was watching his king with apprehension. "What should we do with the prisoner?"

Cadyan ignored him. He was flipping through the pages, counting the different faces. There were several he didn't recognize, but there was no mistaking the healer girl or the man he'd just seen escaping with his sister. And countless pages were dedicated to the man now lying at his feet.

"So many people," he muttered.

The pictures told her life story, a story full of joy and love. No images of fear or pain, no days cowering in the dark, choosing to either hide from violence or let it consume her.

Cadyan's mind spiralled into dark, resentful places, as he wondered why she'd been spared instead of him. Why wasn't she haunted by memories of hate every time she closed her eyes?

And now she was trying to steal the only thing Cadyan ever had, the only thing he'd ever dreamed about. She had the audacity to defy him, to turn her magic against him. Magic that was never meant to be hers.

"I hate her," he said finally, slamming the book closed. "I

hate her with every ounce of my being and I want her dead, do you hear me?" He raised his eyes to glare at the firkon, who were standing around him, looking alarmed.

"She'll be heading to Awnell," said Slaedir. "We should follow her."

Cadyan wrestled back his anger. "We will," he said through clenched teeth. "Julyán, you take the prisoner back to Caerlon and await our return. The others and I will ride on to Awnell. I expect Queen Ayr can be persuaded to help us find our fugitive." He brushed his thumb against the ring on his finger, ignoring the nagging doubt in the back of his mind. "And if not," he continued in a deadly quiet voice. "I will raze her kingdom to the ground."

Cadyan gazed back out at the dark horizon, clenching his fist around the tattered book in his hand.

THE END of
Book One of
THE QUIESCENCE TRILOGY

# ALSO BY KATHRYN KNOWLES

THE QUIESCENCE TRILOGY

The Last Verratrí, a Short Story Prelude

Book Two Coming Spring 2022

# ACKNOWLEDGMENTS

Thank you to my family for always believing in me. Thank you, especially, to Colin for helping me cross the finish line, and to Mom for all the reasons imaginable.

To Rebecca. I remember that day a couple years ago when we sat on your couch and I just talked to you for hours about my wacky idea for a book. I remember how interested you were. You asked tons of questions, and you got really into it. That's when I knew I needed to do this. From that point on, you were nothing but supportive: reading the first book (not to mention all the short stories and poems too!), reading various versions after that, and capping it all off with oodles of comments and notes, pushing me to cross the final threshold from DRAFT908 to FINALDRAFT.

To Heather. I get the sense you knew I could do better and you wouldn't settle for anything less. Thank you for the shrewd insight and detail-oriented comments. Thank you for listening to me and talking with me, and for helping me work through problems. It's an understatement to say that, without your help, this book wouldn't be what it is today!

To MacKenzie. For over fifteen years of friendship, and for

being the bestest bud. You inspire me and make me want to write better characters. Thank you for reading the book, and for helping me work through all the annoying logistical stuff like computers and software and cover photos—oh my! You're a wonderful sounding board. Sitting and talking with you is how I recharge.

Thank you to my friend and colleague (violinist extraordinaire) Karin, whose priceless chapter reactions kept me going and became a source of comfort. You want to #becomelikediyah? Too late, you already are.

To my wonderful Beta Readers, Jeff, Jesse, Martha, and Vicki. You read this when it was still one book. Your feedback gave me the courage and resilience to make it into three. Thank you to my short story Beta Readers, Katerina, Morgan, Peter, and Sherrin. You gave me the confidence to release the short story, *The Last Verratrí*, and officially launch this journey.

To all my friends and family, thank you for cheering me on, for being patient with my obsession(s), and for empowering me to take a chance. I feel unbelievably fortunate to have so many strong, supportive people in my corner.

And finally, to my readers. Thank you for taking a chance on this book. I set out to write a fun story with engaging characters—a story that transports readers. Hopefully, I've achieved that goal. I figured if I wrote a story I enjoyed, there was a strong probability that at least one or two other people would enjoy it too. I hope you are as excited as I am about book two.

# ABOUT THE AUTHOR

Kathryn Knowles is a composer, cellist, conductor, and writer currently based in Toronto, Ontario. Her musical works have been played in workshops by the Toronto Symphony Orchestra, the New Orford String Quartet, and the Penderecki String Quartet.

*Photo Credit: Claire Bouvier Photography*

She holds a Bachelor of Music and a Master of International Business from Queen's University, as well as a Master in Music Composition from the University of Toronto.

In addition to her work as a composer and writer, Kathryn is a Centre Director with Sistema Toronto and the Music Director of Music4Life String Orchestra. Kathryn is a strong advocate for the accessibility and appreciation of music and art in today's society and she values the constant pursuit and celebration of knowledge.

Learn more at www.kathryn-knowles.com

instagram.com/kathryn.knowles_